Embraced By A Highlander

By

Donna Fletcher

Copyright

Embraced By A Highlander
All rights reserved.
Copyright © November 2017 by Donna Fletcher

No part of this publication may be used or reproduced in any manner whatsoever, including but not limited to being stored in a retrieval system or transmitted in any form or by any means, electronic, mechanical, photocopying, recording or otherwise without permission of the author.

This is a book of fiction. Names, characters, places, and incidents are either the product of the author's imagination or are used fictitiously, and any resemblance to actual persons, living or dead, business establishments, events or locales is entirely coincidental.

Cover art
Kim Killion Group

Chapter One

Hannah eyed the three women skeptically. They huddled together whispering... about her. While most had ignored her arrival at the village, the older woman had been kind enough to give her a piece of bread and cheese. It had been a Godsend after not having eaten for a full day. Though, she should have known something was brewing when the woman had whispered to a young lad and he had dashed off. It had not been long after that that the other two women arrived to huddle and whisper with the woman who Hannah had believed generous.

You never get something for nothing. There is always a price to pay. So ask yourself how much are you willing to pay before you accept anything.

For as long as she could remember, her mum had reminded her of that. But she had been so hungry that she had not even considered asking if something was expected of her in exchange for the meager food. Besides, the woman seemed kind enough, even eager to help her.

The older woman, who Hannah had heard one of the women call Blair, had a good girth on her, full, rosy cheeks, a smile that had produced permanent lines, which meant she wore it more often than not, brown eyes that twinkled with their own smile, and brown hair sprinkled with gray that refused to stay pinned to the top of her head.

Whatever could a woman who seemed so congenial want from her?

The other two seemed to be agreeing with Blair, nodding as she spoke.

Hannah turned her head, chewing on the last of the bread, casting her glance around the village and making it seem that she was not interested in their discussion, but keeping an ear turned to them.

"Someone has to go—"

"Soon or else—"

Hannah strained to hear, but only managed to catch snippets of the conversation.

Two more women suddenly appeared and joined in the huddle, making it more difficult to catch words.

"Savage—"

Hannah turned rigid upon hearing it. Was it possible?

She turned with a stretch, so the women would think she was not paying them, or anything in particular, any attention. When what she intended was to get a better look at the keep in the not too far distance.

It was a good size, though the dark stone made it appear more ominous than welcoming. There was also signs of decline here and there, some stone blocks crumbling, and wood rotting. The land around it was overgrown with thickets, some nearly consuming the wood door that hung crooked, yet was shut closed. It was almost as if the edifice warned people away with its prickly nature. If the keep was home to who she thought it was, she could understand why.

Slain MacKewan... the savage.

Hannah stifled the shiver of fear that ran through her.

Slain MacKewan was a fierce Highland warrior who showed no mercy to his opponents, and could fell more men than three Highlanders combined, or so it was told. He had fought beside two other warriors who were just as feared and revered, one more than the other two... *the beast and the demon.* They had battled side by side against invading enemies and had ended land disputes, some for the King, and some for themselves. If the tales were true, and Hannah had always thought that there was a kernel of truth to most tales, then this village she had stopped at belonged to the savage.

She gave another stretch so the women would think that she continued to pay no mind to anything in particular, then pulled the faded blue, thin scrap of cloth from her hair and let her bright red curls break free. Her hair always had a mind of its own, escaping ties and combs that tried to tame it or keep it imprisoned. She preferred to give it free rein, but her mum had told her to beware. That wild, red hair like hers enticed men and she needed to keep it tamed. Her mum had been right about that, but then her mum had been right about many things, and she missed her dearly. She ran her fingers through the soft, long strands and reluctantly gathered them together to secure with the scrap of cloth once again. She did not need to cause herself any more problems than she already had.

She turned once again, slowly this time, wanting to take in most of the surrounding village. Surprisingly, the place seemed to thrive and appeared well-maintained. Gardens had been made ready for planting, thatched roofs—damaged by the winter—were being repaired, and bedding was thrown over tree branches to air and refresh from their long winter confinement.

The villagers themselves seemed well-fed and their garments were in fine shape. If the village did so well, why not the keep? Were people so afraid of Slain MacKewan that they feared going near the keep?

"Hannah."

She turned to face the group of women who now were at nine, and all nine of them were staring at her.

"Hannah," Blair said again, keeping a smile stuck to her face. "You did say your name was Hannah, right?"

"Aye, I did, and once again I am grateful for your generosity," Hannah said and let a smile loose, something she did not often do.

The women's eyes turned wide and small gasps were caught.

Hannah never thought herself beautiful, though her mum warned her otherwise, especially when she smiled. Her mum used to say her smile was like being kissed by the sun, warm and welcoming, making you want to linger in it. Her green eyes, the color of the grass-covered rolling hills on a clear spring day also added to her fine features.

The women started whispering and nodding again until the unease in Hannah's stomach forced her to speak, "Is something wrong?"

The women turned silent and a slim woman nudged Blair in the side.

Blair took a step forward, her smile fading. "We have a bit of a problem and we are hoping you might be able to help us with it."

It was Hannah's turn to remain silent, letting Blair know she would listen, but made no comment until she heard what they had to say.

Blair continued. "Our chief is a good man, but not an easy man to get on with. Most think he is more comfortable when in battle, for he cannot seem to find peace, even with himself, otherwise. He lives mostly alone in the keep, except for Helice." She shook her head and the other women joined in. "He brought her here when he returned from battle one day. She oversees the keep and is the most antagonistic woman God has ever created."

The other women nodded vigorously.

"Between Helice and S—our chief, no one in the village wishes to serve in the keep," Blair explained.

It was not lost to Hannah that Blair stopped herself from referring to the chief by name, which made Hannah believe she had been right. This was the home of the sav—Slain MacKewan. She could not bring herself to think of him as a savage or she might be too fearful to stay and she needed to remain here. Otherwise, she had nowhere else to go and her fate would be sealed.

"The women who have gone to the keep to help—"

"Last not even a day, not one of them able to tolerate Helice and if by chance they happen upon the chief..." a short woman said, interrupting Blair and shivered. "None are willing to go."

"Gwynn," Blair said, shaking her head.

Gwynn threw her hands up. "What? Do you expect us to send her to the keep completely blind as to what she will face? She will run screaming from the place in no time." She threw her hands up again. "Why do we even bother? No one will please Helice or—"

"I will accept the position," Hannah said and every woman's mouth dropped open.

It took several moments before Blair was able to speak. "You will go to the keep and serve there?"

"Aye, I will," Hannah said with a nod. "I have no place to go and I cannot be a burden to your clan. If this is the way I can seek a home here, then I will do what I must."

What other choice did she have?

Her thought was not answered, for she had yet to find one.

"We would be ever so grateful," Blair said.

"Do not get your hopes up, Blair," another woman said. "We have had others who have agreed like this one and were gone before the day was done. Besides, we have not told her how the chief enjoys women."

"He has never forced himself on a woman and he certainly bothers no women from the village," Blair said in defense of Slain MacKewan.

"Then why do the women travelers who stop here and make their wares available to him always leave in tears?" the one woman demanded.

Blair looked to the slim woman. "You know why Wilona. You heard what at least three of those women told us."

Wilona gave a brief snort before reluctantly admitting, "The women told us that they had never known such immense pleasure with a man and they feared they never would again. And that he showed no interest in wanting to see them again should they journey back this way. He even told one, who had been insistent upon returning to him, that he had no desire to poke her again."

"He is a cruel bastard he is," another woman said.

"Or is he a man who knows his mind and speaks it?" Blair asked.

"You always defend him," Wilona accused.

"He is our chief and a good one, seeing that the clan is cared for. We do not starve even in the harshest of winters, our garments are not threadbare and we have a good healer in Neata. What more do you want, Wilona?"

Wilona rubbed her arms. "A chief who does not make my skin shiver when he walks through the village."

"If he makes your skin shiver, I can only imagine how our foes feel when they battle him," Blair said.

All the women nodded, even Wilona.

"It is not an easy task we ask of you," Blair said, turning to Hannah. "And if it is not one you find acceptable, we will understand and hold no ill will toward you."

Easy task.

This was by far an easier task than any she had been through lately, not that she was not fearful of what she would face in the keep. She would be a fool not to fear, for fear instilled courage and strength, or so her da believed.

"I will do my best," Hannah said.

"You still agree after what we have told you?" Wilona asked, not quite believing her.

"I will heed your warnings and do what I can," Hannah said, reminding herself that she had to. No matter what, she had to stay here with the Clan MacKewan."

Blair looked to each of the other women and they in turn nodded. She turned to Hannah once again. "You should go to the keep now, since our chief gave us until today to fill the position or else Helice will come and choose someone herself."

"There is no need of that now, since I have accepted," Hannah said, once again confirming her willingness, and all the women smiled and nodded with relief.

"We are here if you should need us," Blair said.

"Not to help at the keep," Wilona hastily added.

Blair shot her a scolding look before focusing on Hannah again. "You are welcome anytime to share a brew and talk."

The other women nodded.

Hannah kept her smile to herself. *Gossip.* It was the mainstay of any village.

"Am I to bring anything with me?" Hannah asked.

Blair shook her head. "The keep has all it needs or all you need."

With a nod, Hannah took her leave and headed to the keep.

All you need.

Did the keep have all she needed? Would she find what she searched for there?

Fatigue mixed with sorrow weighed heavily upon her, but then she had been walking for days, not sure if she had been going in the right direction. Her body ached, not only from the endless journey but also from the bruises it had suffered, especially her one arm. It had remained weak from the torture and she feared it may never grow as strong as it once had been.

She, however, had remained strong and determined, now more than ever. She would survive. No matter what it took, she would survive.

Her fear grew as she drew closer to the keep. It certainly did not welcome, its neglect even more prominent up close. The thickets had thorns and after one scratch, tearing the sleeve of her already worn blouse, she was careful not to get too close. It certainly served as a deterrent to anyone who approached.

She suffered another tear. This time to the hem of her shift when she stepped up to the door, having caught it on a branch she had to step over.

How the door stayed closed with how crooked it appeared, she did not know, but it was shut firm. She stood staring at the thick door, wondering if anyone would hear her knock. Not sure that anyone would, Hannah pounded on the door with her fist.

She waited and waited, giving time for those within to reach the door. After several minutes passed with no response, Hannah pounded on the door again. She jumped back, almost stumbling into the thickets, as the door suddenly popped open, though only a bit, startling her. It hung on an angle, the one hinge appearing loose. The door began to open slowly, bit by bit, creaking as it did as if in protest of being disturbed or by a slow hand that was not sure if it should answer the summons.

Uncertainty grew her anxious and fright had her heart thudding in her chest as she waited to see who would appear. When no one did, she called out a greeting, "*Latha math.*"

Silence was the only thing that reached her ears.

She called out once again. "*Latha math.*"

When still no response came, she realized she had only one choice, push the door open and enter. Her stomach churned as her hand reached out and pushed at the door. The creak turned to a squeak as the door opened to reveal a yawning darkness. Hannah hesitated, her feet not willing to take her any further and her heart pounding so madly that she feared any sound would be lost to her.

The dark had never bothered her until recently, until she learned that monsters did really live there. Now it held a fear that shivered her down to her soul.

It took all her willpower to push past the fear that prickled her skin and nearly froze her limbs, as she forced herself to step forward into the darkness.

Chapter Two

Hannah blinked her eyes several times, attempting to see through the darkness and called out once more. This time it was not silence that greeted her but her own voice as it echoed back at her. Her eyes were beginning to adjust to the dark and she thought she caught the shapes of tables and benches. Most likely, she was in the Great Hall, but why was there no fire burning in the hearth or candles about?

As if someone had heard her thoughts, she saw the flicker of a candle in the distance. It looked as if it drifted through the air on its own accord as it moved closer and closer.

"Close that door, you fool," a strong voice boomed out of the blackness.

Hannah jumped startled by the stern reprimand and not wanting to lose what little light she had, she closed the door more slowly than necessary.

"Another weak one. Is there not a sturdy woman among you Scots?"

Hannah turned to see a woman, who stood a good head over her, approach. She had a thick girth and her once blonde hair, she wore in a long braid that rested on her chest, was streaked generously with white strands. Deep lines fanned out from the corners of her stark blue eyes and deeper lines curved down from the sides of her mouth, giving her the appearance of a perpetual frown.

Her accent was familiar to Hannah. She was from the land beyond the North Sea, home to the once raiding Vikings. She had to be Helice, the woman the village women warned her about.

The woman stepped around her and with one shove of her hand pushed the door closed and dropped the latch on it, securing it closed to any visitors.

"I was expecting you sooner."

The reason the door had been unlocked, Hannah thought. So Slain MacKewan left his door unlatched for those he wanted to enter, but it remained closed to all others.

"Do you have a tongue?" Helice snapped and held up the candle to cast a light on Hannah's face.

"I believe you will find me sturdy enough for chores," Hannah said and smiled, hoping to keep herself in good stead with the woman.

Helice stared at her a moment, then shook her head and ordered, "You will keep your distance from the chief." She nodded for Hannah to follow, mumbling to herself in a language Hannah did not understand.

As Hannah hurried to keep step with Helice, she gave a quick glance around the room. It was the Great Hall, a ghost of what it must have once been. Tables and benches were covered in dust, cobwebs dripped from the candelabras that sat in the center of the tables, and a mound of ashes was piled high in the fireplace.

Why was there no life to this keep?

Helice blew out the flame of the candle she held as they entered the torch-lit passageway that led to the kitchen.

Hannah could not keep her eyes from spreading wide when they entered the room. Never had she seen such a well-kept kitchen. There was not a spot of grime anywhere and the delicious scent that came from the cauldron that bubbled over the flames had Hannah's stomach gurgling and her mouth salivating.

"That hunger of yours will wait until mealtime. You have chores to do," Helice ordered.

"How wonderful." Hannah smiled again, hoping by staying pleasant the woman might return it in kind. "I have a delicious meal to look forward to."

Helice snapped a finger at her. "And more chores to tend to afterwards."

"Then it is good I will have a full stomach."

"Your stomach will be full here and your hands never idle," Helice said, though it sounded more a warning.

"Then I best get started. What will my chores be?"

"Whatever I decide," Helice said.

Hannah had forgotten to ask the village women if she was to sleep here in the keep or return to the village at night. She had no choice but to ask Helice. "Am I expected to sleep here?"

"You are the first to ask that," Helice said with what Hannah thought was respect. "A pallet on the floor in the Great Hall is all you will get."

"That is more than I have now, so I am grateful for it."

Again Hannah thought she caught a hint of admiration in Helice's cold blue eyes.

"The solar needs cleaning. I will show you what must be done."

Hannah followed Helice to a room tucked away behind the Great Hall. A fire burned in the hearth and several candles helped light the room, and Hannah could not believe what she saw. There were books piled on stools and benches and on top of chests as well as papers and drawings of strange looking things. Books were not something easily obtained. They were reserved more for the wealthy and the literate, and were written in languages many did not understand.

Thankfully, her mum had taught her Latin, a language the clergy often used when transcribing books. She hoped she would have time to sneak a peek at the books and drawings as well.

"You will not enter this room without my permission," Helice directed.

Hannah almost sighed with regret.

"I will bring you here when it needs tending, otherwise you will keep your distance from it," Helice instructed firmly. "You will keep the books piled neatly, though you will not remove them from where they sit. You will keep the dust from gathering, the hearth burning, and the ashes from mounting. You will also keep the wine decanter full and the goblets clean. See to all of that but do not touch anything on the desk."

Hannah nodded, pleased with the chore, for it would give her time to glance over the books.

"You may start here now. I will come fetch you when it is time to eat." Helice did not wait for a response. She walked out the door, shutting it closed behind her.

Hannah looked around at where to start and her glance kept returning to the desk. She had one of many faults as her father often reminded her. The one that annoyed him the most was that he could be sure if he told her not to do something, Hannah would be sure to do it. Her mum had warned her that she was too curious. Her father was of a different opinion. He believed that she was obstinate and simply refused to obey. Of which, her mum would remind matched her father's tenacious nature.

To Hannah, neither were right. She had discovered that people were not truthful, including her mum and da. That secret and lies were the way of life. Who then was there to trust? Who could she truly rely on?

Knowledge. That had been the conclusion she had reached. With knowledge she could protect herself, so obstinacy and curiosity had become her shield and sword. Unfortunately, her shield and sword had not been strong enough against evil.

She went to the desk and looked with interest at the drawings on the parchment. They seemed to be some type of tools. Then there were drawings of buildings. A couple of the drawings struck a familiar cord, but she was not quite sure what it was.

Curiosity had her reaching for a rolled parchment, but a noise outside the door had her hurrying away to straighten a stack of books on a narrow table against one wall. It reminded her that she did not know how much time she would have to complete her chore and she had better show that she had done something before Helice returned or the woman might send her away and, at the moment, here is where she wanted to be... needed to be.

Helice returned sooner than Hannah expected, the older woman giving her a tongue-lashing for not having worked fast enough.

"Keep up your laziness and you will be returning to the village before nightfall," Helice reprimanded. "I will give you a few more moments. Be done with it."

Hannah got busy, ignoring the books and drawings that tempted her. She just finished when Helice returned.

"Learn to be quicker," Helice ordered after glancing over the room. "Time to eat."

Her stomach ached for food and her body ached for rest, having walked since before dawn in hopes of reaching here. The hardy stew was delicious and Helice was generous in her helping of it as well as the freshly baked bread, both easing the gnawing in her stomach.

As she ate, she wondered over Slain MacKewan. There was no sight nor sound of him since her arrival, and she wondered where he could be. After the meal, Helice had her washing garment after garment and laying them over strips of wood positioned between tables in a small room that burned with roaring flames in the fireplace.

Hannah's cheeks were burning red by the time she got done and her sore arm ached beyond belief, though she made no mention of it. By the time the evening meal came, she barely had the strength to eat and she was never so glad to seek the pallet Helice had her carry to the Great Hall and place in front of the cold hearth.

"You will stay here. No matter what you hear, you will not leave this room until I come fetch you in the morning," Helice warned, her blue eyes glaring at Hannah.

Hannah was barely able to force a nod, she was so tired and as soon as Helice left the Great Hall, she collapsed on the pallet. She pulled the blanket, that had been rolled up in the meager bedding, over her and curled into a ball. Sleep claimed her before the chill of the hard wood floor seeped into her.

A noise broke through her sleep and woke her, and she froze at the sound… footsteps. They had found her. They were coming for her. She had to run. She had to get away. Fear froze her limbs. She could not move. She could barely breathe.

Run! Run! Run! She screamed silently to herself.

Her courage broke through the fear and she jumped up, fighting to keep her legs strong as she stared into the darkness, appearing as if it was ready to swallow her whole. There was no time to think. She had to get away. Her eyes caught sight of a faint light in the distance.

Good God, they were here… they had found her.

She turned to run when out of the darkness stepped a man. Shadows followed him, hugging at his shoulders, falling partially across his face, but it was his eyes that stole her breath… they were darker than the pits of hell.

She stepped back away from him so quickly that she lost her footing and tumbled backward, the back of her head catching on the stone fireplace. As she dropped to the floor, she heard the man speak.

"Who is she?"

As darkness claimed Hannah, she thought she heard Helice answer, "A servant, no one of significance."

Hannah woke confused and, surprisingly, to a small fire burning in the fireplace. The warmth eased the aches in her body. Last night's incident returned to her, though she wondered if it was nothing more than a dream, fears of the past haunting her. She stretched as she sat up and winced when a pain struck at the back of her head. Her hand instinctively went there and she felt a small lump.

Last night had not been a dream.

She shivered recalling the man's dark, ominous eyes.

Had she met the *savage*?

She shook her head, though stilled, the movement causing her slight pain. Savage was not his name.

But he was called it for a reason.

"You will keep a small fire burning in here, to keep the chill off you."

Hannah turned much too fast to face Helice and grimaced against the pain that shot through her head once again.

"Eat, for you are already late in starting your chores." Helice placed a bowl of porridge on the table and a tankard with a steaming brew in it. "When you finish come to the kitchen, and do not take long." She turned and left Hannah to eat alone.

Hannah sat at the table and sipped at the brew, while glancing around at the darkness that hugged most of the room. She missed the light, the sunshine and its warmth, even more so with what she had gone through.

Darkness harbored secrets and concealed truths, and festered old wounds, never letting them heal. It tore at the heart and withered the soul until there was nothing left. She did not want that for herself. She was stronger and braver than that.

As soon as she finished her meal she went to the kitchen and Helice wasted no time in shoving an empty basket at her.

"The young, wild onions should be plentiful in the woods. Fill the basket, and stay to the edge of the woods, and do not dawdle. There are still many chores to be done. Wear that cloak." Helice nodded to a worn brown cloak hanging from a peg on the wall near the door. "It may be spring, but winter remains an unwanted guest."

Hannah was pleased with the task that would take her outside. The confines of the dark keep and Helice's constant scowl did nothing to keep hope thriving.

Gray clouds tormented the sun, which managed to shine through now and again and did much to improve her spirits. The air was far from warm, though it lacked the sharp chill of winter. It was perfect and far more refreshing than the musty keep.

She got busy, knowing Helice would keep watch on how long she was gone. She was so pleased to be enjoying her morning task outside that she did not realize she had drifted further into the woods until the basket she carried was near full. She turned to head back when her ears caught a sound. Her head snapped from side to side.

Footfalls.

Fear sent a chill racing through her and she gripped the handle of the basket as she frantically looked for a place to hide. Footfalls would forever frighten her since that night. She had heard them coming, but there had been no place for her to go. No place for her to hide. The steady sound of the boots against the wood had sounded more like the steady beat of the drum of approaching warriors ready for battle, ready to defeat the enemy.

She hurried to a formation of boulders and squatted down behind it, her heart thudding so madly that she feared it would be heard. Her stomach joined in, roiling more strongly as the footfalls drew closer.

They stopped suddenly and Hannah closed her eyes tight and folded her lips in her mouth to keep any sound from escaping, since it seemed as if the person had stopped directly on the other side of the boulder.

A bird let loose with a wobbly whistle and when it was returned, Hannah knew it was no bird, but a signal.

The whistles went back and forth for several minutes before Hannah heard another set of footfalls approach.

"Hurry, I do not have much time?" a whispery voice cautioned as footfalls approached the boulder.

"Either do I," the other man said.

"Have you heard anything yet?" the whispery voice asked.

"Nothing of significance. All continues as is, though a change is expected soon. One that will prove beneficial."

"Good. Patience wears thin and time grows slim."

"Soon it will be done. Soon things will be made right."

"Soon we will celebrate victory," the whispery voice said.

Hannah heard footfalls fade away in opposite directions, but she remained where she was, too fearful to move. Too fearful that she might be discovered. She would give it time before taking a chance and stepping out from behind the safety of the boulders. In the meantime, she wondered over what she had heard. Was someone betraying Slain MacKewan? If so, who would be foolish enough to betray the savage?

"Hannah!"

The relief in hearing Helice's curt tongue made her realize just how long fear had frozen her. She stepped around the boulder quickly and hurried toward Helice's shouts.

"What did I tell you about staying to the edge of the woods?" Helice demanded. "If you cannot follow simple orders then there is no place here for you."

That could not happen. She had to stay.

"Forgive me," Hannah was quick to plead. 'I was so busy with the task that I did not realize I wandered."

"Fail to obey me again and you will be gone," Helice warned her tongue so sharp Hannah felt the sting.

Hannah bobbed her head and followed behind Helice as she turned and stomped off.

It struck her as she was walking to keep pace with Helice that the woman had warned her twice to remain at the edge of the woods. Could she have possibly known of the meeting? Was she part of the possible betrayal?

What secrets and lies did the keep hold?

Chapter Three

Hannah was about to see to her chore the next morning after a hardy meal when Helice announced that she was to follow her. The stone staircase they climbed curved considerably and after traveling two floors up, they stopped on a small landing with a door to the right and one to the left.

Helice took hold of the door latch to the right and gave a nod to the door on the left. "That is the east wing and you are never to go there. *Never.* Do you understand?"

Hannah nodded and followed Helice through the open door, though curiosity had her glancing back at the forbidden door. Why was the east wing forbidden to her?

One glance told her this was Slain MacKewan's bedchamber. It was large. It had to be for the huge sized bed that dominated the room. Three people could easily sleep in it, if not more. The bedding was rumpled and garments lay strewn about. A small table and chair sat by a window and Hannah walked to it as Helice spewed out orders.

"You will change the bedding," —she nodded to fresh bedding folded on a chair near the hearth— "wipe the room of dust, fold the garments and place them in the chest," — she nodded again, this time to the large chest at the foot of the bed— "clean out the hearth and set a new fire. Do not dally. I have another chore for you as soon as you finish here." Helice turned and left, leaving Hannah to her task.

Hannah looked out the window surprised no tapestry covered it and that light was actually allowed to shine through, unlike the rest of the keep that seemed shrouded in darkness. A field of heather laid beyond and she thought how wonderful it would be to collect some and set them in the various rooms and add sprigs to the fire to mask the musty odor that permeated the keep.

She turned away, knowing her time was limited to complete her chore. She got busy changing the bedding first, not wanting to leave it for last since her hands were sure to be covered with soot and ash after cleaning the fireplace.

The potent scent washed over her as soon as she picked up one of the pillows. Her nostrils flared as she breathed in the mix of earth and pine and... the other scent was more potent than the two familiar ones, the unknown one stirring her senses. It was as if she could not get enough of the tantalizing scent. She wanted to bury her face in the pillow and breathed deeply until it consumed her, became part of her.

The foolish thought had her dropping the pillow as if its touch suddenly scalded her. She hurried to the window and fumbled with the latch to open it and let in the chilly air. Then she went about her chore, trying desperately to ignore the tempting scent that refused to leave her nostrils.

She saw to folding the garments which managed to brand her even more with the alluring scent, it was so heavy upon them. Even the dust she cleaned away that had her sneezing did not help rid her of the provocative scent that seemed to grow stronger as she worked.

Finally, she returned to tackle the bed, a more difficult task than she would have imagined. Not only did the scent grow stronger as she pulled the bedding off, but her thoughts betrayed her by thinking of the women that Slain MacKewan had entertained there. That he had entertained so well, they had begged to return to him.

Hannah shook her head, trying to clear her thoughts, but his intoxicating scent continued to hold her spellbound.

Once the bed was done, blankets folded back, the pillows fluffed, she hurried to the fireplace, wanting to be done and out of here. It was after the ashes had been cleaned out and logs piled to start a new fire that Hannah realized that the room was being prepared, but for what? Slain MacKewan's return? Or was someone about to visit him?

Hannah stood staring at the bed, wondering if he would have a companion tonight.

"What are you doing?"

Hannah jumped at the sound of Helice's reproach, though recovered quickly. "I was looking to make sure the room was done." Helice's scrunched expression told Hannah that she did not believe her, though Hannah was glad she did not question her lie.

"I need you to go to the village to the healer, Neata. She has something for me."

Hannah wondered if Helice was ill, though she certainly looked hardy enough, but it would not be polite of her to ask. "Where will I find the healer?"

"Ask anyone in the village and they will point the way. You are to go there and return as soon as you finish. Do not—"

"Dally," Hannah finished with a smile.

"So you know you dally, yet you do nothing about it," Helice accused.

Hannah wondered if the woman ever found anything amusing or even smiled. She would not let that ruin the excitement that stirred in her over being able to get away from the keep for a while.

"A fault of mine, I fear," Hannah said, letting her smile fade.

"A fault that needs immediate correcting."

"Aye," Hannah agreed with a nod.

"Take the bucket of ashes while I see to taking the soiled bedding, which you will scrub on your return home."

Home?

Was this now her home? Was this all she had?

A tear tickled at her one eye and she made sure to turn away so that Helice could not see. By the time Hannah stepped into the kitchen the tear had faded, though it returned as she stepped outside and headed to the village.

She had had no time to grieve over what she had lost or perhaps she simply had not wanted to think on it. She feared the more she dwelled on her situation, the more her heart would break.

Stay strong. Survive.

More of her mum's repetitious wisdom that at one time annoyed her and now gave her strength. It also made her realize how strong her mum had been and how she had survived a marriage that was anything but loving. She had made the most of it and had survived until an illness had taken her.

"I will survive, Mum, and it is because of you I will survive," she whispered her heart heavy with loving memories of her mum.

With tears gone, a smile and a strong gait, she entered the village. It was not as easy as she expected to get someone to speak with her. Every time she approached someone, they would scurry away from her as if frightened. She finally caught sight of Wilona, the slim woman whose long dark hair seemed to be at odds with her and whose dark eyes seemed too large for her face.

Wilona's eyes nearly popped from her head when they settled on Hannah and she looked ready to run.

"Wilona, a moment of your time," Hannah called out and before the woman could run off, Hannah hurried over to her.

Wilona rung her hands as she spoke. "Do not tell me you are leaving us."

"No, not at all," Hannah confirmed and watched the woman's face flood with relief. "I simply need to know where I can find the healer."

"Someone is ill at the keep?' Wilona was quick to ask.

"All I know is that I have been told to fetch something from the healer," Hannah explained, feeling it was not right of her to say anymore, but then she knew nothing more than that.

"I will take you there," Wilona said.

"That is generous of you," Hannah said, though she was aware that generosity had nothing to do with it. It was curiosity that had Wilona offering and it took only a few steps before the questions started.

"How is Helice treating you?"

Wilona sounded more like she demanded than asked, similar to the way Helice spoke to her, so her abrupt nature did not offend Hannah. "She is generous at meal time and her food is the most delicious I have ever tasted. The chores are plentiful and keep me busy. I have no complaints."

Wilona was speechless, though only for a few moments. "And our chief, he treats you well?"

Hannah spoke the truth. "I have not met him yet, though he must be a learned man since he has many books."

Wilona snorted. "Learned in ways of battle. It was his mum who was the learned one. The clan often wondered what the sweet and wise Leala saw in the not so wise, though handsome William."

"It was not an arranged marriage?"

Wilona shook her head, then nodded. "It was both. The two fell in love and their marriage was beneficial to both clans so no objections were made. Slain got his da's fine features and thankfully his mum's intelligence." She stopped walking. "Here we are."

Hannah looked to where Wilona pointed, to a small cottage at the end of a narrow path.

"Neata is a good healer." Wilona went to turn away and stopped. "Welcome to the Clan MacKewan."

Hannah smiled. She had a feeling that Wilona could be almost as cantankerous as Helice, and did not accept people into the clan easily, so she was grateful for the, if not warm but abrupt, welcome.

Though, Neata's cottage was small, a huge garden sprawled out around it, drawing a wide smile from Hannah as she got closer. Fresh spring buds were sprouting everywhere and the leaves on the old oak trees were springing to life. A wreath, abundant with dried herbs, graced the front door that sprung open before Hannah reached it.

The woman who stepped out had seen a plethora of springs and winters, the deep lines around her mouth and cheerful eyes attesting to that. Her long gray hair was streaked liberally with white and laid in a braid on her chest. She was petite and slim, almost fragile looking and yet there was a strength about her that could not be denied.

"You must be Hannah," Neata said as Hannah approached. She waved to her. "Come in. Come in. I have been eager to meet you."

Hannah entered the cottage, a smile surfacing as an array of lovely scents assaulted her. Never had she been in a cottage or a room that smelled so inviting.

"Sit. Sit," Neata directed, pointing to one of two chairs that sat opposite of each other at the small table in front of the hearth.

Hannah glanced around as Neata busied herself fixing them a hot brew. A narrow bed sat tucked in a corner while slim tables, more like high benches, sat beneath the two windows, baskets, crocks, and pouches sitting atop them.

"I have what Helice needs," Neata said as she filled a tankard for Hannah and one for herself, then sat.

"It is none of my concern and I do not intend to pry, but is Helice ill?" Hannah asked, feeling the need to learn more about the woman especially with what had happened in the woods. Was Helice a champion of Slain or a traitor?

"A minor problem that will heal," Neata said and took a sip of the brew before continuing. "But what of you? I see that you favor your one arm."

Hannah had thought she had disguised it well enough, but the chores had taken its toll on her arm. She had felt it growing weaker and without rest, as she had been warned was needed, it would get worse.

"An unfortunate accident that weakens my arm at times," she said, not wanting the woman to know the truth.

"Helice will need more of the salve I send her. Next time you come for it, I will have a look at your arm and see what might be done to help it."

"I am grateful for any help you can give me," Hannah said, thinking of the healer who had so bravely helped her survive the torture she had suffered.

"I am a healer; I heal," Neata said. "Now tell me how you fare at the keep."

"I am learning my way," Hannah said with a smile.

Neata smiled as well, her whole face lighting with it. "And how do you find our chief?"

"I have yet to meet him," Hannah confessed.

Neata nodded. "He can be a recluse at times."

Hannah wished she could stay and talk with the woman, but she was reminded of Helice's words.

Do not dally.

She did not want to chance losing her position there. She needed this place of safety.

"I cannot stay, Helice awaits my return," Hannah said and stood reluctantly. "Thank you for the brew."

"Next time, you will stay longer and I will see to that arm of yours that drags your shoulder down."

Hannah looked down at her arm. She had felt the weight of it herself with the days of heavy chores. But she would not speak of it to anyone, she could not, for she took the chance of revealing the truth.

With a nod and taking the small crock of salve from Neata, she left. She had barely stepped off the path to Neata's cottage and into the heart of the village when she heard her name called. She smiled and returned Blair's wave as the woman hurried over to her.

"Wilona spoke with you," Hannah said as she continued walking, Blair joining alongside her.

"Aye, she did and I wanted to make sure all was well with you," Blair said.

"All is well," Hannah said, not entirely sure, though for now she wanted to believe so.

"I cannot tell you how relieved many—most—in the village are that you are still here, helping at the keep. But what of your family? Will they not miss you?"

Curiosity, or was it fear Hannah would take her leave, that had Blair asking. Hannah eased the woman's mind. "There is no place left for me to go."

Or so she believed, but then there was nothing to prove otherwise. What the future held she did not know, but for now she was safe.

"Then you will stay here?" Blair asked and seemed to hold her breath.

"As long as I am welcome."

Blair grinned. "You are a MacKewan now and always will be. Welcome to the clan."

Hannah smiled, grateful for the acceptance, though worried it would not turn out as well as Blair believed.

"All goes well at the keep?" Blair asked, walking alongside Hannah.

Hannah thought this would be a good time to see if she could learn anything about the keep and Slain MacKewan in particular. "Aye, all goes well, though…" She let her words hang.

"Something is wrong?" Blair asked anxiously.

"More strange than wrong. Why is it that no one is allowed in the east wing?" Hannah asked, hoping to find an answer.

Blair glanced around to see if anyone was near and listening. When she saw that no one lingered close by, she spoke, but in a whisper. "Slain took over the east wing when he returned home from an early battle. He spent many secluded days there. There is speculation about what he did there, but no one was ever brave enough to question him or find out for themselves. Every now and then a flickering light is seen in one of the room's windows. Some believe it is the ghost of Leala watching over her son. She loved him dearly."

Hannah stopped abruptly. "The clan believes the keep haunted?"

Blair shook her head rapidly. "No, no, it is just that when lights are seen in the east wing some wonder—"

"If it is a ghost," Hannah finished.

"It does not happen that often," Blair said.

"When was the last time the lights were seen?"

Blair worried her bottom lip, reluctant to speak.

"Since I have been here?"

Blair was quick to shake her head. "No. No lights have been seen since your arrival."

"But were seen before I arrived?"

Blair gave a reluctant nod. "We should have told you, but we were cowards. While Slain MacKewan is a good man, the savage can be a brutal one."

"You feared he would hurt one of his own if you did not send someone to the keep?"

Again Blair shook her head quickly. "No. He has been good to us, but we have seen the savage released and it puts the fear of the devil into you, though we have heard it is nothing compared to the one he fought for... Warrick."

"*The demon*," Hannah whispered as a shiver raced through her.

Blair shivered as well. "We do not know what goes on with our chief. He has changed and we do not know the man he has become."

Hannah nodded, understanding more than Blair would ever know, for she was not the person she once was and would never be again.

Blair rested a gentle arm on Hannah's. "Listen to Helice and stay away from the east wing. If anything resides there it is sorrow." She patted Hannah's arm. "I hope to see you again soon. We can talk more as friends often do."

Hannah smiled. It would be good to have a friend. "I would like that."

They parted, Blair turning and walking away and Hannah walking toward the keep.

The skies had darkened, a storm approaching and Hannah hurried her steps. She raised her head, curiosity having her eyes go to the east wing. It appeared ominous and bleak against the threatening skies.

What secrets did it hold?

She told herself it did not matter, that it did not concern her. She hurried her step, the first drop of rain splattering on the ground.

She gave one last look up at the east wing and she stopped dead, her heart slamming in her chest as she caught sight of a light flickering in one of the windows.

Chapter Four

Hannah woke the next morning with still no signs that Slain MacKewan had returned. His solar was untouched, as was his bedchamber. Helice had her cleaning out the room off the kitchen after the morning meal. It stored various foods, the ones that had rotted needing to be discarded and room made ready for what late spring and summer blooms would have to offer them.

Her arm ached considerably after the chore, though it was from the accumulation of all the work she had been doing. Her arm would grow worse if she did not rest it, but there was no chance of that. She prayed it would not simply go limp, as it had done before. If it did, Helice might not feel her fit enough to remain working at the keep.

Once finished with the storeroom, Helice ordered Hannah to get busy in the Great Hall. She was to dust and scrub as she had done to other rooms.

Hannah gathered a bucket and filled it with water from the rain barrel outside the kitchen door. She grabbed several cloths from the stack on a chest in the kitchen, added a chunk of soap, the scent pleasing enough, and went to the Great Hall.

She rolled up her worn sleeves and went to the three windows covered with shabby and tattered tapestries and one by one tore them down, coughing as she did from the dust she had disturbed. Not that it was difficult, neglect having rotted them. It was a shame since they must have been beautiful at one time. But what was more of a shame was the light they had prevented from shining through the windows.

The sun was shining brightly and struck the windows, pouring light into the sizeable room and highlighting the plethora of dust motes dancing in the air. Hannah stood where the sun shined the brightest through the one window and let it bathe her face with its warmth, sneezing several times as she did.

At that very moment, it struck her... she was free, though for how long she did not know. But for now, she would enjoy it.

She smiled, turned, and got busy cleaning the Great Hall, using the solitude to think on what to do next. Her thoughts were always clearer when she was busy, allowing ideas to take root and grow. Some would blossom while others withered on the vine. She needed things to blossom, too much had withered of late.

She concentrated on one section of the Great Hall, knowing the task was too difficult to complete in one day. She dusted and swept before she got busy scrubbing the tables, benches, candelabras, anything that needed cleaning, and when Helice appeared with food for her, Hannah was pleased to see the look of surprise on her face, not that it lasted long. The stern woman wiped it off almost as fast as it had appeared.

"Eat," Helice ordered, placing a board with bread and cheese on it on the table along with a full tankard.

"With your permission, I would like to go collect some heather to scent the Great Hall. I saw that it grows on the hill on the side of the keep."

"After you eat, and do not dally, I want the Great Hall half-finished today," Helice ordered.

Hannah smiled and nodded, and Helice shook her head and mumbled in her home language as she walked away. She wasted no time in eating the generous amount of food Helice had provided. She was familiar with hunger and not sure of her positon here, or anything for that matter, she had promised herself she would fill herself with food when given the chance.

Once done, she returned the wood board and tankard to the kitchen, grabbed a basket from the few stacked by the door and hurried outside to collect the heather.

Spring was strong in the air after a cold winter, though a chill continued to linger. She should have worn a cloak, if she had one. It had slipped her mind to grab the one by the kitchen door. If only she had her own, but then she would not be here if she was in possession of her cloak. She would be home.

No time to dwell. Do what you must.

Another of her mum's many warnings rang clear in her head. She would pay it heed, but for now she would do something she had once so enjoyed doing with her mum. She would collect heather and perhaps some branches and make a wreath to place on the mantel. The lovely scent would be pleasing this evening while she sat and further thought on ideas beginning to take root.

Hannah found a spot where the sun beat down the strongest and went to work collecting heather. She lingered in the task, the warmth of the sun on her skin much more inviting than the darkness of the keep as well as the fresh scent of the abundant heather. She breathed deeply of the familiar musky fragrance with a light touch of flowery sweetness. Again a reminder that at the moment she was free.

The basket was nearly full when she reached for another sprig. Her hand cramped and she winced from the pain. She turned her head as she rubbed hard at her palm, trying to force the cramp away, and as she did her eyes caught sight of someone standing at the second window above the Great Hall… Slain MacKewan's bedchamber.

She squeezed her eyes, straining to make out the figure and in the blink of an eye the person disappeared. Had it been Helice? Or had it been the elusive Slain MacKewan?

She glanced up at the empty window and smiled at the strangeness of the keep and how it served her well right now. She remained looking over the dark edifice while continuing to ease the cramp from her hand. It could be a lovely place with the thickets removed and life restored to the inside with laughter and love.

Love.

Would she ever know that?

She shook her head. There was no time for nonsense and something that would never be.

With the cramp in her hand finally gone, Hannah took the basket of heather into the Great Hall and began to place sprigs around the candelabras on the clean tables and along the mantel. She also threw several sprigs in the fire.

She returned to scrubbing a few more tables and benches, leaving the rest for tomorrow to finish. Finally done, she looked around pleased with what she had accomplished… except.

A thorny thicket had grown up along one of the windows and with the sky growing cloudy and the earlier breeze turning to a wind, a thicket branch was tapping against the window.

Tap. Tap. Tap. Tap.

The thorny branch seemed to demand entrance.

She would not be able to sleep tonight if that continued. She hurried off through the passageway into the kitchen and out the lone door. She glanced around and not seeing what she was looking for, almost gave up. Then she spied it. She hurried back into the kitchen and grabbed a small hatchet and returned to the ladder that lay strangled by thickets and vines. She hacked away to free the ladder, thorns stabbing at her hands, refusing to release it.

Hannah was just as tenacious, refusing to give up. She chopped and chopped and chopped until finally a brilliant smile burst across her face.

She did it. She freed the ladder. Or had the chopping been like freeing herself?

She slipped the hatchet in her belt and dragged the ladder around to the other side of the keep and stopped once to push strands of her wild red hair that had broken free of its tie, out of her face. She had to plant the ladder nearly up against the window, behind the thickets thick beneath it.

She made sure the ladder was planted firmly before she climbed it. She had to hurry, dark storm clouds having gathered overhead while she had been busy getting the ladder, and the wind was growing ever stronger.

It took a climb to nearly the top rung to reach the annoying branch and once Hannah did, she began hacking away at it. She cheered when it finally fell to the ground, though it was a brief victory, since a clap of thunder had her drawing her shoulder up and wincing at the sound.

She dropped the hatchet to the ground and went to hurry down the ladder when her left arm and hand lost its strength. She should have expected it. It often happened awhile after her hand cramped. It hung nearly useless at her side. She would have to rely on her right hand to get her down.

She had stepped only a few rungs down when a strong wind whipped around her and she clung to the ladder with her one hand. Hannah felt the ladder sway before she felt the rung beneath her crack. She reached out with her good hand to grab onto a protruding stone just as the ladder gave way beneath her.

She tried desperately to force some strength into her limp arm, but it refused, continuing to hang useless at her side. Her grip was precarious. She would not be able to hold on much longer and when she fell, it would be the thickets that caught her.

Hannah glanced up to the heavens to beg for help, when she caught sight of a black figure with wings rapidly descending on her. And as her fingers slipped from the stone, and she thought she was surely falling to her death, the black figure consumed her along with darkness.

Chapter Five

Home. She was home, the bedding soft and welcoming, and while the scent was more robust than she remembered it, it was quite pleasing to her senses. She went to turn on her side, to bury her face in the pillow and breathe in more of the pleasant scent when she felt a pain slice down her left arm, stirring unpleasant nightmares.

Not nightmares… memories.

Hannah's eyes shot open and she bolted up in bed, grimacing against the pain as memories came flooding back.

"Do not dare move from that bed!"

Hannah stilled at the sound of the potent command that would freeze the bravest of men. She remained as she was, her eyes slowly searching the room. A small fire in the fireplace did little to light the room, darkness and flickering shadows occupying most of it.

"You will remain there until your arm heals."

Hannah shivered against the chilly tone of his forceful command, but she gathered her courage and asked, "Are you the winged creature that saved me?"

"I am the creature you will stay away from," the strong voice ordered.

"Slain MacKewan?" Hannah dared ask.

"The savage," the voice corrected.

"From what I have seen, you seem more a raven."

"I am many things that you should fear," he warned.

Before Hannah could lose her courage, she said hastily. "I have need of you."

"Satisfy your need elsewhere," he snapped.

Before Hannah could say no more, she heard the creak of a door opening and jumped when it closed so hard that it seemed to tremble the room. She sat there waiting in near darkness, thinking perhaps he had stayed and would speak at any moment, but she was met only with silence.

Exhaustion, pain, endless struggle, she did not know which one plagued her the most, though the heaviness weighing on her shoulders suggested it was all three. She eased her head down on the pillow and allowed herself to indulge in the comfort of the bed. Why fight a good rest in a decent bed?

Besides, she could take the time to think on the various plans that had been swirling in her head, not that she thought any were of much worth. One thing was for sure, she could not stay here forever. She would be found, then what?

She could be honest, but she had discovered that honesty often got her in more trouble, especially with everyone that had been around her lying with ease and without care.

She yawned, the warmth and comfort of the bed forcing her eyes to close and surrender to sleep.

~~~

Voices penetrated Hannah's sleepy haze and she lay still listening to them.

"I will send her away."

"No. She stays."

"That is not a good—"

"Your opinion is not wanted and your permission not required."

"I will keep her busy."

"You will not work her hard. Get more help."

"It is not easy to—"

"Nothing is easy. See it done."

"I will move her to another bedchamber."

"No! She stays in *my bed* for now."

Of course, the pleasing, familiar scent, she was in Slain MacKewan's bed, and a tingle of fear washed over Hannah.

His words returned to her. *I am many things that you should fear.*

She did not fight the sleep that rose up to claim her once more. At least in sleep no worries plagued her. She woke again when she rolled on her sore arm, wincing as her eyes drifted open.

"How did you injure your arm?"

Hannah squinted her eyes, trying to see into the shadows as she responded, "Torture."

The voice turned hostile. "Who dared to torture you?"

"That is wiser left alone," she said and rubbed her arm.

A hand, fingers lean and grip strong, covered hers, easing them away. With the fire's light having dwindled, it was too difficult to make out the shadow that hovered by the side of the bed. She could only see his hand that lay on her arm, the fingers beginning to massage the strain and ache from the muscles. His fingers worked along her flesh slowly, kneading and forcing the sore muscles to obey him.

The soreness began to drift away and so did Hannah, his commanding touch forcing sleep on her.

"I have need of you as well."

The words drifted in her head as she thought to ask him what he meant, but sleep claimed her before she could.

~~~

Morning found her trying to stretch out what aches and pains remained. Her arm was still sore, but the strength of Slain MacKewan's hands kneading it had helped greatly. She wondered why he had done that and why he had brought her to his bed after the fall? Most of all, she wondered what he had meant when he had said, "I have need of you as well." If they had need of each other, perhaps they could help each other. A thought, she feared, was more wishful than probable.

She told herself to hurry out of bed and get to work. She had lingered enough, neglecting her chores and she could not lose her position here. She spent a few more moments snuggled in comfort, not knowing when next she would know such ease.

With her mind finally clear, she realized that she was wearing a nightdress, a soft wool one. But who had stripped her and dressed her in it?

The door swung open and to Hannah's relief, Helice strode in.

"Time to eat and then chores," Helice said, approaching the bed.

Hannah hurried to get up.

"These are for you." Helice placed folded garments on the bottom of the bed. "You must look presentable."

Hannah could not hide her surprise at the brown shift, pale yellow tunic, and a soft green wool cloak. "You are too generous."

"The chief's orders," Helice said as if she did not approve.

"May I speak with him? I would like to thank him for saving me from a terrible fall."

"You will not disturb the chief and I gave you no permission to do such a foolish thing. Obey my commands or else."

Hannah wondered over the or else and recalled hearing Slain forbid Helice from sending her away. If so, what had Helice meant by or else?

Hannah ran her hand slowly over the soft white wool. "As you say, and thank you for kindly changing me into this fine nightdress,"

Helice glared at her. "No one has ever called me kind. Hurry and dress. There are chores to be done."

Hannah stood frozen when Helice closed the door behind her. Was the woman telling her that she was not the one who stripped her naked and placed her in the nightdress? If that was so, only one other person who could have done so.

Slain MacKewan.

~~~

Around mid-day Helice informed Hannah that she would be going to the village.

"While I am gone, you will see to the chief's bedchamber, since you disturbed the fresh bedding. Also, see to the hearth. When he returns he will want to rest." She turned to go, then stopped and fixed a stern glare on Hannah. "Remember what I told you about not going to the east wing." She turned again and walked away, calling out," "I will not be gone long." A warning for Hannah to get busy and be finished by the time she returned.

Hannah gathered a few items she needed from the kitchen, then stepped outside to dip a bucket in the rain barrel. Her glance caught Helice walking off in the distance, but instead of going toward the village, she veered off into the woods. Whatever was she doing going into the woods?

The keep and its two occupants held secrets, but then so did she.

Hannah thought of secrets as she climbed the stairs to Slain's bedchamber. Had she been wise in coming here? She had wondered where to go after her escape and when the thought had struck her, she had argued with herself against it. Was it wise and what would it accomplish?

The point was and would remain that she had no choice. Nothing else was left to her. She had made it this far. She had survived. She could not give up now.

She saw to adding more logs to the fire and quickly got busy straightening the bedding that she had rumpled. Why had Slain brought her here to his bed? Why not another bedchamber in the keep?

She grabbed the pillow to fluff. There it was, his potent scent, like the fields when they were ripe for planting. She did not know what it was about it that she found so appealing, so tempting that it made her bury her face in the pillow and inhale deeply, as if taking part of him inside herself.

The improper thought jolted her and she tossed the pillow down, staring at the bed where she had slept last night. Where Slain MacKewan had made love to many women who he had never invited back.

Whatever was she thinking? That had nothing to do with her. It was no concern of hers. She shook her head and kept shaking it as she rushed to finish straightening the bedding. She stopped now and then to stretch out the lingering ache in her arm. It continued to linger, though more as a dull ache, after an incident, more often than not, and she wondered if it would ever truly heal completely. She wanted to hurry through the chore, be done with it, and be gone from the room, but that would only serve to worsen her arm, so she slowed her pace. Once she finished, she rolled up the bedding and rushed out the door, then stopped abruptly.

Never go to the east wing.

Why did Helice's warning have to plague her now?

Most believe the ghost of Slain's mum walks the east wing.

Of course, Blair's tale had to enter her head as well.

What difference did it make to Hannah what was in the east wing?

You will be sorry.

Her mum's never-ending warning about Hannah's never-ending curiosity rang in her head.

No one was here. No one would know.

How badly do you want to know? she asked herself.

Sometimes ignorance could be more dangerous than curiosity or so it was the excuse she used to approach the door that would take her to the east wing. The door was dark wood, a round metal ring attached to the center.

Hannah took slow steps toward it, thinking that perhaps she would be wiser not to know what was behind it. She shook her head at her doubt. It was better she knew all she could about Slain MacKewan, especially the things he wanted to keep hidden.

She reached out and took hold of the metal ring once in front of the door. It squeaked and she stilled. She stayed as she was for a moment, then tilted her head to listen, having thought she heard a distant sound.

Could Helice have returned already? Or had Slain returned home?

She continued to remain still, her ears perked to hear any sound and it came again. She rushed down the stairs as fast as she could, not wanting to be found standing at a door she had been forbidden to enter. The more she descended the stairs, the louder the sound grew until she realized that it was someone banging forcefully on the front door.

Did she answer it with no one home?

She was about to enter the Great Hall when she heard the door creak open. She moved with haste and silence to the dark alcove a mere two steps from the stairs.

Silence hung heavy for a moment before someone finally spoke.

"Are you not going to invite me in?" a man asked.

"No, say what you have come to say and take your leave."

Hannah recognized that voice... Slain.

"The time grows late. Have you got what he needs?" the man demanded.

"Does he not recall my answer?"

"No is not a response he accepts."

There was something familiar about the man's voice, but she could not place it.

"It is the only one I have for him," Slain said.

"He will not accept it."

The harsh warning in the man's voice was not to be denied but Slain's icy, curt response sent a shiver through Hannah.

"I do not care."

"He will not be pleased with this news."

"Did you not hear my last response?"

"You forget what he has done for you?"

A reminder or another warning, Hannah could not tell.

"I thought he did that out of friendship, but then I realized he did it to benefit himself."

"Watch your tongue, Slain."

"Why? Will you cut it out as he has had done to others?"

"If necessary."

"You can try, but you know very well why I am called the savage and I will see your tongue ripped from your mouth before you or any of your men lay a hand on me. Take that message back to him."

"There is also the other matter."

Slain's snort of laughter echoed through the Great Hall. "Again something else that will benefit him."

"That is not the reason and you know it."

"My answer remains the same for that matter as well... no!"

"He can force that one."

"He can try."

"Regardless of what you think, he is your friend."

"At one time, I believed that."

"You will hear from him."

Again Hannah heard a stern warning in the man's voice.

"Will he have the courage to face me himself the next time?"

"Do you have a death wish, Slain?"

This time there was frustration in the man's voice while Slain's remained confident.

"I have faced death too many times to let anything frighten me."

"I will tell him what you said."

"Good. Now that you have what you need... leave."

"This is not the end of it."

"It is for me."

"Do not be a fool, Slain. He will—"

"Enough!"

Hannah jumped at Slain's forceful shout, the word echoing through the Great Hall.

"We are done here. Take your leave now!"

"Until next time, Slain," the man said and the door slammed shut, the latch falling into place with a thud.

Hannah remained tucked in the secluded alcove, thankful to the shadows that concealed her. Her heart pounded as rapidly as a mighty war drum in her chest and her stomach churned so anxiously that she feared she would lose whatever was in it. If Slain chose to go to his bedchamber, he would have to pass by her and she would risk being discovered hiding there. She prayed with all the strength she had that he would go to his solar.

His heavy footfalls drew closer and closer and she shut her eyes as if somehow it would help her from being seen.

She released her breath when his footfalls drifted off in a different direction.

She opened her eyes after a moment and sighed softly. She would wait a few more moments, then hurry to the kitchen and—

An arm suddenly snagged her around the waist and she was yanked up against a hard body, her feet left dangling in the air.

Chapter Six

Hannah recognized his scent... Slain. He brought his face close to hers, his lips resting next to her ear, and his warm breath prickling her skin.

"If you ever hide and listen to a conversation that is none of your concern again, I will see you punished for it. Do you understand?"

Hannah nodded, her voice caught somewhere in her throat.

His lips moved away from her ear to settle near her mouth. "And if you ever dare try to enter the east wing again—"

He brought his lips closer to hers, so close she thought for a moment that he intended to kiss her.

"You will regret it."

He did not wait for a response. He released her after making sure she had steady footing when he lowered her to the floor. She watched as he strode away, not that she could get a good look at him. She knew him more by scent than features, since she had yet to see him clearly. At least seeing him from behind, she now knew he was a tall man, his dark hair barely reaching his wide shoulders. He appeared trim and lean, not bulky as she imagined a savage might look.

"You are to rest your arm. No chores for you today," he called back to her. "I will make it known to Helice."

He turned the corner and was gone from sight and she let out a breath she did not realize she had been holding.

She remained where she was, wondering over Slain, wondering if it was wise for her to remain here, wondering if life would ever be as it once had been. Or if she wanted it to be. A chill ran through her at the same moment, a tear suddenly threatening the corner of her eye and she wiped it away and hurried out of the dark alcove and over to the fireplace.

She had cried enough tears. They had only served to fill her with sorrow and she had had enough of that as well. But sorrow could not always be quashed. It lingered deep and would creep up when you least expected and take firm hold.

Do not dwell, she silently scolded herself and hurried to her feet. She went and fetched the cloak Slain had provided for her and hurried out of the keep through the kitchen. She was grateful Helice had not returned yet or the woman would have stopped her and demanded to know where she was going and at the moment, though she fought the well of tears building inside her, she feared she would not be able to hold them back. Nor did she know if she wanted to.

Hannah took off for the woods, aching to escape, yet having no place to go. She had nothing. She was alone. She dropped down to sit on a stump after only going a short distance. Her life had had its trials, but had been basically good while her mum had been alive, but once she died everything had fallen apart.

A tear ran down her cheek and she let it fall. She had gone through hell the last few months. A hell she feared where death would be her only rescue. Another tear followed and she did not stop it.

She wished she could go home, but she truly had no home left. Her safe haven had died along with her mum. Now she did not know who to trust. She did not know if she would be safe, especially if her step-brother had found out that she was still alive. He would search for her and he would see her dead.

Here was the only place she could find protection.

Here with the savage, where people feared to tread.

Tears spilled freely down her cheeks. How else was she to stay alive? Her only hope of survival was to seek sanctuary with a man feared by many. Then there was her other problem, one she did not want to think about. One she believed there was no solution to and ironically made worse by being here. But it was a chance she had to take.

More tears fell as sorrow filled her heart and squeezed it tight. She let herself cry like she had not cried since her mum died.

"Why do you cry?"

The gruff demand had her jerking her head up. Her tears ceased out of fear or shock she was not sure. Slain MacKewan stood a short distance from her. It was the first time she got a truly good look at the man. He was dressed in a brown and black plaid with shots of red weaved through it and a brown shirt beneath. His black boots rode up his lean calves, the black leather aged and worn. And his features were the handsomest she had ever seen on a man. Strangely enough though, what caught her attention the most was how his brow scrunched not with anger but concern and his dark eyes held even more concern. Her tears actually upset him.

She spoke honestly. "I am not where I wish to be."

"Where do you wish to be?"

His strong voice held interest not annoyance and as he took a step closer to her, it was then his features caught her breath and she understood why women would want to return to him again and again. He was a feast for the eyes. Even an artistic hand could not capture his fine features they were so defined. Dark brows arched over dark eyes and his narrow nose appeared sculpted perfectly along with his high cheekbones. His narrow lips sat slightly parted and looked as if they invited kisses. One would never grow tired of looking upon him. But as before that mattered not to her. It was concern that held strong in his dark eyes that appealed to her, for she had known little of that from a man.

"Home," she said.

He took another step closer. "Then why not go there?"

She wished to speak the truth to him, but she could not chance it, perhaps never would be able to. "I am no longer wanted."

"Why?"

The sway of his broad shoulders and long legs as he took another step toward her added to his not only powerful but confident gait. But then she had heard tales about the savage.

He is confident in victory. It shows in his ever step.

Her response came easier than she thought and held a bit of truth. "I am not an obedient daughter."

"Is that why you were tortured?"

Her eyes could not hide the surprise at his words.

"When I asked you about your arm, your only word was… torture. The bruises on your body also tell me you have suffered at someone's hands."

His words confirmed what she had suspected. He had been the one who had stripped her and slipped her into the nightdress. Heat rushed up to sting Hannah's cheeks at the thought of him seeing her naked and for a moment she found herself speechless.

The words Helice had used to describe her that one night echoed in her head. *No one of importance.*

She regained her wits and said, "Punishment for what someone thought I deserved."

His eyes narrowed as if he did not believe her or perhaps it was that he did not agree.

"You said you had need of me," he reminded.

The words rushed from her lips. "A place where I will be safe from monsters."

"If it is monsters you run from then you will not be safe with me."

Panic struck Hannah and she tread lightly with her words. "Are you telling me that I should leave?"

"A safe place is here if you want it, but it comes at a high price."

She thought of her mum's warning that you never got something for nothing. "What price?"

His dark eyes traveled over her slowly, lingering at intimate places until Hannah shivered and pulled her cloak snugly around her.

"A price I do not think you will be willing to pay. Think carefully on it and seek me out when you have the courage. And, Hannah, never, ever go into the woods alone again."

Hannah shivered once more as he turned and walked away.

~~~

Slain walked the woods that were as familiar to him as was every nook and cranny in the keep. He had been born here like his many ancestors before him. Only endless wars, pointless skirmishes, and greed had been hard on the land and the clan, though foolish decisions by his father had been the costliest. He had managed to restore much of his clan, but it had come at a price that continued to make demands on him.

When he had returned home and had caught a glimpse of Hannah, he had made a point to catch a better look more than once. Her beauty defied his eyes. That raging red hair, her lovely green eyes, her flawless skin touched ever so slightly by the sun, and a vulnerability that she worked hard at hiding had intrigued him and it had been a long time since any woman had intrigued him.

His first thought had been to send her away, to keep her safe from him. Then when he saw her hanging from the window beneath his, he grabbed the rope he kept in his bedchamber, if a quick exit proved necessary, and rushed down to save her from landing on the thorny thickets.

Once he had her in his arms, he had not wanted to let her go. Somehow his actions had made him feel as if he had claimed her. A foolish thought, yet one he could not shed. He had not thought twice about slipping her out of her worn garments and into a nightdress, the torture that it was. And seeing the bruises on her lovely, and far too tempting, body had infuriated him.

He had never touched a woman against her will and he had certainly never taken an unconscious woman, that was beyond cowardly. Besides, seeing her there so vulnerable once again and her telling him that she had need of him had made him want to protect her. He had not known what happened to her, but he certainly wanted to find out... and make the person suffer for it.

He snapped the twig, he had scooped up as he walked, in half. It had been obvious to him that she was not telling him the whole truth. She was running from more than she had told him, which was why he made her the offer that he did... the monster that he was.

She would accept it. She had no place to go, leaving her in no position to refuse him.

It was not right, but he had need of her as well, and she fit that need perfectly... she was a person of no consequence. She would be the solution to his one problem. The other problem? There was time to think on it, but not now.

He would settle the one problem and be done with it and Hannah would help him do that. He had thought to walk away when he had seen her in the woods crying. Normally, he ignored tears on a woman. Too many of them used it against a man. But Hannah had been sitting alone, crying to herself. They had been sincere tears and he wondered what had brought them on. What she had told him about needing him had only fueled the idea he had been contemplating since seeing her. And once she asked to stay and be kept safe from monsters, any doubts he might have had vanished.

Unfortunately, she had run from one monster to another, and monsters had no souls. It was why he had no remorse for what he was about to do to Hannah, and once it was done, there would be no changing it.

Hannah would belong to him.

Chapter Seven

Hannah sat near the warmth of the hearth in the Great Hall, her legs tucked up against her chest, her arms wrapped around them, and her chin resting on her knees. She had fled Helice's presence after supper, the woman so angry that Hannah had expected to see fire spew from her mouth. It had started when Helice had informed Hannah she was not to do any chores until told otherwise. She could not blame the woman. There was much to be done in the keep, far more than two people alone could do.

"You should leave."

Hannah's head shot up to see Helice standing a short distance away.

"There is nothing here for you. Go now while you can. I will give you food to last for a few days. Find someplace safe."

Hannah did not expect to hear the last three words from her. She was telling her it was not safe here. She almost laughed, not with humor, but fear. No matter where she turned, there was no place for her to go. No safe haven. No one to help her out of kindness, except for the healer who had freed her from that hell. She had been the only one who had showed her true kindness, wanting nothing in return for it.

"I have no place to go."

"Any place is better than here. There is no heart to this place, no soul. It will swallow you whole and you will never escape."

"If that is so, why do you stay?" Hannah asked curious of how the woman came to be with Slain.

Helice's chin went up. "I owe a debt and I will see it repaid."

"I guess then we are both stuck here," Hannah said.

"You can find another clan who will surely take you in," Helice said almost as if she commanded it.

"Trust me, Helice, when I tell you that this is the only place I can find refuge and I will do what I must to remain here… for now."

"If you do not leave by morning's light, you will never leave here."

A direct warning that sent a small shiver through Hannah.

"I will leave a cloth wrapped with food for you in the kitchen if you should change your mind, and I hope you do."

Hannah watched Helice turn and walk away and she considered paying heed to the woman's dire warning and advice, but it always returned to the same thing. Where would she go? Her only other choice would be for her to leave the Highlands and go where? This was her home and the only place she knew. The only place she wanted to be. Besides, there was no safety for a woman traveling alone.

When she had been freed from that hellhole of a dungeon, she had kept company with another woman who had been freed along with her. They had traveled at night and had avoided the well-traveled roads. They had parted when their destinations went in different directions and Hannah had to admit she had missed traveling with her. They at least had each other even if the woman had barely spoken a word, but then she had suffered far worse than Hannah had.

Slain was her only hope at the moment, and Helice might think that she would never leave here, but Hannah knew better. There would come a day when one, or perhaps both, of the monsters she had escaped would come claim her.

She had no choice but to agree to pay her due for being allowed to remain here, though she would give herself a few days to think on it. Sometimes solutions could be found for the most improbable problem if one gave thought. Or so she told herself, when she knew better. Sometimes there was no solution... only surrender.

She was no fool. She had known by the way Slain's dark eyes had caressed her body slowly what demands he would make of her and she had to be sure that she was willing to surrender to him. She would be a servant and she would serve the chief of the clan. Was she truly willing to pay such a price to survive?

She would think on it, though she worried her fate was already sealed.

~~~

Hannah could not sit idle the next day. Without her hands busy, her thoughts were chaotic. After making sure Helice did not see her, Hannah grabbed a bucket of water and other items she needed and went to the Great Hall to continue cleaning it. She intended to take her time since her arm remained weak and still pained her. But the pain in her arm was a welcoming relief compared to the endless, disturbing thoughts that plagued her.

She smiled and raised her arm to wipe the back of her hand across her brow, after finishing cleaning one table and the benches along each side. She kept her left arm tucked against her since it was simply too weak to be of any help.

"What did I tell you?"

Hannah jumped at Slain's unexpected and fierce reprimand and turned to see him walk with quick strides toward her. Instinct warned her to back away from him, but courage rose up and refused to allow her to move.

He came to a stop directly in front of her and she could tell he had recently been in the woods, the scent of pine heavy on him. He remained there, his arms folded over his chest. His sleeves were rolled up, the cuffs clinging tightly to the defined muscles in his arms.

There was a sternness to his expression, his brow narrowed and his mouth tauter than pinched, but his eyes told a different tale. A spark of concern flashed in their dark depths, similar to yesterday when he had found her crying, and she wondered if there was a more human side to the savage than he allowed anyone to see.

She realized he waited for an answer. "I cannot sit idle," she explained.

His hand reached out to cup her elbow. His touch was firm as if not giving her a choice and his hand warm against her bare skin, having rolled up her sleeves to work, as he directed her to sit on one of the benches that had been cleaned.

"Tell me of this torture that injured your arm," he said and sat beside her.

She had spoken of it to no one, but then who was there to tell, and she would have preferred not to speak of it. However, his stern tone told her it was not a request. "My upper arm was shackled and I was left to hang from it for long periods of time, my feet unable to touch the ground."

His brow scrunched as he measured her words. "That is how you got that bruise that looks like a band around your arm?"

Hannah nodded, fearful he would demand to know who tortured her. A question she would not answer, so she spoke quickly. "A healer told me it would take time for my arm to mend, though it may never heal completely. That it may always remain weaker than my other arm."

"That is a harsh punishment for a disobedient daughter," —he paused a moment— "Or is it a husband you run from?"

She was quick to say, "I have no husband and no family who wants me."

"Then who are these monsters who chase you?"

He had trapped her with that question. He was searching to find out some truth about her. Hannah's mum had once told her that the truth was not something always to be told, especially if the truth could prove harmful to one's self. In this situation, the truth could prove deadly for her.

"Those who would do a woman on her own harm."

"How long have you been on your own?" he asked.

"Long enough to know there are too many monsters for me to fight alone."

"Why come here? Why the Clan MacKewan?"

"You are feared and respected, and you are a chief who has already fought monsters," she said.

"It takes a monster to fight other monsters," he cautioned.

Hannah shook her head, ready to correct him, "It takes courage—"

"To confront a monster, especially in his lair. With such courage, why would you need me?"

"Courage only goes so far when you are on your own."

"So what you truly seek from me is... friendship?"

An unexpected smile rose on Hannah's face at the thought that that could actually be possible. "It would be nice to call you friend."

Slain leaned his face close to hers. "It is not friend you will be calling me, Hannah."

He brushed his lips faintly across hers with a tenderness that sent a ripple of pure pleasure cascading down along her body to fade at her feet.

He stood. "Have Neata look at your arm and see what she says. She is a good healer," Slain ordered, leaving no room for her to disagree. "In the meantime, you will do as told. No chores for you until I say otherwise."

Hannah went to protest, but a sharp wince replaced her words and she looked down at her hand in her lap. It had cramped, her misshapen fingers resembling more a talon's claw. She went to grab it with her good hand when Slain quickly seated himself beside her once again and took hold of her cramped hand.

She winced again when his thumb dug deeply into her palm, pressing against the taut muscle that sent a stinging pain to shoot all the way up her arm.

"I know it hurts, but it is the only way to ease away the pain," he said, and continued fighting the muscle that refused to relax.

The pain grew and she shut her eyes against it, trying desperately to fight it as she had done endless times. It seemed like forever before the pain began to subside and once it did she realized that she had rested her brow against Slain's.

When had she done that? And why had he allowed her to? She warned herself to ease away, but instead, she opened her eyes.

It was almost as if his dark eyes touched her green ones and this time she saw it clearly... concern. It disturbed him that she suffered pain. If he cared, how could he be a savage? Somewhere inside him had to be a kind heart. Or at least that was what she wanted to believe.

Slain watched confusion swirl in her lovely green eyes. She did not know what to think of him. He confused her and that was not good. He could not let her think that he cared or had a heart. She would only be disappointed.

His hand suddenly grabbed at the back of her neck, holding it stiff as he brought his mouth close to hers, so close his words brushed her lips. "Do not be foolish enough to think I care. You will settle a need I have and that is all." He released her and stood to stand in front of her. "If you cannot sit idle, find something to do that will not require use of your arm."

Hannah watched him walk away, not another word spoken between them.

~~~

"I got a severe tongue lashing because of you," Helice accused as she all but dropped the bowl in front of Hannah where she sat at the table in the Great Hall that evening. "I do not understand you Highland women. You are stubborn to a fault."

"I only thought to help you," Hannah said in a way of an apology.

"If you want to help... leave here and never return." Helice turned and walked out of the room mumbling in her native language.

Hannah ate little, her thoughts once again cumbersome. Why had she ever thought coming here would be a solution for her when there was no solution to her problem?

Hope.

She had held on to the hope that things would turn out well despite all she had been through. That hope, unfortunately, was beginning to fade.

Her churning stomach prevented her from taking another bite and she retreated to her pallet by the hearth. She was tired of thinking, tired of worrying, tired of being strong. She wanted nothing more than the peacefulness of sleep until at least dawn.

Regrettably, that was even denied her. She woke from her sleep and seeing that the logs in the fireplace had not dwindled that much, she realized she had not slept long. And with how awake she felt, sleep would not soon return to her.

She lay on her pallet, staring up into the dark, not looking forward to the long, sleepless night ahead when a sound caught her attention. She lay still, listening.

Was that the crinkling of parchment she heard? Footfalls as well? And the scent of pine and earth was strong.

Slain.

With the scent so heavy, he had to have been in the woods again. He seemed to spend much time in the woods, and she wondered why. The clansmen did the hunting, the meat shared amongst the clan.

The footfalls sounded indecisive, stopping then starting again.

It was not until the whispers started that Hannah realized that it was two footfalls she heard and though the voices were low, she could distinguish them as coming from two men.

She turned her ear to the whispers, straining to hear even just a snatch of conversation.

Whispering mumbles met her ear, then she caught something.

"—anyone to know you are here."

That sounded like Slain. From the words she had caught, he did not want anyone to know the person he was speaking with was here. Did that include Helice? Did he not trust her and if so why?

More footfalls approached.

"Go—follow soon—east wing."

Slain spoke rapidly, the crinkling of parchment making it difficult to hear his words clearly, then footfalls rushed off as another approached.

"Do you need anything?"

Helice's whisper was not as quiet as the men had been.

"I will retire shortly, after I am done in the solar," Slain said, keeping his voice low.

"Are you certain you do not want her moved to a room?" Helice asked.

"No, she stays here until I have my answer," Slain said.

So Helice knew what he intended. Was that why she had told her to leave? Could Helice actually have been concerned for her?

Hannah listened as two pair of footfalls faded away. She lay there wondering what was going on. How had the unknown man gotten into the keep without Helice knowing it. Did Slain not want Helice to know about the visitor?

MacKewan keep held far too many secrets and if she was going to remain here, she had to know what was going on. She could not live with secrets. Secrets could have disastrous results. She knew that from experience.

She quietly got up off the pallet and silently made her way up the stairs to the east wing door and her eyes turned wide.

It sat ajar.

The man who had spoken with Slain must have left it open, since Slain had said he intended to follow. Hannah did not give herself time to decide if it would be wise to follow after the man, she quietly slipped past the door into the east wing.

Chapter Eight

A long, dark narrow hallway with a faint, flickering light at the far end greeted her, though more warned her away, along with a musty odor that tickled her nose. She hurried to pinch her nostrils, feeling a sneeze about to erupt. Keeping hold of her nose until she was sure the sneeze had passed, she made her way slowly down the hall.

She kept alert for footfalls from either end of the hallway, not sure if the man who had disappeared through here was gone and if he was, that meant there was an exit in this wing. And from what Slain had said, he would be coming here as soon as he finished in his solar.

Finished what?

She had little time to explore and little light to do it by. There were three doors from what she could make out. Halfway down on the left was one, another sat across from it to the right, and the other sat at the far end where the light flickered. Knowing her time was short, she hurried quietly and cautiously to try the door to the left and when she found it locked, she turned and went to the door on the right. That one was locked as well. Which meant the man must have gone through the door at the end of the hall. The same room Slain would go once he entered here.

Her knee bumped against something, the sound sending a slight echo along the hall. She froze. If the man had not left the keep yet, he may have heard it. She was relieved when no noise came from the far end of the hall, but fear prickled her skin when she caught the sound of footfalls on the stairs.

Her heart was already pounding against her chest and grew worse as she glanced around frantically searching for a place to hide, but she could see no alcoves or cubbies to duck into.

She was beginning to question the wisdom of her decision to have come here in the first place. What had she thought she would find? Or had she hoped to hear more of an exchange between the two men? Either way she should have given her action more thought, but it was too late now.

The footfalls grew closer and a creak sounded at the end of the hall, someone was opening the door.

Hannah felt along at what she had bumped into, grateful to find it was a wood chest. It was long and narrow. Hannah did not hesitate. She opened the chest and felt down around inside it. From the feel of it, blankets & garments were stored within. It really did not matter what the chest held. She had to disappear and fast. She climbed in and eased the lid down, trying as best she could to bury herself beneath the contents in case the chest was opened.

Footfalls drew near, though she could not tell from which end they came.

"Why have you not left?" Slain demanded.

His voice sounded as if he stood in front of the chest.

"…heard a noise."

Hannah caught only the three words, the man whispered so gently as if not trusting that he and Slain were alone.

The silence grew so heavy that Hannah feared the two men would hear her breathing. She closed her eyes and willed herself to breathe gently and not move a muscle.

Slain finally spoke. "Footfalls?"

"A scratching noise," the other man said. "Rats perhaps."

Hannah squeezed her eyes tight and wrinkled her nose at the thought of the scurrying creatures. She also wondered over the voice that was a bit clearer. She thought it sounded familiar, but the whispery tone made it hard to place.

"Possibly," Slain said, not sounding quite so sure. "You need to hurry. This message must reach him before daybreak."

The man must have given a silent response, since footfalls followed and Hannah heard a door shut. From what she had heard, the man was about to leave on a mission for Slain. But what of Slain? Would he be returning this way again? Did she wait or did she take the chance and run before he made his way back again?

A sudden thought had her easing the top of the chest open. If Slain did come back this way to leave, he could lock the door behind him and then she would be stuck. That was a chance she was not willing to take.

She eased herself up and out of the chest and lowered the top carefully, though she wanted to rush. Any moment Slain could open the door at the end of the hall, and then what?

Once done, she hurried down the hall toward the door she had entered and as she reached it, she heard the door at the other end creak open. She almost sighed with relief when she saw that the door had remained ajar and slipped past it with ease. Though it reminded her that Slain had intended to return this way and no doubt would soon not be far behind her.

Hannah flew down the stairs and hurried to her pallet in the Great Hall. She tried to calm her breathing, but it was difficult, fright still heavy upon her. She turned on her side, keeping her back to the stairs in case Slain approached. She did not want him to see her chest heaving.

No sooner had she settled herself as if asleep, she heard him enter the Great Hall. His footfalls stopped for a moment, then she heard them again… headed her way.

Fear raced through her, rushing to her heart, pounding it like a mighty drum in her chest, and her breathing increased until she thought she would not be able to catch her breath.

He would discover that she had spied on him, then what?

Swift thoughts and instinct to survive had served her well these last few months just as it did now.

She jumped up off her pallet, screaming.

Slain was rarely startled or rattled by anything. It came from surviving endless battles. Yet Hannah's terrified scream had pierced his heart as sharply as an arrow, though it did not freeze him as such screams did to some men. He was by her side in an instant, grabbing hold of her arms.

Hannah struggled to breathe and her eyes were as round as full moons as she stared at Slain. He had not been that far from her. Had he intended to see if she was there on her pallet?

"Ni-nightma-nightmare," Hannah stumbled to say.

"You are safe. I am here with you. I will let nothing harm you," he said and gently rubbed along her arms.

Her heaving breaths began to slow.

Slain slipped his arm around her and guided her to a bench at one of the nearby tables. He held her against his side as he eased them both down to sit. While he held her close, his free hand eased beneath the sleeve covering her left arm to caress and massage the muscle.

That he remembered or even thought to see to her injured arm or offer her comfort touched her heart. Not to mention that the strength of him half wrapped around her made her feel safer than she had in some time.

"Tell me of your nightmare. It will help to chase it away."

That was easy, for all she had to do was share the recurring nightmare she had since escaping the dungeon.

"Voices, footfalls, they rush at me—" She stopped a moment, fear racing her heart and catching at her breath once again. She pushed past both eager to speak it aloud and be rid of it, if only it was that easy. "Hands grab me, pull at me," —she shuddered— "they have come to take me away, to torture me, to see me dead."

"You believe your family wanted you dead?" he asked, his arm remaining firm around her.

She bit at her tongue, having been so focused on her nightmare that she had said too much.

"It felt that way... in the nightmare," she said, hoping the brief explanation would suffice.

"Your nightmare also makes it seem that you believe your family searches for you. Do you believe that?" he asked as if it troubled him.

"They have no wont of me," she said her words partially true.

"Yet you still fear monsters. You still seek safety."

She thought for a moment on her response, concerned she would say too much. "I worry that one day someone in my family might come across me and think to return me home or perhaps finish what they had started."

"You said they had no wont of you, so why would they bother," Slain reminded.

She knew exactly why they would bother, but she could not share it with him.

She sighed. "Memories of what I suffered brings endless fears... and nightmares."

"Then think hard on what you will surrender for the safety you seek from me when you may not need it," he cautioned, his arm slipping off her. He stood. "Monsters come in different guises. Make certain you do not exchange one monster for another."

Hannah sat staring as he walked away. Was that not what she needed? A bigger monster than the one she had escaped to help keep her safe?

"Hannah."

It was the first time she heard her name fall softly from his lips.

He turned and looked at her. "I will give you one day to give me your answer since we both know what it will be."

~~~

Slain sat in his solar, his thoughts not where they should be. He did not know what to make of Hannah. He had known from first meeting her that she did not speak the whole truth of things to him and the more he spoke with her the more he realized he was right.

She kept something from him.

The question was why? What did she not want him to know?

Whatever it was, it frightened her enough to seek refuge here and with him in particular. Again he questioned why. She had had courage enough to escape a horrific situation and courage enough to seek out the savage. She was braver than she believed and yet she still feared.

He should probably speak with her more before forcing the situation, but in the end he doubted it would matter. He had need of her and she would serve that need well.

That he found her appealing was another matter. He also found himself catching a glance of her whenever he could and if by chance he caught a smile on her lovely face, he would find himself growing aroused.

A smile...a simple smile had aroused him.

Not just any smile, though, Hannah's smile. It had annoyed him. He had no time to allow a woman into his thoughts. He had enough on his mind. She lingered there anyway, refusing to leave. Or did he refuse to let her?

He had had the occasional visit from women selling their wares as they passed through on their travels. They had sufficed, though rarely satisfied. There was too much for him to think on, too much that needed to be done to allow himself to get lost in a woman.

That was why Hannah would serve him so well. Though he would have to be careful and not let her into his heart. What heart? It had died and he had buried it along with all he had lost. He had no tenderness, no caring, no love to offer her.

They each had a need and that need was what would be served, nothing more.

~~~

"That offer still remains," Helice said with a sour face and a nod to a wrapped bundle on the table when Hannah entered the kitchen the next morning.

She decided to counter with a smile. "You will miss me if I go, Helice."

"Bah, why would I miss a lazy one like you?"

Hannah snatched a warm piece of bread off the table. "You will miss my smile since it is the only one in the keep and you will miss how I eagerly devour your delicious meals."

"I will not miss your foolishness," Helice argued with a dismissive wave of her hand.

Hannah chuckled. "We are all foolish one time or another whether we want to be or not, or so my mum warned me."

"Then you should have paid her heed," Helice scolded.

Hannah's smile faded. "Aye, I should have."

"I will bring your meal to the Great Hall," Helice said as if dismissing Hannah.

Hannah went and while she did enjoy Helice's meals, she found that this morning she was not hungry. Her mind was on Slain and that he had given her one day to accept his offer and that he seemed sure she would.

But then that was what she had come here for, safety, was it not? Why did she continue to question it? What would it change?

Everything... with what he wanted from her.

She sat at the table alone staring at the bowl of porridge Helice had brought her. She forced herself to take a few spoonsful, then shook her head and snatching up her full bowl off the table, she went to the kitchen and placed it on the table where Helice worked. "I am not that hungry." She then went to the door, grabbed her cloak off the hook, and went outside.

"Where are you going?" Helice called out.

Hannah did not answer.

She headed to the woods out of instinct. It was where she would go when her father let loose his temper, which had been far too often. She shook the disturbing memories away as she kept her gait steady. There was a briskness to the spring air that brought a smile to Hannah's face and a glow to her cheeks. It felt good to leave the darkness and solitude of the keep even though two other people occupied it besides herself. There was simply no life to the place.

"I told you not to go into the woods alone."

Hannah turned, surprised to see Slain not far behind her. He truly tempted the eye and not only his features but the strength of his stance, his broad shoulders drawn back, a slight lift to his chin and the way his muscles strained against his shirtsleeves.

"Why?" she asked before she could stop herself.

He raised his brow as he came to a stop in front of her. "You question me?"

She had forgotten her place as her father had often reminded her. "Forgive me, I thought a walk would, at least, keep me from being idle."

"It is not safe for you to walk alone in the woods."

"Then walk with me," she said, hoping he would accept, hoping he might tell her exactly what he expected in return for allowing her to remain in the safety of his clan.

Slain was about to refuse when he found himself saying, "No more than a brief walk." She smiled and he felt himself stir. It annoyed him that her smile could have such a stimulating effect on him.

Hannah snatched up a small stick as they walked, her smile growing. "This was an ample sword when I was a wee bairn. I would fight the fiercest of creatures with it and always emerge victorious."

"I insisted on a real sword from the time I could grasp one firm," Slain said surprised at himself for sharing it with her. He rarely, if ever, shared anything about himself.

"That was brave of you, since this," —she raised the thin stick and waved it— "did little to help me." She tossed it aside, thinking how unprepared she had been for real monsters.

"What of a brother or did he agree with your father?"

Another question she could answer honestly. "I have no brothers or sisters and I was a disappointment to my father."

"A disobedient daughter could prove a problem, though a courageous daughter brings great pride."

Was he defending her?

"I would prefer courageous over obedient."

Hannah reached out as if it was the most natural thing to do and hooked her arm around his as they continued to walk. "I would imagine your daughter would be more courageous than most other women."

"I will make sure she is," Slain said surprised she had taken hold of his arm, yet enjoying the feel of it wrapped snugly around his.

"Then you hope for children?"

It was one thing he wanted most… a family. He once had hoped for a wife who would love him the way his mother had loved his father—unconditionally. She had known his faults, but they had not mattered to her. He could see the love in her eyes and in his father's eyes each time they looked at each other. It never dimmed or faltered. It had shined like a beacon ever strong.

It was not meant to be for him.

"A marriage is being arranged."

She stopped abruptly, dropping her arm off his. "I have heard no such news."

"I have not made it known yet."

For a moment, she stood speechless. "Then what do you want from me?"

Slain stepped close to her, took hold of her face and brought his lips down on hers.

Chapter Nine

Shocked, Hannah grew rigid at Slain's touch. She had never known a man's lips on hers and she was not sure what to expect. Never would she have expected such warmth, tenderness, and pure pleasure from a man referred to as the savage.

His lips coaxed hers with gentle kisses and slight nibbles into responding and she did with eagerness, pressing her lips against his as if she could not get enough of him and a vague tingling began to spread throughout her body. His tongue faintly brushed between her lips and her mouth dropped open ever so slightly with a soft sigh, and his tongue slipped in.

His kiss suddenly engulfed her and she shivered at the intensity of the pleasure it brought her, that vague tingle turning to sparks that ignited intimate parts of her body. Her limbs weakened and his arm was quick to go around her waist and steady her against him, which seemed to heat her body even more.

Slain held her close, much too close. A kiss. A simple kiss was all he intended, but when his lips touched hers, everything changed, and even more so when she responded so innocently. It was as if she had never been kissed before and that thought not only fired his blood but aroused him.

He warned himself to end it, not let it go any further, but he found the taste of her too intoxicating. One taste was not enough; he wanted more. Much more.

He eased his lips away from hers, though kept his arm tucked around her. "Think on what you are willing to surrender." He stepped away from her, his hand going to take hold of her arm when she appeared unsteady on her feet. "We return to the keep."

Hannah went along with him, keeping silent the whole way until they grew nearer to the keep. She stopped suddenly.

Slain stopped as well, his hand still firm on her arm.

"I think I will go to the healer and have her look at my arm."

Slain's first impulse was to say no, though he kept hold of his tongue. Why he should not want her to go see the healer made as much sense as to why he wanted her to remain there in the keep with him. It was wiser to put distance between them with how aroused he felt.

He had given her until tomorrow to make a decision and he would keep his word.

"Go see Neata and then return here. Do not dawdle," he ordered.

Hannah did not think before she spoke, but then she felt frustrated and annoyed. "What is wrong with dawdling at times? Must everything be rushed? Can one not simply linger and enjoy?"

"When I give you permission," Slain snapped, his own annoyance surfacing, which he should have expected since he had left them both unsatisfied. "Go and do not linger." He shook his head annoyed even more that his tongue had been so snappish, and annoyed that if he lingered any longer with her, he would do more than kiss her.

Hannah turned away in a huff, glad for his retreat. At the moment, she did not care to be in his company, though the more forceful steps she took the more she realized that was not true. She sighed and slowed her gait. The problem was that she had not wanted to leave his side. She had enjoyed their kiss and would have preferred talking to him, asking him why he wanted intimacy with her when a marriage was being arranged for him. Though, it was a question best suited for her to answer. Which would be far worse for her, remaining here, a kept woman to the savage, under his protection or... she shook her head.

Death.

She would be left far too vulnerable if she left here. There would be no place she could go that would offer the protection that the savage could. Besides, while Slain could intimidate at times, there was a kindness to him that he did not want anyone to see. Which seemed at odds with what he was demanding of her in exchange for her remaining here.

He was a bit of a mystery surrounded by secrets, which Hannah intended to unwrap and reveal.

She walked through the village, most nodding to her now, accepting that she was here to stay, no doubt thanks to Blair and Wilona's wagging tongues. But what would happen when they found out that her position at the keep had changed? Would they still nod and call out greetings to her or turn their heads? But what would it matter? She at least would survive.

Neata waved when she saw Hannah approach and stepped out of her garden where she had been busy working.

Hannah smiled and returned the wave.

"You have finally come for a visit," Neata said, resting the hoe she held against the side of the cottage.

"A visit and to have you look at my arm."

Neata grinned. "I was going to suggest that. Come in and we will enjoy a nice chamomile brew, then I will look at your arm."

Do not dawdle.

Hannah chased the words from her head and followed Neata into the cottage.

They talked of various things and Hannah was grateful Neata did not probe. She accepted the answers Hannah gave and questioned no more beyond them.

"I remember how Slain's mum beamed with joy when I handed her squalling, wee son to her," Neata said with a wide smile.

"You delivered Slain?"

"I did and I hope to deliver all his bairns. He wants a slew of them, though he admits it to no one. He cannot hide from me how much he misses his family and the way it used to be here, especially at the keep. The door to the Great Hall was always open to those in need. No one went hungry or unattended. Leala, his mum, made sure of it. It will be nice when Slain weds and his wife restores life to the keep."

Neata spoke as if she knew of the marriage that was being arranged for Slain, but her next words confirmed the opposite.

"I hope Slain weds soon and she loves him with all the strength and courage that his parents had for each other. Then they would both be well loved, for Slain would surrender his heart and soul to the woman he loves."

Hannah felt a strange catch to her heart. To be loved that way would be remarkable, and the strange catch to her heart turned to heavy sadness. She would never know such incredible love.

"I knew such a love," Neata said with a smile and a tear in her one eye. "I lost my Peter far too soon after we wed and never found another like him. But the memories he left me with comfort me and keep me warm on cold winter nights." She brushed a tear away. "Now let us see to that arm, though you must be honest with me in how you truly suffered such an injury. You have my word I will tell no one."

Hannah hesitated, though only a moment. She could tell the healer without revealing certain information that had nothing to do with the torture.

It did not take long for Neata to reach a conclusion. "The healer who tended you was wise and thanks to her exceptional care your arm has healed better than I would have expected. Though, that healer was also right in telling you that your arm may never fully heal properly. It may continue to pain you and grow weak at times."

"I can manage that," Hannah said. "I could have been left far worse off."

"There are not many healers as skilled as the one who treated you. What is her name?"

Hannah remained silent.

"It was Espy, Cyra's granddaughter, was it not?" Neata asked, realizing Hannah had no intention of answering her.

Hannah smiled, but would say nothing, having given her word to Espy.

"Both Cyra and Espy are exceptional healers, though I believe Espy more so since her father had been a physician and had taught her all he knew. Espy is fortunate to have the knowledge of the old and the new ways, and you were fortunate to have had her tend you."

A rumble of thunder caught both their attention and Neata went to the door to look out. "The sky darkens. A storm will arrive soon."

Hannah slipped on her cloak and joined Neata at the open door. "I enjoyed our visit and will come again."

"I would like that, and I hope to be the one who delivers your first born, after you find and wed a man who loves you."

The two women hugged and Hannah hurried off, thunder following her and the sadness returning to poke at her heart. She would never know such a love and the thought seemed to crush her spirit.

People were hurrying to take cover in their cottages from the impending storm and Hannah quickened her own pace, the wind suddenly whipping at her. She lowered her head to avoid the lashing wind and lifted it only now and then to make certain she remained on the path to the keep.

The wind grew stronger, whipping more violently. It would be a harsh storm that soon descended on them. Hannah raised her head once more and scrunched her eyes to make sure of what she was seeing.

It was the creature who had saved her from falling into the thickets headed her way, his cloak billowing out behind him and from his sides like raven wings, almost as if the wind was too frightened to lash at him as it did her. Only this time she could see his face... Slain.

His mouth was pursed tight and his dark eyes wore a scowl that was focused directly on her.

He was coming for her; she had dawdled far too long.

Hannah braced herself for a tongue-lashing and was more than surprised when he raised his arm, the edge of his cloak in his hand, making it seem as if he spread his wing and he wrapped it around her as he turned and came alongside her, protecting her from the lashing wind.

He guided them both to the keep without a word being spoken, but then words would have been hard to hear with the relentless wind. The first drop of rain splattered the ground as they reached the door of the keep. He eased her through the door before him and shut it firmly behind him, then turned and glared at her.

"Forgive me, I lingered too long," Hannah said before he could reprimand her.

"Did you not see the storm approaching?" He reached out and slipped off her cloak and divested himself of his own. With a firm hand to her lower back, he eased her toward the large fireplace that was burning more brightly than usual.

"I was inside visiting with Neata," Hannah said and realizing her hands were chilled rubbed them together.

"Sit by the fire and warm yourself. The storm brings a chill with it." He took her arm gently and eased her down on a bench. "Helice!" he shouted, after turning, his strong voice echoing throughout the Great Hall and no doubt the entire keep itself.

Helice appeared soon after.

"A hot brew," Slain ordered and the woman nodded and hurried off.

Slain sat beside her. "What did Neata say?"

She smiled softly and purposely looked in his eyes and was not surprised to see concern there. Again she was reminded that he was not so much the savage most believed.

"She agreed with the healer who tended me. My arm may never heal properly. The pain may continue as well as the weakness. But I feel fortunate, since it could have been much worse."

"You will take care not to abuse it with senseless tasks," he ordered.

"What tasks would they be?" she asked pointedly, hoping he would define what he expected from her. He stared at her and he looked about to move closer, looked about to kiss her. She did not move away, for fool that she was, she wanted him to kiss her.

"Whatever I command," he said and stood abruptly, not trusting himself to remain next to her. "Tomorrow I will summon you and you will give me your answer." Quick strides had him leaving the Great Hall, passing Helice on the way.

Helice placed two tankards on the table, snatching one up after placing the pitcher there. "You had your chance," she warned and walked off.

Tears brimmed in Hannah's eyes, though she refused to let them fall. She raised her chin and stared after the woman, whispering softly, "You are wrong. I never had a chance."

~~~

Hannah was summoned to Slain's solar before the morning meal. She was glad since she had barely slept and her stomach had not stopped churning, thinking of how her fate had been sealed long before she arrived here.

Helice had shaken her head when she had delivered the summons and reminded her yet again as she had done last night. "You had your chance."

Hannah knocked on the solar door and Slain's deep, sharp voice bid her to enter.

He stood with his back braced against the desk, his arms crossed over his chest. He spoke not a word. He simply waited for her answer.

Before she lost her courage, Hannah rushed to say, "I will do what I must to remain here under your protection."

"You will do whatever I command? I have your word on it?"

He was giving her another chance to leave or escape as Helice had warned. Her next words would seal her fate and she spoke them with what courage she had left. "Aye, whatever you command. You have my word."

Slain walked toward her with hasty strides and startled her when he went past her to the door and opened it.

Helice entered and behind her followed a man dressed in the plain brown robe of a cleric. The short, thin man appeared frightened as if he wished to be anyplace but here. Helice avoided looking at her as they both stepped to the side, remaining silent.

Slain returned to Hannah and with no smile and an icy tone said, "Today, Hannah, you become my wife."

Chapter Ten

Hannah stared at the cleric as he spoke, not truly hearing his words. Her mind was busy trying to comprehend what was taking place. Slain stood beside her as the cleric joined them as husband and wife.

She told herself to stop the ceremony, it could not be. It could never be, but her voice failed her. She had also given her word that she would do whatever he commanded in exchange for protection. Never, though, would she have thought he would choose to wed her. She had been the marriage that was being arranged. He had planned it all along.

Why though? Why wed her?

It was a question that gave her an uneasy feeling, though nowhere near the troubling concern it gave her at what would happen when her father discovered who she had wed.

"Hannah."

Her name spilled so softly from Slain's lips that she was not sure she heard it, though she turned to him with a gentle 'aye' falling from her lips. It took a moment for her to realize that she had just agreed to accept Slain as her husband.

Speak up. Speak up. Stop this farce. She silently warned herself, but again her voice failed her. A sudden thought came to her then. Would this marriage be valid if her father did not agree to it?

No one of importance. That was who he thought he wed. But why would he want to wed a peasant?

"The document must be sealed," Slain said and stepped away from her, the cleric joining him at the desk to make their union official, and consummation would be the final sealing of their vows.

Hannah watched as Slain poured wax into the corner of the document and the cleric quickly pressed his ring into it. Slain repeated the process to apply the MacKewan seal to it as well and as he did, Hannah cast a look to Helice.

The woman gave a nod of respect to her, then looked to Slain.

It made Hannah realize that she was no longer a servant and that things would be different. How different though? Would she be a prisoner here as much as Helice seemed to be? Was that what Helice had been trying to warn her about? Had she traded one prison for another?

"It is done," Slain said, seeing that his wife still appeared stunned by what had transpired. Her lovely green eyes had deepened in color and had rounded considerably when he had announced she would become his wife, and they had remained so.

She had seemed as though she wanted to speak, but could find no words. Nor did he think she had heard any of what the cleric had recited. That he had caught her unware was quite apparent and had served him well, for the shock of his announcement had left her speechless. But then she had given her word and Slain, for some reason, believed Hannah an honorable woman and would not have reneged regardless, which made what he had done that more dishonorable.

It mattered not. Hannah was his wife now and there would be no changing that.

After Helice escorted the cleric from the room, Slain turned to Hannah. "You are free to do as you please during the day unless I summons you. I take my meals alone and I sleep alone. You will come to my bedchamber only when I summon you. You are not permitted to leave the keep without my permission and never ever are you permitted to go to the east wing."

Slain thought she might protest when a slight scowl surfaced on her face, so her question took him by surprise.

"Why did you wed me?"

"I had need of a wife."

"Why me?" she asked, his answer not satisfying her.

"You were here. You were convenient." She appeared ready to question him further and he quickly said, "No more. Go do what you will and do not disturb me."

"May I venture outside around the keep without always asking your permission?"

"*No.*"

It was an emphatic no, and so Hannah asked, "May I go outside around the keep now?" Before he could ask why, she explained. "I would like to collect more heather."

"Stay away from the thickets," he ordered.

Hannah nodded. "Is there anything else—" She paused, not sure how to address him now that he was her husband.

Slain walked over to her and stopped so close to her that their bodies brushed each other. "Slain or husband will do," he said, as if knowing her thoughts. He lowered his head so that his lips rested close to hers. "Though there may be times you want to call me a savage."

Hannah ignored the spark of fright he had provoked in her and called on her courage. She smiled wide. "I would never call you that, my husband." She then placed a hasty kiss on his lips and hurried out of the room.

Slain stood there as speechless and stunned as Hannah had been when they had wed. Until finally, he ran his tongue gently over his lips, tasting the faint flavor she had left behind. He shut his eyes, enjoying the minty sweetness on his lips. Never had he expected her to do that and never had his manhood hardened so quickly at an innocent kiss.

His eyes shot open and he hastily tucked his tongue back in his mouth to spew oath after oath. She was his wife and he would satisfy himself with her and be done with it. He would feel nothing for her. Nothing at all. He would do his duty as a husband and no more. She was simply a means to a way of solving a problem. No more than that.

Why then had he felt a jolt to his heart when she had kissed him so innocently?

~~~

The basket lay near empty at Hannah's side as she stared at the hillside covered in purple heather. She was not so much interested in collecting heather as she was in collecting her thoughts.

Everything had happened so fast that she had yet to accept she was wed. Was it real? Was she truly Slain MacKewan's wife? And the question still begged to be answered... why? Why had he wed her? There had to be more to it than she was simply convenient.

Most of all what would happen when he discovered her true identity? Worse still what would happen when her father discovered who she had wed? Would their union unite her clan with the Clan MacKewan? Could it possibly prove beneficial? Or would her father adamantly reject their union since he had not given his approval?

She shook her head. Of course he would reject the union. When her father found out that she had wed the chief of the Clan MacKewan, he would be furious, for the Clan MacKewan was his bitter enemy.

One thing was for certain, her step-brother would use this to his advantage. He would attempt to convince her father that she ran away to purposely defy him and wed Slain MacKewan. That she was a traitor to her own clan. Constant whispers in her father's ear might well convince him of the accusations until her father finally believed him. When all along it was her step-brother to blame for her disappearance.

She sighed and shook her head again. Thinking on it all, she came to the conclusion that her situation had worsened rather than improved. She had believed her decision to come here to the Clan MacKewan had been a wise one. It was the one place she would be safe from her step-brother once he found out she was not dead. She had hoped to find a solution to her problem before then.

She raised her head suddenly as if something had just dawned on her. Perhaps this marriage was the solution to her problem. A frown fell upon her face. There was no telling what Slain would do once he discovered her identity. He could return her to her father which would infuriate him even more since she would return shamed and useless to him, a beneficial marriage no longer viable.

She did not know what to do, but then what could she do? She was wed to Slain MacKewan. Their marriage only needed to be consummated for it to be sealed, though he could claim that she never spoke up, never spoke the truth of who she was to him. Then what? Would he cast her aside? Return her to her father?

How much worse could her situation get?

She could get with child.

The thought troubled her. What then? What would happen to the bairn?

She shook her head, her worries growing. She knew there was a way of preventing a man's seed from taking root. She could ask Neata about it. She shook her head again. Neata had mentioned how she hoped Slain would have a family. She would not betray her chief.

Hannah had never been with a man, though she was not ignorant to the intimacies between a husband and wife, thanks to her mum. She had been quite blunt about wanting her daughter aware of what to expect from a husband… good or bad.

It was thanks to the healer who had helped her escape that she was still a virgin, left untouched by the prison guards. The woman had convinced the guards that Hannah and the other women prisoners had a disease that was contagious and deadly to men. The healer had been so convincing that Hannah had actually feared it was true until the healer had confided the truth to her.

It was not an excuse she wished to use on her husband. The problem was that once their vows were consummated, there would be a chance that his seed would take root and she would be with child. Her concern was what would become of her and that child if in the end when all was discovered, he no longer wanted her as his wife?

She ran her tongue slowly over her lips, recalling his kiss in the woods and the quiver that had raced through her. She shivered at the memory. He would expect much more from her tonight. Her mum had warned her that if she did not favor the man chosen for her to wed that she should lay there and do nothing and once she was with child he would leave her alone and find his pleasure elsewhere. But if she was lucky and she cared for her husband and her husband cared for her, then intimacy could be something more than just satisfying for them both.

You are here. You were convenient.

His own words reminded her that Slain did not care for her. She was simply a means to settle his need of a wife. But he believed her a peasant woman. Why had he wed a peasant woman? She continued to believe there was more to his reason for marrying her than he would say.

A sudden thought caused her eyes to turn wide. What if he had no intentions of remaining wed to her? What if he was using her with plans to be rid of her? Annoyance stung at her. What had she been thinking in agreeing to whatever he wanted?

Desperation and fear. Desperation had consumed her decision, believing there was no other choice left to her. Fear shivered her, prickling her skin as she recalled the torture she had suffered and how she would do anything never to suffer it again. Then there had been the fear of being returned home only to find herself not welcome or worse, murdered by her step-brother. Desperation and fear had not allowed her to think wisely.

Question after question plagued her and with no answers forthcoming, she wondered if she had sealed her fate today and that she had lost far more than she ever imagined.

Busy your hands.

Another of her mother's sage words. Whenever Hannah found herself troubled, her mum would tell her to busy her hands. Her mum had insisted it emptied the mind so that clearer thoughts could prevail.

Hannah turned her attention to the heather. The sun was shining, though she doubted that would last long. Clouds or a shower would probably roll in bringing with it a deeper chill. She worked in silent thoughts, letting her chore take reign and quash the never-ending questions.

An unexpected tug at her cloak a short time later had her looking down. She was surprised to see a lass of no more than four or so years. Her braided hair was the color of the darkest night and bright blue eyes, full of tears, looked up at her while her small arms stretched out eagerly to her.

"Mummy," she said, her tiny lower lip quivering.

"Wandered off, did you?" Hannah asked softly and scooped her up. "How about we go find your mummy."

The little lass nodded and sniffed back her tears.

Hannah did not think of seeking permission from her husband, the tiny lass her only concern. Her small head rested on Hannah's shoulder as she walked toward the village. Her instinct was for the little lass and keeping her safe until she could find her mum.

Stares greeted her and respectful nods. *They knew.* The clan knew she was wife to their chief. How? How did they learn of it so soon?

Whispers and mumbles followed her and no one dared approach her, which did not make it easy to find the little lass' mum.

Finally, Hannah spotted a familiar face. "Blair!" she called out and the woman turned, her eyes growing wide.

Blair approached her with a bob of her head, then stared at her, at a loss of what to say.

"I am no different than when we first met," Hannah assured her, "and this little lass looks for her mum."

Blair released the smile she had been holding back, and nodded. "That is Cara, Kate's youngest and only daughter. No doubt one of her three older brothers were told to keep watch over her and failed to do so." Blair reached her arms out to take the lass, but the little bairn refused to let go of Hannah.

"She has attached herself to you. She feels safe with you," Blair said. "The wee lass has good instinct."

Odd that Hannah was searching for the same thing that the little lass had found in her... protection.

Blair called out to a passing lad, "Go fetch Cara's mum."

The lad nodded and hurried off.

Blair lowered her voice as she asked, "So it is true? You are wife to our chief?"

"Aye, I am," Hannah admitted without hesitation. Curiosity as to how the news had spread so fast, though having a hunch, had her asking, "The cleric told you?"

Blair nodded. "He did and urged us to pray for you being forced to wed a savage."

Hannah quickly defended her husband. "Slain is no savage. A troubled soul perhaps, but no savage."

"Many would disagree with you," Blair said.

"Cara! Cara!" a plump woman called out as she ran toward them. Her full cheeks were flushed and her blue eyes, identical to her daughter's, shined with fear.

"Mummy," Cara cried out, her little arms reaching out to the woman.

Hannah held the little lass out to her mum and Cara hugged her mum's neck as if she would never let go as soon as she was safely tucked in the woman's arms.

"I am going to box your brothers good for not watching you," Kate said and as if realizing who she stood before, she bobbed her head. "I am sorry—" Abrupt silence followed as she seemed not to know how to address Hannah."

"Hannah. My name is Hannah."

"I am much grateful… Hannah," Kate said a bit hesitantly, "and it is pleased I am that you are wife to our chief."

Hannah smiled and laughed softly. "A surprise to us all."

Her lovely smile and gentle laughter broke the tension that was palpable.

"It will be good to have a smiling face at the keep," Blair said.

Kate agreed with a nod. "It was such a welcoming place at one time."

"Perhaps it can be so again," Hannah said, wishing it could be so.

Blair reached out and laid a tender hand on Hannah's arm. "You are welcome to visit with me any time."

"Me as well," Kate said. "You are always welcome in our home."

Hannah felt a tug at her heart. Her father had allowed her few if any friends. It felt freeing to have women who chose to be friends with her, though like her father's command she would now need to seek permission from her husband to visit with them. That mattered little to her though, since knowing she could visit with them made her feel less a prisoner.

"The clan wonders if there will be a feast to celebrate the marriage of our chief," Kate said, Cara keeping herself occupied by playing with her mum's braid.

A cloud suddenly rushed in overhead, swallowing the sun at the same moment Kate paled.

Blair's eyes turned frightfully wide, and Hannah did not need to turn around to know what had put dreadful fear into the two women. She turned anyway to confirm what she suspected and saw her husband come barreling down on them. His dark scowl was as frightening as his rapid gait and he looked ready to devour all of them whole as he descended on them.

Hannah would have retreated several steps like the two women did, but showing fear of her husband did not bode well for a new wife. She remained as she was and turned a smile on him, hoping to speak to him and explain what had caused her to disobey him.

She never got a chance. As soon as he drew near, his hand shot out and gripped her arm. Without a word to anyone, he swung her around and forced her to walk alongside him to the keep.

Chapter Eleven

Slain had not believed his eyes when he had glanced out the window and seen his wife talking with two women in the village. She had blatantly disobeyed him and his anger had mounted. He had not given it a second thought when he went after her. He had grown even more annoyed when he realized she had forced him to do something he had avoided since returning home… go to the village. And she had had the audacity to smile at him. A damn beautiful smile at that.

Married less than a couple of hours and his wife was already presenting a problem in more ways than he could have comprehended.

He waited until the door closed behind them in the keep to turn a sharp tongue on her. "You dare disobey me?"

She winced, not at his words but at his grip that had tightened considerably on an already bruised arm, reminding her of the all too recent torture she had suffered.

Slain released her arm at her slight gasp and silently cursed himself for not thinking of the bruise he had seen there, his own hand only making it worse.

Hannah rubbed her arm gently as she spoke. "Cara, a wee bairn, had wandered off and I returned her to her mum. I did not think you would expect me to seek permission for seeing to the safety of one of your own."

There was not a woman who had ever left Slain speechless… his wife just did.

"I meant no disrespect. I only wished to see the wee bairn safe," Hannah continued. "The two women I spoke with are pleased to know you have wed and wonder if there will be a feast to celebrate the occasion."

"There is nothing to celebrate," he said, his tongue remaining sharp.

His words disturbed her and had her wondering once again if he had nefarious plans for her. She spoke without thinking. "What do you truly want of me?"

"I want a dutiful wife who gives me no trouble." Slain held up his hand when she went to speak again. "And one that does not ask me endless questions."

"So to be perfectly clear, I am not to disturb you, ever, and I will see you only when summoned."

"Now you understand," Slain said, though found her words annoying to him.

"Then please grant me permission now to take my leave of the keep when I wish and go to the village when I wish. I give you my word I will venture no further than the village without your permission. This way I will disturb you even less and you will not have to suffer my endless queries."

What she suggested made sense. His need to deal with her would then be infrequent, so why did that annoy him even more?

"Renege on your word and you will go nowhere and do nothing," he warned.

"Thank you, my husband," Hannah said with a respectful bob of her head.

Though Hannah seemed grateful and obedient, he wondered if he had just agreed to something he would regret.

His concern had him taking a step toward her and lowering his face close to hers. "Do not play false with me or you will regret it."

"I have no wont to do that, my husband. I will leave you to yourself now," she said and as she did earlier, she brushed a quick kiss over his lips and hurried out of the room.

Slain stared after her, wondering over her innocent kisses, though they truly were not innocent, at least to him. The earlier one had stunned him in more ways than one, arousing him much too fast. This one had left a tingle on his lips that radiated through his body, sparking his manhood and arousing him more than before.

He was on dangerous ground here, his manhood responding so easily and quickly to a woman. His needs had always been plentiful, but he controlled them and never let any take command of him. Not so with Hannah. When he had first kissed her, he knew he wanted more from her, and in time he would have it. But these innocent kisses of hers were proving too difficult to ignore and growing impossible not to respond to.

He had no plans of bedding her just yet. She was more a means to an end of a problem he had not known how to solve. Her presence here had solved it for him, but now he wondered if it had created more of a problem.

He shook his head. It mattered not. She was his wife and would remain so and he would allow her to get only so close to him. He would have no trouble keeping his distance from her. Then why did his lips seem to ache for another taste of her?

~~~

Hannah was elated that she could come and go as she pleased. She would feel less confined that way, less a prisoner.

She stopped a moment on her way to the kitchen, her fingers going to her lips. Instinct had had her kissing him again. Why? Why had it felt like the most natural thing for her to do? She had not given either kiss thought. It had just happened, as if it was what she was supposed to do, wanted to do, and that confused her even more. How could she feel that way toward a man that she barely knew?

She continued to the kitchen and entered with a smile to find Helice scrubbing the table. Hannah was impressed with how clean Helice kept the kitchen and she loved the delicious scents that always filled the room.

"Can I help with anything?" Hannah asked.

Helice stopped scrubbing and glared at her. "Do you not know your place? You are wife to the clan chief." She shook her head. "Forgive me, I should not speak to you so disrespectfully."

"Wife to the clan chief has yet to settle in, so I could use a reminder now and again," Hannah said. "I am used to keeping busy and with only you and me to see to the keep, I wish to do my share, regardless of my position."

"The chief would not approve."

Hannah smiled, knowing full well the answer to the question she was about to ask. "But as his wife, am I not in charge of seeing to the care of the keep?"

"You are," Helice said with a nod more resolved to the fact than acceptance of it.

"Then I will do whatever I feel needs doing," Hannah announced.

Helice had no choice but to say, "Whatever you wish. The chief takes his mid-day meal alone in his solar. I will serve yours in the Great Hall."

Hannah was not used to eating alone. Her meals had always been shared in the Great Hall where many of the clan would gather. There would be talk, sometimes tales told or songs sung. She had enjoyed those times, at least until her mum had died, then everything changed.

"I will return soon. I am going to fetch my basket of heather," Hannah said, though she did not have to tell Helice where she was going, but she wanted her to know if Slain should ask.

Hannah hurried her steps almost afraid that Slain would rush out behind her, having changed his mind, and prevent her from taking another step. Or was it that she worried about him summoning her?

The thought of tonight and performing her wifely duties in bed poked at her and caused a flutter in her stomach.

Slain was a stranger to her. How was she to be intimate with a stranger? But then her father had intended to wed her to someone who she would not have met until their wedding day, so how different was that from this? Did she count her blessings or pray that she had not condemned herself to a worse fate?

Her basket of heather sat untouched where she had left it on the hillside. She snatched it up and returned to the keep with slow steps, much preferring the slight chill the clouds had brought to the dark chill of the keep. It was obvious why no one from the village ventured near it, the thickets with their sharp thorns that had been left to grow wild around it warned anyone away and the crumbling stones only added to its inhospitable appearance. It was no wonder there was no joy to this place that should be the heart of the clan.

She could not help but wonder why the village was so well-kept when the keep sat neglected. If anything, it was usually the keep that outshined the village, so why was it the opposite here?

The question slipped from her tongue upon entering the kitchen. "Helice, why does the village thrive and not the keep?"

Helice shook her head. "That is not for me to say, but you should be aware that there is little wealth here."

"How can that be?" Hannah asked surprised. "The Clan MacKewan is known for their wealth and power."

"I do not have a loose tongue."

Meaning she would tell Hannah nothing, though that did not keep Hannah from persisting. "But how can the village do so well when the keep does not? It makes no sense."

All she received from Helice were tightly pursed lips and arms crossed over her chest, announcing more loudly than if she had spoken that she had nothing to say.

Hannah gave up and turned to leave.

"Your bedchamber is next to your husband's. I set a fire to chase the chill, but I have yet had time to clean it. You will need it tonight since the chief always sleeps alone."

Hannah turned a pleasant smile on her. "You need not worry about my bedchamber. I will tend it myself."

"Whatever you wish," Helice said and returned to her chore, turning her back on Hannah.

Hannah climbed the stairs to the third floor and her new bedchamber. She walked as silently as she could past Slain's bedchamber, not wanting to disturb him if he was there. Or perhaps it was that she did not want to alert him to her presence.

She pushed the door open slowly and stepped inside. It was a nice sized room with a bed big enough to fit two people. A chest sat in front of the end of the bed, dust covering it. Spying a few candles, Hannah sat her basket of heather on the chest and draped her cloak over it, then collected the candles and lit them from the flames in the fireplace and placed them in their holders around the room so she could have a better look.

There were a few personal items on a narrow table that sat against the wall opposite the hearth; a couple of worn bone combs, a few small stones in a shallow crock and a piece of embroidery, dust covering its beauty.

"They belonged to my mother."

Hannah jumped and turned, her hand going to her chest fearful her pounding heart would burst from it, her husband had frightened her so. And as if her heart did not pound enough, it only increased, seeing him standing there shirtless. He was lean, his middle rippling with muscle and his arms defined with them. The fire's light flickered across his chest like hungry tongues licking his bare flesh.

"Wrap them and put them away in the chest. There are garments in there that might fit you or if you are skilled with a needle you can alter them to fit you. Helice will see to readying the room for you."

"She has already lit the fire, I will see the rest done myself," Hannah said, his sudden scowl letting her know he did not approve.

"It is not for you to do."

"There is far too much for Helice to do here without adding more to her chores. I can see to it myself and perhaps I can have a village lass or two come help."

"I will not have my solitude disturbed."

"I will make certain you do not even know they are here," she said.

"See that you do." He turned to leave, stopped, and turned back again. "There is no lock on this door. I will enter at will and you will welcome me."

Hannah did not know what made her ask, "Is there a lock on your door?"

A barely detectable grin surfaced on his face. "I will let you find that out for yourself."

Hannah stared as he left the room, leaving the door open behind him. Was he inviting her to his bedchamber if she dared have the courage to go there? Darn if her curiosity was not itching to find out.

The day wore on drawing closer to night and Hannah kept herself busy except for when she sat in the Great Hall, eating alone. Though the food was good, she did not have much taste for it, her thoughts more on the evening ahead.

She ate some of the meal, not able to finish all of it, and returned to cleaning her bedchamber. Helice had left her clean linens for the bed and she was pleased at the fresh scent of heather that permeated the room from the sprigs she had thrown in the hearth earlier.

There would be no returning to what she once had, but then what she once had had disappeared as well. This room, this keep, this clan was her life now until... those who searched for her found her. Only then would she know if her husband intended their marriage to last.

Hannah ate even less for the evening meal, recalling the memories of how it had felt to feel hunger not even forcing her to take another bite. Helice shook her head when she collected her bowl, but said nothing. Hannah retired to her bedchamber and her stomach knotted even more when she saw the white nightdress that she had worn after her accident laying on the bed in wait. A bucket of water sat near the hearth along with a clean cloth.

Helice had left the items so that she could wash and prepare herself for her wedding night ahead with her husband.

Hannah's hands trembled as she washed herself and used the combs she had yet to wrap and put in the chest, to run through her wild hair that refused to be tamed, letting it fall where it may, often around her face in stubborn curls.

Once she was done, her nightdress on, she sat on the bed waiting for the summons or for her husband to enter her room.

It grew later and later and no word came from Slain.

Finally, too tired to remain sitting there in wait, she lay back and no soon as she did, the day's exhausting events caught up with her and she quickly fell asleep.

The door creaked open slowly and Slain approached the bed just as slowly. He stared down at his sleeping wife, her bright red hair flaring out around her head on the pillow. Her slim lips were parted slightly, a slow even breath escaping in a soft snore. The white nightdress she wore was gathered up, exposing one slim leg and the bruise that was fading there.

She was beautiful and once he touched her, he would tarnish that beauty. He wondered why he had been so reckless to make her his wife. He could have found another way to meet the demand made on him. He did not have to involve Hannah.

Yet there was something about her that he was drawn to with an overwhelming urge he had never felt before. She had strength and courage, but then many Highland women did or they did not survive the wild and unpredictable Highlands. She showed vulnerability at times, though was quick to hide it, and there were things she had yet to share with him.

He could have refused to grant her safe haven here and send her on her way, not caring if she had no place to go. But it was a thought that he had easily dismissed.

He had need of a wife and she had been there, it was as simple as that. Or so he repeatedly reminded himself.

Seal your vows and be done with it, a voice in his head demanded. He would but not just yet. He had to make sure that she understood that while he would protect her, always keep her safe from harm, couple with her, plant his seed in her, he could not now, not ever… love her.

He had no love left to give.

Slain reached for the blanket at the end of the bed and pulled it up over her, tucking it around her. He then surprised himself when he brushed his lips lightly over hers as if returning the light kisses she had placed on his lips twice that day. Once again he grew aroused.

"Sleep well, wife," he whispered, "for the savage will come for you soon enough."

Chapter Twelve

Two days wed and her marriage vows were yet to be sealed and her husband yet to be seen. She had even attempted to enter the east wing to see if he had gone there and to see what else she might discover, but it had been locked. After searching endlessly for Slain, she had decided that he had either vanished from sight or had left the keep altogether. When she had asked Helice if she had seen him, the woman had snapped at her.

"I am not the chief's keeper."

Hannah wondered if Slain had dire plans for her or if he now regretted their union and intended to release her from it since their vows had not been consummated. Then he would send her away and she would be right back where she started. She was a fool to think she could find safety anywhere.

You are a woman. You were born vulnerable.

Another of her mum's wise words and never had she felt the truth of those words more until her step-brother had made his strength known. Even now she was vulnerable to the will of her husband. But did she need to be?

Once, she had thought to find a husband who would love her. She knew now that had been nothing more than a dream. Her mum had warned her that she would be wiser to find a husband who would be good to her, treat her well. That love was rare for women who had duties to uphold. And her mum had been good at upholding her duties to a husband who had shown little wont to spend time with his wife.

Hannah had always hoped for more, but now that was not possible, but did it mean she had to remain vulnerable? If she did not establish a life here with her husband, then was she not leaving herself open to harm from those who would eventually come for her?

She admired the healer who had so courageously freed her from that awful prison. Could she not find courage to free herself with this marriage? Slain was not a demanding husband. He kept to himself, bothering little with her and he had not forced himself upon her.

Was what she had been looking for right in front of her? Could she find a good life here and be a good wife so that her husband would defend her without hesitation?

Know what you are willing to give, to endure, to get what you want or what is necessary.

More of her mum's sage advice that pertained to her situation.

What was she willing to do to stay alive? No, more importantly, what was she willing to do to no longer be left vulnerable to others?

Somehow she would find a way through her difficulties and survive, and be left defenseless no more. Besides, she found her husband's lips quite nice, so perhaps it would be no chore to couple with him. Though, she had wondered how such an intimate act could be shared between strangers. Her mum had talked of it as if it was simply a duty one did. While the servant lasses she had heard talk about it laughed and teased each other about how they preferred men who cared about pleasing a woman and not just themselves. Her curiosity and her own desires that would surface from time to time had her wondering about it, more so when her father had begun talking about arranging a marriage for her.

Now here she was married and still wondering.

Hannah chased her thoughts away as she walked to the village. Thinking on them and doing nothing would do her little good. It was why when she saw the sun shining brightly that she had hurried out of the keep toward the village. After the last two days with rain forcing her to remain inside, she realized just how empty and lonely the keep was. It was as if all inside were withering and dying. Even the heather she had sat around withered faster than usual. Life needed to be stirred back into the keep and that she could not do alone.

She hoped to start by finding at least two women who would help in the keep for a few hours a day. She knew she could demand help as Slain had done, but that had not worked well. Between Helice and Slain, the women of the village were just too fearful to step foot inside the inhospitable place.

How she would get anyone to do that, she did not know, but she would try.

Hannah thought the villagers friendly, calling out greetings to her and bobbing their head in respect. She did not realize that it was her vibrant smile that had them responding to her.

As soon as Blair saw her, she hurried over to her. "You look... well."

"Is there a reason I should not look well?" Hannah asked and realizing what the woman might mean added, "Slain is not the savage you think him to be."

Blair shook her head, her eyes popping wide. "I meant no disrespect."

Hannah's smile grew as she laid a gentle hand on the woman's arm. "I never thought you did. And while I do not know Slain as well as his clan does, he has shown no savage side to me."

"Then be grateful, for it is not a side of your husband you wish to see," Blair warned.

Having heard her father and others speak of the savage and seeing how isolated Slain kept himself, Hannah paid caution to Blair's words. He was a man with a dark side and she would do well to remember that.

"Is there something that brings you to the village today or did you just need to escape that morbid keep." Blair bit her bottom lip as soon as the words were out. "I have a loose tongue," she said in a way of an apology.

"Though you can be blunt, you speak the truth and I appreciate that from a friend."

Blair grinned. "I never thought Slain's wife would call me friend, but it is proud I am that she does."

"You were right about both. There is something I need, and I wanted... some time away from the keep."

"What is it you need?" Blair asked, though cautiously.

Hannah was about to ask if there were two lasses who would be willing to spend a few hours a week helping her, not Helice, in the keep when her eyes caught sight of two men with axes chopping at a tree.

What she requested surprised her as well as Blair. "Are there men who would be willing to chop away the thickets around the keep and some women who would help me ready my garden for planting? The keep has been neglected long enough."

Sorrow filled Blair's eyes as she glanced at the stone edifice. "It was once the heart of the village... of the clan. There were celebrations, tales told, songs sung, and dancing. It was filled with such joy."

"What happened?" Hannah asked.

"The former chief, Slain's father, was not a wise man when it came to choosing what battles to fight and friends to have. The clans and men he had pledged his loyalty to lost heavily and the promises made him were for naught. Slain had tried to warn his father but he refused to listen. That was when Slain went and fought alongside Warrick. He returned with enough riches to refill the coffers, but when he left again, some young warrior convinced the old chief to use some of his wealth to join with other chiefs to fight an encroaching clan. The old fool learned too late that he was helping the clans that his son was fighting against. All that Slain had given him was gone." Blair shook her head. "That was the worse winter ever. We barely had enough food, the harvest being pitiful that year, and Slain's mum took ill and died. She was the most loving and giving woman you could have ever met. Slain's da blamed himself and all believed he died of a broken heart only two months after he lost his wife. Slain returned home to a devastated clan."

"How awful for him and all of you," Hannah said, her heart going out to her husband and his clan.

"We thought for sure the clan would not survive, especially when Slain left two days after his return, though he assured us he would return soon and all would be well. And he did, with an army of men. They helped us repair the village, filled our storehouses with more food than we needed, plowed our fields, and planted them with fresh seeds they had brought with them and stayed until harvest was done, then left. Two of our women wed two of the men and left with them. All was good, except for our chief. He took to the keep after that and was rarely seen."

"The keep was not repaired along with the village?" Hannah asked.

Blair shook her head. "We all figured that our chief spent what wealth he had returned with to see that the clan was taken care of and there was nothing left to repair the keep."

"Then perhaps now would be a good time for the clan to help restore life to the keep and who knows, one day it may be filled with songs, tales, and dance once again."

"It is a hope the whole clan has for it," Blair said, wiping a tear from her eye. "There are plenty of us who would gladly help."

Hannah was thrilled with the news and even more thrilled when twenty men followed her back to the keep with axes and sickles and got busy chopping away the thickets.

Her delight grew when Blair arrived with several women, Kate one of them, to help with the kitchen garden that lay in poor neglect, almost to the point where a garden could not be distinguished from the surrounding area.

Helice stepped out of the kitchen and walked over to Hannah who was busy helping the women clear the garden of dead weeds and debris.

"A moment please," Helice said stiffly.

Hannah brushed the dirt from her hands and walked a distance away where they could not be heard.

"He will not be happy about this," Helice warned.

"He is not happy now. There is no happiness in this keep. It is empty, devoid of any life. So what difference could it possibly make to return a small spark to it?" Hannah asked, though she did not give Helice a chance to answer. "Join us. We will have a thriving garden this summer and fall if we get the seeds in the ground soon."

Helice wrinkled her nose as if in disdain, though said, "It could be made larger. There are some seeds I have saved and have been wanting to plant."

"Kate thought the same and offered us some seeds she has as well. Come and let me introduce you," Hannah said before Helice could refuse her.

The men made quick work of the thickets, carting them off to a section in the village where a pile of debris was set to burn. Some of the men took shovels to the garden and extended it according to Helice's instructions.

By late afternoon all was done and everyone gone, leaving Helice and Hannah to admire the work that had been accomplished.

"It will be a fine garden," Helice said, a slight smile actually breaking through her stern expression.

"It will," Hannah agreed, looking over the large swath of land that had been thoroughly weeded and the soil turned, leaving worms to crawl here and there throughout the rich earth.

The two women were about to walk around to the front of the house when Hannah stopped at the sound of a cart approaching not far off. A quick glance at the man in the seat had Hannah tossing up the hood of her cloak to pull down around her face as she told Helice, "Get rid of him. Send him away. There is nothing we need from him."

Helice appeared ready to question her when Hannah gave a sudden, commanding nod and turned the corner.

Hannah hurried toward the kitchen, keeping her head down when she suddenly collided with a hard body, a strong arm rushing around her to steady her feet and keep her close.

"What goes on here?" her husband asked curtly.

Slain had returned and not at a good time. Hannah needed to get inside, away from the man driving the cart.

"You are trembling. What is wrong?" Slain demanded, feeling her quivers run along his body. Something had frightened her.

"I speak to the chief, not a servant," a gruff voice could be heard from the front of the keep.

Slain kept his arm firm around Hannah, leaving her no choice but to walk along with him as he went to confront the demanding man.

Hannah tucked at her hood, making certain not a strand of her red hair showed and kept her face turned against her husband's chest so that her face was not visible as they turned the corner of the keep.

"Aye, there he is," the man called out and jumped down off the seat of his cart.

Hannah did not need to look at him to see his features. He was a thick man, not hard muscle, but not soft either. She knew well the strength to his thick hands, having felt them on her. They could do harm with one squeeze. She would never forget him. He was the man her step-brother had handed her over to that fateful night and told him to make sure she suffered well before she died.

"I have two women I thought you might be interested in, but I see that you already have one. My two will join in if you like."

"I never accepted your offerings before, Muir, why would you think I would take them now?"

"Heard you were all alone here and knowing your endless appetite for women, I thought you might be interested. And that one you got there tight in your arm does not seem so willing. My lass' can help tame her for you."

Her husband would not do such a thing, would he? Hannah's body turned rigid at the thought and she felt Slain's muscles grow taut against her as his arm tightened around her.

"Get on your cart, Muir, and leave my land and never return or I will cut that ignorant tongue from your mouth and stuff it down your throat."

Muir took a quick step back, raising his hands as he did. "I mean no harm and want none in return. I will do as you say, but the day grows late. I would be grateful if I could camp on the outskirts of the village for the night. The lassies could use a rest."

"Be gone at first light and be warned about bringing any trouble down on my clan. I have gutted bigger men than you."

Hannah shivered at the picture his words painted in her mind. A savage did live inside her husband, something she kept forgetting.

"As you say, Slain," Muir said with a bob of his head and climbed back up on the cart.

Hannah dared take a peek after she heard the cart turn around. Her heart broke for the young lass, whose dirty face and large eyes seemed to beg for help, looked out at her from the back of the cart.

Memories rushed over her of being bound hand and foot and a dirty cloth stuffed into her mouth until she thought she would choke. Then she had been lifted and thrown, dumped like garbage, into Muir's cart.

The fear and anguish of that night settled around her again and tears rushed to her eyes for the young lass left without an ounce of hope.

Hannah found herself suddenly pushed away from the comfort of Slain's strong body.

"Now you will tell me—" Several oaths flew from his mouth when he saw tears running down her cheeks.

Hannah never expected him to scoop her up in his arms and carry her into the keep, Helice hurrying forward to open the front door for him and leaving them alone once inside the Great Hall.

Slain did not know his wife well, but what he had surmised was that she did not shed tears lightly. Something was troubling her and it had to do with Muir.

He sat at one of the tables nearest the hearth, since her trembles had yet to cease along with her tears. He settled her in his lap and when her head dropped to rest against his chest, he exploded inside with a mixture of anger that something had disturbed her so badly it had brought her to tears and an overwhelming need to do whatever was necessary to chase those tears away and ease whatever burden she carried.

"You will tell me why you cry," he ordered, though kept the sternness from his tone and tried unsuccessfully to calm his thundering heart, not wanting her to feel his anger and concern.

Hannah could not tell him that it was Muir who she had been given to, for she had no doubt he would go after the man. If that happened there would be a good chance that Muir would find out that she was here and Slain would learn that she was not a peasant... but the daughter of a clan chief.

"I was carted off like those women, full of fright and despair."

"Your family sold you?" Slain asked with a sharp edge to his voice that bordered on fury.

"Aye," she said, recalling the jangle of the coins in the pouch that exchanged hands, though it was her step-brother who paid to have her taken away. Fearful she would reveal too much to her husband, Hannah turned the conversation away from her. "I could not help but shed tears for those poor lass' and what they go through."

"You were given to men to pleasure?" he asked, fighting to contain his anger.

"No, some of the women were saved for particular men. I was lucky enough to escape before I met that fate." She had been more than lucky, since Muir had kept certain women from being touched so that he got even more coin for the virgins he delivered to the prison leader. He in turn would sell them to any warrior or prison guard who wanted an untouched woman, then the other guards could have at her once the man was done with her. Her luck had come in the form of the healer and she was thankful every day that the woman had saved her from suffering such a horrible fate.

She raised her head and sniffled back her tears. "If you wonder... I am a virgin. I have known no man."

Damn, if that did not make him want to protect her even more, though it should be himself he saved her from.

Slain wiped at her wet cheeks, grateful her tears had stopped, but then they had helped her purge the horrid memories Muir's appearance had caused. "You are my wife and will remain my wife until the end of our days. You will always be safe with me. I will always protect you, that I promise you."

Hannah felt a strange pull at her heart and without thought, she pressed her damp cheek to his and whispered, "I am forever grateful to have such a good husband."

Her warm breath tickled at his ear and sent a shiver rumbling through him straight to his manhood, which grew hard instead of simply aroused. He wanted her so badly that he could almost taste her sweet flavor on his tongue, feel her soft flesh against his, and imagine the intense shudder when he brought her to climax.

He stood quickly, lowering her to her feet and pushing her away from him. "Good is something I am not and something I will never be, but I will keep you safe and protected…"

Hannah watched him storm off and the last of his words drifted in a whisper to her ear.

"Especially from me."

~~~

Hannah waited again that night for her husband to come to her, but when the hour grew later and later, she knew he would not come.

Before she lost her courage, she changed from her nightdress to her shift and tunic, pinned her hair up as best she could, a few stands falling loose to brush the sides of her face, slipped on her shoes, tossed her cloak over her shoulders, and pulled up her hood.

She went to the door and eased it open, cringing when a faint creak sounded more like an echo through the entire keep. She waited a few moments to see if her husband had heard it and when she heard nothing from his room, she stepped out of hers, closing the door ever so slowly to avoid another creak.

With light steps, she hurried cautiously down the stairs and through the keep to the kitchen, grabbing a knife as she passed through and out the door.

Chapter Thirteen

Hannah could not live with the thought of what those two young women would suffer if she did not at least try to help them escape. If someone could do it for her, then it was her turn to do it for someone else. She had planned it out in her head. She would free them and have them hide in the woods until Muir left, then they could seek a permanent home with the clan, since she doubted they had anywhere to go.

The biggest threat to her was Muir catching and recognizing her, but she could not let the fear of discovery stop her.

She made her way to the village, keeping to the shadows. The night and its strange sounds had once run a chill through her, but having been forced to travel in the darkness when she had escaped the dungeon, she had soon made friends with the night and all it offered her, just as it did now.

She had to enter the woods once she neared the edge of the village, since there was an open swath of land between it and where Muir had settled his cart, that would provide no cover. She kept to the trees, using the thick trunks to slip behind and conceal her presence. It helped having a half moon that filtered through the tree branches, but then that could also prove a hindrance.

Once close enough, though safely hidden, Hannah heard the familiar noise before she cast a look to the cart.

Muir was snoring as he had done when she had been his captive. Oddly enough, she had been glad to hear it, for it meant she was free of torment for the night. He would take great pleasure in pinching her hard or grabbing the flesh of her arm or leg between two fingers and twisting it so viciously that she could not help but cry out in pain. He also loved to yank her hair until she thought he would rip it from her head.

The awful memories only strengthened her resolve to free the two women.

Hannah saw what she had expected. The two women, their hands tied at the wrists and raised above their heads and secured to the wheels of the cart. It was a terrible position to be kept in all night, for the arms were left aching and weak in the morning, but then that had been the purpose to begin with, leaving them weak and more vulnerable.

Hannah listened to Muir continue to snore where he lay not far from the two women but not close enough so that they might do him any harm. She would have to be cautious and as quiet as possible so as not to wake him.

She stepped slowly out of the woods and took light steps toward the cart. When the one young woman's eyes fluttered open and caught sight of her, Hannah was quick to rush a finger to her own mouth, cautioning the woman to remain quiet. She held up the knife to her wrist, showing the woman that she intended to free her.

The woman's eyes turned wide and she nodded vigorously. She turned to the other woman, her eyes closed in sleep, and gently nudged her foot until her eyes fluttered open, then she gave a nod of her head toward Hannah.

The other woman's eyes opened fully and filled with tears as she nodded.

Hannah made her way toward them as silently as possible and squatted down before the one woman who had seen Hannah first. She cut through the rope, fearing the noise would wake Muir. After some effort, she broke through the rope that held the woman's hands to the wheel and was about to turn and do her feet so that she was at least free to run, when the woman's eyes suddenly filled with fright.

Hannah turned and saw Muir staring at her. He jumped to his feet and headed toward her, his meaty hands clenched in fists. She dropped the knife to the woman, knowing if she kept it, Muir would use it on her.

"Free yourself," she warned and did what she knew would draw Muir away from the two women. She pushed back her hood off her head, several strands of her bright red hair springing free of the combs, and turned to face him.

Muir glared at her, then suddenly stopped in his tracks, recognizing her. Fear suddenly spread across his face.

Hannah was well aware of the man's thoughts. He was frightened to think what her step-brother would do to him when he discovered that he had not done what he had been paid to do... see Hannah dead.

She rushed for the woods, knowing he would follow, the two women no longer important to him. His life now depended on him catching her, making certain she died.

Hannah hoisted her cloak and shift, then ran with all the strength she could muster, darting around trees, dropping her head to avoid low hanging branches, jumping over large rocks, ever so grateful that she had learned to maneuver the night so easily.

His heavy footfalls followed much too close behind. The man could run. She had seen him catch a younger man half his size. She needed to get to the village and scream as loud as she could in hopes that someone heard and came to help her.

Her legs burned with pain, she ran so fast, twisting and turning to remain out of his reach. She spied the village through the trees and turned, headed for it, and realized her mistake too late. Muir had figured out her intention and had turned before her.

She had to turn quickly to stop herself from running into him and her foot caught on something, sending her stumbling. Though she managed to stay on her feet and right herself, Muir was quicker and her head snapped back as he grabbed the back of her hair and yanked hard.

The pain had her screaming out and her scream was her last chance at surviving… if only someone heard her.

Muir tossed her to the ground, knocking the breath and scream out of her and dropped down on top of her, stealing even more of her breath.

"I am going to have my fun with you before I slit your throat."

Still fighting for breath, Hannah was too helpless to do anything, though she swatted at him with what little strength she had.

Muir was suddenly ripped off her and sent flying through the air, his big body smashing against a tree and dropping to the ground. A dark figure descended on Muir and hoisted him in the air once more, throwing him with such strength against another tree that he bounced off it and crashed to the ground again.

Gasping to regain her breath, Hannah forced herself to sit up and when she did, she saw that it was her husband throwing Muir around as if he weighed nothing. What shocked her even more, though, was that his barbaric expression made him barely recognizable.

This was what Blair had warned her about.

This was the *savage*.

"You dare touch my wife."

Hannah backed away, Slain's voice sounding more animal than man.

Muir was barely able to move from the last toss against a thick tree trunk, and she watched as Slain picked him up and flung him as he released a fierce roar that had Hannah cringing.

This time when Muir landed on the ground, his head lolled to the side, his wide, lifeless eyes staring at Hannah.

Hannah feared looking at her husband, for what she might see. She slowly raised her eyes to him. He stood over Muir's dead body, his eyes narrowed, glaring at her. She saw then that he wore no shirt, only his plaid and boots. His chest heaved as heavy breaths racked his body and flared his nostrils.

He was trying to control the savage.

He walked toward her, every powerful step a warning that he would not go easy on her.

Her own breathing was still labored, though it may have been out of fear from what she had just witnessed.

He came to a stop so close in front of her that she had to crane her neck to look up at him. Fury swirled in his dark eyes and his scowl was so harsh that she thought it might bruise her skin.

She would suffer for this, but first she had to make sure the two women were safe. "The women... I must see that they are all right."

Slain pursed his lips tightly, his hand shooting out to grab her arm and hoist her roughly to her feet. He rushed her out of the woods at the edge of the village and she was not surprised to see that the cart and the two women had not waited. They were gone. They had their freedom.

He swung her around and hurried her back through the village. People had stirred from their cottages, no doubt having heard Slain's vicious roar.

Hannah caught sight of Blair and wished that she had not, the fright on the woman's face when her eyes fell upon Slain and the worry when her eyes went to Hannah, caused her own unease to twist in her stomach.

No one whispered a word, though a few people crossed themselves, and there was a tear or two in some eyes. But not one single person attempted to stop Slain.

A voice raced through Hannah's head.

Beg him for mercy. Beg him for mercy.

Her worry grew when he rushed her through the Great Hall and up the stone stairs, keeping her from slipping a couple of times. But then his hold was so firm on her arm that there was not a chance of her falling.

He released her with a shove into her bedchamber, slammed the door closed, and turned to face her. The fury had not subsided in his dark eyes, though his breathing was not as heavy.

His lunging step toward her had her stumbling back away from him and once again his hand was there to prevent her from falling, though it left her when her feet were steady.

"You gave me your word."

Hannah thought she saw a spark of hurt in his eyes, but it was so faint, so foreign there amongst his anger that she could not be sure if she had only wished it there. He was right, though, she had given him her word that she would not leave the village.

"For that I am truly sorry," she said, sincerity filling her every word. "I was all too familiar with what those poor women suffered and I could not stand by idle. I had to do something."

"It was not for you to do."

"If not me," —Hannah slapped her hand to her chest— "then who? I felt as helpless seeing them as I did when I was in their position. How do I justify doing nothing when I am fully aware of what they suffered?"

"You could have died," he challenged.

Hannah's hand dropped away from her chest and her shoulders drooped. "I would rather have died trying to save those women, then have died a little each day because I was too cowardly to do nothing."

Slain's fury rose and fell with her every word. While he was angry beyond reason with her for what she had done, he also admired the courage it took to do it. Not only the bravery it took to free the women, but the sheer strength it took to defy him. No woman ever had and any man who had dared tried, regretted it.

"Please believe me when I tell you that I truly regret betraying my word to you, but I will never regret what I did for those women."

"You should have come to me."

"And what would you have done? Tell me it did not concern me and dismiss it without thought?"

"You think that little of me?" Slain snapped, annoyed that she may have been right and wondering what he would have done.

"I know little of you."

"You do not want to know more of me," he warned.

"You are my husband yet a stranger to me. How do I trust a stranger? How do I bring any concern of mine to you when you will not even share a meal with me and," —she silently warned herself to hold her tongue, but her words were out before she could stop them— "how am I to be intimate with you when you do not even speak to me?" She shook her head. "Why did you truly wed me?"

"To settle a debt."

His curt words pierced her more painfully than she had expected. What did it matter though? As she had expressed to him… they were strangers. Their marriage had served a purpose for them both, his to settle a debt and hers for protection.

"We mean nothing to each other," she said, though she had not meant to say it aloud.

"On the contrary, wife. You are my responsibility and I take that seriously. As I have told you before, I will protect you and see you kept safe."

"Aye," Hannah said with a nod, "so you have shown me."

"And you will show me respect by keeping your word to me."

It was not a question nor a warning, simply what would be, and Hannah nodded once again.

"A dutiful wife," she said on a sigh not able to keep the disappointment out of her voice.

You cannot live on dreams and wishes, Hannah.

Another of her mum's warnings she had learned the hard way, and her present situation confirmed it even more. There would be no love or an ounce of caring from the man she wed. She was no more than a responsibility to him. And after seeing his savage side for herself, she should be relieved. Why then did the thought pain her heart?

"Is that possible for you?"

Hannah turned a scrunched brow on him, not understanding his question since she had been lost in her thoughts.

"To be a dutiful wife… is it possible for you?"

Hannah went to answer and stopped, holding her tongue a few moments before she finally spoke. "At one time I would not have thought so, but now with what I have seen and been through, I wonder if it will be difficult for me. I cannot honestly say that if I came across women who needed help that I would not help them even if it did place me in danger."

Though her response did not please him, that she did not lie to him did please him. She had integrity and that was something rarely found in a woman or a man.

"Then I will have your word that you will come to me if that should ever happen again," he ordered.

"You will help?" she asked hopefully.

"Aye, I will help, if help proves necessary."

"Who will decide if it is necessary?"

"We will decide together," he said and felt a punch to his gut when she smiled at him. She truly was a beautiful woman in more ways than one.

She could not keep the joy from her eyes or her smile from spreading as she said, "I am grateful, my husband."

The pure joy in her green eyes and growing smile not only sent another punch to his gut, but it also sent a twist to his heart and stirred his loins. He dared not say another word to her or remain there. He walked to the door, warning himself not to do it, not dare go near her, but his warning fell on deaf ears. He turned and reached her in quick strides, his arm reaching out to hook her around the waist as she backed away from him.

His other hand caught at the back of her head, holding it firm as his lips came down on hers in a bruising kiss. He wanted to leave his mark on her, wanted her to know that she belonged to him, wanted her to feel how much he ached to taste her. And she did, since after a brief hesitation she returned his kiss in kind, greeting his tongue eagerly as he slipped it into her mouth.

He did not think he would ever be able to smell the scent of mint again without thinking of her, the refreshing taste of it forever on her lips, but then he already thought about her all the time. And he grew hard every time he did, just like now.

End it. End it now!

He ignored the warnings bellowing in his head, telling himself he would end it in a moment... just a moment more was all he needed. But she grew as hungry for more just as he did and he had yet to safely contain the savage to chance coupling with her now.

It took more strength than he ever would have imagined to end the kiss, resting his brow to hers after he did and whispering, "Never frighten me like that again."

He released her and walked to the door, leaving a stunned and silent Hannah staring after him.

Chapter Fourteen

Hannah sat at the table in the Great Hall alone, lost in thought, her morning meal growing cold. She could not forget the way her husband had kissed her last night or his words.

Never frighten me like that again.

If she had frightened him by what she had done, then he had to care at least a little for her. Did he not? And the way he had kissed her, as if he could not get enough of her, had to have meant something. She had felt it herself. His kiss had awakened and stirred something inside her that continued to stir her whenever she thought about him. She wanted him to kiss her again, though if she was truthful she would admit she wanted more from him than just a kiss.

They were wed and their vows needed to be sealed and her curiosity satisfied. If coupling with him would be anything like the kiss, then she would be overjoyed. She would rather look forward to welcoming her husband to her bed than dreading his every visit.

"Your food grows cold... eat."

Hannah looked up so startled by her husband's presence that a tingle raced through her. Or was it that he looked so handsome and his lips so inviting? She stopped herself from shaking her head at the thought and said, "How do you know it grows cold?"

"I have been standing here watching you for some time now."

"Why?"

"Do you always question?"

"What other way am I to find the answer?"

Helice entered then and stopped, as startled as Hannah to see Slain there and though she knew he had already eaten, she asked. "My chief, may I get you something?"

"A hot brew for me and," —he walked over to the table and snatched up Hannah's bowl of porridge— "a fresh, hot bowl of porridge for my wife."

Helice hurried to take it from him.

Hannah and Helice could not hide their shock when Slain slipped onto the bench opposite Hannah, though Helice quickly recovered and hurried from the room.

"What are your plans today, wife?" Slain asked.

Hannah stared at him dumbfounded for a moment, then said, "I was going to go to the village to see if a couple of women would help here at the keep." She did not add that she also wanted the clan to see that her husband had not harmed her, since they had all stared at him last night when he had practically dragged her through the village, most appearing as if they feared for her well-being.

"They will be glad to see you are safe," Slain said and he was surprised when she smiled.

"And glad to know their chief saved me from my own foolish actions."

That she would make sure his clan knew what she had done to draw the ire of the savage astonished him. But why should it, when she had proven to be an honest woman?

"The clan does not need to know you rescued those women." He raised his hand when she went to speak, though remained silent as Helice entered the room and spoke again after she placed a tankard, steam rising from the top, in front of him and a bowl that steamed with heat as well in front of Hannah. "Muir did not work alone in his capture of women and men alike who failed to pay their debt. If his partner discovers the two women are free, he could very well send someone to track them down."

"Then I will make sure to say nothing," she said, glad he reminded her that Muir had a partner, not that he knew she was aware of it.

"You also will not *request* help for the keep, you will *demand* it. It is the clan's responsibility to serve the chief and his family. They did so gladly with my mother and father and they will do so with their present chief and his new wife."

Hannah grew excited, thinking perhaps last night had given him a change of heart. "Then I will make sure to have enough servants to tend the Great Hall so it may be open to those who wish to seek a meal or companionship here."

"No!" he said firmly. "I prefer my privacy."

Her joy faded. "Do you not get lonely?"

"I have you now."

"But it cannot just be the two us and what of when children come along? They will need friends."

Slain stood abruptly. His leg caught the end of the table jostling it and splashing the hot brew over the edge of the tankard. "Do not question me, and," —he paused with a glare— "I gave you no permission to cut down the thickets."

"They were far too prickly," —she smiled— "much like you."

"You think you can cut the sting out of the savage as easily as you cut away those thickets?"

"We shall see," she said, her smile remaining strong and determined, even though inside she quaked with uncertainty.

That she even thought she could soothe the savage gave him pause. He, himself, had a difficult time controlling the fierceness within him. What made her think she had any chance in calming him?

"Be careful, wife, a savage has no heart or soul." With that he left the Great Hall, not having touched his hot brew.

Hannah watched him go, her smile fading. The man who kissed her last night certainly had a heart and soul, which meant the savage had to have both as well.

~~~

Tears sprang to Blair's eyes when she caught sight of Hannah, though she cautiously asked, "You are well?"

"I am," Hannah said and offered no more explanation. She knew the clan wondered and gossiped over what had happened last night. Over why they had heard the savage roar. But they would say nothing and either would Hannah.

"I am glad to see you," Blair said and wiped the few tears from her eyes.

"And I you."

"What brings you here today?

Slain may have told her to demand not request, but she could not do that. She wanted people who agreed to help, not forced to help. "Help is needed at the keep,"

Blair shook her head. "That is not going to be easy after last—" She bit back her tongue, stopping herself from saying more.

"If there are two women who would agree to help and see that it is not as bad as everyone believes, then perhaps more will follow and the keep can once again be brought to life." She hoped Blair understood that she was not only speaking about stirring life into the keep, but into Slain as well.

"It is not an easy task to rid—a place—of darkness once it has taken hold."

Hannah smiled, Blair understanding what she had implied. "Perhaps, but I'm encouraged by a spark of light I have seen."

Blair's eyes turned wide. "Many would be pleased to hear that and perhaps help after all."

"That pleases me greatly," Hannah said, reaching out and giving Blair's arm a gentle squeeze.

Blair smiled. "I have some time to give to the keep and I think I can get Kate to help as well as long as she can bring Cara with her, since she has not trusted her sons to watch after the wee lass since last they failed to keep her with them."

"I think the keep could do with the sound of a child's joy and innocent laughter."

Blair patted Hannah's arm as her smile faded some. "We have prayed for our chief for he has suffered much, lost much, and I believe the heavens have answered us... you were sent to him. You are his salvation."

Hannah was glad that Kate approached, Cara balanced on her hip, since Blair's words had struck Hannah silent. She was also glad that Blair explained to Kate what she and Hannah had discussed, for her thoughts turned troubling.

The Clan MacKewan was accepting her as one of them. What would they do when they discovered she was not who they thought she was?

"I can spare some time now," Kate said.

A joyous smile grabbed hold of Hannah's face. "That would be wonderful. I started cleaning the Great Hall a few days ago, but have not been able to complete the task."

"All on your own?" Blair asked and when Hannah nodded, Blair shook her head. "That is too big of a task for one woman."

"I would be pleased with the help and even more pleased with the company," Hannah said and the three women and wee bairn walked to the keep.

Helice confronted the three when they entered through the kitchen, ready to dictate orders to the two women, but Hannah stepped forward and took charge as she had seen her mum do countless times.

"You may continue with what you are doing Helice. Blair and Kate will help me in the Great Hall, though, if you like, you are welcome to join us."

With the two women standing behind her, Hannah did not see how their eyes filled with respect for how the chief's new wife handled the far too ornery woman. It also surprised them the way Helice acquiesced with a simple nod and not a curt word.

The three women soon were busy in endless chatter as they swept and scrubbed their way through the Great Hall. They were so busy enjoying the task and the companionship that none of them noticed Cara slip out of the room.

She chased the dust motes, believing them fairies, reaching out with her tiny hands trying to catch at least one to have as a friend.

~~~

Slain sat at his desk working on one of the sketches, though his mind was not on it. Hannah had taken over his thoughts and would not leave them, and it had worsened since last night when he had kissed her.

He had been beside himself when he had gone to her room, why he had not been certain, to find it empty. His first thought had been that she had run away, but he had soon dismissed it. She looked for protection. She would not leave what she had found.

So the question had been, where had she gone?

That was when he had thought of what she had shared with him about suffering at the hands of a man similar to Muir. He knew then where she had gone... to free the two women.

Anger had taken hold of him at first, but as he ventured through the woods fear had begun to creep over him. What if he was too late to save her from her own foolishness, as he had been too late to save his parents and clan from his father's foolishness?

When he had heard her scream, the anger that had been boiling up inside him spewed out, but it had been when he had seen Muir on top of Hannah that the savage broke loose. It had not been until he returned with Hannah to the keep and had spoken with her that the savage was soothed, but not entirely. He had wanted to taste pure innocence, or had it been that he wanted to corrupt it as he had been corrupted?

If anything, it had been Hannah's honest response that had forced the words from his lips.

Do not ever frighten me like that again.

He had not realized how much it meant having Hannah there in the keep with him. The savage seemed to stay at bay with her around. She had been in his life for a little more than a week and she had already changed it. His only fear was that he would change her and not for the better.

Slain tried to turn his attention to the sketches. He owed a debt and the time to pay it was ticking away. His friend would wait only so long. Then there was the debt he owed his da, to revenge what had been done to him and the clan. It had taken time, but he would soon have what he needed to see it done and restore the MacKewan name and honor. But it would be he, himself, who made the man pay for making a fool of his da and almost destroying his clan. He would enjoy letting the savage loose on him.

"I caught a fairy."

Slain was not only startled that he had failed to hear someone enter his solar, but that it was a wee lass who had done so. She was a pretty little thing, no more than four or five years, with eyes as blue as a summer's sky and hair as black as raven feathers. She had full cheeks that were flushed pink and she clutched her tiny hand tightly in a fist.

"Want to see?" she asked, though did not care if he did or did not, she intended to show him since she hurried her little legs toward him and once around the desk, stretched her arms out to him. "Up."

Slain obeyed the little bairn without question, reaching down to scoop her up and sit her on his lap.

"I show you," she whispered as if it was a secret and pressed her tiny finger to his lips. "Quiet, no scare her."

Slain nodded, trying not to smile, but she was so adorable, and so serious about the fairy she had caught, that it was difficult not to.

She unfurled her tiny fingers slowly and her eyes turned wide when she saw her palm was empty. "She gone."

Slain felt a tug at his heart when her bottom lip began to quiver.

"Fairies are sneaky creatures and can slip easily between fingers. You were very lucky to have caught one at all, even if it was only for a few moments," he said, hoping to ease her disappointment.

She raised her tiny hand to almost shove it in her face and scrunched her eyes as if to make sure the fairy was not hiding somewhere there. She suddenly dropped her hand and looked to the parchments on his desk. "What?" she asked as she leaned forward, pointing at the drawings.

Slain gave a snug tug of his arm at her waist to stop her from toppling off his lap. "Those are drawings."

"Me do," she said with a broad smile, her round, chubby cheeks popping high as her smile spread wide.

She was too impossibly cute to deny and he moved them both closer to the desk, giving her a piece of charcoal. It was only then he wondered who she was and how she had gotten into the keep.

~~~

"It is looking much like it did when Slain's da, William, led the clan. Slain's mum, Leala, welcomed all who entered here. She was a good woman," Blair said, sniffling back an unshed tear.

"That she was," Kate agreed and wiped away a tear before it could fall. "Leala would be proud that her son wed such a kind and caring woman."

"That she would," Blair agreed with a smile.

Hannah hoped that whatever she accomplished here would benefit all.

"I think with you in charge of the keep, Hannah, you may very well have some women looking to help here," Kate said, casting a pleased eye over the Great Hall that now showed not a bit of grime or dust.

Hannah had hoped for just that. "That would be wonderful."

Blair turned her head quickly as she cast a frantic look around the Great Hall. "Where is Cara?"

Kate gasped and hurried to search the room. "Here I am scolding my lads for not keeping a good eye on their sister and I go and do the same thing."

Hannah joined in the search as well, praying the little lass had fallen asleep in a corner and had not wandered out of the room and, heaven forbid, had come across Slain.

"Is this who you search for?"

Hannah froze, as did the other two women, at the sound of Slain's stern voice.

The three women turned to face him and their eyes bulged wide with shock.

Slain stood, holding the tiny lass, appearing even tinier in his powerful arms, her face smeared with charcoal, and his face streaked with it as well.

Cara grinned and pressed her little finger against Slain's smudged cheek. "I draw."

Chapter Fifteen

"Please, forgive her, my chief," Kate said, approaching Slain, worried for her daughter. "She is just a wee bairn, much too young to know any better. It is my fault. I should have kept a more watchful eye on her."

"Aye, you should have," Slain said, casting a scowl on the woman before looking at Blair, to lastly settle on his wife. "Things are done here for the day."

The three women nodded in unison.

Kate cautiously reached out to take Cara and was shocked at what her daughter did next.

Cara turned, her little arms going around Slain's neck, as much as they could fit, to give him a hug, then she kissed his cheek, and tapped his chin as she said before stretching her arms out to her mum, "I visit again."

Kate did not wait to see what her chief would do, she latched onto her daughter and ran from the Great Hall, Blair close on her heels.

Hannah tried to stop the smile that had been fighting to break loose, but it was impossible to keep contained. Seeing her husband's face smudged with charcoal and how Cara had spoken to him without an ounce of fear and that she planned to visit him again, simply warmed her heart.

"You think it humorous, wife?" Slain asked when Hannah's smile turned to a soft laugh, a laugh that soothed and tempted, if that was possible.

"Heartwarming," Hannah said on a faint laugh.

"You will clean my face," he ordered with a scowl, whether over his wife's word or that he should have her clean his face, not a wise choice, he was not certain.

"As you wish," Hannah said, a smile still tempting the corner of her mouth. "Sit by the fire, a chilled rain descends on us."

Slain watched her leave the room, then cast an eye to the windows. The day had darkened and rain pelted the windows and he could almost feel the chill that it brought. He did as Hannah said and sat by the fire, though not before noticing that the Great Hall looked as welcoming as it had when his mum had been in charge of the keep.

He missed those days when the Great Hall was full of talk and laughter and his da would pay heed to his advice. He blamed himself for what had happened to his clan. He should have known his da was vulnerable. He had seen it on his last visit home and also that his mum had not been faring well. He had warned his da to make no decisions until he returned home. He should have known he would pay his warning no heed. All that had happened was more his fault than anyone and he intended to make certain to see that his clan never suffered again.

Hannah returned with a bucket of water and a cloth. She sat next to him on the bench near the fire, enjoying the warmth of the heat. A chill had settled into the keep and she wished she had a shawl to keep the cold from hugging her shoulders.

She dipped, then rinsed the cloth in the bucket of water, she had made sure to warm, and started on her husband's cheek, her smile returning along with the image of Cara kissing it.

"However did your face get smeared with charcoal?" she asked.

Slain wanted to shut his eyes and soak in the gentleness of her touch. Her strokes were soft and easy, even when an area needed more than a mere swipe, she was tender in her repeated ministrations.

Her caring touch relaxed him and he responded without thought. "Cara's little fingers were covered in charcoal and she insisted on turning my face to where she wanted it to go."

"You were patient with her."

Slain opened his eyes settling them on hers, bright green with curiosity. "Cara is part of my clan and a mere bairn at that, therefore, it is my duty to protect her."

"Duty?" Hannah wondered if it had been only duty that had had him being so patient with Cara.

"Aye, I have a duty to my people and I will see it done. I will see my clan kept safe, no matter what it takes."

His response seemed strange to her. If he felt so responsible to keep his clan safe where were his warriors? He had had them at one time, for her da had spoken of Clan MacKewan victories with anger and envy. Where was that contingent of men now who would go to war and battle for him tomorrow if necessary? Had they chosen not to return home with him from battle? Had they fled to another clan because of what had happened here? Unlikely since Highlanders were devoted to their clans, though riches could entice.

Hannah turned her full attention to his face, something she had been avoiding since taking the cloth to his cheeks. Her husband was a handsome man, his features finer than she had ever seen. They not only pleased the eye, but the senses as well and try as she might, she could not help but feel an attraction to him. But then he was her husband and she had a right to find him appealing and to also think that it would not be such a chore to couple with him.

It may have been seeing how easily he had held Cara in his arms that made her think he would make a good da. And though there had been an annoyance in his eyes when he had first appeared in the Great Hall, it had softened when his eyes rested on the wee lass.

The savage had more of a heart than he wanted people to know, or at least she hoped he did.

Slain warned himself to say nothing, let her finish, then take his leave, but he was finding it difficult, if not impossible, to ignore her moist, rose-colored lips. They ached to be kissed. Or was it he who ached to kiss them? Recalling the last time, he had kissed her, and had so enjoyed it, only managed to make him want to kiss her again.

Hannah wiped the last of the charcoal off his face, using her thumb to catch the small spot near the corner of his mouth.

It was Slain's undoing, his hand went to hers, taking hold of her thumb and running it faintly and ever so slowly over his lips. It sent an intense rush of passion through him, turning him hard, his manhood growing even harder when the tip of her tongue peeked out from between her lips and licked them slowly, then she worried her bottom lip with nibbles.

Her innocent actions were much too tempting to ignore. His hand fell away from hers to cup her neck as he brought his lips to hers, brushing them faintly. Once. Twice, before nibbling softly along her bottom lip until it was plump and red, then he kissed her.

Her lip had grown so sensitive from his gentle bites that she gasped with the pleasure that shot through her and her breath caught again when his tongue darted in her mouth to mate with hers.

Hannah got lost in the exquisite pleasure, instinct having her respond as her tongue met his with desire and determination. His hand rode up under her breast to cup it, his thumb brushing over her nipple and it shot a shudder through her that was so intense that if she had not been sitting, she would have collapsed. Tingles followed, rushing to settle between her legs and left her feeling damp. That she responded to and loved her husband's touch was undeniable.

His one arm suddenly coiled around her waist to swiftly move her off the bench to his lap. She gasped again when his hard manhood rubbed against her as he settled her there. All the while, he continued to kiss her, stir her, have her aching for him.

When he moved his lips off hers and rested them at her neck to tease with kisses and nips, she found herself whispering his name in his ear as if she begged him for something, "Slain."

He raised his head, resting his brow to hers. "What do you want, wife? Tell me."

Her response came fast and easily. "You, my husband. I want you."

He got to his feet with her in his arms in a mere second and headed for the stairs when a powerful pounding at the front door seemed as if it shook the Great Hall.

Slain let a slew of oaths fly silently in his head.

The heavy pounding came again.

Disappointment gripped Hannah when Slain lowered her to her feet and moved her to the shadows. "Stay here. Do not move."

Hannah had no time to nod, he all but flew to the door, though opened it only partially. The exchange with whoever was there was brief and when he turned and walked toward her, she saw that the passion that had flared so strongly in his eyes only moments before was gone. Sheer determination fueled by anger replaced it. Hannah wondered if that was how he looked when heading into battle.

"I have to go," he said when he came to a stop in front of her.

"Where?" she found herself asking.

"That does not concern you."

"I am your wife," she said as if that should settle it.

"And are told what I choose to tell you."

His words sent a shiver through her, but it was not passion his voice evoked this time, but an icy chill that delivered a warning. It annoyed her that the precious loving moment had turned so cold.

"When will you return?" she asked, not able to keep the frustration from her voice.

"Not your concern." His voice turned curt when she went to speak again. "Not another word, wife, and make sure to remain in the keep until my return." His finger pressed against her lips when he saw a protest spark in her eyes. "You will do as I say."

Realizing it would get her nowhere to argue with him, Hannah relented with a nod and as soon as she did, he turned and left the Great Hall.

Hannah returned to sit at the table alone, wondering where her husband was off to. Her brow wrinkled. She had assumed Slain spent most of his time secluded in his solar, but had he? Had he been away from the keep the two days after they had been wed? And what of other times she thought him here in the keep? Had he been gone as well? And if so where had he gone and who had summoned him?

He had secrets, but then she did as well.

Helice appeared and set a hot brew in front of her.

"There is a chill," she said and turned to leave.

"How did you come to know Slain?" Hannah asked.

Helice did not even stop walking as she said, "He will tell you if he wants you to know."

It is not your concern. Her husband's voice was clear in her head. *I will tell you what I want to tell you.*

Why did this place hold so many secrets? Was that why Slain had buried himself in here, to keep its secrets? She glanced around the Great Hall, empty, the crackle of the fire the only sound. Could she get it to reveal its secrets to her?

The one place that might reveal something to her was Slain's solar and with him gone... she hurried off the bench.

Once she was in the solar, Hannah quietly closed the door behind her. Slain's solar was vastly different from her father's, not that she had been allowed in it. Young and being more curious than wise, she had snuck into her da's solar one day. It had been nothing like Slain's. No books. No parchments with drawings, not even a crude map or a tapestry that told a tale. It had held the barest of furnishings, giving no hint to the man who occupied it. She had wondered what her father did there.

Her mum had found her and had punished her with confinement to her bedchamber for the remainder of the day and the next entire day. It had been torture for her, especially since her peek into her da's solar had been for naught. Though thinking on it now, she had found something... emptiness. There had been nothing in that room that spoke of her da, unlike here in Slain's solar.

She walked over to the chair that sat near the fireplace, a narrow, squashed pillow a sign that someone had sat braced against it. A small wooden footstool was positioned a distance away from the chair, evidence it was for a person with long legs who wished their feet close to the heat of the hearth.

Hannah imagined Slain's long legs stretched out as he sat there reading a book from the few that sat stacked on the small table beside the chair. Her mother had taught her to read, she having learned from an aunt who had felt it important. Her aunt, a woman of daring courage, had transcribed several poems and presented the small volume to her mum. Her mum had first read them to her, then used them to teach her to read. It was a cherished possession of her mum's that she wished she had.

Hannah made her way slowly over to the desk, her interest drawn to the parchments there. She sat in the chair, surprised by the cushioned seat that felt welcoming. She studied the top parchment, the drawing having such fine detail that it was easy to see that it was a wheel device of some sort. There were written words as well, but Hannah was not familiar with the language.

Another parchment seemed as if it had been drawn by a different hand, the drawing crude, more symbols than detail. The wiggly lines obviously represented water, tall triangles not enclosed at the bottom, mountains, and straight lines with angled ones coming off it, trees, leading Hannah to believe it was a map.

She came across the one that she had seen the first time she had been in the solar. More detail had been added to it, and the little bit of writing, in Latin there was, she understood.

Results depend on the amount of force used.

She tilted her head, trying to make sense of what the drawing depicted. She thought it was some type of weapon since it appeared as if several spikes protruded from a narrow board. Of course results would depend on the amount of force used in striking someone. But weapons were created to inflict damage or death, so why would he write the obvious?

Hannah shook her head and placed the drawing aside, smiling at the next drawing. It was the keep in better days. She smiled, thinking that Slain had drawn it from memory, a happy time when things were going well for the clan. But on closer study she realized that there were differences from the keep now and in the drawing. The square front door that now hung crooked had been changed to an arched doorway and a barbican had been added around the upper portion of the keep, allowing sentries a vast view of the surrounding land.

This drawing showed a significant change to the keep. Was it something Slain planned to do, though how could he if his wealth was gone?

Hannah looked around the room. It spoke of a learned man, a man of many interests, a man of many talents, a man who was far from being a savage.

"It is not good for a wife to spy on her husband."

Hannah jumped startled by Helice's sudden presence rather than her reprimand, though she refused to let the latter stand without comment. "Since one of my tasks had been to keep the solar clean, I assumed the room was not off limits to the chief's wife."

Helice looked contrite, though only for a moment.

"One can learn much about someone from their interests," Hannah continued, "and since I know little of my husband, I hoped his solar would tell me more about him." She smiled. "Especially when others refuse to tell me anything."

The reprimand was not lost on Helice, though she pursed her lips, reaffirming that she would share nothing about Slain.

"I have learned many things about you since arriving here," Hannah said.

Helice's only response was a scowl.

It did nothing to deter Hannah in continuing. "You enjoy cooking, preparing the meals with care and love. You say you owe a debt to Slain, yet I believe your debt has long been paid, if Slain ever thought of it that way, and you stay because you wish to be here or perhaps you cannot return home."

Helice bit at her bottom lip as if forcing herself to hold her tongue, though it lasted only a moment. "You think you know, when you know nothing. I gave you fair warning to leave when you had the chance. That chance is gone. You now belong to the savage and if you think Slain is no savage think again. It took a savage to save me and it took a savage to survive the fires of hell with the demon lord... Warrick."

Chapter Sixteen

Hannah sat in the Great Hall the next morning eating her meal alone, her husband still not having returned home. Though sun shined through the windows brightening the room, it still felt dismal. The keep was barren, not an echo of a voice or burst of laughter. No voices raised in conversation or footfalls heard. Nothing but emptiness.

It made the heart ache.

"For someone who claims my food is delicious, you eat little."

Hannah looked up at Helice, her face pinched as usual. She wondered if the woman was ever happy. "I am not hungry." She pushed the bowl away. "Where is my husband?"

Helice shrugged. "I do not know. I am not his keeper."

Hannah stood with a flourish and a bit of annoyance, snatched up her cloak off the bench, and went to the door.

"Where do you go?" Helice asked.

"You are not my keeper either," Hannah said.

"Your husband will want to know if he returns while you are gone."

"Then let him find out for himself," Hannah said, her hand on the latch to open the door.

"You will tell me now, though better still you will remain in the keep."

Hannah turned to see Slain standing behind and to the right of Helice, his arms folded across his chest. He looked no different from when he had left, though there was a tiredness to his dark eyes that she had not seen before. Otherwise, he appeared as imposing as ever.

Helice gathered up the remnants of Hannah's uneaten meal and with a respectful nod to Slain went to walk past him.

"Wait," Slain ordered and cast an eye at the full bowl of porridge.

Helice responded as if knowing what he would ask, "She has eaten little if anything since you have been gone."

"Bring us more food," he ordered and Helice gave a nod before leaving the room. He walked to the table Hannah had just vacated. "Join me."

She did not protest or argue, she was too pleased to see him. Her heart thudded a bit faster as she walked over to him and the flutters in her stomach would not stop. And though tiredness lingered in his eyes, there was also concern that had been there many times before when he looked at her.

A large flutter erupted in her stomach as she wondered if it was more than concern she saw there. Could her husband actually care for her? They had been on the verge of going to his bedchamber, before he had taken his leave, not just to consummate their vows, but to satisfy a passion that had sparked easily between them. Were they beginning to care for each other?

Slain watched her take slow steps toward him, slipping her cloak off her shoulders as she did and dropping it on a bench all the while her lovely green eyes seemed alight with joy at seeing him. She had missed him and annoying as it was to admit to himself, he had missed her. It was the strangest feeling being eager to return home. He had had no wont to return to this empty place since his parents had died and all had seemed lost, even this crumbling edifice. Obligation had him returning and doing what was necessary, though truth be told it was more revenge that drove him. Revenge that kept him going. Revenge that would finally satisfy him.

Slain sat opposite her at the table, trying to ignore her beguiling smile and the way passion flared in her green eyes now and again, turning them a brighter green.

"Your arm does well?" he asked as Helice placed bowls of porridge in front of them and a plate of bread and a crock of honey, then took her leave.

"Aye, it does well," Hannah said.

Slain wanted confirmed what he already suspected. "You have missed me?"

She nodded, her smile spreading. "Aye."

"Why?" he asked, her smile feeling as if it reached across the table and stroked his face with the slightest of touches.

She stared at him a moment, a small piece of bread clutched in her hand. "I do not know."

"You are honest, wife."

"As much as I can be," she said, "I only know I am glad to see you."

"I am glad to see you as well," he found himself admitting.

"Perhaps it is a start to a marriage that will do well," Hannah suggested.

"Perhaps, we shall see." He dared not hope to be so fortunate, since misfortune had been all that had prevailed of late. "Now tell me where you were going."

"To the village to find someone to talk with, though now that you have returned, I have no need to go there. It would, however, be nice to welcome clan members here again."

"Maybe in time."

His response gave her hope, though she also realized that the more she made herself known here, the more news spread of the chieftain's new wife, the more chance she took of being discovered. But in the end it would be inevitable anyway.

"I have seen your drawings. You have a talented hand."

"Given to me by my mother along with a passion for the written word."

"My mum had a book she would read to me again and again."

"Wherever did your mum learn to read or come by a book?" Slain asked puzzled.

Hannah had been enjoying speaking with her husband so much that she had not guarded her words. A woman of the peasant class certainly would not know how to read let alone own a book, a rare possession. At least she had kept a smile on her face, not showing the alarm his question had raised in her.

She shrugged. "I do not know, my mum never said. I only know she cherished the book as did I." Hannah feared he did not believe her since his mystified look remained.

"Where did your mum learn to read?"

She assumed he would follow with that question and was prepared with an answer that was partially true. "She spent time in a keep when young and the chieftain's wife taught her." She did not expect his next question.

"How did your mum feel about your father selling you?"

Hannah's smile faded, thinking of her mum and how protective she had been of her only child. "My mum would have never allowed him to sell me. She would have protected me with her life, if she had been alive. But then I do not have to tell you about the love of a mother for her child. From what I have heard you had loving parents."

"The clan still speaks of them fondly?"

"Aye, I hear nothing but good and kind things about them."

"Even my father?" he asked.

"I am told he loved your mum beyond reason."

"An attribute I greatly admired about him," Slain said with a sense of pride.

"Then you are fortunate, for I have no attributes to admire about my father."

Slain did not care for the sadness that stole the joy from her eyes. He reached across the table and took hold of her hand. "You are safe here."

She wanted to believe him, she truly did, but she wondered if the woman she had escaped with had been right when she had repeated over and over that no place was safe. *No place.*

Her thought jogged her memory of that day in the woods when she heard what she believed was someone betraying Slain. Now would be a good time to alert him to the incident and she hurried to explain.

"I should have told you of this sooner, but I was not sure if I should speak of it to you or not, but now I feel it is important I tell you," she said and continued on before he could stop her. "When I was in the woods I heard two men exchange information about something happening soon and how victory would be theirs, though there was nothing else for either of them to report this time, so it appears as if the two have met before."

"What were you doing in the woods alone? Did I not warn you that you were not to go alone into the woods?"

Hannah was surprised that he focused on her and not the incident. "Aye, you did, and Helice told me to keep to the edge of the woods when she sent me on a task."

"And you saw fit not only to pay no heed to Helice's order but mine as well?" Slain accused. "Do you know what could have happened to you if those men had found you?"

"I hid—"

He squeezed her hand. "Listen well, wife, you will obey me this time and never go into the woods alone again."

Hannah was more concerned with the incident than her foray into the woods. "As you say, but what of the man who betrays you."

"I will see to that. You are not to concern yourself with it."

She should have expected the dismissal. After all, what did he know of her that should make him trust her? Though she thought he would question her more about what she had heard or seen, making her wonder if he was already aware of it.

"I have some things I must see to, but we will sup together tonight," he said and released her hand.

Dismissed again, although the way his dark eyes held hers, Hannah sensed they would do more than sup together this evening.

"You have something to busy yourself with?" Slain asked, not wanting her to sit idle, since she just might get herself in trouble that way.

"There was something I intended to seek your permission on."

That she asked cautiously, had Slain worried as to what she might be up to. "What is it?"

"I noticed in your one drawing that you made improvements to the keep, the front door in particular. I thought I would see if some of the clansmen would be willing to do the work." Seeing he looked ready to shake his head, Hannah quickly added, "You take good care of your clan. I believe they wish to return the favor for a chieftain they admire greatly."

"Though fear more," Slain corrected.

"All the more reason to change that and let them see the keep restored," Hannah said, though kept the thought that followed silent. *And their chieftain as well.*

"The door, no more," he grudgingly agreed, hoping it would keep her busy, and stood.

Hannah smiled, jumped up, and hurried around the table to hug her husband.

Her arms circled him and she pressed her cheek to his chest and instinctively his arms wound around her. She favored his embrace, it having been far too long since she had felt such a caring one.

She raised her head and his lips claimed hers, possessively and eagerly. She responded in kind, having wanted to kiss him since he entered the room. His kiss was even better than she remembered and she lingered in it along with him, exploring, demanding, responding, and enjoying the wonderful mix of sensations that consumed her.

Slain stepped away from her and hastily said, "Until this evening, wife."

Hannah sighed, disappointed he chose to leave. She would have preferred he stayed. She shook her head. Whatever was the matter with her?

Do not be a fool, she silently warned herself.

He has secrets, as do you and secrets never fair well.

Guard your heart well, for once you lose it all good sense goes with it.

More of her mum's advice that Hannah wondered if she had learned from experience. Had she lost her heart to Hannah's father only to discover he was not the man she thought he was? Was she losing her heart along with her good senses to Slain?

She stood and reached for her cloak, tired of worrisome thoughts. She would be cautious and guard her heart and hope it was not already too late to do so.

The village was busy with activity, the onset of spring bringing everyone out of hibernation. Fields and gardens were being planted, cottages repaired, women were deep in chatter, and children were running around in play and laughter.

Hannah smiled and allowed herself to enjoy the moment. She did not know what the future would bring, but for now she intended to enjoy what she had.

Blair waved to her and Hannah walked toward her as she approached.

"It is a good day when the sun chooses to smile on us," Blair said, greeting Hannah with a smile of her own. "All goes well with you?"

"Aye, all goes well."

Blair lowered her voice. "A light was spotted in the east wing the other night. You have not gone there have you?"

Instinct warned Hannah to mind her tongue and say nothing about her experience in the east wing. She shook her head. "I have no wont to meet a ghost."

Blair shivered and rubbed her arms. "Either do I. It is good you stay away from that section of the keep. So what brings you to the village today?"

"I was hoping to get some men to repair the keep door."

"Slain allows it?" Blair asked, her brow rising with surprise.

"He gave me permission just a short time ago and I am eager to see the task started. If not today, then soon."

Blair turned and shouted at two men in conversation near a cottage, "Imus."

The larger of the two men turned to her, though said not a word.

"A moment," Blair called out with a wave for him to join her.

Imus' pace was quick and steady for one so large. He had pleasant features and his long, red hair and beard were heavily streaked with gray.

He was only a few steps from them when Blair said, "The chief needs some men to repair the keep door." A scowl surfaced on his ruddy face and before he could say a word, Blair continued. "The chief gave permission for the work to be done. Can you gather some men and see to it?"

Imus gave a nod and turned and walked away.

"My husband wastes little time on words," Blair said with a laugh. "He will see the work gets done and be glad about it, though not show it. He says little but does much. He is a good husband."

Hannah and Blair continued to talk and were soon joined by Kate, then Wilona. It was pleasant to chat with the women on a variety of things, and it made Hannah wish life could be like this, more pleasant moments rather than ones fraught with uncertainty.

When a group of about ten men headed toward the keep, Hannah bid the women good day and hurried on ahead of them. She wanted to inform Helice of the repair work that was about to begin so the woman would not rage at the men and chase them away.

Helice glared at Hannah after she finished explaining what work was about to begin.

"You bothered him with that?" Helice snapped as if scolding Hannah.

Hannah did not know what happened to the woman to make her so unpleasant and quarrelsome, but she was tired of it, hoping to bring more happiness to the keep than misery, and snapped back at her. "What I discuss with my husband does not concern you, and I do not appreciate your hostile manner. You will watch your tongue with me or I will seek your removal."

"Slain will never allow that," Helice said with confidence.

"And why is that?" Hannah asked, doubting the woman would answer.

Helice raised her chin. "I am his mother-in-law."

Chapter Seventeen

Hannah's mouth dropped open, though no words spilled out.

"*Was*," Helice corrected, "now that he has wed again."

Hannah did not know what to say. She remained silent, words failing her, staring at the woman.

Helice's chin went up. "So no matter what you say, I will remain here."

Stunned, Hannah stared at her a moment more before shaking her head, gathering her senses and walking out of the kitchen. She entered the Great Hall to be greeted by the door being ripped from its hinges.

Blair's husband stood in the open doorway and acknowledged her with a respectful nod, then returned to work. Soon the sound of splintering wood and stone being chipped away echoed through the Great Hall, yet Hannah paid it no heed, her thoughts on Helice's shocking reveal.

How was it that no one knew, or did they? That Slain had been wed once before? What had happened to his wife? Why did Slain not speak of the marriage?

Secrets revealing more secrets, would they never end?

How could she complain when she had her own secrets? Still, the news troubled her and also reminded her of how little she knew about her husband.

"Your head will pound soon enough, if you sit here and continue to listen to that noise."

Hannah looked up to see that her husband had entered the room, her heart swelling at the sight of him. Why was it that he seemed to grow more and more appealing to her every time she laid eyes on him? And what was it with the little lurch and tug to her stomach that grew as he neared her?

Guard your heart or you will lose it.

She feared it might already be too late.

A silent reminder of what she had just learned raised disturbing questions. What of his first wife? Did she lose her heart to him as well?

He snatched her cloak off the bench. "Come, we will go for a walk and leave Imus and his men to work."

Hannah stared at her cloak, not even remembering that she had taken it off. She walked over to him and he slipped it over her shoulders. She caught her gasp before it could slip from her lips when his hand drifted down along her arm to take hold of hers, closing around it with strength. He led her out of the room and through the kitchen, Helice nowhere in sight. She thought he intended to walk in the woods and was surprised when he led her around the back of the keep and down a path, open land to either side of them, with woods bordering the land a distance to the left. Not so to the right, rolling hills rippled over that land, extending around to the side of the keep where the heather grew in abundance.

She looked out over the beauty of the land as they walked. Something familiar about it caught her eye and she turned to him. "There is a creek up ahead."

Slain's brow creased as he asked, "How did you know?"

"You did a drawing of this area, a map of sorts." He seemed to tense beside her, his grip slightly tighter on her hand. "It is good to know the lay of the land and its vulnerability to attack."

That mystified look, he had gotten when last she had said something strange, for a crofter's daughter, appeared once again on his face.

"Your croft was vulnerable to attacks?" he asked.

She was quick to offer an explanation. "For a keep, attacks. For crofters, strangers who may mean harm. My father kept open land around us, so he could see who approached and make ready if necessary."

"You are well versed in many things," he said.

Hannah was not sure if he meant it as a compliment or if it puzzled him that she was well-versed... for a crofter's daughter.

They continued walking, silence falling between them.

Slain wondered over Hannah. The more he spoke with her, the more he learned about her, and the more he questioned her story. She kept something from him, but what and why?

They reached the bank of the stream, its water flowing rapidly. On the opposite side of the stream was a brief stretch of land before one reached dense woods.

"Your land extends beyond the woods?" she asked, though knew his land was vast, having heard her father speak many times about it.

"Far beyond the woods. My ancestors were granted part of the land by various chiefs and rulers. Other areas were claimed from the spoils of battle. My grandfather allowed the chiefs of some of the defeated clans to keep their lands as long as they pledged their fealty to the Clan MacKewan, most have remained loyal."

Hannah slipped her hand out of his and dropped down to sit on the ground, patting the spot beside her for him to join her, and smiling as she did. She wanted some time to speak with her husband. Not only to come to know him better, but because she actually enjoyed his company.

Slain stared at her a moment before lowering himself down and sitting close enough for their arms to brush each other. Her beauty never ceased to get his heart racing and his loins stirring, but it was her smile that really did him in. It invited and tempted.

"Tell me of your family's croft," he said, wanting to avoid kissing those far too tempting lips of hers, fearing one kiss would not be enough. He would want more, much more.

Hannah thought of the only croft she had ever visited with her mum. The crofter's wife had claimed to be a healer and her mum had sought her out when she had taken ill and their own healer had done little for her.

"There is not much to tell. It was a good piece of land or so my father said. He worked it hard and expected my mum and me to do the same." That was not so with the croft she had been to. The healer and her husband had four sons to help tend the land, while the healer tended those who sought her skill.

"That is the way of crofters, the land and survival demands it," Slain said. "Why did your father truly sell you? It had to be more than being a disobedient daughter?"

She thought about what her step-brother had said to her and spoke the words aloud. "Plans changed."

Slain caught the distant look in her eyes and he could see she was reliving a memory. He hated for her to revisit such a horrid time, but he wanted to know what had truly happened to her.

Again her thoughts went to her step-brother's words, though she changed them to fit her response. "I became a burden who stood in his way."

Anger rumbled through Slain, hearing the sadness in her voice. How could her father have treated her so cruelly? He reached out to take her hand in his and tempered his annoyance when he spoke. "You are no burden to me."

She favored the way his strong hand devoured hers, clutching it firmly, and that he should consider her no burden warmed her heart and made it beat a bit faster. Her instinct was to move closer, rest her shoulder to his, turn her face up for a kiss that she sensed was wanted, and one she would not deny she wanted as well, yet she did none of that.

Instead, she could not help but ask a question, one that had plagued her since learning the news. One she needed an answer to. "What happened to your first wife?"

Slain dropped her hand as if it was suddenly hot to the touch, stood, and walked closer to the edge of the stream, keeping his back to her.

Hannah did not relent. She needed to know for her own sanity or was it her own safety? "Helice told me when I warned her I would let her go if she continued to be troublesome."

He turned then, a flash of anger in his dark eyes. "This is Helice's home. She remains here."

"I have no wont to send her on her way. It was nothing more than a false warning. I simply wish she was not so cantankerous."

"It is her way."

"Tell me so I may understand," she offered.

"You need not know."

"I need to know why you made no mention of your first wife," Hannah persisted.

"It is of no importance."

"It is to me." Hannah stood.

Slain approached her with quick strides. "Tell me what secret you keep from me and I will tell you of my first wife."

Hannah took a step back away from him, his words startling her.

Slain snagged her arm with his hand before she could put too much distance between them. "I am no fool, wife. There is more to your story than you tell me."

Stunned that he recognized the truth, Hannah found herself speechless.

Slain stepped closer to her, lowering his head as he spoke. "Secrets can only be shared when there is trust. Do you trust me, wife?"

Her response came easily. "Do you trust me, husband?"

It was Slain's turn to be startled. She had turned his question on him and he responded in an angry tone. "How do I trust you when you do not tell me the whole of your story?"

"I could say the same of you," she accused annoyed that while she wanted to trust him, caution warned against it.

He looked ready to spew his anger at her when a shout in the distance caught his attention.

Hannah turned and saw Helice waving for him to return.

He kept hold of her arm and their return walk was far different than when they had ventured this way. Their pace was rushed and they spoke not a word to each other.

When they reached Helice, she said, "You have a visitor."

Slain's hand fell off Hannah's arm and he rushed off, saying not a word to her.

Helice walked off as well, though not before warning, "If you know what is good for you, you will keep hold of your tongue."

Hannah entered the keep wondering over the visitor that had Slain rushing to meet and curious about why Helice would warn her to hold her tongue. About what and who? What Helice had told her about Slain? If that was so, it was too late and she was glad of it. She wanted to know about Slain's first wife and he would be the only one who would tell her.

She drifted past Slain's solar and heard voices raised in argument. They quieted again, as if they realized their mistake, though they raised again a moment later, stopping Hannah suddenly. Her eyes turned wide and her heart pounded in her chest. The voice sounded familiar. But what would Melvin, one of her father's most trusted warriors, be doing here?

Was it him? If it was, did his presence here have anything to do with her?

Please, Lord, no, she silently prayed. Going home would mean certain death for her.

She listened, straining to hear what was being discussed, but she could catch only snatches that made no sense.

When quick footfalls approached the door, Hannah scurried away to hide in the shadows in the Great Hall. Her heart continued to pound and her stomach roiled so fearful was she if it was Melvin that he would see her.

Angry shouts followed the two men into the Great Hall and Hannah's legs almost failed her when she saw that she was right. It was Melvin, though he looked to have aged since she had last seen him only two or was it three months ago? He was already an aged man, but he had grown more so, the gray in his long hair having devoured what dark strands had been left. The few wrinkles on his face had multiplied and fatigue seemed to fill his blue eyes that once were bright but had since dulled. He had always been kind to her and her mum, but first and foremost his allegiance had been to her father.

Melvin's anger spewed out with his words. "You will regret that you did not accept his generous offer."

"Generous?" Slain said his voice so strong it echoed in the Great Hall. "Ross MacFillan has never been generous. He is a greedy, ruthless man who takes what he wants or believes should be his. Clan MacKewan and all its holdings will never claim fealty to him."

"You are a fool, Slain MacKewan," Melvin shouted and shook a raised fist at Slain. "You leave your clan vulnerable with no warriors to defend it and refuse a generous offer to keep them safe."

"Safe?" Slain shouted. "MacFillan leaves destruction wherever he goes."

"Chief MacFillan is a—"

"Do not say generous man again or I will cut out your lying tongue," Slain threatened. "MacFillan demands more and more from the clans he decimates, leaving them to starve while he grows his coffers and land."

"You will regret this," Melvin warned.

"The only regret I have is that I have yet to kill the foul, despicable, lying Ross MacFillan."

Melvin turned and stopped, the men who had been working on the door having entered the Great Hall and spread out in front of the open door, axes, picks, and hammers in hand.

Melvin turned to Slain and had no time to protest, Slain ordering, "Let him pass. He has a message to take to Ross MacFillan. The Clan MacKewan will never bow, claim fealty, or surrender to the Clan MacFillan."

Attack. Her father would attack the Clan MacKewan, as he had done to other vulnerable clans, and lay claim to it. What had Slain been thinking not making certain he had an army of warriors to defend his clan?

Slain had powerful friends. Would he call on them for help?

Either way, her presence here would be revealed to those she had been hiding from, leaving her where? Would her husband protect her as he had said he would or would it be easier for him to surrender her?

The men parted only enough for Melvin to slip past them, his feet taking flight to hurry through the crooked doorframe that was nearly repaired.

Slain nodded to the men and they returned to work.

Hannah held her breath, hoping her husband would return to his solar so that she could hurry up the stairs to her bedchamber and make it seem that she knew nothing of what had just happened.

She should have known better.

He walked straight to her, his hand reaching out to snatch her arm and she had to ask as he yanked her out of the shadows, "How did you know I—"

"I see in the darkness," he answered before she could finish and rushed her to his solar.

She would have thought that impossible until the healer had told her how to use the darkness to see. She had learned that shadows, movements, sounds, and smells shed light in the darkness and that knowledge had helped her keep her sanity while imprisoned.

"Why were you hiding?" Slain demanded after shutting the door behind them.

She had not expected that question, though she had no difficulty answering it. "I did not think you would want me there."

"So you hid instead of taking your leave."

He trapped her with that one, but she was quick to respond. "I am unfamiliar with wifely duties in such a situation, so my instinct told me to conceal myself."

"From this moment on, you will not now or ever *conceal* yourself. I want all to know I have wed and to meet my wife."

That should be no surprise to her and yet it churned her stomach, for it meant it would not be long before it was discovered that she was Ross MacFillan's daughter. Did she tell Slain now and be done with it?

Consummate the marriage first and seal your vows.

Oddly enough, she could not do that to him. She had grown to care for this man, though of late she wondered if she could possibly be falling in love with him. Or was she simply grateful for what he had done for her since her arrival here. He had saved her life twice and their marriage had offered her even more protection. But would that last if he knew the truth? And what of her father? How would he respond to the news that she had wed his enemy?

Time. She needed time to sort through it all. Time to come to know her husband better. Time to see if love was even possible between them? Unfortunately, Melvin's unexpected presence here showed that time was something that was running out for her.

Hannah had not realized that her head had drooped, her chin nearly to her chest, until Slain slipped his finger beneath it and gently raised it. It was not his fine features that fluttered her stomach, it was the concern so potent in his dark eyes. It spoke louder than words… he cared. He did not hide it. It was there for her to see and she felt a tug to her heart.

"I want no worry burdening you. You are my wife and will remain so. You are stuck with me."

Hannah had to look more closely to catch the slight teasing smile that caught at the corners of his mouth. Her smile was far from slight, it lit her face. "It is no chore being stuck with you."

"You say that now, but you have yet," —he paused and brought his face close to hers— "to hear me snore."

Hannah erupted in laughter.

Her burst of laughter had an unexpected and unfamiliar laugh spilling from his lips. How long had it been since he had last laughed? He could not recall, but it felt good.

Hannah's eyes softened when she stopped laughing and said, "I would not mind hearing you snore."

The message in her remark was clear to Slain… she would be pleased to share his bed. It sparked his manhood, rousing it, and it also poked at his heart. As clear as her remark had been, he wanted his just as clear.

His hand had fallen off her face when she had laughed and he returned it there now, running a finger along her cheek and down to her chin. "Think well on it, Hannah, for I have a strong appetite for coupling. I may demand more than you want to give."

"What if I want more than you are capable of giving me?"

Slain could not help but laugh lightly, especially since she said it so seriously as though it was possible. "The only problem I see with that is that you would probably be with child more often than not."

Having a large brood pleased Hannah, her husband thinking her question humorous did not. "So you are telling me that you will never fail to pleasure me?"

"That, my dear wife, I can promise you."

That he gave another little laugh annoyed Hannah. "And what recourse do I have if you do not? Do I seek another man's bed?"

Slain grabbed both her arms and yanked her close, anger sparking his words. "Do not even joke about that. No man will touch you but me, and the day that I cannot please you will be the day I am put in the ground."

Hannah felt a jab to her heart at the thought of him dying and she reacted without thought. She pressed her cheek to his, her whisper sounding like an edict. "You will not die before me." She brought her lips to his and kissed him gently as if sealing her command with a kiss.

Both her words and kiss were demanding and tore through something inside him, breaking past some of the shields and barriers he had erected. He felt them shatter as her kiss deepened and she worked her way further into his heart.

His hands dropped away and his arms circled around her, pulling her close, needing her there snug against him as his lips took charge of the kiss. It was as if he was kissing her for the first time, tasting, savoring, and enjoying every bit of her. Her lips tasted like no other. There was a sweetness, a freshness to her that he favored. It snuck inside him and spread, stirring and churning, making him want more and more.

His hand cupped her one breast, squeezing it lightly and running his thumb over her nipple, hard beneath her garments. He wished she was naked so he could feel her smooth flesh and taste her rosy bud grow harder in his mouth.

He wanted her. He wanted to slip between her legs and sink into her and get lost in pleasure. But not here in his solar.

She whimpered sorrowfully when he moved his mouth off hers, a smile quickly replacing it when he whispered, "Come to my bed."

She nodded eagerly and as they grasped hands as if they intended never to let go, a knock sounded at the door.

"Message," Helice said from beyond the closed door.

Slain took a deep breath, fighting to calm the mounting need inside him. Reluctantly, his hand fell away from hers, though her slim fingers tried to keep hold of it, and it was like a jolt to his heart.

He went to the door, opened it, and it surprised Hannah when he stepped out, closing the door behind him. She stood staring at it, wondering if she should go over to it and see if she could hear anything. Before she could decide, Slain returned. The passion that had ignited in him all but drained away.

"I must leave. I should return by this evening."

"I will wait your return."

"No," he snapped. "I will see you in the morn."

He opened the door, a sign that she was to leave, and it upset Hannah that only moments before he was so loving and eager to be with her and now he dismissed her so coldly. Was the savage sneaking in and stealing her husband away?

She had no choice but to take her leave and when she reached the door, Slain's hand caught her arm, stopping her.

"You will not await my return."

Hannah went to speak, but his sharp words stopped her.

"Do not defy me on this, Hannah."

He released her arm and Hannah walked out the door without a word or a nod to him.

~~~

The keep was quiet, no wind whistled around the windows or rain slashed at them. It was as if nature itself held its breath.

Hours had passed since she had left Slain in his solar. Imus and his men had long since finished working on the door for the day, one of his men had let her know they would return on the morrow. She had eaten supper alone in the Great Hall. Helice spoke not a word to her and she did not try to engage the woman in conversation. How she would deal with Helice from this point on was questionable, but she had little choice.

Her thoughts jumped around, keeping her from sleeping.

After another hour or so past, Hannah sat up in bed, punched her pillow, then dropped back, her head sinking into it. She let out a sigh.

So much had happened to her in such a short time that she was not sure how to comprehend it all. She recalled something the healer had once told her mum when her mum had asked the woman a stream of questions.

We are often left with more questions than answers and often do not like the answers we get. Life can be wicked. Life can be good. But there is one thing certain about life… it is unpredictable.

The healer had been right about that.

She twisted and turned some more until finally she wore herself out and dropped off to sleep.

She woke suddenly and, casting an eye at the hearth, saw that the fire had burned down some, a couple of hours had past. But what had woken her? She lay listening and realized a strong wind whipped at the window. She burrowed beneath the soft wool blanket and snuggled her head against the warm pillow, thankful sleep was creeping over her once again.

Her eyes barely closed when a loud pounding had her springing up and looking about. For a moment, she thought someone had pounded on her door, but there was no lock on her door and the only person who would enter this time of night would be Slain.

Unless something had happened to him and Helice...

She did not wait to finish the horrid thought that it could be Helice outside her door to deliver bad news. She scrambled out of bed and to the door, opening it cautiously to peer out.

No one was there.

She jumped when the pounding sounded again and she realized it came from Slain's room. Someone pounded on his door from the inside. It had to be Slain.

It shivered Hannah when the door shook again from the pounding. He would hurt his hand if he continued to pound it. She went to the door, her thought on what he had once said to her. That her door had no lock and it was up to her to discover if his did. She was about to find out.

She grabbed the latch and swung the door open.

Her husband stood there, naked from the chest up, his fist raised, ready to swing at the door again. His knuckles were scraped and bleeding from the previous blows. His dark eyes raged with animalistic fury, much like they had done that night in woods when he had viciously ended Muir's life, and a tremble of fear rippled through her.

"Get out," Slain shouted, his muscled chest heaving from his heavy breaths, as if he had run a distance.

"You are hurt," Hannah said and took a couple of steps inside the room.

"Get out now, Hannah!" he shouted again and shook his fist at her.

"After I tend your injured hand," she said more calmly than she felt. Inwardly, she trembled, fear crawling along her skin, prickling it as she realized it was not her husband she spoke with but the *savage*. Yet somewhere in there was Slain and she had the overwhelming urge to protect him from himself.

"Out!" he ordered, shaking his fist at the door, fighting to keep his eyes off her body naked beneath the white wool nightdress that hung off one soft, smooth shoulder, begging to be kissed and nipped in playful pleasure. But he was in no mood to be playful. He was in the mood to hurt, to rage, to pound away the fury that consumed him.

"I will tend your hand, then leave," Hannah said firmly, compassion for her husband outweighing her fear of him or was it her own foolishness? She licked her lips, her mouth so parched she worried she would not be able to speak. "I will be quick."

The tip of her tongue circling her lips, leaving them moist and inviting, broke him. "No, wife, it will not be quick."

He moved with such speed that he was standing in front of her before she realized it and just as fast his hand shot out past her head. She cringed, feeling the room tremble as the door slammed shut behind her, and fear jumbled her stomach when the latch clicked shut.

She was locked in here not with her husband, but with the *savage*.

Chapter Eighteen

Hannah stared at Slain's naked chest so close to her that if she puckered her lips she would kiss his hard flesh. It heaved in and out, his solid muscles rising and falling and, for a moment, a brief moment, no more than a blink, she thought she heard the mighty thumping of his heart.

She called on her courage—no—her stubborn foolishness. That was what her mum had called it one time when she was young and had climbed on a horse to ride it, to prove to her father she could do it. It was the first time and the last, she had seen any pride in her father's eyes for her.

Whatever it was, courage or foolishness, she needed it now.

Hannah raised her head slowly and when her eyes met his dark ones, she stifled a gasp. Anger warred with passion in his dark depths and she wondered what had been the cause of his fury. It was, however, not the time to ask.

"Are you all right, *husband*?" she asked, hoping to remind him that she was his wife, Slain's wife.

"Aye, *wife*, I will be as soon as you shed that nightdress."

"Your hand," she said, brushing his remark aside, and reached for it, but he pulled it away.

"Your nightdress... rid yourself of it."

"Slain," she said softly, hoping to wake that part of him that was her husband.

"Now!" he demanded and his hands went to his plaid and began to unfasten it.

With his shirt already off and his boots as well, he would be completely naked soon and he expected the same of her.

"If you leave it to me, I will rip it off you."

Hannah had no doubt he would do just that, so she slipped the nightdress over her head and tossed it aside. It mattered not, since he had already seen her naked. At least that was what she told herself.

A chill sneaked in from somewhere or perhaps it was her courage waning that brought on the shiver that puckered her nipples and turned her skin to gooseflesh. Or was it the way her husband stood staring at her, his eyes slowly taking in all of her.

She felt vulnerable, much too vulnerable and she had felt that way far too much of late. Something inside her refused to allow herself to feel that way with her husband, for if she did so now, it might never change.

Hannah looked him in the eye and began to slowly let her eyes roam over him from top to toe, stopping in the most intimate of places longer than necessary, and finding herself growing quite aroused as she did. Her eyes returned to settle on his eyes and she thought she saw a spark of admiration there.

He stepped closer to her and leaned his face down near hers to whisper harshly, "Are you ready for the savage?"

She did not know where her response came from, but it flew from her mouth before she could stop it. "It is not if I am ready for the savage, but if the savage is ready for me."

She threw her arms around his neck with a forceful lunge that sent her body slamming against his and if Slain did not throw his arm around her waist and steady them both with his strength they would have tumbled to the ground.

She captured his lips before he could say a word and her aggressive kiss fired his blood and turned his already hard manhood, the results of his eyes lingering on her gorgeous naked body, even harder. She tasted and demanded of him as if she would never be satisfied, and he fed her hunger as well as his own.

He kept his arm snug around her waist and brought his other hand to the back of her head, holding it firm, not letting her move it, keeping her lips locked to his. He maneuvered them toward the bed, stepping back while keeping her tight against him, the feel of her hard nipples digging into his chest, poking, igniting, and firing his loins.

When his leg hit the side of the bed, he tore his mouth away from hers, scooped her up, and dropped her down on it. He was stunned when she spread her arms and legs, welcoming him as he lowered himself down over her.

She showed no fear of him, not an ounce, and she wanted him as badly as he wanted her. His manhood ached for satisfaction, but it was the strange feeling that gripped his heart that he noticed more.

He could easily love this woman.

Not now, not yet, he silently warned himself, but knew the warning did little good.

He took her lips this time, in a kiss so demanding it would frighten most women, but not Hannah, she returned it with a demand of her own. He slipped off to rest at her side so that his hands could touch her, explore her, caress every intimate part of her.

Her hand was quicker, running eagerly down his chest and he jumped when she grasped his manhood, then began to stroke it, as if she was not only familiarizing herself with it but laying claim to it.

What amazed him even more was that he felt her chuckle when he jumped, yet she never broke their kiss. It actually intensified.

He was the one who finally ended their kiss, much to her annoyance, though once he began feasting on one of her nipples that changed and her moans of pleasure heightened his own. He rolled his tongue across the tight little bud and tugged at it with his teeth, eliciting moans and squirms from her.

Though he loved her touching him, he was relieved when her hand fell off his manhood and gripped his arms. If she had continued, he would have climaxed much too soon and that was not what he wanted.

He wanted to slowly enjoy every inch of his wife and seal their union, securing her as his wife forever.

His hand drifted down along her flat stomach, her skin so smooth and soft that he never wanted to stop touching her. And when his hand slipped between her legs to find her wet and ready for him, he almost surrendered to his urgent need.

"Slaaaain," she moaned his name, though it sounded more as if she begged.

Hannah had never expected to find coupling so intensely pleasurable, though she did not think it would be that way with anyone other than Slain. That she had lost her heart to this man was now obvious to her. She could never lay naked like this, be stroked and kissed so intimately by anyone but Slain.

She trusted him. She trusted him more than she had ever realized.

"Slaaaain," she moaned again as his fingers found their way inside her and his thumb brushed the nub hiding in her nest of red hair between her legs. The more he stroked her, the more she moaned, the more her pleasure grew.

His mouth left her nipple and moved down along her heated skin and the further down his kisses went, the louder her moans grew. When his tongue flicked across her hidden gem, her body arched and he quickly spread her legs and settled his face between them.

What he did to her next had her definitely thinking him a savage, for he tasted, nipped, and licked, his hands firmly clasped to her backside so she could not move or writhe or even breathe the pleasure was that intense. And if that was what the savage would do to her in his bed, she would welcome him every time.

"Slaaain!" she pleaded with an aching whimper.

He heard her pleading ache, felt it himself, but she tasted like no other woman, sweet as well as potent, a perfect blend that was irresistible.

"Ohhh!" she cried and squirmed, desperately trying to free her bottom from his grip.

She was near to climax and he wanted to be inside her when she did. He moved up and over her, his arm going around her waist to lift her up along the bed until her head rested on a pillow. Then he lowered himself to hover over her, her legs already spread in eager anticipation of him. His manhood was so hard it was easy to slip it between her legs and push the tip gently into her.

Hannah's moan was more a sigh and she arched her back, wanting more of him.

He pushed further in and she arched higher against him and he slipped deeper in her. She was so wet, yet so snug, and so welcoming. He pushed further in with a bit more force and he stopped when she gasped.

"I hurt you?" he asked, appalled at the thought.

She shook her head, her red hair flaming from the fire's light. "No. No. Do not stop. Please do not stop."

He realized he had hit her maidenhead and it was tight. He did not want to hurt her, but it was better done fast or so he had been told since he had never coupled with a virgin.

"Hold onto my arms tight," he ordered. "It will be over quick."

Her eyes flew open wide, a spark of concern in them. "I do not want it quick. I want this pleasure to last."

He could not help but smile. "It is your maidenhead I must take quick. As for your climax, I will see you have more than one."

Hannah grabbed his arms, loving the feel of his strong hard muscles. "My maidenhead is for you to take, husband, but I beg you do not stop once you do."

Damn, if her words did not have his manhood throbbing unmercifully, and with one swift thrust he drove into her and he almost stopped when she cried out, but she shook her head and locked her legs around him and tightened her hold on his arms.

He kept a steady rhythm for a few moments to let her accept the fit of him, then he increased it again and again and again, until their bodies pounded against each other.

Hannah gripped his arms tighter and tighter as pleasure mounted throughout her body. It grew and grew and grew with every thrust and so did her moans. Until... her whole body burst with the most exquisite sensation and she shouted out, "Slaaaaain!"

Slain did not stop. He would come, but not just yet. He would see her come again before he did.

Hannah's moans turned soft, the exquisite pleasure beginning to fade when suddenly it sparked again and she turned wide eyes on her husband.

"You will come again for me, wife."

She nodded and smiled and her moans began again until once again she burst with pleasure, and he joined her, surprised at the strength of his own climax. It gripped him and rolled through him with an intensity he had never felt before or satisfied like ever before.

After he was completely spent, he moved off her to lay beside her and took her hand in his, and he liked that she curled her fingers around his, not ready to let go of him. His breathing had yet to calm as well as his heart, it thumped a mighty beat, and there was something else. Something he wanted to ignore but was having difficulty doing so.

His wife had actually calmed the savage in him. She had chased away the fury that had raged like a violent storm ready to ravage the land, and what had she used to combat it?

Love.

Impossible. She did not love him. She was being a dutiful wife.

He almost chuckled aloud. It had not felt like duty. It had felt like she could not get enough of him. That she wanted him with as much desire as he did her. Or was it that he wanted to believe that someone would break past the savage within him and love him… all of him?

Hannah rolled on her side, slipping her leg over his, resting her arm across his chest, and placing her head on his shoulder with a contented sigh. She looked up at him. "Can we do this again tonight?"

Once again Hannah left Slain speechless. It took him a moment to push aside his shock, then he gathered his wife in his arms, kissed her lips lightly, and said, "We can do it as often as you want."

He was startled again when she turned a joyous smile on him, though worried when it was suddenly replaced by a frown. "I will not wear you out, will I?"

He could not help but laugh, a deep resounding laugh.

She jabbed him in the side. "I am serious."

Her curt tone and scrunched brow told him she was very serious and though he could not keep the smile and light chuckle from his words, he reassured her. "Trust me, wife, when I tell you that you will not wear me out."

Her smile returned. "Good, I will move my things in here in the morn."

He would love to have her share his room, sleep with her, couple endlessly with her, but there were other things he needed to consider.

She spoke before he could. "It would be foolish for me to remain in the other room and make so many trips back and forth throughout the night."

He smiled at the thought, but being more experienced than her knew that was unlikely, though he would not discourage her. "A wise decision," he said, realizing too late he should not have agreed, but then he was better off knowing where she would be since she could be too curious for her own good.

Hannah yawned, feeling more comfortable and comforted in his arms than she had ever been. Or had it been from making love with her husband? She wanted to believe it was their joining that had brought her a satisfaction and comfort she had never known. She wanted to believe that Slain cared for her, could possibly love her, since she knew without a doubt that she loved him. How impossible it might seem, she loved Slain, and she wanted desperately to spend the rest of her life with him.

Regret poked at her, not for making love with him, but for not telling him who she was before they did. Now their vows were sealed and there was a chance his seed could take root in her, a thought that thrilled her. But would he be as thrilled when he found out who she was? She had to tell him. She could not wait any longer. Not now, though. She did not want to ruin this night with him. Tomorrow would be time enough.

She yawned and shivered, a slight chill running over her. She tightened her hold on her husband when he went to move. "Where are you going?"

"To stoke the fire and then get us snug under the blankets, a storm brews outside." He kissed her cheek and slipped out of bed as reluctant to leave her, as she was to let him go.

Hannah remained on her side, her head resting on her arm as she watched her husband tend the fire. She kept her eyes fixed on him. She wanted to tuck this moment away in her memory and have it there to recall, should this be the last time they shared such a precious moment. She did not want to think that way, but after the last few months of hell, the healer's words to her mum had proven all too true… life was unpredictable. She did not know what tomorrow would bring, she only hoped she would share it and all the days to follow with Slain.

She stretched her arms out to him as he approached the bed and her heart swelled at his smile and the look of affection in his eyes, the fury that had raged in them before completely gone.

He tucked her against him close after covering them with the warm wool blanket.

"You will share the morning meal with me?" she asked.

"Aye," he said, softly and found himself looking forward to it. He wished he could spend more time with her, but there were important matters for him to see to. His months of planning would finally see fruition and he could let nothing stand in the way, not even his wife.

Over the morning meal, Hannah planned to confess her identity and be done with it, and see if it would change anything between them. Tonight she would enjoy every moment with her husband and pray that tomorrow changed nothing.

She turned sleepy eyes on him and saw that his eyes were closed, his lips slightly parted, a soft breath coming from them. She eased her head up and pressed a faint kiss on his lips, not wanting to wake him and let a soft whisper spill from her lips, "I love you, Slain, and always will."

With her head settled on his chest and her body tucked close against him, she drifted off in a peaceful sleep.

Slain opened his eyes after her body went limp against his in sleep.

She loved him.

Her words thrilled him and worried him. Now was not the time to have someone fall in love with him or for him to fall in love. She could be used against him and he would kill, as he had done, anyone who dared harm Hannah. If he had not owed a debt, he would not have wed, not now. To have wed Hannah to settle a debt was not fair to her, though honesty had him admitting that the debt had been an excuse to have what he wanted… Hannah.

The night he had saved her from that fall, stripped her of her worn garments, he knew he wanted her. The more he came to know her, the more she intrigued him, the more he wanted to know.

Not the time for love.

His mum had enjoyed telling him how she had helplessly fallen in love with his father and always finished with, *love arrives when it wants, but it is up to you if it stays.*

There was not a shred of doubt in his mind that he wanted Hannah to stay.

He would have to be more cautious in his plans and once it was done, once he stripped Ross MacFillan of everything just as Ross had done to his father and see that miserable, lying step-son of his dead, then, and only then, could he start a life with Hannah.

His eyes drifted closed, though sometime in the middle of the night he woke too Hannah stroking his manhood. It was a quick joining, since she had turned him so hard. His need could not wait and either could hers.

He woke her next, teasing her nipples with his tongue while his fingers pleasured her.

It was another quick joining since Hannah pushed him on his back and climbed on top of him. He helped her ride him, but when her climax drew near, he took charge, lifting her off him to drop on her back and spread her legs to enter her, her protests turning to moans as he thrust into her eagerly.

Sleep wasted no time in claiming them again and even the slashing rain and wind pounding at the windows did not wake them.

Hannah stretched herself awake and winced at the soreness between her legs, then smiled thinking it had been worthwhile. She turned, reaching for her husband's warm body and found the bed empty.

Chapter Nineteen

Hannah ate the morning meal in the Great Hall alone, her husband nowhere to be found. He had promised her that he would share the meal with her. No, she was wrong. He had not promised... he had simply said *aye*. What had happened to take him away from her?

When Helice told her she had no idea where he was, Hannah had searched the keep. She had even tried the door to the east wing, but it had been locked. She had no recourse but to wait his return.

The Great Hall was much too quiet. With the rainstorm, Imus and his men could not work on the door and she could not venture to the village in the heavy rain. She was trapped here and that would not have been bad if her husband was here with her, but she was alone.

When Helice came to collect the remnants of the meal, the woman shook her head and scolded. "You need to eat more."

Hannah's appetite had returned to what it once had been, but worries had a way of making it wane and remaining so until whatever worried her was settled. While numerous worries plagued her, there was one concern she chose to address now.

"I want peace between us, Helice," she said and raised her hand to still any response. "When I am finished you may speak." Helice pursed her lips and rested her arms on her ample chest and Hannah continued. "Your home is here and I have no wont, now nor did I before, to change that. What I would like is for us to be friends."

Helice remained stoic, not speaking or moving.

"Is that possible?" Hannah asked, knowing it would take work, not even sure if she would be here to see it done, but determined to give it a try. For a moment, Hannah thought the woman would remain silent, then she took a step closer to the table.

"You speak to me as one familiar with directing servants and your knowledge is considerable... for a peasant. Your hands show no signs of hard work, yet peasant families work the fields together. You are no crofter's daughter. When you tell me who you are maybe then we can become friends." She picked up Hannah's bowl and tankard and turned.

Hannah words stopped her before she could take another step. "You have your reasons to keep secrets and I have mine."

"Secrets can destroy."

"Like they do to this keep?" Hannah asked.

"Aye, secrets crumble this keep. When you discover them will you stay or will you run?" Helice turned and walked out of the Great Hall, as if no answer was necessary, as if she already knew it.

Hannah thought on Helice's words. Was the woman trying to warn her that she may not be able to live with the secrets harbored here in the keep? Could they be that bad?

She decided to go to her husband's solar and look around. His drawings had shown promising improvements to the keep and at least one small one had already begun. Would the other drawings show her something else?

She tapped at the door, in case Slain had returned, but got no response. She eased the door open, stepped in, and eased the door closed behind her. The fire had burned down some and she went and added a couple of logs to it.

The wind and rain was lashing against the window and she wondered over her husband's whereabouts and if he was safe. A burst of thunder had her jumping and made her anxious for his fast and safe return.

She went to the desk, the pile of drawings still there. She sat in the chair and made her way through each drawing. Some were more detailed than others were and the more she saw, the more she was impressed with her husband's talented hand. The one where the keep appeared fully restored was beautiful. It appeared to welcome with open arms, flowering bushes surrounded the once neglected keep and, surprisingly, the window in the east wing stood open.

The drawings that followed showed the keep from different angles. The kitchen garden was larger and overflowed with plants and two buildings sat off to the left of it. Slain's plans were substantial, but how could he do all this if his coffers were empty?

The next drawing had her eyes narrowing at first, as if she was not quite sure what she was looking at, then they popped wide. It was her home, drawn on a smaller scale and expanding out to the surrounding area. There were Xs in various spots. She recognized the one spot. It was where one of her father's sentinels caught her trying to sneak off into the woods alone. She realized then what the Xs signified. It was where her father stationed his sentinels.

She quickly looked at the next drawing and it showed tiny Xs completely devouring the land around the keep. Was this something Slain planned or was this nothing more than what he wished he could do? He had no army, no warriors to fight for him. Or did he?

She stared at what seemed like thousands of Xs. Even if Slain had an army of warriors it would never be this large. There was only one who commanded such a large show of warriors.

Warrick.

Her stomach roiled so badly she feared she would lose what she had eaten. Slain might be considered a savage warrior, but it was nothing compared to Warrick. He showed not an ounce of mercy and cared not for the pain he inflicted on others. Many believed him one of the devil's demons, and she knew all too well what pain he could bring.

With the amount of Xs on the drawing, her clan would take a savage beating, countless lives would be lost, homes destroyed, and her father... she closed her eyes, which only made it worse. Images assaulted her of what her father might suffer. He may have showed her little love throughout the years, but he was her father. As for her step-brother, Nial, she cared little of what happened to him.

Her unease grew as she continued to stare at the drawing and the more she stared, the more she saw endless carnage and suffering. What should she do? If she told her husband who she was, would it make a difference? Would he spare her clan or would he cast her aside? And what of her father? Would he see it as a strong union between two strong clans or would he think it an affront and demand the marriage be nullified?

Why did she ever think she could escape who she was and hide amongst her father's enemy? It always went back to what choice had she? Anyone else would have turned her over to her father for a price? But what of Slain? What would he have done if given a choice?

The day wore on with no sign of her husband. She kept herself as busy as possible, listening for the sound of his steps or his voice. She spent some time going through the garments in the chest by her bed and found a couple she could stitch to fit her since they were slightly large for her. She also placed a few of her items in her husband's bedchamber.

By evening she went back and forth from concern to annoyance that he had still not returned, nor had he sent word to her. The rain had not helped, having confined her to the keep all day. She finally retired to his bedchamber with the hope that he would return some time during the night.

Her hopes were dashed when morning arrived and she found herself alone. She was pleased the rain had stopped and as soon as she finished the morning meal, she hurried to get her cloak, intent on going to the village.

When she returned to the Great Hall, Imus and his men were working on the door and he acknowledged her with a nod as he stepped aside to let her pass. Blair had been right, her husband was a man of few, if any, words.

She smiled and waved when she spotted Blair walking toward the keep and went to meet her.

"Finally, the sun," Blair said, casting a smile to the sky, "though who knows how long that will last."

Hannah nodded. "Spring brings the rain."

"You mean more rain." Blair chuckled and raised her arm, a basket draped over it. "Brought some food for my husband, since he rushed out early this morning without eating and he can get grumpy when he does not eat."

A shout had the two women turning.

"Sweeney, you owe me," yelled a thin man weaving from side to side and looking as if he would tumble over at any moment, his steps so unsteady.

Blair rolled her eyes and shook her head. "That is Potsman, Wilona's husband. He drinks more than he does anything else."

"Sweeney, do you hear me? I want what is due me," Potsman called out and looked about to fall back but caught himself. "You drank all my ale."

Sweeney, a short wiry man put his shovel aside and approached Potsman. "You are daft, Potsman. I was not drinking with you last night."

"Do not think me a fool," Potsman garbled. "I know who I drink with."

"It was not me," Sweeney argued.

"Leave Sweeney be, you drunken fool, you were drinking alone last night and started again this morning as soon as you opened your eyes," Wilona called out as she approached the pair.

Potsman nearly toppled over when he turned to wave a fist at his wife. "Stay out of this, woman, I know who I drink with."

"Yourself, that is who you drank with," Wilona said, waving a raised fist back at him, anger flashing in her eyes.

"Go mind your duties and leave me be," Potsman ordered.

"Mind my duties?" Wilona said, stopping in front of her husband with her hands on her hips. "I have no time to mind my duties since I am constantly looking after you, the drunken fool that you are."

"Do not talk to me that way, woman," Potsman said, though the words were barely understandable.

"Go home with your wife, Potsman," Sweeney said, dismissing him with a wave of his hand.

"You owe me and I will not be leaving here until you give me what is owed me," Potsman said and fisted both hands, raising them as if ready to fight.

"Be gone with you, Potsman, and sleep off your drunk," Sweeney said and turned away from the man.

Potsman swung, barely tapping Sweeney on the back. "Cheat. Coward."

"Go home," Sweeney said, moving further away.

"Coward," Potsman cried out again.

"Go home," Sweeney repeated.

Wilona went to her husband's side and grabbed his arm, ready to drag him home.

Potsman threw himself into his swing as he jumped in the air and brought his fist around with all the strength he could muster, sending him in the wrong direction.

Wilona ducked and her husband's fist caught Hannah on the jaw near her mouth and sent her stumbling. She landed sprawled out on the ground, in the mud left from yesterday's rain.

"Good Lord!"

Hannah was not sure who said that, though right afterwards several faces were peering down over her. All stared wide-eyed at her and though her vision was a bit blurry, she saw that it was Blair, Wilona, and Sweeney. Imus suddenly appeared as well and two more men.

"God help, Potsman, when the chief finds out about this."

Hannah was not sure who said that either, but a couple of hands reached down to help her to her feet.

"Are you all right?" Blair asked, staring at Hannah's jaw.

"It was an accident."

Though the voice sounded as if it shivered with fear Hannah recognized it as Wilona's.

"What difference does that make? Your husband struck the chief's wife," Blair said, her own voice trembling with as much fright as Wilona's.

Hannah's senses finally cleared and she agreed with Wilona. "It was an accident. There is no need for worry."

Sweeney shook his head and looked to Wilona. "I would worry plenty. Look at how her jaw is already swelled and bruising."

Hannah raced her hand to her jaw. She winced and her eyes turned as wide as the others upon feeling the large bump.

"It looks even worse," Blair said.

"That was some unlucky punch," Sweeney said.

"You deserved it and what do you mean unlucky. I got you good," Potsman said as he struggled to get to his feet.

"You stupid fool," Wilona screamed at her husband. "You did not hit Sweeney. You hit the chief's wife."

Her words hit him like a bucket of cold water being thrown in his face. His eyes bulged and he turned whiter than fresh fallen snow.

"You might as well start digging your grave now, Potsman," Sweeney said, "the chief will kill you for this."

"No." Hannah defended her husband. "Slain would not do that."

Every one of them stared at her as if she had lost her mind.

Their attention was quickly diverted when Potsman began weeping, a heavy, gut-wrenching weeping, and copious tears ran down his face. "I am a dead man," he said through heavy sighs.

Wilona shook her head. "I will be a widow soon enough."

"Nonsense," Hannah said. "I will speak to Slain and explain everything."

Sweeney turned to Potsman. "Run while you can."

"No, all will be well," Hannah encouraged, though no one paid her mind.

Potsman clung to his wife as they walked off together, mumbling over and over. "Dead. I am dead."

"For once, he is right," Sweeney said, shaking his head and returning to work on the door.

The other two men followed him and Imus turned a sad shake of his head on his wife, took the basket from her, and walked off.

"Potsman is right. The chief will kill him for laying a hand on you," Blair said.

Hannah tried reassuring all and herself, since the thought of the man dying because of an unfortunate incident involving her was not something she could live with. "I will not let that happen."

"You will not be able to stop him… the savage. He will show himself and that will be the end of it and the end of Potsman." Blair patted Hannah's arm before turning and heading to the village.

A gray cloud suddenly devoured the sun as if confirming Blair's prediction and knowing a visit to the village now would only worsen things, she returned to the keep.

Hannah changed garments and kept to herself, not letting Helice see her bruise. By evening her jaw pained her and seeing her reflection in the window she almost cringed. The corner of her mouth down to her jaw was swollen and a dark spot covered a good portion of it.

She kept her hand over the area when Helice brought her the evening meal. She found eating a bit painful, though it was her worry for Potsman that had her appetite waning after only a few mouthfuls.

"You miss your husband so much that you cannot eat."

Hannah was so happy to hear Slain's voice that she did not think about her bruise. She jumped up from the table, her hand falling away from her face and a smile spreading across it, though it turned to a wince fast enough.

Hannah watched her husband transform before her eyes. Ferocious anger flared like a fiery flame in his dark eyes, his lips appeared to take on a feral lift, and she thought she heard him give a low animal growl.

He sprung so fast toward her that Hannah jumped and gasped when his hands took hold of her arms, turning her to face the hearth's flame for him to see better.

She spoke quickly, hoping to soothe him. "It was an accident."

Slain could not take his eyes off his wife's swollen and deeply bruised jaw. She had taken a hard punch, though not as hard as the one he intended to deliver to the person who did this to her, accident or not.

"Who?" Slain demanded.

"It was an accident and best forgotten," she said and foolishly tried to smile in hopes of softening his anger. She winced instead, which only served to spark his anger even more. She could almost feel the low rumbling growl stir in his chest. "I am unharmed. It is nothing."

Slain fought to contain the fury that mounted in him. "You are not unharmed and you say it is nothing when your jaw is swollen and bruised so badly that you cannot smile without it paining you." His growl was stronger this time as he raised his eyes to the rafters for a moment, shook his head, and took a strong breath. "You cannot eat without pain either, can you?"

"It is a bit sore, nothing more."

"You lie," he accused though softly and eased her down to sit on the bench, joining her. With a faint touch, he ran his fingers over the bruise. "Tell me the truth. Does it pain you?"

The anger in his eyes had quieted, though remained stirring there and his touch was ever so gentle and caring. She decided the truth would serve her best, as it would be later when she revealed her identity to him. Something she was not looking forward to, but was necessary.

"It pains me to smile and to chew, but it is not an unbearable pain," she admitted.

"It is an unnecessary pain none-the-less."

Hannah gently rested her sore jaw against his hand. "It truly was an accident. No one needs to suffer for it."

"That is for me to decide," Slain said his heart going out to his wife for her suffering. When he first saw her injury, he could not contain the savage within him. He rose with a fury ready to tear someone from limb to limb, something he was still thinking of doing. Though first, he would tend his wife. "Has Helice seen to your injury or the healer?"

Hannah moved her head away from his hand reluctantly and shook her head. "It is not necessary. It is a bruise and will heal in its own time."

"What happened?" he asked instead of who did it, intending to find out one way or another.

Hannah hoped to avoid names. "The punch was meant for someone else. I was hit by accident."

"So there were others present," Slain said, something he was glad to hear, for if his wife would not give him the name he needed, someone else would.

Hannah realized the same as her husband. "You will find out so I may as tell you it all."

"You are right. I will find out all of it, though I prefer it come from you."

"I will tell you, but please give me your word you will not harm the man over a foolish accident."

"Foolish or not, that is for me to judge." He leaned forward as soon as Hannah appeared ready to protest and brushed his lips gently over hers. "Tell me, wife."

What choice had she? He would find out and perhaps the telling of the incident might be better coming from her.

Hannah explained it all, impressing on her husband that it was an unfortunate accident. Her husband showed no reaction as she spoke, but anger remained stirring in his dark eyes. She finished with, "So you see no malice caused it."

"No, drunken foolishness did," Slain said and shouted out for Helice.

The woman must have been lurking nearby since she appeared quickly and Hannah was surprised at the concern on her face when she looked upon the bruise.

"See to my wife's wound and if you feel she needs the healer, fetch her. Also brew a broth for her since it pains her to chew. I will return shortly and share the meal with her."

Hannah grabbed his arm when he went to stand. "There is no need to harm Potsman."

"I remind you again… my decision," Slain stood and left the Great Hall.

"You should have come to me," Helice said her voice gentler than Hannah had ever heard it.

"You would have told Slain upon his return."

"Of course, I would have. He is your husband and chief of the clan. He must know," Helice said as if Hannah's question made no sense.

"You know him better than me," Hannah said a bit of envy poking at her. "Slain will not harm Potsman, will he?"

"Slain will do what is necessary. He always does."

Hannah waited until Helice took her leave and knowing she would return soon hurried out of the keep, not even bothering to stop for her cloak.

Chapter Twenty

Light was just fading from the land when Slain walked through the village, his strides strong and his anger apparent. Mumbles and whispers followed him, as did the villagers. He paid them no heed, his thoughts on Potsman alone. His wife may have had sympathy for the drunken sot, but he did not.

"Potsman!" Slain shouted when he came to a stop in front of the man's cottage. It was small and well-kept thanks to Wilona, since the worthless fool did nothing to help. He shouted his name again. "Potsman!"

The door creaked open and Wilona stood there, her eyes red from crying.

Slain's anger grew that the man was such a coward he would send his wife to face him, but then Wilona was nudged out of the way and Potsman stepped out the door, Wilona following so close behind him that they looked as one.

Potsman stood with his shoulders drawn back. "I would beg for forgiveness, my chief, but what I did was unforgiveable. I deserve whatever punishment you inflict on me."

Potsman was soberer than Slain had ever seen him and far cleaner as well, no foul odor emanating from him, but that only infuriated Slain more since it had come at the expense of his wife's suffering.

Wilona went to step forward to speak, but Potsman stuck out his arm, stopping her, and whispered something over his shoulder. She remained as she was, though tears pooled in her eyes.

"I am sorry for hurting Hannah, for she has been nothing but kind and gracious since her arrival here, and it is good you have found such a fine woman to take as your wife."

"How generous of you, Potsman."

Everyone turned, except Slain. He rolled his eyes to the heavens at the sound of his wife's voice. The woman had far too strong a mind of her own. But was that not what he loved about her?

Love.

He had been struggling with the thought since he had left her the night before last after they had coupled for the first time. Though they had not coupled, they had made love, and having been separated from her for a mere day had made him realize that, whether he wanted to admit it or not. *Love*. It was something he was still trying to come to grips with and this matter did not help any.

He had failed to be here and protect her and now he wanted to make it right. He wanted his revenge.

Slain heard people shuffling behind him, clearing a path for Hannah to join him and he knew next he would hear her speak.

"I explained the unfortunate accident to Slain," Hannah said as she stepped beside her husband and took his hand. "He knows you meant me no harm."

"I would never harm you. I would lay down my life for you if necessary," Potsman said with a sincerity that touched Hannah's heart.

"A fitting punishment," Slain said, wrapping his fingers tightly around his wife's hand.

Hannah spoke up. "But not at all necessary."

Silence fell over the crowd, hearing Hannah all but correct her husband.

"Your chief knows mistakes are made and mistakes can be forgiven," Hannah said, thinking of her own mistake of not telling Slain the truth before they wed and fearing the consequences.

Though they had not known each other very long, she could not imagine life without Slain. Somehow he had filled a void in her, an emptiness she had not known she had until she had met him. The thought of life without him frightened her and realizing that now frightened her even more, since she may have no future at all with him.

Slain remained silent, wondering over her words and if they were meant for Potsman or herself. Had she made a mistake and feared to tell him? But what mistake? She certainly had been agreeable enough when they made love, so it could not be that. And he did not believe that she regretted their marriage, since she seemed to have planted herself firmly in it, wanting to get busy making changes to the keep.

"Mistakes can be forgiven, unless they are grievous," Slain said and thought he felt her body gasp, but she quickly shook her head as if shaking it away.

"It is good then that this incident is not grievous," she said with a slight smile, fighting off the wince that rose up to grab at her.

The crowd remained silent, waiting to see if the new bride of the Chief of Clan MacKewan could contain the savage.

Slain stared at Potsman, his dark eyes smoldering, ready to ignite at any moment. "You will report to Imus in the morning and help with the work on the keep door. You will continue to work on the keep until I say otherwise."

"Aye. Aye, my chief," Potsman said with a look of pure shock.

Wilona nodded vigorously behind him, her own expression one of shock as well.

Hannah was pleased with her husband's wise decision to keep Potsman busy working on the keep so that he would be too busy to drink, at least as much as he usually did.

What happened next stunned everyone, leaving them open-mouthed and staring.

Slain moved with such speed no one knew what happened until it was over and Potsman lay on the ground, blood flowing from his mouth and his lip, and his jaw swelling so badly he would be lucky if he could eat or drink for days.

"Touch my wife again and I will kill you... and not slowly."

Hannah's breath caught along with the crowd's and she got the distinct feeling there was more to her husband's warning that they understood than she did.

He took her hand and the crowd parted once again to let them both pass this time.

Hannah felt the blood on his knuckles but said nothing until they left the village. "Your hand is bleeding."

"Aye, and it feels good, though he deserved much more."

What did she deserve for deceiving him? She would know soon enough since she did not intend to let any more time pass without telling him. The burden of the truth had become too heavy for her to carry or perhaps it was the possible consequences that burdened her the most.

Hannah planned on speaking to her husband alone as soon as they entered the keep, but her plans went astray when she saw that Helice had food waiting for them and her husband made it quite clear that she was to eat.

The hot broth Helice had made for her was tasty, though she had to force herself to drink it since her stomach rolled in waves of worry.

"You barely sip the broth. Does it pain you to do so?" Slain asked, trying to keep the annoyance out of his voice, since it was not meant for her.

"No, the broth causes me no pain," she said, "though what does pain me is that I woke alone yesterday morning and today, and you left no word of where you went or when you would return."

"It does not concern you," Slain said, turning his attention to the stew in front of him.

"You are my husband and anything that takes you away from our bed concerns me," she said, laying a gentle hand on his arm and managing a soft smile without wincing.

Slain loved when she smiled whether softly or exuberantly it did not matter, and that she should bear pain to do so made him want to make Potsman suffer even more. Though, what touched his heart and stirred him to arousal was that she had missed him in their bed.

Their bed.

That he shared his bed with her, wanted to share it with her, continued to surprise him. He had given no thought to falling in love, had no time for it. Yet love had struck him whether he wanted it to or not. It had hit him hard, harder than he had ever thought possible. And while his first instinct was to fight it, he had soon learned that it would be a battle that would know no victory for him.

He turned to her and whether it was a wish on her part or real, she thought she saw a spark of love in his dark eyes. It had been brief, but she had seen it or was it that she believed strongly enough that she had, which propelled her to speak before giving thought to her words?

"You have stolen my heart, though I gladly give it to you, for my love for you runs deep."

Slain stared at her, shocked that she felt as he did and that she had the courage to admit it.

Hannah shook her head. "I do not know when I fell in love with you or even why. I only know that my heart beats ever faster when you are near and flutters fill my stomach, and I want to forever hug you close, forever make love with you, forever be with you."

Slain went to speak when Helice entered the room.

"The healer is here, wondering if Hannah requires her skill," Helice said.

While Slain did not want to lose this special moment with Hannah, he also did not want his wife's injury to go unattended and possibly turn worse. Reluctantly, he said, "Bring Neata here."

Hannah was disappointed. That was until her husband spoke.

"We will resume this discussion later, for there is much I have to say to you, wife." Slain placed an ever so gentle kiss on her cheek.

It did not take Neata long to let Slain know that Hannah was fine and only time would heal her injury.

"I will tell Helice to make a comfrey poultice for you to help with the bruising. For tonight, I advise rest and sleep," Neata said.

Hannah covered her mouth and her wince at the unexpected yawn that took hold, confirming Neata's counsel.

"She will rest," Slain said as if he commanded it.

"I would have come to you sooner, but I was attending a birth at a nearby croft and only learned of it upon my return," Neata said. "I am surprised Helice did not already treat your wound with a comfrey poultice."

"I did not tell her about it," Hannah confessed.

Neata shook her head. "Helice may have a prickly nature, but she is a good woman and knows well the healing ways. Trust her." After a gentle pat on Hannah's shoulder, Neata took her leave.

Hannah hoped to resume her discussion with her husband, but Helice appeared once again to let him know he had a message.

"Finish your broth and go to our bedchamber and rest. I will join you when I can." Slain kissed her cheek and walked off with Helice.

Hannah could not stem her annoyance. Where did these sudden messages come from and why did they always seem to take him away from her? The thought that he would be gone again annoyed her all the more. There were things she needed to discuss with him before he discovered them on his own.

She ignored his order to finish her broth. Instead, she hurried off to his solar to let him know that she would wait in the Great Hall for him. She stopped abruptly not far from the door, having heard voices. He was not alone. The voices were low and barely distinguishable. Helice had told Slain a message awaited him, but it was a messenger who had delivered it.

Mysterious comings and goings, messages at all hours, visitors as well, and the locked east wing had her curious to learn what exactly was going on.

"He is busy. I can relate a message for you," Helice said, causing Hannah to jump from the woman's sudden presence.

Hannah turned to face Helice. "You know what goes on here. Why keep it from me?"

"Why keep the truth from your husband?" Helice countered.

Hannah was in no mood for the woman's contentious nature. "Say and think what you will, Helice. I want nothing more than to see my husband kept safe so that we may share a decent life together."

Her own words were nothing more than, wishes, hopes, and dreams. But wishes, hopes, and dreams had been what helped her through this difficult time and she would not let go of them now.

She continued, since Helice remained silent. "I will be in our bedchamber resting... as he commanded."

"A wise choice, since he would be upset if you suffered any more than you already have."

Hannah left Helice standing guard by the door to Slain's solar.

Her feet took the stone stairs slowly as her mind swirled with thoughts. Helice remained a mystery to her. She kept a watchful eye on Slain and seemed protective of him, but was it a ruse? Helice had warned her to not go deep into the woods that day she had heard one of the clan betraying Slain. Hannah had wondered then as she did now if Helice had known about it, hence the warning. Slain had also warned her not to go into the woods alone. Could it possibly be that Helice and Slain both knew of what was going on there?

Hannah dropped down on the bed after entering the room. There was far too much going on here that she did not know about, Melvin, one of her father's trusted warriors being one of them. There was a good chance Melvin would return or—God forbid—her step-brother would show up, the message Melvin returned with not to Nial's liking. She had to tell Slain who she was, she had to before it was too late.

She changed into her nightdress, intending to wait for her husband. She would tell him everything then and face whatever consequences befell her. And whether wise or not, she was glad she had told him that she loved him. She hoped he felt the same since she believed, wanted desperately to believe, that love was strong enough to conquer evil, not that her mother would agree.

Or would she?

Her mum had warned her endlessly about foolishly losing her heart and the disappointment of love. Yet there were times, rare as they were, that her mum had spoken about love differently and Hannah often wondered what had happened to have her mum be so disappointed by love.

Hannah stretched out on the bed, hoping to stay awake to speak with her husband. If not, she would certainly wake when he slipped into bed with her and she would have a chance to speak with him then. She drifted off soon after cuddling beneath the warm wool blanket.

~~~

Slain sat alone drinking in his solar. The message he had received was a good one. All was going according to plan. It would not be long now before he had his revenge. Nothing could stop it.

Love.

He had planned for everything but love. He had long known that he might not survive the battle that was brewing and had made arrangements for his clan's protection if it proved necessary. He would gladly die revenging his father and clan's honor. That was until he met Hannah and lost his heart to her.

Now death was something he was not yet ready to meet. He wanted a life with Hannah. He wanted to have children with her, laugh and love with her, and grow old with her. He wanted what he had seen his mum and da had once shared, and had once thought not possible for himself... family and a love that grew through the years.

He stretched his feet out by the fire. He fought the desire to go upstairs to his bedchamber and join his wife in bed, take her in his arms, hold her close, and...

He shook his head. She needed rest. She did not need to be worn out even more by making love and that was what would happen if he slipped in bed with her. It was not his own aching passion that concerned him, for he could contain it. At least he had with other women, he was not so sure about that when it came to his wife. Especially since she had proven to enjoy making love so much. She held back nothing and gave everything. She was more than he could have ever dreamed of or hoped for, she was an amazing, courageous, and loving woman. And she belonged to him and always would, as he always would belong to her. They were one now and never to be parted.

He would have his revenge and he would fight to stay alive for his wife and the future they would have together.

~~~

Hannah grew annoyed when she once again woke to an empty bed the next morning. Her husband was neglecting his husbandly duties and she intended to let him know that it was not acceptable. She hurried into her garments and with a quick comb of her hair that did little to tame the fiery, stubborn curls, she rushed out of the room in search of her husband.

She did not have to go far. She found him in the Great Hall. Her steps stilled and familiar flutters filled her stomach when she saw him. Where her red hair was wild and free, his dark hair lay tamed just above his shoulders and while it was hard muscles he wore beneath his garments, it was strength and dignity that he carried for all to see.

His smile when he looked upon her stole her heart all over again and when he stretched his arms out to her, she ran into them.

Slain had grown impatient waiting for her to wake. It had been too long since he had last held her and his arms had felt the emptiness of her absence. Now with her wrapped close around him, he felt whole. Something he had thought he would never feel again.

"You are feeling well?" he asked, after placing a kiss on her forehead.

She honestly had not given thought to her injury, since waking. She had been too annoyed to find her husband absent from their bed to pay it any mind. "I would feel better if my husband did not neglect his husbandly duties," she said with a soft smile and felt some discomfort, which to her meant her injury had improved some.

Slain could not keep his smile from growing. That she was more concerned he had not joined her last night than her injury squeezed at his heart. He did so love this woman and he wanted her to know it, but he held his tongue when he saw her smile fade.

She rested her hand to his cheek. "Promise me you will always seek our bed each night no matter what happens between us."

Slain turned his face just enough so that his lips brushed her palm. "That is an easy promise to give and an easier one to keep, wife." He was pleased when her smile returned and he placed a gentle kiss on her lips.

His sudden scowl had her asking, "What is wrong?"

"I should have given Potsman more than one punch for robbing me of the one thing I love to do the most."

"What is that?" Hannah asked with a curious scrunch of her brow.

"Kiss you," Slain said and placed another tender kiss on her lips.

"Though," Hannah said with fiery spark in her green eyes, "there are other places than the lips you can kiss."

Slain laughed. "You are a wicked woman."

"And I do hope you are a wicked man."

Her suggestive whisper aroused him and he had to fight against his mounting desire not to scoop her up and rush her to their bedchamber. "You tempt me, wife," he warned playfully.

"My intentions," she said proudly.

He eased her toward the bench. "You need to eat,"

"I need the nourishment you can give me more."

"Later," he whispered.

"Now," she insisted.

"Your injury—"

"Is far less painful than my need for you," she begged.

"Hannah—"

She went up on her toes to press her cheek to his and whispered, "Please, husband, I need you."

It was impossible to deny her soft pleas and besides, he wanted her as much she did him. Why deny themselves?

"You will not kiss me anywhere," he ordered when she moved away from his cheek to look at him with pleading and playful eyes.

She frowned.

"It is that or nothing," he said, "and just so you know, it is as difficult for me to order that as it is for you to obey it."

Hannah's frown quickly turned to a smile, his words pleasing her. "I will obey your command… for now."

Slain hugged her tight. "I do love you, wife."

Hannah felt her breath catch and her heart soar. He loved her. He truly loved her, she could not be any happier and her grin showed it.

"Stop smiling so wide when it pains you," Slain ordered, a slight wince marring her brow. "I love you, wife, and I will tell you that often so you never forget it. You broke past the shield I kept over my heart and stole it without me knowing, and I am so very pleased that you did." His hand brushed over her bruise so faintly it could barely be felt. "And I am so sorry for not being here to protect you."

"We love each other. That is all that matters," Hannah said filled with more joy than she ever imagined possible.

"It is all that will ever matter," Slain said and kissed her cheek.

"I ache for those lips of yours to kiss me in other places," Hannah whispered teasingly.

"I will gladly and most enjoyably satisfy that ache, wife." He went to scoop her up in his arms when a bell tolled loudly, followed by a pounding on the door.

"Stay here," he ordered Hannah and looked past her. "Make sure she stays here."

Hannah did not care what order he gave her or Helice, she intended to see for herself what was happening. She rushed behind her husband before Helice could reach out and grab her.

Slain threw open the door to find Imus and several clansmen standing there, swords and axes in hand. Imus whispered something to him and Slain nodded, turned, and took Hannah's hand to step outside with her.

Hannah's joy was washed away by fear. A short distance away a troop of warriors approached and in the lead was her step-brother Nial.

Chapter Twenty-one

Hannah turned to Slain, tugging at his arm. "I need to speak to you before Nial reaches us."

"You know him?" Slain asked, annoyed that she was familiar with the man he hated beyond reason.

Hannah nodded. "I have been meaning to tell you since shortly after we wed."

"Tell me what," Slain asked sharply, sensing her words were not going to please him.

She prayed her confession would not rob her of the man she had come to love with all her heart. "Ross MacFillan is my father and Nial is my step-brother."

Slain shot her a glare that sent a nervous tremor racing through her. "I should have—"

"Do not say another word," Slain ordered gruffly, "and hold your tongue in front of your step-brother."

"That might be difficult," she admitted.

He brought his face close to hers. "Obey me on this, wife, or the consequences will be severe."

His harsh tone alone warned her not to defy him and she bit lightly on her tongue, reminding herself to keep hold of it.

Hannah turned to watch Nial ride toward them as if he had already conquered the clan and it now belonged to him. He had about twenty warriors with him and Melvin rode alongside him. Everyone in the village followed to either side of the troop, carrying swords, axes, picks, whatever would serve as a weapon, letting Nial know they were ready to defend themselves.

When Hannah had met Nial, it had not taken her long to realize he was not to be trusted. It was three years ago when she was just turning ten and six years. Her mum had been dead barely over a year when her father had announced he would wed again. She had been surprised how frail and ill the woman had been that he wed. She died not even a year after they wed. Her father had gotten so angry, screaming viciously at her when she had asked him why he had wed the ill woman, that she never spoke of it again to him.

She came to realize soon enough that her father treated Nial like the son he never had and that she was the daughter who would wed a man who would benefit the clan, ensuring his vision of a powerful and wealthy clan.

Hannah watched her step-brother approach, wondering how he would react when he saw her there beside Slain alive and well. He had his mother's features, common enough, and dark long hair, wearing one side braided. He was slim and of good height, not as tall and muscled as Slain, though he had strength to him, and he was skilled with a sword.

His smug expression changed as soon as his eyes fell on Hannah and she squeezed her husband's hand and moved closer to him when she saw the look in her step-brother's eyes turn murderous.

That his wife leaned against him and took firmer hold of his hand, spoke more loudly to Slain than if she had voiced her fear. Her step-brother frightened her and that made him hate the man all the more.

Nial was off his horse as soon as he brought the animal to a stop. He approached Hannah with quick strides, his eyes blazing with fury. "What are you doing here?"

Slain stepped in front of his wife, not letting go of her hand. "You will address me, not *my wife*."

Nial stumbled back as if Slain had struck him. "Your wife? It cannot be."

"Hannah is my wife and our vows have been sealed."

Nial shook his head. "No. Impossible. Her father did not consent to this."

"Consent or not, we are wed and will remain so. I suggest you return home and inform Ross MacFillan that Slain MacKewan is wed to his daughter. "

"This union will never stand. You forced her to wed you," Nial claimed.

Slain stepped aside for Hannah to stand beside him. "Did I force you to wed me, wife?"

Before Hannah could speak, Nial blurted out, "You beat her. Look at her face. You have taken a hand to her. Ross MacFillan will never stand for this. He will see this farce of a marriage annulled and he will make you pay for what you have done to his daughter." He stretched out his hand. "Come with me, Hannah."

"Never!" she said, moving closer to her husband, wrapping her arm around his and clinging to it tightly. "You sold me to a man and told him to make sure that I suffered before seeing me dead. He took me to hell on earth... Warrick's dungeon."

The shock of her words sent an angry burst through Slain, though he showed no outward sign of it.

"I did no such thing," Nial said. "You ran away and got yourself snatched up by some villainous man."

"Is that what you told my father?" she asked, wondering if her father had worried about her disappearance.

"Your father knows your penchant for disobeying him," Nial said and looked to Slain. "You must know by now she is not an obedient wife."

Hannah hated Nial at that moment, since by speaking to her step-brother she was disobeying her husband. But how could she stand there and not defend herself against this man who did nothing but lie?

"Hannah is a courageous wife who does not fear confronting a liar," Slain said.

Nial's face flushed with anger. "How dare you call me a liar."

"I dare speak the truth. Something you never do," Slain said and took a quick step toward the man, startling him enough to have him take a stumbling step back. "Now be gone from my land and tell Ross MacFillan that if he has an ounce of courage or honor that he will come speak with me."

"Ross MacFillan will come here that is for sure," Nial said, waving a raised fist at Slain as he stepped back, not stumbling this time. "But it will be his warriors he comes with to rescue his daughter and lay claim to this land."

He mounted and turned, his warriors following, though not Melvin. He remained where he was.

"You are well, Hannah," the older warrior asked concern heavy in his thoughtful expression.

"I am well and happy, Melvin. My husband does not raise a hand to me. He is good to me and I love him," Hannah said, trying to hold back her tears.

"I am glad to hear that, but you know that your father will come for you," Melvin warned, a sadness in his eyes for what would come.

"I will see to her father," Slain said.

Melvin nodded at Slain, then turned to Hannah. "I did not believe you ran away, though I would not have blamed you. Stay safe, Hannah."

"I will keep Hannah safe," Slain assured the man.

Melvin gave a nod to Slain, turned, and rode off.

Hannah found her tears difficult to contain and she turned her face to her husband's chest to hide the ones that slipped out. She did not want to show weakness in front of the clan, but her heart was breaking at the thought that her father would attack the Clan MacKewan because of her, and how, without an army of warriors, would the clan defend themselves?

Slain's arms wrapped around her and held her close as he spoke to the clan. "Fear not, I will see you all kept safe."

Hannah kept her face buried against her husband's chest. She felt ashamed for not revealing her identity sooner, but what if she had? Her father would have been informed and she would have been returned home to what? Her stepbrother devising another way to see her dead? But would not one death be better than a whole clan's death?

But then she had never intended to wed Slain MacKewan let alone fall in love with him.

Slain kept his arm around her as he led her inside the keep and to his solar. After shutting the door behind them, he lifted her head gently and placed a tender kiss on her lips. "You will tell me everything, wife."

Hannah could not contain her tears any longer, they fell freely down her cheeks, and once again she buried her face against her husband's chest and cherished the feel of his strong arms wrapping protectively and comfortingly around her.

Slain wanted Nial dead even more so now after hearing what Hannah had said he had done to her. Her tears strengthened his resolve to see it done. He would enjoy taking the man's life and he would make sure he suffered unimaginably before he did.

He walked his wife over to a chair to sit, but she refused to let go of him, so he stood there holding her until her tears subsided.

A knock at the door had Helice entering with a tankard that she placed on the small table next to the chair. "Chamomile."

Hannah raised her head when she heard the door close. "Sit and drink the hot brew, and we will talk."

She went to wipe her tears away, but his hand brushed hers gently aside and he wiped at her wet cheeks.

"No one will take you from me. I promise you that," he said and kissed each cheek, then with a firm hand on her shoulder forced her to sit. He picked up the tankard and handed it to her. "Drink."

Hannah did as he said, her mind awash with where to start, what to say, when it came to her. "Forgive me for not being honest with you from the start."

"You need not apologize for making a wise, if not difficult, choice and I commend you for doing so. Where else would you be safe from your heartless step-brother but in the home of your enemy. It was not your fault I forced a wedding upon you."

"I should have told you before we wed."

"It would not have mattered. I had already hopelessly lost my heart to you whether I wanted to admit it or not. And once I would have learned what your step-brother had done to you, it would have only reinforced my resolve to keep you safe. Now tell me what happened."

Hannah did not hesitate, she told him all. "I knew Nial was a liar from the moment I met him and I could not understand why my father wed his mother when she was so gravely ill. My mum had been dead barely a year, and my step-mother died not even a year after my father wed her. Nial became like the son my father never had. As for me, I mattered less and less to him, not that I ever mattered that much to begin with, until he began to speak of an arranged marriage that would prove beneficial to the clan. My father and I argued over it, since I wanted to wed someone of my own choosing. Before anything could be arranged or settled, my step-brother sold me to Muir."

"So that was why you wanted to help free those two women from him," Slain said.

She nodded. "He would sell them over and over to men until there was nothing left of them and then discard them. Those sold to him for a higher price, women and men alike, were the ones who were meant to suffer before they died. Those he took to Warrick's dungeon."

"That is where you were tortured?" Slain asked, knowing too well what was done in Warrick's dungeon. When she nodded, he had all he could do not to hit something, rage racing through him rapidly. Wise or not, he would confront Warrick about this. A sudden thought came to him. "You escaped Warrick's dungeon?"

Hannah nodded again.

"How did you ever do that?" he asked, shaking his head. "No one has ever escaped from there."

Hannah was careful in telling the tale, not wanting to bring harm to the healer. "There was a fire in the dungeon and in the commotion some prisoners escaped."

Slain held his tongue a moment, then asked, "Do you trust me, Hannah?"

He seemed upset and she was quick to answer. "Aye, I trust you."

"Then why are you not telling me the truth? The guards would have been too busy saving their own lives in a fire, then to worry about freeing the prisoners that death waited to claim."

Hannah gave her husband what he wanted—the truth. "You are friends with Warrick, and I will not see the one who helped me escape punished for it."

"Either will I. I would prefer to reward him for saving your life."

Hannah hesitated, then said, "A woman saved a few prisoners."

"It was a woman who saved you?" he asked in disbelief.

"One I will always be grateful to," Hannah said.

"As will I," Slain said, more than grateful to the unknown woman.

Hannah continued on, not wanting to say another word about the healer. "Once free, I knew there were no clans who, once learned my identity, would offer me shelter. They would return me to my father, some for coin and others to gain favor from him."

"You would have been discovered here eventually, what then?" Slain asked, not liking what her fate may have been.

Hannah shrugged. "I was not sure what I would do. I needed a safe place where I could take some time for my arm to heal and think of possibilities. None had included returning home since I feared my step-brother would do me harm. I felt the safest, if not foolish, place was with my father's fiercest enemy. I suppose I hoped, maybe wished, that someday I might be able to return home." She smiled softly. "I never dreamed I would find a new home, a more loving home, and one I would never want to leave."

"And one you never will," Slain said, reaching out to ease Hannah out of the chair and into his arms. "You are stuck with me wife until one of us no longer takes a breath."

"I love being stuck with you, husband, and it pains me to think of ever being separated from you."

"We are one now and can never be separated. You are never without me or I you. I will always be with you wherever you are, remember that. And remember that my love for you is eternal."

Hannah kissed him without thinking of her injury and winced when a pain shot through her jaw.

"No kissing, wife," Slain reprimanded gently when he rather would have roared with anger over her suffering. He was going to make certain Potsman worked his fingers to the bone for what he had done.

She poked his chest as she responded. "Need I remind you there are other places on me to kiss?"

"My lips are going to have to roam all over you to discover those places." He kissed her cheek ever so lightly.

Hannah shivered, his faint kiss a preview of what he would do to her naked body, and she whispered, "Aye, all over me."

Her whisper not only encouraged, it grew his arousal, but then he grew aroused anytime he held his wife in his arms. Unfortunately, he could not satisfy either of their urgings right now. There were matters that needed his immediate attention.

"Later I will see to it," he said, not only to her disappointment, but his as well. "Now, I must attend to some important matters."

"Like gathering an army to defend against my father?" she asked, shaking her head as she stepped away from him. "He will come with his troop of warriors and your clan will be defenseless… and my father will show no mercy." She waved his response away and continued. "He may come and speak with you, but only to warn you. Our marriage, one he did not sanction, is the perfect excuse for him to attack you."

Hannah grew annoyed when a knock interrupted them and got even more annoyed that a message had arrived for Slain.

"Where do these messages come from and who brings them to you?" Hannah asked once Helice left the room.

"Worry not about—"

Hannah did not let him finish. "How can I not worry and since I confessed my secret, it is time for you to confess yours. What goes on here that you do not tell me? Why does the east wing remain locked? What do you hide from me?"

"Enough!" Slain snapped and annoyed at himself for raising his voice to her, he reached out to take her in his arms once more. "You say you trust me, then trust me and let it be for now."

Hannah laid her head on her husband's chest, not wanting to let him go. "You will be careful?"

"I have good reason to be more careful now than ever before. I have a wife I love and a future I look forward to sharing with her." He kissed her cheek and reluctantly released her and walked to the door, stopping after he opened it, and turned to her. "I will be awhile. Do not place yourself in any danger or get in trouble while I am gone."

"What could happen?" Hannah asked with a shrug.

"With you, dear wife, I never know."

Hannah smiled at her husband's remark, thinking her mum would have agreed with him. Her mum had often told her that for a wee bairn and a female at that, she could get herself into the most troubling situations.

She remembered one time when she was young and wanted desperately to play with the new kittens in the barn, a place forbidden to her. Naturally, she paid the warning no mind and went anyway, the kittens too much of lure to ignore. She had hidden in the corner of an empty stall when she heard someone coming. It had been her father and mum. They were laughing and dropped down on the mound of hay in an empty stall and made love, not that she had realized it at that time. She had thought they were playing, though she had grown worried when she heard her mum begin to moan. It had been why, later that night, she had asked her mum if she was ill.

Her mum, wise woman that she was, managed to get the truth from her. She had never seen her mum get so angry. It had frightened her so much, she did not go into the barn again until she was older. It was not until she grew a bit wiser that she realized it had not been her mum her da had been playing with.

She had continued to defy orders, finding she discovered and learned so much more when she snuck off on her own. Or had gone places forbidden to her. She supposed her thirst for learning had never abated.

Sneaking off, hearing things she was not supposed to be privy to had actually helped her make the decision to came here to the Clan MacKewan after her escape. Her father disliked Slain, but admired his exceptional warrior skills. She had heard him admit, not that he knew she heard, that Slain might be one warrior he might not be able to conquer. That had been enough for her to believe she would be safe here.

Hannah stretched out her aches as she left the solar. She decided to go to the village and face the people before she lost the courage to do so. She only hoped they still thought her a friend.

She grabbed her cloak off the bench in the Great Hall and approached the open door, the men having returned to work on it.

"We need more wood and stone, Potsman, and do not take all day to fetch it."

Hannah froze halfway to the door, recognizing the voice. It was the same voice she had heard betraying Slain and the clan that day in the woods.

She stared not believing who it belonged to… Imus.

Chapter Twenty-two

Hannah nodded to Imus as she passed by him. It seemed impossible to believe that Imus would betray Slain. He had stood with axe in hand at any sign of trouble, ready to defend Slain and the clan. And what of Blair? Hannah could not comprehend the woman betraying her clan. Or did she know anything about what Imus was doing? If she looked at it another way, could it possibly be that Imus was making it appear that he betrayed Slain, but that he actually was gathering information for Slain?

She shook her head, not knowing what to believe. Imus had no reason to betray Slain or did he? Did he feel Slain could not defend the clan and so he sought out help from someone who he believed could? And what of Helice? Did she protect Slain or did she blame him for her daughter's death?

Hannah simply did not know enough to reach a conclusion, though her husband would probably remind her to trust him. But did he know what was going on here? Her father had always said that Slain MacKewan was not only a skilled warrior but a wise one.

Do you trust me?

She did trust him, but did she trust those around him? Slain certainly seemed to trust Helice, and Imus seemed a friend. She hurried her footsteps, wanting to see what she could learn from Blair.

Some of the villagers acknowledged her with a bob of the head while others turned their heads away.

"Some believe you while others think you came here to trap our chief. Which is it?"

Hannah turned to see Blair standing there with her arms crossed over her ample chest and a slight scowl marring her brow. "I came here with no such intentions of hurting the clan or Slain. I only wanted a safe place to hide from my step-brother. I never imagined falling in love with the Chief of the Clan MacKewan and now I cannot imagine life without him."

Blair's scowl turned to a smile. "That was all I needed to hear confirmed, since you can see the love in your eyes for him and you have the courage it takes to be his wife. They needed reminding of how you saved Potsman from the savage and how you calmed the savage. You are good for him and they will learn that in time." Blair hooked arms with her. "Come and have a brew with me."

Hannah followed along with her, eager to speak with Blair, but careful how she went about it. "Have you and Imus always been part of the Clan MacKewan?"

"Born and raised," Blair said with pride.

"Then Imus knows Slain well."

"They have been friends since they were bairns. They have shared good times and bad together, including the loss of Slain's parents. They had treated Imus like a son, he having lost his parents to a fever when he was young. His grandmother was there for him, but it was Slain's parents who saw to raising him."

"They do not seem to spend much time together," Hannah said, thinking how she had never seen them exchange more than a few words.

"It might seem that way, but their friendship is strong, built even stronger over the years."

Hannah was glad to know that, it made her less suspicious of Imus.

"They both love their clan and would do anything to keep it safe."

Upon hearing that, her suspicion sparked once again. Would Imus think Slain incapable of keeping the clan safe and have turned to someone who he thought could provide the clan with protection? Or was his friendship with Slain too strong to ever betray him?

"Your step-brother truly sold you?" Blair asked once they were inside her cottage sharing a brew.

Hannah was relieved to share the truth with Blair. It had been a heavy burden to carry and she was glad to be free of it.

Blair shook her head after hearing all Hannah had to say. "Nial is an evil one and, in the end, Slain will make sure he gets what he deserves."

"I do not want blood shed because of me." Hannah was quick to say.

"It is not only because of you Slain will see Nial dead. His hatred is already strong for the man. It is vengeance Slain seeks for his parents and the clan, and the clan will celebrate the day it comes to pass."

Hannah leaned forward at the table, her hands cupped around a tankard. Curious and concerned, she asked, "What did my step-brother do?"

Blair shook her head slowly, sadness filling her eyes. "Remember when I told you about a young warrior who talked Slain's father into emptying his coffers to help aid in battles that would benefit the Clan MacKewan?"

A rash of anxious tingles raced over Hannah as she nodded, fearing what Blair would say.

"It was Nial. He lied and robbed William and the clan of all the coin and treasures Slain had earned fighting alongside Warrick. All of us believe that it was what turned Slain's mum, Leala, ill and brought on her death. William was not the same after his wife died and no one was surprised when he died shortly after her. Nial robbed Slain of everything." Blair wiped a lingering tear from the corner of her one eye.

Hannah remained silent, at a loss of what to say.

"Slain will see Nial suffer for what he did and he will deserve every moment of pain."

Hannah took lingering steps back to the keep, thinking over what Blair had told her. She wondered if her father knew what Nial had done and if he had condoned such deception? She hoped the heavy gray skies covered her shame for it weighed heavily upon her for her step-brother's misdeeds.

The keep was quiet upon her return, Imus and his men having finished for the day thanks to the dark clouds that promised imminent rain. Hannah draped her cloak over the bench near the fireplace glad for the fire's warmth since a chill ran through her.

"Where have you been?"

Hannah jumped and turned at Helice's scolding tone. "I went to the village."

"You are supposed to rest and have the comfrey poultice applied to your bruise," Helice continued to scold. "Slain has enough to worry about without worrying about you. You should pay your husband's situation more heed and do as he directs. And you need to eat more, since he worries you do not eat enough."

Hannah stared at the woman, for the first time looking through her prickly nature, as Neata suggested, and seeing the woman differently. Helice cared for Slain and Hannah believed the ornery woman cared for her as well. In a way, Helice reminded her of her mum, abrupt and to the point, no nonsense about anything. Funny that she had not noticed that before now and her heart softened toward the woman.

She voiced one of her thoughts. "You care for Slain."

"His is a good man," Helice said as if it was explanation itself.

Hannah realized then that Slain had done something that had made him a hero in the woman's mind. "What did Slain do for you, Helice, that you care for him as you would a son?"

Helice's chin went up. "He made a wish of mine come true. Now you will go upstairs to your bedchamber and rest while I prepare the comfrey poultice for your bruise."

"Could I get a chamomile brew and some bread and cheese along with that? I find myself hungry."

"Good, then you will finally eat as you should," Helice said and turned, walking out of the Great Hall, though calling back as she did, "afterwards you will remain in bed and rest."

Hannah had to smile. The cantankerous woman was looking after her in her own way, and it felt almost as good as when her mum would order her about and look after her when she was ill. Something she had missed greatly.

She stretched out on the bed, wondering over the wish her husband had fulfilled for Helice. It had to have had something to do with her daughter. She wished she could find out more, but both Helice and Slain were tight-lipped about it. Perhaps time would change that.

Hannah laid still as Helice applied the poultice, noticing what a tender hand she had and how focused she remained on the task.

"I will bring drink and food shortly. In the meantime, you will lie still and let the poultice help you," Helice ordered.

"I could use a brief rest," Hannah said, a small yawn proving the need for one.

The day wore on with Helice tending Hannah, which the woman seemed to enjoy doing. She fussed over her, encouraged her to eat, though it did not take much since Hannah found herself hungry.

It was evening, twilight barely noticeable with the dark sky bringing promise of a rainstorm when Hannah asked Helice, "Has there been any word from Slain?"

"Not yet, but he will be home some time tonight," Helice assured her.

"How can you be so sure?"

"It is obvious he does not want to be away from you," Helice said, tucking the blanket around Hannah's waist where she sat in bed. Where Helice had insisted she stay and rest most of the day. "And it is good you were finally honest with him, though you delayed it far too long. You should have trusted him."

"I was frightened," Hannah admitted.

"Slain will protect you. He will always protect you. Now rest," Helice ordered for the umpteenth time that day.

Surprisingly, her jaw and lip were far less painful than they had been and the rest had proven helpful as well, her arm causing her no discomfit and the few aches she suffered had disappeared.

"Thank you for looking after me, Helice," Hannah said and the woman stopped before reaching the door.

Helice turned. "It is my duty to look after you, but it is also an honor. You are a courageous woman with an understanding heart, keep strong hold of both, for you will need them. And never forget how much Slain loves you."

Why did Hannah feel as if the woman was warning her about something?

Secrets.

There were still secrets to discover about Slain and this keep, but what would they matter? She loved him and nothing would stop her from loving him.

Hannah closed her eyes, wishing her husband was there beside her and she was wrapped in his arms. She had slept a full night with him only once, but it had been enough to know that she never wanted to sleep without him again.

The strength of his arms, the warmth of his body, his gentle breath against her face, she sighed at the remembrance and soon after fell asleep.

A clap of thunder woke her and she sat up, her heart beating madly and her eyes searching the room. The fire looked as if fresh logs had been added to it so she could not tell how long she had slept, and the door sat ajar.

Someone had been in the room.

Had Slain returned home?

She pushed the covers off her, swinging her legs off the bed and standing. She took light steps across the room to the door and cautiously peeked around it. A faint light flickered from the wall sconce, otherwise the narrow area was empty. She was about to turn around and return to bed when her eye caught something.

The door to the east wing sat ajar.

It was always locked. Why was it open now? Who was in there? Or what was in there that Slain did not want anyone to see?

She told herself to go back to bed and leave the east wing alone with its secrets. That, however, was something difficult, near impossible, for her to do. She quietly hurried across the wood floor to the door and slowly peeked her head around it.

Her breath caught at what she saw... a gigantic bat, its wings spread wide, eyes glowing red, flying straight at her.

She turned to run and ran right into the edge of the door with such force that she feared she would lose consciousness. Though not from the knock to her head, but from the sudden arm that coiled around her waist and the black wing that all but smothered her.

Though lightheaded, instinct had her fighting. She tore at the wing that cocooned her as she struggled to free herself. She gasped as she felt herself lifted as if the creature was taking flight and she fought harder.

"Stop!"

The creature's voice was muffled near her ear, but she paid him no mind. She would not stop fighting. She would not let him take her away from Slain.

"Stop!"

She would never surrender. Never.

Chapter Twenty-three

"Stop, Hannah, stop! You are safe."

At the sound of her husband's voice, Hannah's eyes sprang open. She was in bed, struggling against the blanket that had wrapped around her. Her husband sat beside her, his hands at her shoulders.

"You were caught in a nightmare," Slain said, his one hand going to gently push her hair off her face where it had fallen over her cheeks and nearly covered one eye. "It is good I got here when I did."

"A nightmare?" she said, her breathing heavy. "It seemed so real."

"Most nightmares do." He leaned over her and kissed her brow. "It is gone now and I am here with you. There is nothing to fear." He stood and shed his garments, then climbed in bed and took her in his arms.

Hannah snuggled tight against him, relieved he had chased away her nightmare, though her fright still lingered, keeping any passion away. All she wanted to do was lay there in her husband's powerful arms and know she was safe.

"Sleep," he whispered and she closed her eyes.

Her thoughts, however, would not let her rest and while sleep quickly claimed her husband, it avoided her. Restless, she turned in his arms that tightened around her when she settled back against him. Even in sleep, he was making sure to keep her close.

The nightmare would not leave her. Never had a nightmare seemed so real. She glanced over at the hearth and stared at the fresh logs that had recently been added, the flames only beginning to eat away at them. Who had placed them there? When Slain had arrived to find her thrashing about the bed he would have gone to her aid immediately. Had Helice returned to the room?

You are being foolish, Hannah, she silently warned herself. *It had been nothing more than a nightmare.* Besides, bats were small creatures. The one in her nightmare had been the size of a man and had looked just as Slain had when he had dropped down from the window to save her from a deadly fall.

Her eyes narrowed at the thought and what it all might mean.

Something caught her eye in the corner of the room, something dark strewn over the chair.

Slain's cloak?

She recalled tearing at, what she believed, had been the wing of a bat. Had she torn it? Too restless to sleep and her thoughts having her too curious, she decided to slip out of bed and take a look at the cloak.

Hannah had to maneuver herself carefully and gently out of her husband's arms, slipping her pillow into them so he believed he still held of her. Her foot barely touched the floor when she felt a pain run through the bottom. She hobbled over to the fireplace, snatching up the small footstool as she went and after sitting on it pulled her leg up to rest on her knee so she could get a look at the bottom of her foot.

She lowered her head and spied a splinter embedded in the skin just below her big toe. It was a good size splinter, not just a sliver and it appeared to be a deeply embedded one. She continued staring at it. She could not have just gotten it since she felt it as soon as her foot had lightly touched the floor and it would have taken more force than a light step for the splinter to have gone so deep.

So when could she have gotten the splinter?

Fighting the bat?
That would mean her nightmare had been all too real.
"Is something wrong?"
Before Hannah could turn, her husband stood in front of her, dropping down when his eyes went to her foot.
"That is a large splinter," he said, his hand going around the front of her foot to turn it some for him to get a better look.
Hannah agreed with a nod, too busy enjoying the way the fire's light danced across his fine features and the way his dark eyes were scrunched with concern. Good Lord, but she loved this man.
"I woke you," she said softly.
Slain looked up at her. "A pillow is no replacement for my wife."
She smiled lightly, pleased he favored her by his side. "I was restless and did not want to disturb you."
"Not having you in my arms in bed disturbs me more." He tapped her foot. "This needs to come out now." He stood and walked over to a small chest, retrieved something within it, and returned to Hannah, once again dropping down in front of her.
"I will do my best not to hurt you," he said.
It was over so quickly that Hannah barely felt a thing. "Your touch is gentle."
His eyes seemed to darken for a moment and his lips appeared ready to spew words, so his response surprised her.
"With you, Hannah, always with you." He ran his finger faintly over her bruised jaw. "Does it pain you?"
"No," she said as if her response surprised her. "It actually does not. Helice treated me with a comfrey poultice and made me lie abed the remainder of the day. She took good care of me."
"She is a good woman."

Hannah wanted to ask more about Helice, though it was really Helice's daughter—Slain's first wife—who she was curious about.

Hannah stood when Slain walked over to the small chest to return the bone needle to it, and when his arms opened as he walked back to her, she went into them. He hugged her close for a moment, then stepped back to Hannah's dismay, though that quickly fled when he took hold of her nightdress and slipped it off her.

"I want nothing between us in bed," he said and scooped her up in his arms and walked to the bed, laying her down gently. He joined her, taking her in his arms again. "Sleep," he ordered.

She raised her head off his chest. "Sleep?" She sat up. "You stand naked in front of me, touch me gently, strip me of my garment, carry me to bed and tell me to *sleep*?" She poked him in the chest. "You disappoint me, husband." She grew angry when she saw him smile and it spread as if he were about to laugh. "If you laugh, so help me—"

Hannah let out a gasp as her husband's arm coiled around her waist, yanked her back, and slipped over her, his hands quickly going to either side of her to brace himself so that he hovered over her. His lips lost no time in seeking out her sensitive neck and she gasped lightly when he began to nibble along it.

"You teased me," she said through a gasp as his nip hit an extra sensitive spot and she playfully slapped his arm. "I will do the same to you."

Slain lifted his head and laughed. "Not possible, wife. You will never deny me, since you want me too much." Passion chased away all trace of laughter. "Just as I do you. Besides, I have not forgotten that you told me there were other places I could kiss."

Gooseflesh raced over her not just from his lips returning to her neck to nip and kiss, but from the anticipation of where else his lips would touch.

The loud warning toll of the bell echoing outside in the dark night drowned their passion like a dunk in a cold stream and had them jumping out of bed and hurrying into their garments, Slain not bothering to slip on his shirt.

Helice was running out the door when they entered the Great Hall and they hurried after her. The sky was ablaze with light and flame from the roaring fire. A building that housed food was up in flames. People were already forming a bucket brigade, though not for the building that was beyond help, but to keep it from spreading to the buildings close by.

Slain turned to his wife, the look of fright on her face had him ordering, "Go back to the keep and stay there."

Hannah shook her head and shook away her initial fright. "No, I will stay and help."

Slain grabbed her arm. "I will not have you to worry about while all of this is going on."

"I will not go and hide while the clan battles this fire. I am either part of this clan or I am not." Hannah's eyes widened, seeing Imus rush toward them. Never had she seen the man move so fast.

Slain turned, following his wife's glance.

"We found tracks. We are following them," Imus called out as he approached.

Slain looked to Hannah.

"Go," she urged. "I will be safe here among the clan."

"Do as she says," Helice said, joining them. "I will look after her."

"Do nothing foolish, wife," Slain ordered and hurried off with Imus.

"I will help," Hannah said, turning to Helice.

"All hands are needed if we are to keep the fire from spreading."

They were lucky that there was no wind and that rain had fallen recently, the buildings not completely dry and not fast to ignite. The added soaking would help. Two bucket brigades were formed to work on the buildings that sat to either side of the one consumed by flames.

Hannah joined the line, passing bucket after bucket, and it did not take long for her arm to begin to pain her, but she ignored it. It would not be right of her to walk away while the whole clan fought to prevent the fire from spreading. It was Helice who finally ordered her to stop.

"Enough," Helice said, tugging Hannah out of the line. "Your arm will be useless to you if you continue."

"Helice is right," Blair said from a short distance down the line.

Wilona voiced the same. "You have helped enough."

Hannah felt differently, though she did not argue. She stepped away to let them continue and keep their mind on their work. She watched the building begin to crumble from the flames. There would be nothing left of it or its contents.

Hannah felt helpless standing there, doing nothing, while everyone worked so hard, though Helice had been right in stopping her. Her arm hung limp at her side, the little she had done having taken its toll. She hated that her arm may never regain the strength and ability it once had. It made her feel vulnerable and she did not like that.

She turned her head away, annoyed at thoughts that did not serve her well and caught a glimpse of movement just at the edge of the woods, down away from the fire. She stared, waiting to see if she would catch it again when suddenly a head popped up from behind a bush and a hand waved at her.

Hannah gave a quick glance back to see everyone busy fighting the fire and she hurried off before her absence could be discovered. She knew who it was and she knew he would be alone. Her father would not chance sending anyone with him. Warriors would be too easily detected, a small lad of eight years would not.

"Conlan?" Hannah whispered as she rounded the bush.

"Aye," the young lad said, his head popping up. His round face was smudged with dirt and his clothes far too big for his scrawny body.

Conlan had been a wild one and fearless since he was little and when his mum went off with a warrior from another clan, two years ago, she did not take him with her. He had fended for himself ever since and her father had taken advantage of it.

He learned quick and was much wiser than anyone thought and he and Hannah often talked and they also enjoyed fishing together. She had come to know him well and they had become friends.

"Come. Hurry. I will get us home." Conlan said his young eyes darting about, keeping watch that no one approached.

"This is my home now, Conlan," Hannah said, reaching out and placing a gentle hand on his shoulder.

He shook his head and sneered. "No, the savage took you against your will. I am here to free you."

"Who told you that?" Hannah asked, though knew.

"Nial told everyone how the savage abducted you and has kept you prisoner, even forcing you to wed him."

"That is not true, Conlan. Slain never abducted me. Nial sold me to a man and told him to do me harm. When I escaped, I sought refuge here among the Clan MacKewan and Slain has kept me safe. I not only wed him willingly, I love him. He is a good man."

Conlan appeared confused. "Nial has told everyone that you ran away, though I did not believe him. Then when he returned from here he told everyone that you had not runaway that the savage had abducted you and forced you to wed him."

"I would never leave my home and my friends willingly," she assured him, giving his shoulder a soft squeeze.

"I knew it. I knew Nial was lying. He always lies, but your da will not believe me."

"My father sent you to set this fire?" Hannah asked.

Conlan shook his head. "No, the fire had already started when I arrived. I came to rescue you. I was going to wait until morning and enter the village, ask for a few days of shelter, find you, and be on our way."

Most would think him foolish for believing he could accomplish such an unlikely task, but Hannah thought differently. "That is very brave of you, Conlan."

His chin went up, his shoulders went back, pushing out a barely noticeable chest. "You have been nothing but kind to me, unlike the others. I wanted to help you as you have helped me so many times."

Hannah's heart went out to him. So few even bothered with him let alone had said a kind word to him. He needed a home, a good, caring home.

"We are friends, Conlan. We always will be."

"Step away from him!"

The powerful demand echoed through the trees and instinct had Hannah stepping in front of the lad, hiding him from view.

"Stay behind me, Conlan," Hannah whispered.

"He will not believe it was not me who started the fire," Conlan said

"Step away from him, Hannah," Slain ordered again.

"He did nothing—"

"He lies."

"I will miss you, Hannah," Conlan said for her ears alone.

Hannah knew he was letting her know that he was taking his leave and she would protect the vulnerable lad as long as she could.

"I will not repeat myself, Hannah."

Hannah waited, knowing that Conlan needed enough time to gain some distance, then he would take to the trees. He climbed them as if he had been born in them. Once he was lost in them, they would never find him.

It was when she heard a crunch of a branch crack beneath her husband's approaching footfalls that she finally stepped aside.

"Find him," Slain ordered the men, a short distance behind him, when he saw the lad was gone.

"He did not set the fire," Hannah said.

Slain cast a heavy scowl at her. "And you believe him?"

"He is my friend."

"He is my enemy."

"No, you are wrong. He is nothing more than an innocent lad."

"Go wait for me in my solar," Slain ordered.

Hannah did not argue. She left him, casting a glance back to see her husband following after his men. She walked back to the keep, taking a wide path around the fire so that she would not have to speak with anyone. Just as Slain had assumed Conlan guilty so would the clan when they learned he had been there.

She paced in front of the hearth, a low fire burning in it. How did she explain it to Slain? How did she let him know that Conlan was not his enemy? Her father was his enemy.

The fire dwindled after a while and so did her pacing. She added more logs and sat, waiting. They would not catch Conlan, which would not please her husband. And what of the clan? What would they do when they learned she had protected the culprit they believed had set the fire? Would they think she betrayed them?

The door swung open and she stilled at the sight of her husband. Soot and sweat covered him and anger flared in his dark eyes. He entered the room and went to the sideboard and poured himself a goblet of wine, downing it before he turned to her.

"He got away."

Chapter Twenty-four

Hannah closed her eyes a moment and her shoulders slumped in relief that Conlan was safe, her reaction further flaring Slain's anger.

"Why did you protect the lad?" he demanded. "Did it not matter to you what he did here?"

"He did not set the fire," Hannah insisted and from the way her husband shook his head at her, she knew he did not believe her.

"Then why was he here?"

Hannah spoke the truth, though worried he would continue not to believe her. "He came to rescue me."

"You believe such foolishness?"

"Nial told everyone that I had run away when he sold me to Muir. Then after finding me here, he told the clan that you abducted me and forced me to wed you. Conlan is a wild one, abandoned by his mum, and manipulated by far too many, including my father. I befriended him when none would and our friendship means much to him and to me. He came here to help me and I believe him. He said the fire was already burning when he arrived here."

"Could someone have followed him here?"

Hannah was pleased that her husband was at least giving her words thought. Unfortunately, her response would not help Conlan. "It is doubtful. He is far too quick on his feet."

"So I learned."

"He takes to the trees and climbs them like he was born to them," Hannah said, hoping her husband would see she was not trying to keep anything from him.

"I wondered how we lost track of him so fast." Only a slight scowl lingered on his face as he asked, "You truly trust this lad?"

Hannah placed her hand to her chest. "With all my heart. As wild and fearless as Conlan can be, he has always been truthful with me. Besides, my father need not set a fire to further ignite his feud with you. Our marriage alone gives him righteous cause to attack you."

"Let him," Slain challenged, slamming the goblet down on the desk and taking quick strides toward her. "You are my wife. Nothing will change that and no one will ever take you from me."

He seemed to dare her to argue with him, though he gave her no chance to do so. His lips came down on hers in a kiss that was meant to confirm his words. She belonged to him and he belonged to her, for she would let no one take him from her. She threw her arms around his neck and returned his kiss, letting him know she felt the same and not caring about the pain to her bruised jaw. She wanted this kiss, ached for it, and ached even more for what they would share.

Slain's passion spiraled so fast that he warned himself to slow down, to take her to their bedchamber and take his time making love to her. His manhood thought differently. It had swelled and hardened so fast, that taking it slow was impossible. He wanted to bury himself inside her now and take her hard and fast.

Then he tasted the blood in his mouth and he yanked his mouth off hers, horrified to see blood dripping from the corner of her mouth. In his thought of nothing but his need for her, he had forgotten about her injury, and now he had made it worse.

Hannah grabbed his arm as he went to step away from her. "No, do not do this. Do not deny us… do not deny me. I need you now. Right now."

"I hurt you," he said, angry at himself for continuing to swell with desire for her.

"No, you did not—"

"Do not tell me I did not hurt you," —he shook a finger at her— "the blood is there for me to see and I taste it on my lips." He wiped at his mouth and his anger grew when he saw blood upon his hand.

"I do not care—"

"I do. I will not bring harm to you," he said, ripping his arm out of her grasp.

"You harm me more by denying me," she accused.

"I do not deny you," he said, fighting to temper his passion and his tone. "We will go to our bedchamber and I will make certain I cause you no more pain."

Her frustration had her shouting at him. "No! I have waited long enough. I want you here and now."

"That is not going to happen. We will go to our bedchamber." He turned to walk to the door.

Hannah scooted around him and braced herself against the door, her legs and arms spread, blocking him from leaving. "Here. Now."

His wife's legs and arms spread wide only served to fire his passion that raced as uncontrollably through him as the fire had done to the building tonight. His manhood had never throbbed with such an unrelenting ache as it did now and he worried he would not be able to contain it.

"Move," he ordered.

"Make me," Hannah challenged, seeing his need was as great as hers was by how his manhood had jutted up, strong and stiff, beneath his plaid.

"Do not push this, Hannah," he cautioned.

She moaned, dropping her head back against the door. "I want you to push deep inside me over and over and ov—"

"I am warning you, wife," he said, a rumbling growl rolling out with his words. "Move away from the door." He was relieved when with a heavy sigh of defeat, she stepped away from the door, though he should not have been fooled that she would obey him that easily.

Hannah whipped off her garments as her feet worked off her boots and she stood naked in front of Slain so fast he stood there stunned, though not for long.

He undid his plaid as he approached her. "You asked for this, wife."

Hannah tossed her chin up. "I begged for it, something a wife should not have to do from her husband."

That rumbling growl spilled from his lips again as he stepped naked in front of her. "It is not your husband that will have his way with you tonight."

Hannah poked him in the chest, a slight smile on her face. "I hope the savage will be able to satisfy a neglected wife."

His arm snagged her around her waist so hard and fast that her head snapped back.

"You will not be able to walk by the time I finish with you."

Hannah grinned. "Or will it be you who will not be able to walk?"

He grabbed her by the arm, dragged her over to the desk, bent her over it, and entered her so swiftly and so hard, she gasped and grabbed the edge of the desk. He pounded into her and she loved every mighty thrust. Her only disappointment was that it would not last long, for their challenging exchange had fired her passion much too strongly.

Slain's fingers dug into her backside, holding her firm as he drove in and out of her with a rapid rhythm. He increased the speed along with her moans, knowing she was near to coming. He was as well, but he refused to allow himself to climax. He intended to make certain that his neglected wife got her fill tonight.

"Slain!"

His name so passionately screamed from her lips almost had him losing control, but he caught himself and with a few hard thrusts, she was screaming out in climax.

Hannah relished every wave of satisfaction that rushed through her, consuming her from head to toe until she thought it would ripple on forever, and she wanted it to. She felt Slain lean over her and a twinge of guilt stabbed at her for having been so wrapped up in her own pleasure that she did not know if he had climaxed.

Slain grabbed a handful of her hair and pulled her head back to press his cheek to hers. "I'm just getting started, wife."

The last shiver of her climax was fading away but spiraled when he once again moved, hard and quick inside her. Hannah found herself coming all too quickly for a second time and when her climax was near to ending, Slain pulled out of her, turned her over, set her on the desk, tilting her back, and threw her legs over his broad shoulders to enter her again, and damn if she did not build toward another climax.

Slain could not hold himself back any longer. He needed to climax, wanted to empty himself into her until he was completely spent, until he felt completely one with her.

Hannah could see he had denied his own pleasure to satisfy her and she loved this man even more for being so selfless. She wrapped her legs around his waist, determined to make him climax, maybe not as much as she had, but at least as hard as she had.

Slain lost it as soon as her legs wrapped around him and she clamped down tight on his manhood. He groaned long and hard as he exploded in a blinding climax that, for a moment, he thought would collapse him.

He fell down over her, his hands slapping down on the desk to either side of her head and keeping him hovered just above her.

She would have none of that. She wanted to feel him against her. She reached out, wrapping her arms around him and pulled him down on top of her. She sighed when his damp, warm body rested against hers. She could even feel the strong, rapid beat of his heart as it pounded in his chest.

"I love you more each day," she whispered in his ear.

He had yet to catch his breath and her words robbed him of more breath since they gripped strongly at his heart. How had he been lucky enough to have gotten such a beautiful, loving, giving wife?

When he finally found his breath, labored as it was, he barely got out a whispered, "I love you."

They lay there for a few moments, calming their breathing and their senses until finally Slain stood, went and retrieved a blanket from a chair and returned to lift his wife off the desk, wrap the blanket around her, and scoop her up in his arms.

"Our garments," Hannah said as he walked to the door.

"Not important," he said.

Hannah yawned and laid her head on his shoulder. "We go to bed."

"Aye, wife, but not to sleep. I have not finished with you yet."

Hannah smiled and snuggled her face against his bare chest.

~~~

Morning brought a misty, cloudy day and an empty bed. Hannah grew irritated at first to be left alone to wake after an endless night of lovemaking, then she recalled the fire. She scrambled out of bed, wincing as she did so. Her husband had kept his word about her having trouble walking the next day. She was sore, but it was worth every wince.

Hannah smiled at the memories she and Slain had made last night and her hand rushed to her stomach. They had to have made a bairn with as often as he left his seed inside her and the thought thrilled her. Then once again she recalled the fire and wondered if her father had anything to do with it.

She hurried into her garments and down the stairs to find her husband talking with Helice at the table in the Great Hall. They broke apart when they saw her and she wondered what secrets they shared.

"I will prepare another comfrey poultice for your jaw today," Helice said and stood as Hannah approached the table.

"Not necessary, my jaw feels fine," Hannah said, jealousy nipping at her that the woman shared something with Slain that she knew nothing about.

"You will make use of the poultice," Slain ordered, "and anything else you may need."

His grin annoyed her since he was so confident that he had done what he said he would... leave her too sore to walk.

However, she was walking fine, concealing the tenderness she suffered.

"I need no healing. I am well," Hannah said about to lower herself on the bench across from her husband.

"I want you beside me, wife," Slain said, tapping the spot next to him.

Hannah rounded the table and knew it would be a chore to lift her leg over the bench without wincing. She kept a forced smile on her face as she did, trying hard not to show her discomfort. She was grateful when the door opened, without a knock, and Imus entered. She quickly seated herself before her husband could notice her grimace.

Imus spoke as soon as Slain gave him a nod. "We picked up some tracks, but they led nowhere."

"The fire?" Slain asked.

"It's nothing but embers. Everything was lost," Imus informed him.

"Hannah has told me that the lad says the fire was already burning when he arrived here," Slain said. "Any thoughts?"

"Is the lad prone to setting fires?" Imus asked.

Hannah hated having to admit, "He has set fires before for my father."

Imus shrugged. "Then he did not set the fire."

Slain's brow drew together in question. "Why do you say that?"

"If the lad has set fires before, he would have boasted to Hannah about setting this one," Imus said.

"Then who set the fire?" Slain asked.

Imus looked down at his boots as if they had suddenly drawn his attention.

"If you know something or think you know something, tell me," Slain ordered.

"I do not like adding to a man's misery," Imus said.

"Potsman," Slain said.

Imus nodded reluctantly. "He was well into his cups when I saw him last night and later that evening Wilona was looking for him, worried that he had drunk himself stupid."

"Find him and bring him to the fire's site," Slain said. "I will be there waiting."

Hannah wondered if Imus could possibly be trying to divert attention away from himself since he had been the one to take coins from the man in the woods. Had he been instructed to set the fire? Yet he and Slain had been friends since young. Would the man truly betray such a longstanding friendship?

Slain turned to his wife as soon as the door closed on Imus. "There is much I must see to today. Rest and recover from last night," he said with a grin, "for I will make sure you are not neglected again." He kissed her cheek gently. "Your mouth does not pain you?" He felt a twinge of guilt for having made her bleed when he had kissed her.

Hannah laughed softly. "You definitely made up for your neglect."

He brushed his lips over hers. "I am glad I have redeemed myself."

"More than redeemed," she said her smile spreading before a pain reminded her that her bruise had yet to heal. "As for my wound? Your kiss was worth the pain and I would suffer it ten times over for you to kiss me like that again."

"You tempt me, wife," Slain said and kissed the tip of her nose. "That is why I will go see to my duties."

Hannah stood along with him. "I will go with you." She gave him no chance to deny her. "If they believe Conlan responsible for the fire, they will look no further and that will leave the clan in danger. We need to know who did this and we will not know if we keep making assumptions."

"You can walk?' he asked teasingly and held his arm out to her.

"With your help."

"Truly?" he asked his tone filled with concern.

She did not wish to see him suffer needlessly and took his arm. "Your help is unnecessary but greatly desired."

Slain slipped her cloak on her shoulders before they left the keep, then took hold of her arm again.

A gentle mist rolled over the land and clouds hovered overhead. The dismal weather matched the bleak faces of the clansmen, the fire having upset everyone. All gave a respectful nod to their chief, though cautious eyes fell on Hannah.

"News of Conlan has spread and they wonder if they should trust me," Hannah said, worry roiling her stomach.

"The truth will be known," Slain assured her as if his words alone vindicated her.

At least he believed her and that mattered the most to Hannah.

Embers were still being doused with water as they approached the crumbled building.

The few men working there stopped and looked to Slain, their faces covered with soot and grime and their eyes filled with exhaustion and despair.

"Stay as you are," Slain said softly to Hannah and approached the men. His voice rang with command and his tone with confidence. "No lives were lost. The building will be built again, its contents replaced. We lost little yet gained the strength of our clan that unites in time of trouble and grows ever stronger. The Clan MacKewan will never be defeated."

The men let out a roar, their arms rising high in the air, and gloom left their eyes, replaced by a spark of pride.

A shout from the edge of the woods drew everyone's attention and Slain turned just as Imus and another man emerged, Imus carrying a body in his huge arms.

Chapter Twenty-five

It took Hannah a few moments to recognize the lanky, bloody body in Imus' arms. It was Potsman and he had been beaten badly.

"Take him to his cottage and someone fetch Neata," Slain ordered and stretched his hand out to Hannah.

She hurried over to him, his hand wrapping solidly around hers and she walked with him as they followed behind Imus.

Wilona and Blair turned from where they stood by the cottage garden talking and when Wilona saw that it was her husband Imus carried, her eyes turned wide with shock, then she let out a screeching wail.

"He is not dead," Imus said as he reached the two women, "but he has been beaten badly."

Hannah left her husband's side and followed Wilona and Blair into the cottage, wanting to help.

Wilona turned once at the door and screamed at Hannah. "This is your fault. You let the one who set the fire go and look what he did to my husband. You are not welcome here."

Hannah drew back, feeling her words like a slap in the face.

Slain stepped forward. "Watch that sharp tongue, Wilona. The young lad who got away could not have done this to your husband."

"The lad was a ruse and is still to blame for everything," Wilona said angry tears falling from her eyes. She pointed at Hannah. "And she let the lad go. Is she a ruse too? Has she—"

"Silence!" Slain shouted. "Disparage my wife with one more word and you will suffer the consequences."

Wilona lowered her head. "Forgive me, I speak—"

"Foolishly," Slain finished. "Go see to your husband and do not let me hear you speak badly of my wife again."

Wilona nodded and hurried inside, her tongue silent.

Neata appeared, hurrying past everyone, heading straight inside the cottage.

Imus came out after Neata went in and walked over to Slain.

"Was Potsman able to speak to you?" Slain asked.

Imus shook his head. "He is barely breathing. Neata will let you know if he says anything. Some of the men are searching where we found him. I go to join them."

Imus gave Hannah a quick glance before his eyes returned to Slain, and with nod, he took his leave.

"He believes I know something," Hannah said, having seen a questioning look in his eyes.

"Imus worries for the clan as do they all and you letting the young lad go does not sit well with them. You should have trusted me."

"I do trust you, husband, it is the savage I am not sure of."

While her words hurt Slain, though they were all too true, she was better off not trusting the savage. There was no telling what he would do. Right now, however, he had no time to dwell on that. He needed to find out what happened to Potsman and if it was in any way connected with the young lad Conlan.

"We return to the keep," Slain said. "You will wait there while I join Imus and the others in their search."

"I will go with you. I might be able to help," she offered, hoping he would not refuse her. She would feel more helpless than she already did if she was left in the keep to wait.

"It is better if you stay in the keep."

She was ready to argue when a thought came to her. "You worry that the clan thinks I had something to do with this and might—"

"No clansmen would dare harm you. They fear the savage too much to do anything so foolish," he said, his hand leaving hers to slip around her waist and draw her close. "They would, however, turn their heads away from you and not speak with you."

Hannah shrugged. "I have suffered such before and survived."

"Who did such a thing to you?" His demand held more concern than gruffness.

With a tilt of her head and a playful smile, she said, "You might not believe this, but I was not always obedient."

Slain chuckled. "And you are now?"

She pressed her fingers to his lips as if in a kiss. "I try to be."

"You do well enough, wife, I would have you no other way." He kissed her cheek, fighting not to capture her lips in a loving kiss.

"Then let me go with you. I want to help and I want the clan to see that I help. I also want to prove that Conlan had nothing to do with this."

His response was to take her hand and continue walking. Hannah was disappointed until he turned toward the crumbled building, men still keeping watch over the smoldering debris.

Hannah was relieved and gave his hand a grateful squeeze.

"You will do your best to obey me, wife," Slain ordered.

"Aye, husband," she said, pleased that he requested she do her best and not demand or threaten that she obey his word.

"You mentioned your father had used Conlan before to set fires. Did he ever send someone along with him?" Slain asked as they entered the woods.

"Not that I know of. Conlan was always sent on his own. He is too quick on his feet for anyone to match his pace."

"I would doubt that if I had not seen it for myself. The lad is faster than any I have ever seen."

They continued to walk deeper into the woods, spotting Imus and a couple of men in the distance. One of the men had squatted down, looking at something more closely on the ground while the other two looked on intently.

"They have found something," Hannah said anxious to see what it was.

The men looked up at Slain and Hannah as they approached and Slain waited for a nod from Imus before he hastened their pace, wanting to make certain what they had found was something Hannah need not see.

"A small pool of blood," Imus said when Slain and Hannah were close.

"From Potsman?" Slain asked.

Imus shook his head. "Potsman was found closer to the edge of the woods. This could possibly be where someone stopped to tend a wound."

"Potsman looked to have suffered too much of a beating to have inflicted any damage on his opponent," Slain said, turning his head as his dark eyes searched the ground around them. "That is odd... no tracks."

"We thought the same," Imus said and the other two men nodded in agreement. "We have searched deeper into the woods and have found nothing."

"No tracks at all?" Slain asked, a questioning wrinkle settling between his eyes.

"None," Imus said, scratching his head.

A shudder caught Hannah along with a rush of fear.

Slain turned to his wife, feeling the sudden ripple that ran through her and concerned the scene had disturbed her. "What is wrong?" he demanded, seeing how deathly pale she had turned.

"Did your men use any weapons against Conlan?" she asked.

"He was too fast we could not—" Slain turned silent, realizing what had upset his wife and he tilted his head back, his eyes going to the tree branches overhead.

Imus and the other men followed suit, though did not know what they were looking for.

One of the men scrunched his eyes, scratched his head, and pointed. "Is that a body sprawled over a branch?"

Hannah's heart lurched in her chest and she grabbed her husband's arm. "Hurry and get him down, Please. He is hurt." She was ever so grateful the leaves had yet to fully bloom or Conlan would have never been spotted.

His wife did not have to plead with him, he had every intention of getting the lad down and discovering what had happened. If the lad was still alive.

Hannah watched with a fearful heart as the men worked to get Conlan down and while she hated to hear him moan in pain, at least the moans let her know that he was alive.

When they finally laid him on the ground, Hannah went down on her knees beside him, her trembling hand swallowing his small one in a loving grip.

"Conlan, it is me Hannah. I am here. You are not alone. All will be well."

His eyes fluttered open. "A dream."

"No. No. It is not a dream. I am here. The healer will take care of you."

Conlan groaned, his face scrunching in a painful wince. "Tried to stop him."

"Who did you try to stop and stop him from what?" Slain demanded, squatting down beside his wife.

"He beat the man—" a painful groan devoured his words.

"He needs Neata." Hannah looked to her husband through misty eyes. "Please have him taken to the keep and send for Neata."

Slain stood, tugging his wife to her feet along with him. "I will not pull Neata away from Potsman to tend the lad."

"Please," Hannah begged.

Slain looked to Imus. "Your cottage sits close to Wilona's, take the lad there so that Neata can tend him when she finishes with Potsman."

Imus did not argue. He picked the lad up gently and carried him off, Hannah hurrying behind him and Slain keeping pace with her.

Neata was outside Wilona's cottage speaking with Blair when they approached and both women hurried over when Imus turned up the path to his cottage. This time Hannah would not be chased away. She did not care who might yell at her or who would grow angry with her, she entered the cottage, intent on remaining at Conlan's side.

Slain let Hannah be, needing time to speak with Imus alone and she needing to be with her friend.

"He saw something," Slain said after he and Imus stepped around the side of his cottage to talk.

"He beat the man, those were his words," Imus said. "It sounds as if he might know who it was, perhaps someone who was sent with him to see the deed done?"

"But why stab the lad if they were to work together?"

"Maybe the lad protested the beating?"

"That would be cause for a hand to be used against him but not a knife, and from what Hannah has told me her father used the lad often. He would not be pleased with his loss." Slain shook his head. "No, there is more here than we are seeing."

Imus shook his head as well. "You do not think it is someone in our clan that has done this, do you? All know you would never let this clan fall to MacFillan or to anyone."

"I ask them to trust without seeing."

"You asked us to trust once before and you returned to us with a troop of men who helped rebuild the village. They know you have powerful friends you can call on for help. I do not believe there is one among the clan who would betray you. This falls on Ross MacFillan."

"The only way we learn the truth is from Potsman or the lad and I fear the lad might not make it. He took a wound to the stomach. Whoever delivered it meant to kill him."

"Why kill the lad and not Potsman?" Imus asked.

"I wonder the same."

~~~

"I cannot leave him," Hannah said when Slain came to collect her. "I do not want him to wake to strangers. He will try to run and make his wound worse. Neata did all she could, searing the wound. She says he is young and strong and being as willful as he is should help him. Rest and care is all that will help him now, and prayers. Time will see to the rest."

Neata's conclusion did not surprise him and either did his wife's words. Looking down on the deathly pale lad, Slain could not blame her for wanting to stay with him. He was so scrawny Slain wondered if he ever ate. He got annoyed at himself for not having had the lad taken to the keep. At least then, Hannah would have remained home.

Home.

It was her home regardless of what others might feel or think and that was where she should be right now. Home with him, but there was no way she would leave the lad and he would not force her. He would stay there with her.

Slain took a chair from the table and placed it against the wall where he would have a view of his wife where she sat beside the bed holding the lad's hand.

"What are you doing?" she asked softly.

"I am staying with you," —he continued before she could protest— "if he wakes I want to speak with him."

"What of Blair and Imus?" Hannah asked, knowing that was only partially the truth. He did not want to leave her there alone.

"They will find a place for the night. Tomorrow I will have the lad moved to the keep so that you may watch over him."

"I am grateful for that, Slain." She brushed the lad's hair off his brow with a soft sweep of her finger. "Who could have done this to him? My father had no cause to harm him."

"Hopefully, he will be able to tell us when he wakes," Slain said, wanting to keep her hope strong for the lad.

"Conlan will not be going back to my father. He will stay here with us," Hannah said as if it had already been decided.

Slain made no comment. If the lad survived, he would see what he had to say and only then decide his fate.

The door opened and Imus stepped in. "Potsman is awake."

Chapter Twenty-six

Slain entered Potsman's cottage to see a similar scene. Wilona was sitting in a chair next to the bed, staring at her husband. Neata had informed him that Potsman was severely bruised and battered but she could find no broken bones. Rest would help him, though Potsman felt copious amounts of ale would do him more good.

Potsman did not look as bad as when Slain had first seen him now that the blood had been cleaned from his face and neck. His one eye was closed shut with bruising, his jaw was swollen, and he winced any time he moved.

"I will get you some of the brew Neata made for you," Wilona said and went to stand.

"Ale, woman, ale. It will kill the pain far better than that tasteless brew."

Wilona moved away from the bed, an annoyed look marring her brow, and gave a respectful bob toward Slain before leaving the cottage.

Slain stood at the end of the bed angry that Potsman had taken such a beaten. Not that he did not deserve one for what he had done to Hannah, but if he was to suffer one it should have come from Slain's hands not a stranger's.

"Tell me what happened," Slain said

"There is not much to tell," Potsman said, finding it difficult to speak, the pain robbing him of breath.

"Why would that be, Potsman?" Slain asked when the answer was known to him.

"I was behind the storage shed well into my cups, brooding over a fight with Wilona." He shook his head and winced. "I never saw it coming. I only felt the blow, then I was dragged off and fists slammed at me over and over." He paused for a much needed breath. "I thought it was the end and I would die." He shook his head again. This time slowly. "Then suddenly it stopped. I heard a grunt of sorts and several oaths spewed from someone's mouth, then silence. I dragged myself away and hid as best I could afraid the culprit would return." Another needed pause. "After that, I remember nothing until I woke here."

"Did you see who did this to you?"

"No. It was dark and he was like a shadow in the night, and fast with his fists, pummeling me so rapidly so that all I could do was try to protect myself."

Slain saw the bruises along his arms from where he must have raised them to shield himself. "There is nothing you can tell me about this man?" he asked annoyed, having hoped Potsman could have provided him with at least some details. He prayed the lad would survive and could tell him more.

"A shadow in the night, that was what he was," Potsman said, his face scrunching against the pain as he attempted to shift himself in the bed.

"You should have gone for help or yelled out for it," Slain said and pointed a finger at him. "Fail me again and you will not like the consequences."

"Aye, Chief," Potsman said with a shiver of gooseflesh rushing over him.

Wilona hurried inside as soon as Slain stepped out of the cottage.

Slain motioned for Imus to join him as he walked back to the cottage where Hannah kept vigil over Conlan. "He saw nothing that will help us."

"Hopefully the lad will be able to tell us something," Imus said.

"If he survives. Neata did not seem too hopeful about it."

"We found nothing in the woods that would help us," Imus said.

"What troubles me is that if this fire was a warning, what comes next?"

~~~

Two days since the attack and Conlan continued to drift in and out of wakefulness, though not wake entirely. He had been placed in the room next to Helice's sleeping quarters, Slain having informed Hannah that the lad was in skilled hands with Helice being so close. Helice had taken to caring for Conlan and remarkably he had responded well to her after Hannah had told him, during a brief waking period, that she was a friend.

The fire had brought a change to the clan, particularly to the keep. The Great Hall was awash with activity. Men coming and going, talking with Slain, and Imus who sat often in conversation with the chief. Women arrived, offering Helice help in the kitchen and with the duties of the keep and she did not turn them away or balk at their efforts, her time spent more with Conlan.

When there was a lull, no one about in the Great Hall but her husband, Hannah approached him.

Slain waited until his wife was close enough, then he reached out and pulled her down on his lap. "You appear displeased, wife," he said and pleased her bruise was fading more each day, placed a feather-light kiss on her lips. She turned her head slowly, soft laughter spilling along his cheek and falling over his ear, raising gooseflesh along his arms and causing his manhood to flare.

"Aye," she said with a teasing whisper to his ear, "I found the bed empty when I woke and you had promised me a morning tryst last night."

"After wearing you out last night, I thought I should let you rest."

Her soft laughter fell against his cheek along with her lips. "Or was it you who needed the rest?"

He couldn't resist nipping along her neck to her ear. "It is you I need... always."

Gooseflesh prickled Hannah's skin and she rested her brow to his. "I do love you, husband."

"Forgive the intrusion," Helice said and they both turned to see she had entered the Great Hall. "Conlan is awake if you wish to speak with him."

Hannah jumped up off her husband's lap and rushed around the table. "How is he?"

"He is in pain, though bears it well," Helice said.

For once Hannah was glad for the woman's blunt nature. She would rather know the truth of the lad's condition than be fed lies and live on false hope. She turned to see that her husband would join her, but then he had been waiting for this moment when he could finally talk with Conlan.

Hannah hurried into the small room before Slain and Helice, going to the narrow bed and sitting on the chair beside it. She was disappointed that Conlan's eyes were closed, thinking he had drifted back to sleep once again. She smiled when they sprang open.

"Hannah," Conlan said, his attempted smile turning to a grimace.

Hannah took his hand, squeezing it gently. "You are safe here and here is where you will stay... in your new home."

Another grimace struck Conlan when he went to display his surprise with a smile. It took a moment for him to be able to speak. "Truly?"

"Truly," she said, not bothering to see if her husband would consent to Conlan joining the clan. She would not see the lad returned to her father and be treated badly.

"I tried—" He stopped, his breath suddenly lost to him along with his words, then once able he rushed his words out before the pain could rob him of them. "To stop him."

Hannah helped him finish, seeing that speaking was causing him pain. "You tried to stop the large man from beating on the smaller one."

Conlan nodded.

Slain stepped up behind his wife. "I admire your courage, Conlan."

Conlan had to tilt his head back some to look up and when he saw who spoke to him, his eyes turned wide. "Savage," he whispered.

"Slain," Hannah corrected, "your new chief."

Conlan did not take his eyes off Slain. "Did not set fire."

"I am aware that you did not set the fire. The man you saved saw a large man with a torch. Did you know this man?"

Conlan shook his head slowly.

"Would you know him if you saw him again?" Slain asked.

"I did not see him." Conlan scrunched his brow against the pain. "Laughed when he stabbed me." He grimaced again.

Hannah was about to end the questioning, seeing how much pain it was causing Conlan when Helice spoke up.

"Enough, he needs to rest."

"We will talk again when you are stronger," Slain said, "and welcome to the Clan MacKewan."

A tear slipped from the lad's eye as he struggled to speak. "Will serve you well, my chief,"

"You serve me well by resting and growing strong and doing as Helice says."

Conlan looked to Helice, another tear slipping from his eye.

Helice walked around in front of Hannah and nearly snatched the lad's hand out of hers to tuck beneath the blanket. "You will drink more of the brew I fixed and sleep. No more talk today."

"Tales?" Conlan asked eagerly.

"Aye, after you rest."

He closed his eyes, then opened them quickly, settling them on Hannah. "Grateful."

Hannah stood, Helice moving back as she leaned over the bed and kissed Conlan's brow. "Get well, we have fishing to do."

He wore a soft smile as he closed his eyes.

All three left the room and before Helice could walk away, Hannah said, "I am grateful to you for taking such excellent care of Conlan."

"He is no chore," Helice said and hurried off.

Hannah stared after her, sure she had seen tears in the woman's eyes. She was about to ask her husband if he had seen Helice's tears as they entered the Great Hall when she saw that Imus and Wilona waited there.

"A word," Imus said to Slain.

Slain nodded and looked to Wilona.

The woman wrung her hands as she spoke. "I came to apologize to Hannah for speaking wrongly of her the other day and ask about the lad who, I am told, saved my husband's life."

"I am pleased to hear that, Wilona, and I will leave you both to talk," Slain said and with a kiss to Hannah's cheek, he took his leave with Imus.

"I regret my words to you that night," Wilona said.

Hannah pointed to the table. "Sit, we will share a brew and talk."

"Was the lad able to tell who did this evil thing to him and Potsman? Wilona asked, slipping along the bench to sit.

"Unfortunately no," Hannah said, sitting as well and filling two tankards with the heated brew.

"Everyone worries."

"Understandably, but I am sure the culprit will be caught soon," Hannah assured her.

"You believe so?" Wilona's eyes turned wide. "That would be most reassuring."

"The men who search will find something that will help lead us to the person who did this. He will be caught and punished."

Wilona hugged herself, her face paling some.

Hannah reached out a comforting hand. "Worry not. Potsman will recover and all will be well."

It was an hour later that Hannah stood outside the keep watching Wilona walk off, the woman's steps were burdensome, but then she had troubles enough to carry. She was about to turn and enter the keep when she thought she caught something out of the corner of her eye. She was surprised to see Imus enter the woods, casting a glance around as if he watched to see if anyone followed. She quickly hurried to a spot by the keep wall where she hoped she would not be seen and braced herself against it. After a few moments, she took a chance and peeked to see where Imus had gone. She spotted him disappearing deeper into the woods.

Her mother once told her that she lacked good sense, plunging into things without thinking and that was what she did now. She plunged ahead without thought to possible consequences, though that did not matter to her. If Imus was betraying Slain, she had to know. She had to protect her husband and new clan.

Cloudy skies made it a gloomy day, casting darkness and shadows over the forest and making it appear uninviting as Hannah entered and hurried to follow Imus. A soft wind stirred the branches and sent a chill through Hannah as it swept down around her. She rubbed her arms, wishing she had her cloak, but there had been no time to spare. She had to follow Imus and settle her doubt about him once and for all.

She kept a good distance behind him, barely keeping sight of him, for fear of him detecting her steps. It did not take long for her to realize Imus was headed to the same spot where he had last seen him meet a man. Confident she was right, she changed direction and came upon the boulder she had hidden behind when she had first accidentally intruded upon Imus and the stranger. She waited and it was not long before she heard voices.

Hannah strained to hear what they were saying, the voices lower and more cautious than the last time. She caught a few words with hopes she could make some sense of them.

"Not long now."

"When."

"All is ready?"

"Knows nothing."

"Not prepared."

Frustration jabbed at Hannah, the few words she caught making it seem as if Slain was not prepared for what was to come. Was Imus telling the man that the Clan MacKewan was vulnerable, not prepared to defend itself? What was not long now? An attack?

The voices drifted off, sounding as if the two man were walking off together. As the voices got further away, she decided to dare take a peek in hopes of possibly identifying who Imus was speaking with. She moved to peek her head past the boulder when a hand suddenly covered her mouth with such a strong grip that she could not breathe. An arm coiled around her waist equally as tight and before she could fight the culprit, a whisper settled against her ear.

"Silence, wife."

Fear fled, leaving her body so rapidly that she fell limp against him.

He dropped his hand away from her mouth, turned her around to face him, and pressed his finger to her lips.

She nodded, understanding his gesture for her to remain silent. He gave a nod in the direction of the keep, took her hand, and pressed his finger to her lips once again. Again she understood what he silently conveyed to her. They would return to the keep in silence.

Hannah dutifully obeyed, agreeing with him that they should remain silent, not chance being discovered, since they truly did not know if anyone else lingered in the woods.

Once they stepped out of the woods she went to speak, but he cautioned her with a shake of his head.

Not another word was spoken until they entered his solar.

"Now do you believe that Imus is not the friend you believe him to be?" she asked, knowing he had to have heard some of the conversation between Imus and the stranger.

"Imus, unlike my wife, obeys my orders," Slain said, pointing to the chair for her to sit.

She walked, instead, to the hearth, standing near its warmth, staring at the flames for a moment, then turning to him with a shake of her head. "I do not understand. Are you saying that you instructed him to make it seem like he was betraying you?"

He ignored her question and instead demanded, "Did I not forbid you to go into the woods alone?"

"Why do you not answer my question?" she asked.

"For your own safety," Slain snapped.

"Or is it that you do not trust me, since I am the daughter of your enemy?"

Slain walked over to her, his hand shooting out to cup the back of her neck tightly. "Listen well, wife. If I thought I could not trust you, you would have been long gone from here. I keep things from you to keep you safe. I could not bear anything happening to you. You have given me something I never thought I would have again… hope for a future. A good and loving future."

"I want the same," she said, "and to have that I need to know you trust me."

"I do trust you, Hannah, but you have tasted the suffering of torture. Would you not confess anything to save you from such a horrible fate?"

Hannah shut her eyes against the memories and his hand loosened from around the back of her neck to ease her into his arms—strong, protective arms—that tightened around her.

"At one time, I would have believed myself strong enough to protect whatever secret was entrusted to me, but after experiencing torture, I know better. It takes a heartless person to create such torture devices, knowing what they are intended for and may he rot in hell for doing so."

Slain tightened his arms around her.

She turned her head up, meeting his eyes. "What do you fear that you do not tell me?"

That was an easy question for him to answer, for it so often troubled his mind. "That you will see me for what I truly am—a savage—and you will love me no more."

"That will never happen. Nothing can rob me of my love for you. It is there deep inside my heart, my soul, forever and beyond. As much as you want no harm to come to me, I wish to keep you from the same. I would fight until my dying breath to keep you safe and with it I would make sure to tell you one last time… I love you."

"Do not speak such nonsense," he demanded, feeling the weight of her words. The thought of losing her too much to bear. He rested his brow against hers. "It is I who will always protect you and every one of our bairns."

"We shall have many," she said eagerly.

"And we will enjoy making every one of them," he said with a playful smile.

"I do so love you, husband," Hannah said softly, "and I will trust you, since I believe you have plans in motion and I will not chance upsetting them."

"You are a wise wife and much appreciated."

Hannah turned a teasing smile on him, her response interrupted by the village bell tolling loudly.

The two rushed out of the solar and into the Great Hall, Helice following behind them. Fright twisted tightly at Hannah's stomach and her heart beat madly in her chest. She had a dreadful fear of what awaited them as they stepped outside.

Hannah's hand rushed to grab her husband's when she saw that her fear had not been misplaced. She watched her father lead a troop of his warriors toward the village, her step-brother riding beside him.

Chapter Twenty-seven

Slain kept his grip strong on his wife's hand, her tremor of fear rippling along his arm. "You are safe, wife."

"My father brings many warriors," she said, her eyes on the troop of about fifty men, all carrying weapons, marching in precision behind her father and step-brother. They looked ready for battle. She turned soft green eyes on her husband. "I trust you, husband."

He leaned his head down and whispered, "Others may have failed to protect you... I will not."

His dark eyes held a fierce determination, but it was his love for her burning so strongly for all to see that brought an instant smile to her face. "Of that I have no doubt."

Hannah was pleased and proud to see the clan, men and women alike, approach the keep, weapons in hand. They formed two lines, opposite each other, creating a path that would force her father and step-brother to travel up to reach their chief.

Helice stepped around Slain and handed him his sheathed sword, then went and joined one of the lines of clansmen. Hannah saw that a sword hung from the belt around her waist. She was prepared to fight along with the others.

Slain released her hand and while he secured the belt around his waist, Hannah cast curious eyes over the clan. They stood with confidence. There was not a tremor of fear among them. Was it confidence in Slain that had them standing there with certainty? Or did they know something she did not? That thought plagued her far too often.

When her husband's hand closed around hers once again, her glance drifted back to him, and with great pride she stood beside him as her father drew closer.

Her fearful tremor returned when her father was close enough for her to see the anger on his face. He was a man of fine features, something that probably had first drawn her mum to him, but over the years his constant scowling and anger left deep lines on his face that turned permanent, leaving him appear forever angry and aged beyond his years. His long, pure white hair also added years to him that he had yet to claim. His size was substantial, broad and thick, and his height fair. He was easily a man who could intimidate, though nowhere near as intimidating as Slain.

Ross MacFillan's eyes went to his daughter as soon as he brought his horse to a stop. "I gave you no permission to marry. You will return home with me this day."

Slain did not bother to hide his wrath. "I gave you no permission to speak to my wife, MacFillan. Keep a civil tongue or leave."

Ross laughed. "How will you make me do that when you have a mere pittance of a clan to defend," —he stretched his arm out behind him— "and I have a troop of warriors."

Slain took a step forward, his hand still firm around his wife's trembling one. "I care not about your troop. It is you I will capture and all will see what I do to those who threaten me."

Hannah did not believe the tremble of fear her father visibly displayed.

"Have your say and be gone," Slain commanded.

Slain's sharp demand did not sit well with Hannah's father and as was his way, his temper took flight.

"You had no permission to wed my daughter. You will release her to me immediately or there will be war between us."

"I warned you about threatening me," Slain said his tone more menacing than Hannah had ever heard it.

Her step-brother joined in, turning an accusing eye on Hannah. "You did this on purpose. You married this *savage* to defy your father."

Slain turned a harsh tone on him. "Speak to my wife without permission again and I will take great pleasure in killing you slowly."

Slain glared at him with such hatred that Hannah thought Nial would drop dead there and then.

"You do not frighten me," Nial said, keeping his voice strong.

"Then you are a foolish man," Slain said.

"I demand you return my daughter to me," Ross shouted, shaking a tight fist at Slain.

Slain punctuated each word with distinct sharpness to make himself perfectly clear. "My wife stays with me. And why is it you arrive here and demand Hannah's return, but yet not ask how she fares? Do you care more to war with me than you do with your own daughter's safety and well-being?"

"You have no right to question me," Ross said.

"I have every right to question you when you ride onto my land ready for battle."

"If it is a battle you want, it is a battle you will get," Ross warned, his hand going to grip the hilt of his sword at his side and a fierce hunger in his eyes to use it.

"We will battle, MacFillan, that is for sure, even though our clans are united through marriage," Slain said, a hunger in his own eyes to see it done.

"Never!" Ross screamed, shaking his fist in the air. "I will conquer your clan and you will get on your knees before me, in front of all, and pledge allegiance to me. And my traitorous daughter will be given to another man to wed. One who cares not that she has been soiled by... the *savage*."

Hannah felt his words like a slap in her face and she turned her head away.

"You should turn away in disgrace, daughter, for the shame you have brought to me and your clan," her father shouted for all to hear.

A low growl rumbled deep in Slain's chest, his eyes turning darker, narrower, and his glare deadlier, ready to spew vile words at the man, but his wife spoke before he could.

"It is you who shames the clan, Father," Hannah said boldly, turning to face him. "With this marriage, you have a chance to unite two strong clans, but you let your greed, hatred, and selfishness stand in the way. I wed Slain freely. He did not force me and I take great pride in calling him my husband. The one and only husband I will ever have. So say and do whatever you will, but I stand by my husband, Slain MacKewan and the Clan MacKewan, now and always."

"Your father is right, you are a disgrace to Clan MacFillan," Nial spat.

Slain wanted to reach up and tear the man off the horse and beat him until he was a bloody mess. He could not have been more proud of his wife and the courage it had taken her to speak to her father like that in front of so many, and Nial had the audacity to say she was a disgrace. Now he had even more reason to kill the fool.

"I will speak to my daughter alone," Ross said to the surprise of everyone, especially Hannah.

"No!" Slain said with such force it sounded like an edict.

"You deny me to speak with my daughter?" Ross accused.

"I deny you to speak with her alone," Slain corrected.

"I agree with the savage," Nial said, "she may try to do you harm. I will stand by your side and protect you."

This time it was Hannah who spoke, though her tone was even. "No, I will speak with my father alone." She turned to Slain, slipping her hand out of his to rest on his arm. "Please, husband, grant me this."

Slain had asked his wife to trust him and he needed to do the same for her. "I will remain close by, if you should need me."

She turned a soft, grateful smile on him.

Nial dismounted along with her father and they exchanged low, angry words until her father finally walked away from him and approached her.

Hannah turned as he neared her and walked a distance away from Slain, her father following.

Though the distance was short, Slain had a difficult time with it. He did not believe MacFillan would do his daughter harm. She was too useful to him, a pawn in a game he intended to win. Still, he did not like leaving his wife vulnerable in any manner and alone with her father left her susceptible enough. The man could be vicious with words and words could sometimes leave far deeper scars than wounds to the body, and sometimes they never healed.

"I should have taken my hand to you years ago, then you may have been a more obedient daughter, though I have my doubts. You are far too obstinate," Ross said when they stopped not far from the keep.

"Like you?" Hannah asked, having had expected unkind words from him, not that they did not hurt. They seemed to confirm what she always believed, that her father cared little for her.

"Watch your tongue or I will do what I should have done," he warned.

"I would be careful, Father, my husband would not take kindly to you raising your hand to me."

"Is that a threat?" he snapped.

"It is the simple truth," Hannah said. "My husband will not let us linger so I will have my say and be done with it."

"As will I," Ross said with a firm nod.

Hannah did not know if her father would believe her or not, but she wanted him to know the truth of her disappearance. "I do not know what lies Nial filled your head with, but the truth is he sold me to a man and paid him well to make sure I would suffer before killing me. That man took me to Warrick's dungeons where I would have died if it had not been for a brave soul who helped me to escape."

"Nial told me you would tell me such a tale, but I saw how hard he searched for you and how upset he was when he returned home after coming here only to find you had been abducted by Slain MacKewan and forced to wed him, the bruise he left upon you still vivid and obvious to all."

"Nial was upset because his plan to get rid of me failed—"

"Stop the lies and nonsense, Hannah. I know well the truth. You ran away because I would not let you choose a husband. Your anger purposely brought you here to Slain MacKewan and you wed him to spite me. Well, it will not work. You will leave here with me today or the next time I return it will be with the full force of my warriors and I will devastate the Clan MacKewan, see Slain dead, and see you wed to a man whose hand will soon tame you."

"You are a fool, Father, if you believe any of that will truly come to pass."

Ross clenched his hands at his sides, fighting to stop from striking his daughter, though he lashed out with his tongue. "I regret the day you were born. You robbed me of ever having more children and the son I always wanted, and you robbed me of a dutiful wife. Now you try to disparage the man who is like a son to me, who means more to me than you ever could and whose mother unselfishly gave to me what your mother no longer was able to."

Hannah felt the sting of his words. "What do you mean? How did I rob you of these things?"

"It was torture for your mother to deliver you. I listened for hours to her endless screams. You left her bleeding and torn, never to have more bairns, never to be able to perform her wifely duties again, forcing me into the arms of another woman."

"Mum never said anything to me about this."

"She did not want you to know. She wanted no one to know what a failure she was as a wife. I care little of what happens to you and truth be told your refusal to return home with me is exactly what I wanted. It gives me the excuse to finally attack the Clan MacKewan without objections or condemnation from anyone. I will ravage this clan and you along with it."

Hannah could not believe the hatred she heard in his words or saw in his eyes. She never felt her father loved her, even when her mum tried to assure her that he did. But to know she had been the cause of her mum and da losing whatever love or compassion they once had for each other stabbed painfully at her heart.

"Hannah."

She lifted her head, not even realizing her father had walked away, or that she had been staring at the ground.

Slain reached out, slipping his arm around her waist, her face so pale he thought she would faint. His worry grew when she stood staring speechless at him. "Hannah," he said softly.

His tender voice broke through her shock and hurt and when she saw the deep concern in his eyes, she said, "I am fine."

"You are not fine," he whispered.

"My father wants no peace between us."

Slain instinctively knew that was not what had left her speechless. Now, however, was not the time to discuss it.

"Either do I," he admitted and he thought he saw a tear in her eye, though it never fell. "It is time for your father to take his leave."

She nodded and reached for his hand and together they walked toward her father.

Slain's hatred for Ross MacFillan multiplied tenfold. He had nearly destroyed his clan, caused his mum and da's death, and now had said something to his wife that had hurt her deeply. The man would pay for what he had done and pay dearly.

Ross had already mounted when Slain and Hannah reached him and Nial was about to do so as well.

To Slain's surprise Hannah spoke. "Conlan is here and will be remaining with us."

Her father looked ready to roar to the heavens, his face turned so red, and Nial approached her with rapid steps and a roar of outrage.

"He will not stay here."

Slain was in front of his wife in a flash, his hands going out to shove the man away from her with such force that it sent him tumbling and landing flat on his back.

Nial's face raged with fury, but before he could get up and retaliate, Slain's boot slammed down on his chest, grinding into it, planting him firmly to the ground.

"Get on your horse and leave before I release the savage on you," Slain warned with a snarl that showed he was dangerously close to doing just that.

"You forget the warriors we have with us," Ross said.

Slain never took his eyes off Nial as he responded to Ross. "We both know you did not come here to battle today. That will be left for another day. Now take this lying fool with you and get off my land." He lifted his boot.

Nial looked ready to lunge at Slain, but a shout from Ross for him to mount his horse had him turning away.

"I will return and you will kneel to me and surrender your clan," Ross said.

"Enjoy that dream for it will turn into your worst nightmare," Slain said. "Now leave, for my patience runs thin and I might just kill you here and now and be done with it."

Nial's nostrils flared with anger and once again Ross commanded him to remain on his horse and with great restraint Nial remained as he was and they turned and rode off, his warriors following.

Imus suddenly appeared out of nowhere, Hannah not having noticed him among the clansmen who lined the path.

Slain turned questioning eyes on him and Imus nodded. "You are sure?" Slain asked and Imus nodded again only this time firmly as if it there was no doubt. "See it done, I will join you shortly," Slain ordered and Imus took a quick leave.

Hannah was disappointed that he would leave her now. She needed his caring and strong arms around her, but with battle on the horizon she could not be selfish.

Slain called out to his clansmen. "I will see you protected, worry not."

A cheer went up in the air and the villagers began to disperse.

Hannah wished she was privy to what was going on, but she had told him she would trust him and so she would, just as his clan trusted him.

Slain tugged at his wife's hand. "I want to return to the keep with you and know what your father said that upset you so much, but I must take my leave and see to an urgent matter. Later we will talk, but know whatever he said could never come between us. I love you and nothing will change that."

"What if we could not be intimate again? Would you still love me? Or would you seek another woman's bed?"

Hannah asked worried that her mum's fate might also be her own.

"What nonsense do you speak?" he asked, tucking her close against him.

She shook her head, not wanting to distract him from something far more important than her worries. "It is nothing."

"It worries you, therefore, it is something. We will talk later, I promise, but know one thing. There is nothing that would ever make me stop loving you or make me seek another woman's bed. You are all I want, all I will ever want." He captured her lips in a kiss that confirmed his words and when he left her side, Hannah felt as if a part of her went with him.

Hannah entered the keep, her steps sluggish, her heart hurting at what her father had told her. She was about to go see how Conlan was doing when Helice stopped her.

"He is sleeping and he needs his rest," Helice said, blocking her path.

Hannah did not know what made her do it, especially in front of Helice, but she burst out in tears. What surprised Hannah was that Helice reached out and wrapped her in her arms.

Chapter Twenty-eight

Hannah's eyes were red and puffy by the time she finished crying. Helice had held her in her arms until her tears had subsided, then she had sat Hannah at a table in the Great Hall and ordered her to remain there. Hannah, far too distraught to argue, did as she was told and Helice returned a short time later with a pitcher and two tankards and joined Hannah at the table.

"Drink," Helice ordered, passing a tankard she had filled to Hannah.

Hannah sipped slowly at the hot chamomile brew and after a few moments, she said, "I am sorry."

"For what? Crying?" Helice asked and shook her head. "Your father hurt you. You have a right to cry."

Helice's words reminded her how the clan had heard some of the things her father had said about her when he had first arrived. She wondered if they believed any of it.

"Your father should be grateful he has such a courageous daughter."

Hannah found herself saying, "He hates me." Did she think by saying it aloud it would ease the pain? If so, it did not help. It only hurt more. She continued, not able to stop herself. "I am the reason my mum grew to hate my da. My birth ruined everything for them."

"Your father is no man, and he was certainly not a good husband, if he lays the blame for his failed marriage on the birth of his daughter," Helice said.

"My mum could not be a dutiful wife to him after I was born," Hannah explained.

"That is nonsense," Helice said with a dismissive wave of her hand. "There are different ways a husband and wife can satisfy each other than the most common way. Your father makes excuses for his own ignorance. And if you do not believe me go ask Neata. She is a wise healer and knows much."

Hannah had not thought of that, perhaps Neata could provide more insight as to what may have happened during her mum's delivery that had caused the problem. She also worried that what had happened to her mum could happen to her and the thought frightened her.

"Worry not about when your time comes to birth your first bairn. Neata and I will tend you and all will go well," Helice said.

Hannah smiled softly. "How did you know that was my worry?"

"It would be any woman's worry who loved her husband as much as you love Slain. Also you do not want to rob him of something he has long wanted... a large family."

"I want one too," Hannah admitted.

"From the passion that shines forever in your eyes for him and the way you chase him about, it is a very large brood you and Slain will have." Helice smiled to Hannah's surprise. "And those heated cheeks of yours prove me right."

Hannah chuckled, having felt the heat rush to her cheeks.

"It will be good to hear the footfalls of little feet, bursts of laughter, and the hugs of little ones."

"You will make a good grandmother, indulging them with treats and hugs," Hannah said. Helice's mouth dropped open at Hannah's unexpected remark, giving her the time to continue. "The bairns will have no grandmother, so I do hope you do not mind filling such an important role in their lives."

"I am too cantankerous to be a grandmother," Helice said with a hint of sorrow.

A bubble of laughter welled in Hannah and a spark of joy returned to her heart as she spoke. "Somehow I do not believe that will be your nature with your grandchildren."

"You give me this honor when you have seen for yourself how I can be?" Helice asked.

Hannah nodded, her smile spreading, chasing the sadness that had consumed her. "It can be a chore dealing with you at times, but I have also seen how protective you can be of those you care for and those in need of care. You have taken excellent care of Conlan and he is healing well thanks to your kindness. You have also cared for me and I must admit it was nice having your gentle hand tend me. It reminded me of when my mum would do the same for me. You must have been a wonderfully loving mother to your daughter."

A hint of a tear flashed in Helice's eye. "I would be honored to be grandmother to yours and Slain's children."

"That pleases me and it will more than please Slain."

Helice stood, her eyes now pooling with tears. "I must go look in on Conlan and you should go speak with Neata."

"I will do that," Hannah said.

Helice stopped before stepping out of the Great Hall and turned to Hannah. "I had a son. He died when he was Conlan's age."

Hannah's heart went out to the woman. "I am so sorry, Helice, though I would very much like to know about him and your daughter one day, when you are ready."

Helice nodded and hurried off.

Hannah could not imagine losing a child and Helice had lost two. She felt tremendous sorrow for the woman. She had no family to love her. It was no wonder she looked after Slain like a son. Hannah had sensed something different about Helice from the way she had held her when she cried.

It had been as if her strong arms had suddenly turned loving and were willing to suffer the hurt and pain so Hannah would not have to. Something a loving mother would do.

Helice would be just as selfless and kind with grandchildren. Besides, she was family as Conlan now was and that was what mattered most.

Hannah's smile turned tender. Her family was growing and she could not be happier. Still, though, there was her father to deal with and she would be glad when that was done. Then there would be nothing left to come between her and Slain.

Hannah made her way to the village and this time she was met with smiles and genuine greetings. Blair approached her when they caught each other's eyes.

Blair reached out and gave her a hug. "The clan is proud of the way you defended Slain and the clan in front of your father. If there had been any doubt about your loyalty to the Clan MacKewan, it is gone."

"I am pleased to know that," Hannah said, "though there is one thing I have been wondering about. Is there something that goes on here that everyone but me knows about?"

Blair placed a hand on Hannah's arm and kept her voice low as she said, "Leave the secrets of MacKewan keep alone. You might not like what you find."

Hannah got the feeling that Blair was not talking about what Hannah had been eluding to, that Slain was well prepared for any attack. What then was the secret Blair advised her to leave alone?

"I must go help Wilona with Potsman. Where are you off to?"

"I am going to see Neata," Hannah said.

"All is well?" Blair asked concerned.

"All is good," Hannah assured her.

"Then the clan will hear good news soon?" Blair asked, glancing at Hannah's stomach with a wide smile.

Hannah's hand went there, pressing lightly against it. "That would be wonderful, but not yet."

"Soon, I am sure," Blair said and after another hug the two women parted in opposite directions.

Hannah found Neata outside, sitting under a tree, and she waved Hannah over to join her.

Neata patted the ground beside her. "Sit and enjoy this rarity of the sun breaking through such a heavy gloom.

Hannah looked up at the skies and smiled at the radiance of the sun. She had been so consumed in thought upon leaving the keep she had not even noticed that the day had turned lovely.

"A good sign," Neata said, nodding.

"That it is," Hannah agreed and lowered herself down beside the healer.

Neata wasted no time in asking, "Your bruise is healing well, so what brings you to me?"

Hannah remained silent a moment, worried what she might learn, but courage, or was it fear for what she and her husband could lose, had her soon asking, "My mum had a difficult time birthing me and was left unable to see to her wifely duties. I was—"

Neata interrupted her question. "Are you saying that your mum could no longer couple with your father?"

Hannah nodded, the pain of her father's words returning.

"Who told your mum this?"

"I do not know who tended the delivery," Hannah said. "My mum never spoke of it."

"I have heard of this occurring, actually more often than one would think. But it is rarer to find any truth behind it."

"What do you mean?" Hannah asked, not understanding.

"There are women who beg the healer who delivers their bairn to tell the husband she can no longer couple with him or bear any more children. It is usually after three or more births that his happens. The women simply do not want to go through another painful childbirth or they simply do not want to couple with their husband any longer. Some healers agree, others refuse for fear of the husband finding out."

Hannah thought on her words and shook her head. "I believe my mum loved my father." She sighed. "At least, I believe there was a time that she did."

"Where there is true love, this problem does not exist. There are ways a husband and wife can please each other without coupling. Though as I said, it is extremely rare that a woman is left unable to couple because of a difficult birth. There may be some healing time, possibly a lengthy period that is necessary, then coupling can be resumed."

Hannah was more confused than ever.

"I would not worry over this. You will do fine when your time comes," Neata assured her just as Helice had done.

Hannah sat for a while longer with a Neata, talking of other things and when a young lad with his mum approached the cottage Hannah stood to take her leave, helping Neata to her feet first.

"Worry not, all will be well," Neata said with a pat to Hannah's arm.

Hannah hugged the woman and left her to her work while she returned to the keep.

~~~

The hour grew late and Slain still had not returned home. Hannah had spent some time with Conlan, though he slept through her visit. It was better he did, since he was in constant pain when he woke. Helice kept careful watch over him, feeling his brow to make certain fever had not set in, and keeping him and his bedding clean. She spoon-fed him a brew Neata had advised her to make along with a broth she made fresh daily.

Hannah ate supper alone, and after going back and forth from the solar to the Great Hall—impatiently waiting for her husband—and yawns coming one after the other, she decided to retire to their bedchamber. She slipped into her nightdress, not that she intended to go to sleep, she pulled a chair nearer to the hearth and with her knees tucked up close to her chin she sat there waiting for Slain.

The warmth of the fire and the long day soon had her eyes closing and she would snap back awake each time her head lulled heavily to the side. It was during one of those times that the sound of voices brought her fully awake.

Hannah went to hurry out of the chair, but her limbs, having been scrunched too long, protested and she had to stretch the ache out of them. All the while she listened, her ear turned toward the door that sat closed. If she could hear the voices through a closed door, then it meant the voices were raised. But where were they coming from.

Hannah finally got her limbs moving, though it was cautious steps she took to the door and even more cautiously eased it open. She heard the voices again and realized they were coming from the east wing, the door sitting ajar. It was easy to tread lightly, not make a sound, since her feet were bare, and she stopped at the door to listen.

Chapter Twenty-nine

"Lies!"

Hannah jumped at the vicious accusation from a voice that held a familiar cord, but anger masked it.

"What if it is not?"

Her husband's voice held an edge of frustration and a hint of anger.

"Why, though, for what purpose?"

"A question I asked myself," Slain said.

"I must get this news to him. He will not be pleased."

"He is rarely pleased."

"Have ready what he wants from you upon my return."

"I cannot do that even more so now than before," Slain said.

Hannah wondered over their words, none making sense to her.

"He will not see it that way."

"Then let him speak to me himself about it," Slain said.

Their voices grew lower, more distant, and Hannah knew their talk was near done. She returned to the bedchamber, not wanting to be caught. She went to sit in the chair she had slumbered in when a sudden thought struck her, freezing her where she stood. She realized who the voice belonged to.

Roark.

What lies did he claim Slain had told him and what would not please Warrick? Had it been something to do with her? With their marriage? Would Warrick demand her return to his dungeon? She shuddered at the thought, jumping in fear as an arm coiled around her waist.

"You were expecting someone else besides your husband?" Slain teased in a whisper at her ear, then nibbled along it before turning her around in his arms. When he saw the worry in her eyes and the wrinkles in her brow, he tried to keep his voice gentle but was unable to keep the demand out of it. "What is wrong?"

Tired of secrets and since he had spoken of trust between them, Hannah spoke up, "I heard you speaking with Warrick's man, Roark."

"Then you heard me tell him of how you suffered there."

"That was why he had shouted *lies*?" Hannah asked, wishing she had held her tongue since now Slain knew when she had come in on the conversation.

"I told him you were sold to the guard there and Roark oversees the dungeon guards. Learning that is a reflection on his command and Warrick is not tolerant of such matters. You do not fail Warrick and you never disobey him, the consequences are much too severe."

Another shudder ran through her. "Yet knowing this, you refuse to give Warrick what he wants from you? What is it he wants from you?"

"You are not to concern yourself with it. That is between Warrick and me," Slain said.

"If you do not obey him," —she shook her head and stepped away from her husband— "you said yourself the consequences of such actions are severe." She gasped at a sudden thought. "He would not make you return me to the dungeons, would he?" Hannah took a step back when a feral snarl curled his lip.

"No one, not your father, not the demon lord, not the devil himself would I let take you from me. You are mine and will forever remain so."

Hannah felt the strength of his words. They settled deep inside her and wrapped around her heart, squeezing tight, and she took quick steps back to him.

His arms spread out to welcome her and not only did they wrap around her, but his lips claimed hers in a kiss that confirmed his every word. His loving kiss had her ignoring the pain that stung at her bruise. It was a small price to pay for the pleasure his kiss ignited in her.

Slain had been thinking about his wife since he had left her, but then she was forever in his thoughts and his heart. He hated being separated from her, especially with all that was going on. He would not take a chance of anything happening to her, of losing her. His heart would not just break... it would stop beating.

He scooped her up and carried her to the bed, slipping off her nightdress after placing her on her feet, then shedding his own garments and lifting her once again to place on the bed before following down after her.

He had been thinking of getting her naked in bed since he had left her earlier and of running his hands over every inch of her, kissing her in tender, intimate places that caused her to moan softly at first, just like she did now.

Hannah had longed all day for his touch even though they had only been intimate last night. She could not seem to get enough of him, of how when he touched her, slipped into her, joined with her that they seemed to merge as one. It was at that particular moment that she felt a part of him like she never felt before. That there was no separating them, that they truly were one.

She tossed her head back and let herself get lost in their lovemaking.

~~~

They lay in each other's arms, their bodies damp with sweat, their lips swollen from endless kisses, and the last of their climaxes fading away. Not long after, they both fell asleep.

Hannah woke suddenly, her eyes opening wide. She did not know what woke her, though as she lay there she realized it had been her father's angry voice in her mind that had woken her. She lay there trying to rid herself of it, to think of anything but him. It did not work. His words came back again and again to haunt her and along with them came the guilt.

Had she truly been the cause of her mother and father's problems? If it had not been for her would her mum had not stopped loving him? She turned her head to look at her husband, sleeping soundly beside her, his arm draped over her waist. The thought alone of losing his love was so painful it brought a tear to her eye and heaped even more guilt on her for possibly having robbed her mum of what she now had.

With her mind in turmoil, she eased out of bed so as not to disturb her husband and walked quietly over to the hearth. She added another log to the fire and watched it catch, the flames dancing high.

No matter how hard she tried, she could not get her mind off what her mum and da had lost and how it could possibly happen to her and Slain. Her heart ached and she could not stop tears from falling.

A warm arm circled her waist and she turned and buried her face against her husband's naked chest.

Slain felt her tears fall on his chest and he wrapped strong arms around her and held her close as she wept. As difficult as it was for him to remain silent, he did so. She needed him to hold her while she cried, not question her tears, though he had a good idea of who had caused them.

Though her tears seemed never-ending, it did not take long for them to stop and when they finally did and the after sobs had subsided, Slain said softly, "Talk to me, wife."

Hannah raised her head, the lingering tears blurring her vision, though not enough that she could not see concern in her husband's dark eyes. She told him everything her father had said to her and before she could express her own fear of it happening to them, Slain was quick to speak.

"That will never happen to us."

"You cannot be certain," she argued.

"I can be certain."

"But what if—"

"I do not waste my time on what if," he said.

Hannah stepped out of his arms. "You dismiss it as if it is unimportant."

"It is, since it will never come to pass," Slain insisted.

Hannah shook her finger at him. "You do not know that."

"I do know that and do not shake that finger at me, wife," he warned.

Hannah threw her hands up and took several more steps away from him. "You are not taking this seriously. You think you can dictate this, make it go away, and yet you cannot. It is a very real possibility that could eventually divide us."

Hannah gasped as Slain rushed at her, grabbing her by the arms and pinning her up against the closed door.

"Do you love me, wife?" he demanded.

His question stunned her but did not keep her from saying, "Aye, I love you, husband, and always will."

"Then what else matters?" He did not give her time to respond. "There are different ways to be intimate between a man and a woman and if your father truly loved your mother, he would have seen to keeping them both satisfied. He has no one to blame but himself for his failed marriage."

Hannah went to speak and Slain pressed a finger to her lips. "Now, wife, I am going to show you one of those ways a husband can please a wife, though you are already familiar with it."

He went down in front of her, his hands spreading her legs gently and she gasped, her arms flinging out from her sides as his mouth settled between her legs and his tongue licked and teased her tender nub.

It was wicked, simply wicked and she loved every minute of it. When his fingers slid inside her, she thought she would climax and yelled out his name. It was not until she called out his name three times, each more frantically than the previous one, that he finally scooped her up and carried her to the bed.

She spread her legs and reached her arms out to him after he laid her down and he quickly dropped down over her and into her in one fluid motion that had her gasping with pleasure.

Hannah held him tight, never wanting to let him go, aching to feel that moment when they became one, when their hearts joined, and their souls met. She could not stop a tear from falling at that moment, since it made her realize that nothing could ever come between them. Their love would never let it.

Slain's climax was so intense that he roared with pleasure, though it was cut short when he saw the tear slip down his wife's cheek. He almost pulled out of her, thinking he had hurt her, but she shook her head, smiled, and held him tight, refusing to let him go, and he let the last of his climax carry him to complete satisfaction.

Slain wiped at her tear with his thumb before slipping off her and taking her in his arms as he rolled on his back. "I am assuming that is a tear of joy?"

"It is," she claimed happily.

"I am glad, since your other tears break my heart."

"Truly?" she asked, raising her head off his chest to look up at him.

"Truly, so I will endeavor to keep you from those tears as much as possible."

She went to kiss his cheek and he grabbed her chin tenderly, stopping her.

"Damn, I ached for you so badly I forgot about your bruise and now it looks more swollen than before."

"I do not care. The bruise will eventually heal, but I will never get back the time you were unable to kiss me."

"I will not see you in more pain. We will be careful," he ordered.

Hannah smiled sweetly. "As you say, husband." She settled her head on his chest and snuggled comfortably against him.

"I mean it, Hannah," Slain warned.

She raised her head once again and this time her smile was wicked. "I tell you what, husband, I will make certain we are careful and not disturb my bruise if you promise to show me more ways a loving husband and wife can please each other."

Slain smiled just as wickedly. "You have my word on that, wife."

Slain woke the next morning to Hannah slipping her tunic over her shift. "Where do you go, wife?"

"To fetch us food so that we may eat undisturbed and have more time alone," she said and hurried into her shoes.

A thump at the door had Slain saying, "Too late, Helice has brought us food and as soon as she leaves you can shed those garments and get back in bed with me, where you belong."

"You read my mind, husband," Hannah said with a grin and hurried to the door.

She threw it open with a flourish and screamed as a man, his face too bloodied to recognize collapsed against her, taking them both to the floor.

Chapter Thirty

Slain sprang out of bed, rushing to his wife's defense, grabbing the man and yanking him off Hannah, ready to do even more damage to him. Slain's anger fled him when he recognized the man.

"Melvin."

Hannah rushed to her feet. "Take him to my bedchamber while I get Helice."

Slain lifted the injured man with little difficulty while Hannah fled down the stairs. Her mind was filled with questions. What had happened to Melvin? Who had done this to him? Why had he come here? How had he even gotten here?

The east wing. It always seemed to come back to that mysterious wing of the keep and this time she intended to get answers.

"You are needed," Hannah said as she flew into the kitchen, grabbed Helice by the hand, and hurried her out. Helice did not hesitate and Hannah knew the woman feared something had happened to Slain.

When Helice saw the bloodied body on Hannah's bed, she paled and her hand went out to brace herself against the doorframe.

Hannah hurried to alleviate her fears. "It is Melvin."

A relieved breath shot from Helice and she hurried to the bed.

"Tell me what you need," Hannah said anxious to help.

"We need Neata, but I believe she was to leave today to visit the outer crofts," Helice said.

"Hopefully, she has not left yet. I will go see," Slain said from the open doorway, tucking his plaid in at the waist as he turned to leave.

He had dressed after placing Melvin on the bed and was ready to do whatever was necessary to help the man, and Hannah was grateful.

"Stay with him while I get what is needed," Helice ordered.

Hannah pulled a chair close to the bed and gently took hold of Melvin's hand. His knuckles were scraped and swollen, blood caked on them. He had fought, but then Melvin was a seasoned warrior and would have it no other way, even if victory was not possible.

"You are safe, Melvin," she said softly. "Slain fetches the healer Neata and between her and Helice they will make sure you get well."

Melvin fought to speak, but he grimaced horribly with pain when he did.

"It is all right. Do not worry. You are safe."

He struggled to speak and though Hannah urged him to stay quiet, he managed to say, before passing out, "Nial... fears."

What did Melvin mean? Was he saying Nial feared something? Nial always seemed fearless to her, but then no one was completely fearless. What could Nial possibly fear? If it was even Nial he had referred to.

Helice entered the room and chased Hannah out of the way. She got busy cleaning the blood off Melvin's face. It became obvious that he had taken a bad beating. One eye was completely swollen shut and the other close to it. It appeared as if his nose had been broken and the one corner of his lip was caked with blood and had swollen considerably. She prayed the rest of his body had not suffered as badly.

Hannah felt grateful that her silent prayers had been heard when Neata arrived, though she was not happy when Neata insisted that Hannah and Slain leave her and Helice alone to tend Melvin. Hannah hesitated to comply, worried for her friend, but Slain's firm arm around her shoulder had her out of the room before she could protest and when the door closed in her face, she buried her face in her husband's chest.

His powerful arms always comforted and protected, leaving her feeling that she was not alone and most of all that she was loved.

"Neata and Helice will take good care of him," Slain said.

Hannah had no doubt they would and with that reassuring thought, she glanced up at her husband. "Melvin tried to speak, though managed only two words. Nial fears."

"That is odd," Slain said. "Nial does not seem to fear anything. Come, we will get ourselves food and talk."

Hannah nodded and continued to offer silent prayers for Melvin as she followed her husband down the stairs.

It was not until they sat at a table in the Great Hall, clouds outside the windows and thunder rolling in the distance, did either of them speak.

"Does Melvin betray my father?" Hannah asked the thought having crossed her mind more than once.

"He does what is best for his clan," Slain said.

"He always has, but to go against my father," —she shook her head— "I never would have thought that. So Imus meets with Melvin to get information from him. Melvin is the one who betrays, not Imus."

"Things, events, happen to change people," he said, handing her a chunk of bread, determined to see that she ate since she had done nothing but poke at the food there. "You have learned that yourself as have I."

"I suppose," Hannah said, though she shook her head. "Still, I find it difficult to believe." She shook her head again. "If this attack had anything to do with his betrayal, my father's rage would have had him running a sword through Melvin. And what brought Melvin here?"

"That I do not know. No meeting was presently planned. Unless he learned something of importance and was bringing it to me. Someone could have followed him." Slain pointed to the piece of bread she held. "Eat. We will have answers as soon as he is able to speak."

Hannah did not know if it was a good sign or bad that Neata appeared, though the grave expression she wore seemed to signify the latter.

Neata wasted no time in delivering the news. "What injures I see are not enough damage for him not to wake, and he refuses to wake. I fear that he suffered more damage than I can see."

"Is there nothing we can do for him?" Slain asked.

"You know from what you have seen in battle that once a deep sleep claims someone, there is nothing we can do but wait, and pray. I will keep vigil at his side, but beyond that—" she shook her head.

Slain waited until Neata took her leave to say, "You need to eat so you can stay strong for Conlan and Melvin."

Knots twists in her stomach so badly that it revolted at the thought of food. "It is my fault they suffer. I should have returned home and faced whatever fate awaited me."

"Do not even think such nonsense," Slain said, taking hold of his wife's hand and finding it chilled, tucked it inside his shirt against his warm naked chest. "Melvin had made his decision before your arrival and Conlan helped Potsman because he is an honorable lad. This is not on your shoulders. This is your father's weight to bear and your stepbrother's. And this trouble between our clans has been long in the making. It is time to bring it to an end."

It pained her heart to ask, "You will kill my father?"

It troubled him to speak the truth to her, but he would have it no other way. "If he leaves me no choice. As for your step-brother... I will see him dead, not only for what he did to my father, but for what he did to you."

"I care not what happens to Nial, and I do not know why I should care what happens to my father. He cares nothing for me."

Slain brushed a delicate kiss on her cheek. "Whether good or bad, he is your father. Now eat." He handed her another piece of bread.

Hannah went to nibble at it while Slain reached for a piece for himself and stopped. "There is a secret passage in the east wing, is there not?" She nodded, answering it herself. "Of course there is. The east wing is how those who help you come and go. That is why a light is seen in the east wing and the villagers believe it is haunted. You meet with people, who must not be seen, and you come and go from there when you want no one to know what you are up to. That is how Melvin found his way to our bedchamber. He has been through that area before and knows the way." Her eyes spread wide, a realization striking her. "It was not a dream that night. You snatched me up after I hit my head on the door and carried me to bed. You were returning from somewhere you wanted no one to know about. Who else comes and goes so freely in our home?" she asked and her eyes widened again, though this time with fear. "Roark knows of it. You spoke with him there. Does Warrick know?" She shivered, just thinking that the dreadful man could enter the keep at will.

"Warrick always makes his arrival known."

Hannah stared at her husband, her heart pounding in her chest. "You plan just as my father plans. Only you have made it seem that you and your clan are vulnerable. That you have no warriors, no way of protecting yourself so that a trap could be set. When my father attacks, you will unleash your warriors." She stared in silence at him for a brief moment. "Your warriors or Warrick's warriors?"

"My warriors and some of Warrick's," Slain admitted, knowing it was useless to keep the truth from her.

"That is why Roark is here?" she asked. "He brought a troop of warriors to help you?"

Slain kept his voice low, not that there was anyone about to hear him. The brewing storm outside kept the villagers in their homes and Neata and Helice were busy with Melvin. Still, what he was about to tell her was for her ears alone. "I made a pact with Warrick."

Hannah shivered. It was like making a pact with the devil.

"I needed help in repairing the damage my clan had suffered due to your step-brother deceiving my unwitting father. Without Warrick's help my clan would have starved and lives would have been lost that winter. Your father was well aware that Warrick helped and it was the one reason he did not attack. He knew his warriors would suffer a dreadful defeat if he dared attack when Warrick's men were here. It gave me time to strengthen my defenses and prepare my warriors."

"That is where you go when you leave here?" Hannah asked.

"Aye, my warriors stay with a neighboring clan. The chief there fears your father and has offered his help so that his clan will remain safe from MacFillan. When Roark first arrived, the time you listened from the shadows, he was here to remind me that my debt was to be fully met if Warrick was to continue helping me."

"The reason you wed me... to settle part of the debt."

"I wed you because I fell hopelessly in love with you from the moment I saw you, though at the time I refused to believe it. The debt could have been settled easily since

Warrick wanted me to wed the daughter of a clan to the north of your father."

"Joining two clans that would be loyal to Warrick and essentially trapping my father between them."

"You have a sharp wit, wife. From what Roark has told me, Warrick feels our union will prove beneficial once your father accepts it. If not…"

"He will be forced to," Hannah said. "No wonder you have been slipping away and returning late, you have been busy planning."

"And adapting to unexpected changes."

"Me?" Hannah asked softly.

"Aye, you, wife," Slain said and kissed her lips gently. "Much changed when you entered my life and for the better. Perhaps Warrick is right. Perhaps our unexpected union will prove beneficial for all and battle can be avoided."

"I do not see how that will happen. My father is too hungry for power." Sadness filled her eyes for a moment, then they suddenly brightened. "Show me this secret passageway so that I may use it if necessary."

"No," Slain snapped.

"Why not?" Hannah asked, drawing back away from her husband. "I know the secret now so why not make me aware of the passageway?"

"I have my reasons."

"Then share them with me so I may understand," she said perplexed by his refusal and annoyed that the Great Hall door suddenly opened, preventing Slain from responding.

Imus struggled against a strong wind to shut the door before he made his way to them. "We must speak. It is urgent."

Slain nodded and stood. "You will remain inside today, the brewing storm no place for you to be."

Hannah could not understand why he was so reluctant about showing her the secret passageway in the east wing. It could prove helpful to her one day or at least that was her excuse for satisfying her curiosity. And what was this other part of the debt that her husband refused to settle or discuss with her? And why did Slain not seemed concerned that it would stop Warrick from helping him?

Sitting there brooding would do her no good, she cleared off the table, then went to see how Conlan was doing or if he needed anything. The lad was sound asleep. She was pleased to see he was no longer pale and there was no stench of a rotting wound. His bedding looked fresh as did the nightshirt he wore and his hair looked to have been combed, not a single tangle in it.

Helice took excellent care of him and Hannah could not be more grateful, and now she was doing the same for Melvin.

Hannah left Conlan sleeping, stopped by the closed solar doors to hear her husband and Imus' muffled voices, then made her way upstairs to see if she could be of any help to Helice and Neata.

The two women were talking quietly when she entered the room and she went to them.

"Can I be of help?" she asked softly.

After only a few moments, Helice was headed to the kitchen to prepare a couple of brews that Conlan and Melvin would need and Neata left to gather more of her healing plants while Hannah remained to keep an eye on Melvin.

His pale face alarmed her as did the way he lay there so lifeless, not even making the slightest movement. His face was so badly bruised that he was unrecognizable. She prayed he would wake. Prayed he would survive. Prayed that whoever did this to him would be caught and punished.

Hannah almost jumped off the chair when his eyes suddenly sprang open and he struggled to speak. It was a good sign, and she leaned over him, wanting to offer encouragement and hope. "You are doing well. You need rest and time to heal."

Melvin continued to struggle to speak and Hannah hurried to scoop up the ladle in the bucket nearby and dribbled some of the water slowly into his mouth.

Melvin took it eagerly and once his lips were moist he managed to say, "All lies." He winced in pain and once again his eyes drifted closed.

Hannah sat back in the chair frustrated. He was obviously trying to tell her something, and something important if he was willing to bear the pain it cost him, but what was it?

"We must talk, Hannah."

Hannah jumped out of the chair and turned to see her husband standing in the doorway, his look solemn.

"Is Conlan all right? I just left him and he was fine," Hannah said, rushing over to him.

"Conlan is doing well."

"Then why do you wear such a solemn face?" A thought hit her and she gasped. "Is the attack imminent?"

His hand gently took her by the arm. "Come with me."

Hannah's heart began to beat wildly. Something was wrong. Very wrong. "What is it, Slain?"

They were about to enter their bedchamber when the bell sounded an alarm that penetrated the keep walls.

Hannah pulled away from her husband and ran to the stairs. "We must hurry."

Slain grabbed her arm, stopping her before her foot hit the first steps. "Your father is dead."

Chapter Thirty-one

Hannah stared at her husband, shaking her head. "How is that possible and how could you know this? He is on his way home."

Slain had not wanted to deliver the news so bluntly, but he had little time and even less now knowing who had arrived. "I had men following your father. I thought he might not leave, but camp somewhere until his army could join him here and they could attack. It was what I would have done and your father thought the same. They camped not that far from here."

"How?" she asked, shock more than sorrow sending a tremble through her.

"I do not know how he died only that he is dead, and I am sorry I had to tell you so directly, but that bell warns of your step-brother's arrival and I wanted you aware of your father's passing before you faced him."

Hannah reached for her husband's hand, needing his strength. "Then let us go and see what he has to say, though I fear it will be mostly lies we hear from him."

Slain pressed a gentle hand to her cheek. "You are up to this?"

"As long as you are by my side." She clutched his hand tighter. "Besides, I want to know what happened to my father. It might help me shed a tear for him since right now I have none."

"I will not leave your side," he assured her.

Hannah followed behind her husband, wondering what this would mean for her clan with her being her father's only heir. Could peace finally exist between the Clan MacFillan and the Clan MacKewan? It certainly was not a legacy her father would have wanted to leave.

The villagers had formed a path to the keep as they had done before and once again they stood with weapons in hand prepared for whatever may come.

Hannah stood beside her husband, thinking it had been barely a full day that she last spoke with her father and now he was dead. It simply made no sense to her. All he had planned. All he had strived for gone in an instant. What could have happened?

Slain turned to his wife and gave her hand a squeeze. "I am here with you. You are not alone."

It hit her then. Her mum and da were both gone, if not for Slain she would be alone. Or worse, she would be stuck with her step-brother.

"I love you, wife, and always will. We are family and we will share a good life together."

He was letting her know that while she had lost one family, she had gained another, and he planned on having a long life with her. His strong message touched her heart and filled her with strength.

They both turned at the sound of approaching horses and there in the lead rode Nial. Behind him was her father's body draped over his horse. Nial rode up to them, dismounted without a word, and went and tugged her father's body off the horse to drop a short distance in front of Hannah.

"See what your husband has done to your father," Nial accused, pointing at the bloodied body.

"Watch how you speak to my wife or you will lose your tongue," Slain warned. "And I remind you only one more time, do not speak to Hannah without my permission."

Hannah's limbs turned weak upon staring at her father's brutally beaten body and she fought to keep her composure, not giving her step-brother the satisfaction of seeing her crumble. It helped that her husband stood close and defended her, but she would have her say.

"My husband did no such thing and how dare you disrespect my father by dropping him on the ground like nothing more than a dead animal," Hannah chided. "How did this happen with so many of his warriors around him?"

"He went into the woods alone and never came out. We searched for him and this was how we found him, pummeled so viciously that he is barely recognizable."

Hannah thought of Melvin and how badly he had been beaten. Could the same person have beaten both men, the two beatings being so similar?

"You have brought shame on your clan and death to your father and I am here to tell you that I will revenge his death as the new chief of the Clan MacFillan," Nial announced for all to hear.

"The chief of a clan is not a position you can appoint yourself to," Slain reminded. "If there is no heir than the clansmen decide who will be the new chief of a clan," Slain said.

A sneer of a smile spread across Nial's face. "But there is an heir."

"Aye, Hannah is Ross MacFillan's heir and since she is my wife that makes me Chief of the Clan MacKewan," Slain informed him, though Nial's sneer told him there was more to it than the man was saying.

Nial raised his chin. "I am no step-son to Ross MacFillan. I am *his son*. My mother gave MacFillan something her mother," —he gave a nod at Hannah— "never could... a son. In time, my father intended to rightfully claim me as his heir, future chief of the Clan MacFillan. I now claim that right."

"What proof do you have?' Slain asked.

"A letter from my mother to Ross MacFillan telling him I am his son," Nial said.

"That proves nothing but the rantings of a woman who looks to secure a future for her son," Slain said.

Hannah listened as if from a distance as the two continued to exchange words. If this was true, why had her father not made mention of it when they talked? Why wait? Why not tell her that Nial would be chief? This could not be happening. It was a nightmare and she had yet to wake. It was not real. Not real. It was all lies.

All lies.

That was what Melvin had said to her. He knew something. Melvin knew something. Was that why he suffered a beating? Had Nial something to do with it? Had he tried to keep Melvin from telling the truth?

"Take your foolish rantings and leave my land," Slain ordered.

"I will leave, but I will return and revenge my father's death."

"As I will revenge mine and it will not be a fast death I deliver upon you... I promise you that."

Nial raised a fist, anger sparking in his eyes. "This land will be mine and my sister will suffer for the shame she has brought to her clan."

"You tempt the savage and he will make you suffer far worse than I will. Now leave!"

Nial went to pick up Ross MacFillan's body.

"Leave him! It is his daughter's right, his *heir's* right, to bury him," Slain ordered.

"He is my father," Nial said, his fist pounding his chest.

"That has yet to be proven," Slain said.

"He needs to be buried on MacFillan soil," Nail argued.

"Ross MacFillan was willing to fight for this land. It is only fitting that at least in death he gets to claim a small spot of it."

"You dishonor your father like this?" Nail said, turning to Hannah.

Hannah agreed with her husband. "I give my father what he always wanted, a piece of MacKewan land,"

"You will rue this day, both of you," Nail said, his face pinched in anger.

"Be gone!" Slain commanded with a sharp tongue and dismissed him with a quick snap of his hand as if he did nothing more than swat away an annoying gnat.

Nial mounted and rode off, the first drop of rain falling on his angry red face.

"We need to get your father out of the rain and prepared for burial," Slain said and a few men stepped forward at his command.

Blair approached of her own accord. "Some of the other women and I will prepare him for you."

"I should do it," Hannah said, though did not know if she wanted to. With her mum, it had been different. She had wanted to help the women prepare her for her final resting place. She had selfishly wanted as much time with her mum before she was laid to rest, never to see her again. Her father not so much. He had no time for her while alive and she felt no need to spare him any time now.

"Conlan and Melvin need you more," Slain said. "Let Blair see to it."

Hannah did not argue. She cast one last look at her father and turned to enter the keep. A chill had crept into her bones and she walked over to the fireplace and stood in front of it, rubbing her arms to warm herself. She tried to call on some good memories of her father, but she could find none. She had been a disappointment to him since the day she was born. He never loved her.

A tear dropped from her eye and splattered on the hearth. Why cry for a man who cared nothing for her? It was not the man she cried for, but what he had failed to be for her... a da. Another teardrop fell, then another and another.

Strong hands took hold of her arms, turned her around, and powerful arms wrapped around her tight, her husband easing her close against him while she cried. She did not let herself cry long, sniffling the tears back as she looked up at him. "Wasted tears."

He wiped at her wet cheeks with his thumb. "Tears help heal in their own way."

Hannah let another tear fall, though not for her father. "I am so grateful you love me."

Slain ran his thumb lightly over her lips. "Promise me nothing will ever change that."

"I promise," Hannah said and kissed the tip of his thumb. "You have no worry of that." Yet Hannah saw worry swirl in his dark eyes. "I love you, Slain, nothing can change that."

Hannah felt his doubt as he kissed her lips gently, and she wondered over it.

~~~

Slain had left Hannah sitting with Melvin. She wanted to be there if the man woke again and see if she could find out if what Nial had told them was all lies. He wanted to go see her father's body and he wanted someone else to see it as well. He had sent a message before joining Hannah in the Great Hall.

Slain walked with his hood tucked down over his head to keep the rain from slashing at his face as he approached the cottage where MacFillan had been taken for preparation. There were things about the beatings and even Conlan's stabbing that disturbed him, familiar things, and he wanted someone else to confirm what he believed.

"Is he here?" Slain asked Imus, waiting outside the cottage door for him.

Imus nodded and opened the door and entered after Slain.

Slain did not greet Roark, the man was far too engrossed in looking over the body to be disturbed. Slain had known Roark would waste no time in responding to his message and with Warrick's warriors camped nearby it would not have taken him long to get here.

"I thought your message foolish, so I had no choice but to see for myself," Roark said, not taking his eyes off the body that had been partially cleaned for burial. "Tell me about the other attacks."

"Potsman was attacked and beaten about the face when he caught someone setting fire to a storage shed. The young lad, Conlan, suffered a stab wound to his side attempting to help Potsman. Conlan somehow managed to escape his attacker. I believe it was because the lad is quick on his feet. Both of them described their attacker as a dark shadow. The next person attacked Melvin. He is barely recognizable from the beating he suffered and barely able to speak when awake. If my assumption proves true, then I would say that Melvin managed to escape his attacker before he could stab him. That brings us to Ross MacFillan, my wife's father. You can see for yourself he was not as lucky as the others."

"He was stabbed, his death not quick," Roark said.

Slain walked over to the body on the table and looked to where he knew the wound would be, then turned his eyes on Roark. "Now you know why I summoned you."

Roark shook his head. "I cannot believe that one of Warrick's warriors would do this. Every one of them has seen what Warrick does to anyone who betrays him. Yet the signs say differently."

"I watched myself as Warrick had his enemies beaten until they were unrecognizable, stabbed in the side to die slowly, and those he deemed the worst offenders he had stripped of their garments so no one could identify them when they were dumped near their clan to die."

"Warrick returned the brutality in kind," Roark said in defense of the mighty warrior.

"In more cases than not," Slain agreed. "But we both stand here and see with our own eyes what was done to this man and I have seen what was done to the others. All of it points to the attacker being one of Warrick's warriors, and since you seemed as troubled by it as I am, I assume these attacks have nothing to do with orders from Warrick."

"Not one," Roark confirmed, "and I find it difficult to believe that a warrior in my troop would do this and yet…" He shook his head again. "The proof is before me."

"Who and why? That is what I do not understand. Why chance Warrick's wrath, if it is one of his warriors? The warrior must know that Warrick will see him suffer horribly before he dies. What could possibly be so important for him to take such a chance?"

"I do not know, but I intend to find out if anyone of them is foolish enough to do so," Roark said and rubbed at his brow. "Warrick is going to be furious when he learns of this and if what you tell me of your wife's suffering in his dungeon is true," —he shook his head again— "he will unleash hell."

"We should find out all we can before—"

"Do you suggest I wait to notify Warrick of what goes on here?" Roark snapped.

Slain's response was sparked with anger. "You think I would condemn you to death?" It was Slain's turn to shake his head. "You know better than that, Roark. I believe it would be best if we found out all we could before Warrick's arrival since we both know this news will bring him here."

Roark rubbed his brow again. "You are right. Warrick will come. He has debts to collect from you and Craven."

"Craven is indebted to him as well? How is Craven? It has been a year now since he lost his wife, but I know how much he loved her. It cannot be easy for him." Slain felt Craven's loss now more than ever since he loved his wife and could not see life without her.

"Craven owes Warrick. He wed Warrick's healer who set fire to his dungeon."

Slain recalled his wife mentioning a healer's help. "So that was how Hannah escaped. I owe the woman my gratitude and Warrick should consider the same since innocent people were being sold to the guard for disposal."

Roark groaned. "Hell will be nothing to what Warrick will unleash when he learns of all this."

"Then it is best if we can discover what goes on here and have good news for him."

"Agreed," Roark said.

"I wonder over the reason for these attacks. Potsman stumbled on the fire being set and Conlan came to his aid, so they were not planned. Those attacks were to protect the culprit from being discovered. Melvin may have discovered something himself and was on the way to tell me when he was attacked. As for MacFillan?" Slain's brow wrinkled. "I wonder. Was it planned or had something happened that precipitated it?"

Roark asked the questioned that remained a complete mystery to both men. "Most of all, though, why would one of Warrick's warriors be involved in this matter?"

~~~

Hannah sat staring at Melvin, though her mind was elsewhere. She was trying to comprehend the news that Nial claimed to be her father's son. Nial was two years older than her and that would mean that her father knew Nial's mother well before Hannah was born. Yet if she understood what her father had made mention of, he did not turn to another woman's bed until after Hannah was born. It also continued to disturb her that he would not have told her there and then when they had spoken that Nial was his son. It would have been the perfect time to denounce her as his heir and claim Nial his son, especially since he had been so angry with her. Why had he not done that?

All lies.

It always brought her back to Melvin's words and she wondered how many lies she had been told through the years.

Hannah had been so engrossed in her thoughts that she had not heard Neata enter the room so she jumped when the woman was suddenly standing in front of her with several poultices heaped in a basket.

"Go. I have work to do here," Neata ordered.

Hannah did not hesitate. She took her leave so that Neata could see to healing Melvin.

She headed for the stairs in search of her husband when she noticed that the east wing door sat ajar. In all the excitement, someone had forgotten to lock it.

Never go in the east wing.

The warning, she had heard so often, rang clearly in her mind, but the need to learn all the secrets of the keep tugged stronger at her. Her decision was made without hesitation and she pulled the door open and stepped into the east wing.

Dim torches produced enough light to guide her way and she hurried her steps, not knowing how long she had before she was discovered. Her heart beat faster with every step she took, wondering and a bit fearful of what she would find behind the door at the end of the hall.

Her courage waned as she got closer and, fearful she would turn and run, she rushed her steps and grasped the door latch and pushed the door open.

A chill hit her, shivering her down to her bones and nothing but darkness greeted her, much like it had when she had first entered the keep. Not a candle flickered or a hearth burned.

She stepped away from the open door and walked over to the nearest torch cradled in a wall sconce. The torch did not burn strongly, but it would be enough light to at least guide her. She had to stand on her toes to reach it and even that was a struggle, but she managed to get it.

Hannah gripped it firmly in her hand and the torch quivered as she approached the open door, her hand trembling so badly it was difficult to hold it still. For a moment she hesitated, the quiver running down through her legs and before she lost all courage, she plunged into the darkness.

Chapter Thirty-two

The torch only shed so much light and Hannah could not hold it high if she was to see where she walked. She caught sight of something and approached cautiously. The closer she got, she saw that it was a desk, pieces of parchment strewn across it. She held the torch closer to the top of the desk once she was upon it.

The drawing she had once seen in her husband's solar lay on top of several other drawings. The one that had appeared to be a board with small spikes protruding out of it. Only now there were ropes attached to the ends. She moved it aside and looked at the next drawing. There were different size chairs and stools all with various size spikes sticking up out of them.

Her eyes glazed over for a moment, a memory flashing before her. A man being pushed down on a small stool, on the spikes, his screams echoing in her ears.

Hannah's eyes sprang open.

Torture devices.

These were designs for torture devices.

She froze, thinking what this meant and something caught her attention in the darkness, and she raised the torch up slowly over her head.

Hannah stared in disbelief as she turned around slowly in a circle, staring in horror. On every wall hung some type of torture device. When her eyes fell on an unlit torch in a wall sconce, she hurried over to it and lit it with her torch and did the same to three more in the room. The last sconce sat empty and she filled it with the one in her hand.

Shock had her continuing to stare and turn, trying to comprehend what she was seeing and what it meant. She gasped a few times when she recognized some she had seen when held prisoner in Warrick's dungeon. Ones that would have been used on her if she had not escaped. When her glance settled on the shackles and chains, she winced, remembering the pain those had brought her.

She continued to turn slowly, disbelief and horror growing in her, roiling her stomach and gripping at her heart. Never had she expected to find this. Never had she expected her husband to…

Hannah gasped when she turned to see the dark outline of a man standing in the open doorway until light flickered across him… Slain.

"You designed these," Hannah accused, hoping she was wrong.

"Aye, wife, I designed them." Slain admitted, hating himself for being the cause of the fear and horror that burned in her eyes. He had feared her discovering his secret, feared he would lose her love, and from the look on her face, he feared he had been right.

"Why?" she demanded, fighting the tears that threatened her eyes.

"War brings out the worst in people and torture is part of war."

"Warrick made you do this?" she asked, wanting to lay blame on someone else, not wanting her husband responsible for all this horror.

"It would be easy for me to say it was his fault, but it would not be true. Torture devices have long been used. I took what I had seen and expanded on it. I created the first device of my own volition. No one forced me to do it. After the results proved more beneficial than expected, I continued to create them."

"How could you? How could you do that to people?"

"I have seen far worse things done to people than these torture devices can do," Slain said, unable to keep anger out of his voice or the horrible memories from his mind. "I hoped these would prevent more suffering."

"How could suffering prevent more suffering?" Hannah asked, shaking her head.

"By learning things before they happened and saving people from being brutally slaughtered."

"What about the innocent ones?"

Slain knew she was referring to herself and she had every right to. "There were no innocent ones and I do this no more."

"Do not lie to me. She went to his desk and held up a drawing, shaking it at him. "I saw this in your solar shortly after my arrival and you have added to it."

"That was the other thing Warrick wanted from me, to create something he could use himself on someone. It is made of leather and can easily be used by one man and I finished it in case I had no choice. Then I met you and learned of your suffering. That ended any thought of giving that drawing to Warrick."

"Then why keep this place? Burn these things and be done with it," —she gasped, the drawing falling from her hand to the floor— "you plan on using some of these."

"That had been my plan, but no more. It is a quick death I will deliver to Nial and be done with it, so that we may live in peace."

"Peace?" Her voice trembled. "How could there be peace with these horrible devices in our home, not far from our bedchamber?"

"I keep them as a reminder of what they cost me... my soul."

"Your soul is not lost to you, but I will be if you do not rid the keep of these horrible things," she threatened.

"You will not dictate to me, wife," he commanded.

"On this I will," Hannah said, the tears she had kept at bay shining in her eyes along with defiance. She took strong steps to the door, to her husband, intending to push past him. He had a different thought and grabbed her arm. She yanked it free, stumbling and turning as she did.

Slain did not hesitate to grab his wife around the waist and swing her around as he shifted his body to keep her from falling into the spiked devices on the wall. He saved her, but one of the devices with long protruding spikes caught his shoulder, tearing his shirt and ripping at his flesh.

He let out an oath.

"You are hurt," Hannah said with alarm.

"More than you will ever know," Slain said through gritted teeth.

A section of the wall suddenly opened and in stepped Roark. He looked from one to the other, then settled a look on Slain. "This is important."

"I will send Helice to tend your wound," Hannah said and eased out of her husband's arms, though she felt his reluctance to release her.

"No, you will tend me when I finish here. We have things to discuss. Go wait in our bedchamber," he ordered.

Hannah nodded and hurried out of the room, Slain closing the door behind her. She was far too distraught to do as her husband said. She was also upset that he had gotten hurt protecting her. He had not hesitated to keep her safe and had done so without thought to his own safety. That he loved her and would do anything to keep her from harm was not in question.

She made her way down to the Great Hall in search of Helice and found her coming out of Conlan's room.

"The lad does well. He is sleeping," Helice said a scowl crossing her face. "What is wrong? You are pale and upset."

"Slain needs you to tend him. He suffered a minor injury. He is in the room at the end of the east wing. Roark is with him," she said and went to turn away.

"You discovered his secret," Helice said.

Hannah nodded.

"Now what will you do?" Helice demanded. "Run away in fright? Stop loving him?"

"I will never stop loving Slain," Hannah snapped.

"Yet you look ready to run."

"I wish he had told me from the beginning."

"And what would you have done?" Helice shook her head. "You would not have bothered to stay here and discover Slain's true worth. You would have condemned him and hated him without giving him a chance. You have come to know him and love him. He is a good man. Do not make him pay for something that has already cost him dearly."

Hannah turned away without a word and left the keep through the kitchen, grabbing a cloak from the hook as she went. Once outside, she stopped and glanced around. She had no desire to speak with anyone. She wanted to be alone to think or perhaps it was better if she did not think. So much had happened today that she felt overwhelmed and there would be more to come, Nial would make sure of it.

She made her way to the nearest barn and was not surprised to find it empty. Her husband had purposely made it appear as if he had nothing, not horse nor weapon, and certainly no warriors to defend his clan. She could only imagine the army of warriors he had put together and with Warrick's warriors here to help, Nial did not have a chance. Her husband would defeat him and take his life.

A shiver ran through her. Nial was not foolish and he was good at making people believe him. She had believed him when her father had brought his new wife and step-son home. He had been kind to Hannah, at least she believed so until her father started accusing her of things she had not done. That was when she learned how well Nial could lie.

That no longer mattered. Slain would protect her just as he had done a short time ago.

Hannah found a small stool and placed it by the door to sit. The rain had stopped, but the clouds remained. She looked out over the land, the village, a short distance away, clansmen going about their chores, children at play, women in chatter. This was her home, her clan, her family. Here was where she would raise her children, live her life, love her husband until she took her last breath, though her love for him would never die.

She could never stop loving Slain. It was not possible. Her heart belonged to him. The thought had her recalling a remark her husband had made.

I fear you will stop loving me.

Had he been worried about what would happen when she discovered his secret? She was upset to learn it. Actually, it had shocked her to see all those torture devices. It had flooded her with memories. Ones she wanted desperately to keep locked away. But not once while in that room did she feel hatred toward him. Not once had her love for him been in question.

Helice was right. If she had learned of this before she had gotten to know him, she would have run. She would have thought him a monster or the savage everyone claimed him to be, but he was far from either. He was an honorable man who put his clan and family before himself and did what was necessary to keep them safe.

She swept at the tear that fell from her eye, annoyed she was crying again today. She had not cried so since her mum died and her father had warned her to stop with a hard slap to her face. He had told her she was weak, but now she wondered if it was simply because he had hated her.

Slain did not mind her tears. He held her every time she cried and comforted her. He never chided her for being weak and was generous in sharing his strength if he thought she needed it.

Find a husband who will be good to you.

Hannah smiled recalling her mum's words and looked up to the heavens. "I found a good husband, Mum."

~~~

"You are bleeding," Roark said when Slain turned and walked to the desk.

"Hannah will see to it," Slain said.

"She did not look like she wanted anything to do with you."

"Mind your tongue, Roark," Slain warned, all too aware of how his wife had looked at him and his heart ached having seen the hurt in her eyes and having felt how she did not want to be near him. He wanted nothing more than to go find her and make it right. No matter what it took. First, he had to see what brought Roark here without notice. "Tell me what is so important that you come here unannounced."

Roark wasted no time in explaining. "You are aware we travel with two black shrouds in case something happens we have another to wear."

"And put the fear of God in people upon first sight just as Warrick intended," Slain said.

Roark nodded. "That it does, and it seems that one of my warriors lost one of his shrouds and did not think it important to tell me."

"Or was too fearful to."

"He is fearful now for his punishment will be severe."

"Does he know where he lost it?" Slain asked.

"He believed he did but when he went to collect it, he was told it was not there."

"And where is there?"
"Here with a woman in your village," Roark said.
"Who?" Slain demanded.
"Your healer, Neata."

~~~

Hannah left the barn to return to the keep. She would go wait for Slain in their bedchamber so they could talk. It was foolish of her to hurry off in anger when the only way things could be settled was for them to talk. One thing was certain, though, the torture devices had to be removed from the keep, better still was for them to be destroyed.

"Hannah."

She turned to see Wilona approaching.

"Neata has sent me on an errand and thought you might want to help. I am to collect," —she waved a plant in the air— "whatever this is for her. She needs it to brew for not only my husband but the other two injured as well."

Hannah did not recognize the plant but then she was familiar with only a few of the plants a healer used. What concerned her more was going into the woods when Slain had strictly forbidden her from going there alone and though she would be with Wilona, she wondered if it would be wise to do.

Wilona seemed to sense her reluctance or perhaps it was her own concern that had her saying, "The plant grows near the edge of the woods, so we do not have to fear going too far."

Hannah would have preferred to return to the keep and to her husband, but she also wanted to do her part in helping Neata with whatever she needed to get Conlan, Melvin, and Potsman well.

"We keep to the edge of the woods," Hannah said.

Wilona shivered. "I have no wont to go any further with what has been happening."

~~~

Slain went to his bedchamber to take Hannah with him to speak with Neata. He wanted to include her with what was happening. He wanted no more secrets between them. She was his wife and needed to be kept apprised of all that went on in the clan and see that he kept nothing from her. Though, more than anything, he wanted to make certain that her discovery of his secret had done no irreparable damage to them. That she still wanted to remain his wife. That she still loved him.

He shook his head and felt a jolt to his heart when he found their bedchamber empty. He did not think she had run off. It was that she had not gone to their bedchamber that spoke louder than words. It announced to him that she no longer wished to share it with him.

It hurt to realize it, but he had faced difficult battles before and though this probably would be one of the most if not the most difficult one he would face, it was one he intended to win.

He went to her bedchamber, intending on filling it with a bairn as soon as possible so that she did not have another room to retreat to, hoping she was there keeping watch over Melvin. He did not find her there, though he did find Neata.

"He still sleeps, though it was good he woke and spoke with Hannah," Neata said when she turned as he entered the room. "Time will only tell if he survives."

"Old warriors never stop fighting," Slain said.

"Then he should survive, but you did not come here to see how Melvin does. There is something else on your mind." She frowned. There is blood seeping into your shirt at your shoulder."

He dismissed her worry with a wave of his hand. "It is not important."

"It most certainly is," Helice said entering the room.

He would learn nothing if he did not let the two, motherly women tend his wound. He quickly slipped his shirt off and sat on a chair. "Hurry and be done with it."

They both went to work on him.

Slain did not waste another minute in asking, "Did one of Roark's men come to you for healing, Neata?"

"This is about the black shroud." Neata nodded, confirming it before Slain could. "I should have told you when the warrior came in search of it. That day got busier and it completely slipped from my mind. I will tell you what I told the warrior. I do not recall seeing it, but he could have very well left it in my cottage only to be picked up by someone else." She shook her head. "I saw needier clansmen than usual that day he came to me."

"Tell me who may have had a chance to take it without you noticing."

Neata scrunched her brow, searching for memories of that day. "I remember the day was warmer than usual and I tended some minor wounds outside, so some never entered my cottage."

"The warrior had been in your cottage?"

"His problem required privacy."

"Who did you see in your cottage after him?" Slain asked.

Neata shook her head. "I cannot recall tending anyone in my cottage after that."

"If that was so the shroud should still be there." Slain never once thought Neata would betray him. She had been with the clan far too long and had been far too faithful to his parents.

"I remember now," Neata said. "I needed something for someone I was tending and Wilona offered to get the dried plant from the cottage for me. She was the only one to enter there after the warrior left."

Chapter Thirty-three

"Look," Wilona said, pointing to a batch of plants a short distance into the woods. "More than enough." She hurried toward the blossoming batch."

Hannah followed, wanting to be done, not comfortable being in the woods with what had gone on here and especially since her husband had warned her against it. She stopped suddenly, her eyes on the plant Wilona rushed toward and her heart quickened. She recognized the plant now that she saw it blooming and realized it had no healing properties. It simply brightened the forest with its beauty.

Hannah did not hesitate, she turned to run, and she took no more than a few steps when she was shoved to the ground. She had no time to scramble to her feet, strong hands yanked her up and she was not surprised to see it was Nial. The only thing Hannah could think to do was scream, hoping someone would hear her.

Her scream barely made it out of her mouth when Nial's fist connected with her jaw, plunging her into darkness.

~~~

Slain barely let the two women finish dressing his wound when he slipped his torn shirt back on and rushed out of the room, Helice following him.

"You say you saw her leave the keep?" Slain asked as they entered the Great Hall.

"Aye, she was upset after discovering what was in the east wing, though she did say she would never stop loving you."

Slain stopped and turned to Helice. "She still loves me?"

"One can see in her eyes how much she loves you. They shine with concern, desire, joy, and so much more whenever she looks at you. It is like you are a gift to her that she gets the pleasure of unwrapping each day. She would not be so foolish to cast such a loving gift aside."

"I should have told her. If anything has happened to her," —he shook his head— "I need to find her." He hurried to the door, his heart pounding viciously against his chest in fear. He swung it open to find Imus running toward the keep. He rushed to meet him.

"Blair thought she saw Hannah going into the woods with Wilona and a scream was heard not too long after."

Slain took little time to explain about Wilona, then ordered Imus to gather the men.

"I will join the hunt," Helice said. "I should have stopped her, knowing she was upset."

"The blame is mine and mine alone. You will remain here and see to Conlan and Melvin and be ready to tend my wife when I return with her."

"I have not been kind to her, mostly for fear that she would bring you pain when she has brought you only love. Even with my harsh nature, she asked me to be grandmother to your children since they will have none. She claims I will be a good one."

"You will be a good grandmother and I will see that you get that chance. I will bring my wife home safe."

"No more secrets, Slain. It has done neither of us any good. I will wait for your return. Do not disappoint me." Helice turned and entered the keep, her steps slower than usual.

It did not take long for the men to gather and orders to be given, and Slain took the lead as they entered the woods.

When Hannah finally had her wits about her, she saw that she was sitting on the ground her back braced against a thick tree trunk and her hands tied in front of her. Her bottom was damp from the chilled, wet ground, though she was glad for it, since it was probably what had helped her to wake. She tasted blood in her mouth and her jaw, that had yet to heal from her previous injury, ached terribly.

She watched Wilona talking with Nial and wondered about the pair. Why did the woman help him when she seemed to care for her husband? Or was that a ruse? Nial persuaded with lies like no one she had ever known. Had he persuaded Wilona?

Nial turned and seeing her awake, smiled and walked over to her. "Unlike your husband, I know how to make a woman obey."

"Like you have done with poor Wilona here?" Hannah asked with a nod to the woman.

"We love each other. I am going to be his wife," Wilona said, wrapping her arm around Nial's.

Hannah shook her head, not knowing if it was sorrow or annoyance she felt for the foolish woman. "You are a peasant and beneath what he wants for himself. He will not wed you. Besides, you already have a husband."

"Potsman would be gone by now if Conlan had not interfered," Nial said.

"The lad was too fast for you and you never expected Potsman to hide, leaving you unable to finish him," Hannah said, baiting him to show Wilona his true worth and hoping it might make her realize she was not safe with him. Then perhaps she would help Hannah and they both could escape Nial. It was all she could presently think of to do while praying Slain had discovered what happened and was on his way to her. Wherever it is she was.

"Do not forget Melvin. Your father always claimed Melvin was his strongest and bravest warrior, he never realized how his brave warrior had betrayed him."

"Melvin betrayed no one, he did what was best for the clan," Hannah argued.

Nial laughed. "You are a fool. His reason was far different than you ever imagined. An opportunity presented itself for him to finally get what he always wanted... revenge."

"Revenge for what?" Hannah asked perplexed, not understanding at all.

"For me killing the only woman he ever loved... your mother."

Hannah glared at him in disbelief.

"You truly are ignorant of what went on in your own home, but then your mother was good at keeping secrets."

"What are you talking about?" Hannah demanded, her anger rising. Could it be true? Did Nial kill her mother?

"Your mother needed to be out of the way if my mum's plan was to work."

Hannah listened, feeling more the fool with each word he spewed.

"My mum realized your father was barren after coupling with him for a few months, long before your mum had you, and not getting with child. Your father was not the loyal husband that he claimed to be. My mum never let him know that she already had a son. She kept me hidden away so that she could later claim me as his child. The opportunity presented itself when your mum learned of his liaison with my mother. Fearful she would never bear him a child, your mum turned to Melvin who had loved her at first sight, and he believed she loved him. I believed she used him to get with child to give your father the heir he wanted, expected of his wife."

"How do you know this?' Hannah demanded, not believing him.

"The lass that tended your mum saw most of what was going on, your mum thinking her trustworthy or perhaps invisible, never believing she would say a word. Never knowing how persuasive I could be with a woman. Never knowing I would do whatever was necessary to see that secrets were kept."

Hannah realized what he was saying. The servant lass who had tended her mum had not died of an accident. Nial had killed her. She looked to Wilona who did not seem at all to understand that Nial was admitting to using women to achieve his goals and disposing of them when they no longer served his needs.

Nial went on. "Your father was a fool, never thinking his wife would betray him with another man. He may have been disappointed his wife gave him a daughter, but to him you were his blood. When you were born and your mother claimed she and your father could couple no more, something that came more from anger than truth, according to your mum's servant, your father returned to my mum. Her plan once again took shape." He grinned proudly. "My mum planned to wed your father one day and when the time was right reveal me as his son. When I was old enough, my mum explained her plan to me and I was more than pleased with it. The time finally came when we had to do away with your mum. Poisoning her was easy, the cook always making something special for her. With me entertaining the lass that looked after your mum, it gave me the perfect opportunity. A concoction here and there applied to her food or drink worked well, making everyone think she was ill, beyond help so that when she finally died no one suspected anything."

A pain ripped through Hannah's heart so badly, she thought she would die. Never had she ever suspected that her mum had been poisoned. That it had happened in front of her own eyes and she never saw it, was never able to help her, never able to stop it from claiming her mum's life.

"Unfortunately, my mum took ill and was not able to enjoy the fruits of her hard earned work. But she encouraged me to achieve our plan and I had no intention of disappointing her after all she had sacrificed for me," he said. "Unfortunately, I had not counted on Melvin's betrayal. I knew he did not trust me, and though he betrayed your father, I never thought he would betray his clan. I also never expected your father to defend him." He shook his head. "Your father came upon me in the woods beating Melvin. He attacked me, defending his friend, not knowing who I was since I wore the black shroud of Warrick's warriors and knowing intimately of their ways."

Hannah listened, her heart breaking that one man could do so much to destroy her family, her clan, and that she, Melvin, and Conlan had been the only ones to have seen him for what he truly was, a lying, vile man.

"I tried to explain that Melvin had betrayed him and the clan and I was doing what was needed to protect him. He would not believe me. He claimed that Melvin was like a brother to him and would never betray him. Then I told him that Melvin and your mum had been lovers and that Melvin was your father. But all was not lost that I was his son. He had a true heir to the Clan MacFillan. He roared with fury, called me a liar, insisted Melvin would never betray him, and denied my claim as his son. Then he made the fatal mistake of telling me I would never lead the Clan MacFillan." Nial grinned. "He was wrong. I beat him unmercifully, then slid my dagger into him and left him to die slowly alone in the woods, a fitting punishment for denying me. While I unleashed my anger on your father, Melvin managed to slip away. No doubt he is feast for the beasts in the woods by now. And now I will lay claim to the

Clan MacFillan and all its lands and eventually all the lands around me."

Hannah made no mention that Melvin had survived and her heart went out to the man who possibly was her father, the news still to startling to comprehend. "You are insane if you believe that. You will never defeat my husband. He will rule over the Clan MacFillan."

Nial's nostrils flared in anger. "I cannot wait to be rid of you."

"The feeling is mutual, *brother*."

"Time to leave," he snapped and turned to go to his horse.

Hannah had to borrow time. She could not let him take her away from here. Away from her home, since she doubted they were that far from the keep. He would not bother dragging Wilona along, since she had served her purpose. He would want to be rid of her sooner rather than later.

"He is deceiving you, Wilona. He is going to kill you. You have done all you can for him. He needs you no more," Hannah said, hoping to incite with words and delay their departure.

"You lie. You have lied since your arrival here," Wilona spat.

"Wilona," Nial snapped and the woman looked contrite.

At least Hannah now knew she was still on MacKewan soil. "He prays on the weak and the vulnerable."

"I am neither," Wilona defended. "I am strong, having put up with Potsman for as long as I have. Nial and I found each other by accident. I did not know who he was until after we secretly met a few times."

"By then you knew you loved him and would do anything to be with him," Hannah said, "which was exactly what he intended." She turned to Nial, having realized some time ago that he liked to show how superior he was to others. "What did you do, Nial, watch from the woods and pick the woman you knew would be the most vulnerable, the easiest to accept your lies?"

"Please, Hannah, you are talking about my beloved," Nial said, walking over to Wilona and slipping his arm around her waist. "Wilona has kept me abreast of how negligent Slain has been in protecting his clan. How the Chief of Clan MacKewan barely leaves the keep. How there are no warriors to defend them. I gave her my word that with me as chief she had nothing to fear."

"Except constant lies," Hannah said, understanding now why Slain had kept all but the most trustworthy in his clan ignorant of his plans.

"It is you who lies," Wilona accused, shaking a finger at her. "You hate him and have told nothing but lies about him."

Hannah feared she would not be able to open Wilona's eyes to Nial's true deceitful nature before it was too late. The only thing was to continue delaying their departure and pray that Slain would arrive shortly.

"Open your eyes, Wilona. Nial cares for no one but himself and he lies to suit his purpose."

"Not true," Wilona said. "He hated that I had to stay with Potsman and make it seem like I loved the fool so that no one would know I gathered information for him. He promised me over and over when this was done that I would have to worry no more."

"Of course you will have no worries, you will be dead," Hannah said, hoping the woman might come to her senses and see the truth.

"Enough of this nonsense," Nial ordered.

"You mean enough of the truth, something you avoid at all times," Hannah said and looked to Wilona. "Have you not heard what he has said? He lies endlessly. It was his doing that saw me shackled and dumped into a cart one night with the sole purpose of seeing me dead, though not before I was made to suffer. And he paid good coin to see it done."

"Then why are you not dead?" Wilona asked.

The smile on the woman's face made it clear that she believed she had caught Hannah in a lie, but it was the smirk on Nial's face that angered her the most. It was obvious he believed he was victorious yet again.

"I was fortunate that someone helped me escape and that I learned what true evil was. I fear you will not be so lucky, for you are blind to evil."

"I am not blind, but I was a fool for thinking Potsman would make me a good husband and that Clan MacKewan would be a good home. I hate Potsman, and I mourn the time lost I could have spent with Nial."

It struck Hannah then. "How long have you—"

"I met my beloved Wilona," —Nial kissed her cheek— "when I came to speak with Slain's father and fell in love with her at first sight. She worked in the keep while her useless husband did nothing but drink himself senseless."

Hannah glared at him. "You saw her vulnerability and made sure to use her in case you needed her one day."

"I offered my help," Wilona argued. "Nial did not force me to do anything."

"Of course, Nial never forces anyone," Hannah said, seeing his grin broaden. "He makes them believe they submit to him freely."

"You are wrong," Wilona said her chin going up with the confidence of her words.

"I truly wish I was, Wilona, for I think you are a good woman and I believed you a friend, and I do not want to see you die."

"You will not see her die," Nial said.

Wilona turned a smug smile on Hannah.

"She will linger long enough to let Slain know that I have you and where he is to meet me and surrender."

Hannah watched in horror as Wilona's eyes bulged in fright and she tried to break free of Nial's arm that had captured both of hers as it tightened around her.

He pressed his cheek against hers and his dagger to her stomach. "Stay still, my beloved. It will hurt less if you remain still."

"Please, I helped you," Wilona begged, tears gathering in her eyes.

"That you did. You served me well, my beloved, but I have no further use of you. Tell Slain that I have his wife and if he wants to see that she remains alive, he is to surrender to me in the northeast field that borders our land. Tell him not to keep me waiting or I will entertain myself with my *sister*."

The sheer horror and helplessness in Wilona's eyes had Hannah scrambling to her feet to try to help her.

"Stay where you are, Hannah, or I will stab her more than once and make her suffer even more," Nial ordered.

Wilona's eyes turned wider in fright, though Hannah did not know if it was because the woman wanted her to stay where she was or take a chance and help her.

Nial pressed a kiss to Wilona's cheek. "You do not want to suffer more, do you my beloved?"

Wilona shook her head, tears running down her cheeks.

Hannah cringed and tears rushed to her eyes, her heart breaking for Wilona as Nial began to slide the dagger slowly into her.

Chapter Thirty-four

As soon as Slain saw the body lying on the ground, he ran, his heart pounding furiously against his chest. *Please do not let it be Hannah. Please I beg of you.*

He dropped down beside the lifeless body relieved to see it was not his wife laying there so pale in death. He had not wished death upon Wilona for what she had done, though he had seen no other way for her with Nial. He had no doubt Nial would dispose of her when he was done with her, and he had.

Wilona's eyes suddenly shot open.

"She is not dead?" Imus asked nearly breathless, looking down at the woman as he tried to calm his breathing, having run twice as hard as Slain to keep pace with him, and failing.

Slain did not answer. He brought his face closer to Wilona's pale one. "Where is my wife?"

Wilona struggled to speak. "Field... north," —she fought for a breath— "east... border." She gasped, her breath nearly gone, but still trying desperately to live. "Forgive... m—"

"That will be for Hannah to say," Slain said, though Wilona had taken her last breath.

"I will see that she is returned home," Imus said as Slain stood.

Slain's eyes were heavy with anger as he said, "Time for battle."

All Hannah had to do was be patient and wait for her husband to come for her or so she told herself as she rode in front of Nial on his horse.

"Your husband will come for you and I will destroy him," Nial said.

He had taken great pleasure in telling her what he intended to do to her husband. How he would use her to anger him, bring out the savage, and see the beast destroyed. He would use her as he used Wilona and all the other women that came before them. Time and time again women had served Nial. She did not intend to be one of them.

"You have tempted me since I first laid eyes on you, but I restrained myself, knowing one day it would serve a greater good. And patience has served me well, since now I will relish the look on your husband's face before he dies, when he learns I had the pleasure of enjoying his wife."

Hannah kept herself from gagging at the thought. This was no time to give into any weakness. She had to stay strong and find a way to escape him, find a way back to her husband before Nial's madness destroyed the happiness she had finally found.

"Nothing to say, dear sister?" he asked with a laugh.

Hannah tried biting her tongue to keep from striking out at him with it. After looking at the trail they traveled, she thought better of it. They rode along the edge of a hill. It could be her chance to escape him, to make sure Nial could not use her against Slain.

"You have to lie to have a woman couple with you or you lie to yourself to see it done, if it ever is," she said.

Nial laughed. "You try and bait me. It will not work."

"Perhaps, but I do not feel you rise to the occasion, so I would think I speak more the truth than you," she said and turned her head to grin at him. The spark of anger in his eyes told her she had hit her mark.

Nial glared at her.

Hannah wasted no time, since she feared she had little of it. She rubbed her bottom against his groin. "Still nothing."

Nial's temper flared.

Hannah realized then that Nial needed a woman who was subservient to him. A woman who showed strength deflated him, and she charged forward. "All is not lost, after all, you are a consummate liar and no doubt have convinced many women that you have pleased them, since they would not know any better."

That did what Hannah had hoped. Nial raised his hand and delivered such a stinging blow to her face that it knocked her off the horse. Though stunned, once on the ground she rolled quickly to the edge of the hill and keeping her arms tucked around her face and her legs crossed, she rolled down the hill.

It seemed like forever that she kept rolling when suddenly she found herself swept up by rushing waters. With her wrists tied, she fought to keep herself above water. It was not long before her arm began to ache and she knew what would follow. She would lose strength in it and once she did, she was finished. She fought as much as she could to survive, to keep herself above water.

She thought of Slain and how much she loved him, how much she had looked forward to a long life with him, to having his bairns, to waking up in each other's arms when they were withered with age. The thought made her fight harder and she saw that the shoreline was not far to her right. If she could only get to it before her arm lost all strength.

She let herself go under and kicked and fought as hard as she could to get to shore and when she broke the surface once more, she saw that she was a short distance from it. She could make it. She had to. She had to get home to Slain. She had to get home to the man she loved with all her heart and then some.

Hannah fought with all her might and she was not far from shore, sure she would make it when her arm lost all strength and she went under.

With a sharp jerk, she was pulled out of the water and was relieved for a moment when she saw it was not Nial, until she realized the warrior who had dragged her to shore was wearing the Clan MacFillan plaid.

~~~

Slain sat his stallion, not as the Chief of the Clan MacKewan, but as the *savage*. He was ready to ride and kill any and all who stood in his way of rescuing his wife. He approached the field Nial had designated as their meeting place, alone, though spread out behind him a group of men from the Clan MacKewan sat atop their horses. A distance away, Nial sat atop his horse, his troop spread out behind him, an impressive sight, though nothing that worried Slain. He knew well the extent of the Clan MacFillan warriors and they were no match for his. He was sure he would defeat Nial. It was his wife's safety that concerned him and that would make him do whatever was necessary to see her safe.

It troubled him that he did not see Hannah anywhere and he would do nothing until he saw that she was unharmed. And if by chance Nial had foolishly done something to her, he would make certain to use every torture device on him before Slain did to him what he had done to Conlan, Melvin, and Wilona.

Slain rode forward as did Nial and they met somewhere in the middle of the field, Slain thinking him a fool for the way he approached with such bravado and confidence. He foolishly thought that victory was already his.

Nial did not give Slain a chance to speak, he spoke up as soon as they brought their horses to a halt near each other.

"Surrender now and save yourself the embarrassment of defeat."

"Where is my wife?" Slain demanded.

"You will see her once you surrender to me," Nial said.

"I will see her first."

Nial laughed. "You think to defeat me with that paltry troop?" He nodded to the small group of men behind Slain.

"My wife," Slain said, his eyes remaining steadfast on Nial.

"Surrender and she is yours."

Slain's dark eyes narrowed. "I have no time for play. You will bring my wife to me."

Nial leaned forward on his horse. "You are defeated. You can demand nothing. Surrender and be done with it. You are as foolish as your father."

Slain glared at him. "And you are more the fool for believing that." He raised his arm and gave a snap of his hand. Out of the woods that bordered the field where a few of Slain's men stood, rode a contingent of warriors that fanned out on both sides until they were nearly on top of Nial's men. Stepping out between the warriors on horses was a contingent of archers who took up a stance, raising their bows with arrows pointed at Nial's men. And what followed caused even the bravest warriors to shiver, since Warrick's warriors, draped in black shrouds, made their way past them all led by Roark. There was not a warrior there who did not fear them.

"My wife," Slain said, "and this is the last time I will ask you."

Fury had Nial's nostrils flaring and his temper near to exploding. How had he not known this? How had Slain kept his army of warriors a secret? There was no way he could defeat such a mighty force and defeat held a bitter taste. One he would not easily accept. "You will give me your word that you will let me live?" he asked with an air of demand.

"You have no room to bargain." Slain grew concerned, seeing how the man's eyes darted about and how sweat broke out heavily across his brow. "Bring Hannah to me now."

"As you say," Nial said with a sharp nod. "I will go fetch her."

"Delay in bringing her to me and I will turn you over to Warrick's man and see done to you what you intended for Hannah."

Nial glared as he gave a nod, then turned and rode off.

Slain watched as Nial's men parted for him and he was relieved they remained that way, for he did not trust Nial. If the warriors had closed rank behind Nial, he would have ridden straight at them, brandishing his sword, ready to kill anyone who stood in his way of getting to his wife.

There was a flourish of activity where Nial had stopped and then he once again rode past his parted warriors, though slowly this time.

Hannah struggled against the pain in her arm made worse with her wrists being shackled with rope that Nial held while she was forced to walk behind his horse. Her body had been plagued with shivers since having been pulled out of the cold stream. She fought to take step after step.

"He has come for you," Nial said, catching her attention. "He has brought warriors, far too many for me to see victory against."

Hannah's heart filled with joy at the news. Slain was here. Soon she would be safe. She bit back a response, wanting to remind him that she had warned him he would see no victory against Slain, but thought better of it. He still held her captive and anything could happen with him holding the end of the rope that bound her wrists.

"He will not let me live," Nial said.

Hannah wondered if he spoke more to himself than he did to her and it disturbed her, for Nial was not a man to accept defeat easily.

"Your husband planned well, hiding his army of warriors, living as if he only had those present in his clan to defend his land. But then many believed Warrick would be there to help him if needed. It was why your father offered you in marriage to Warrick. Though if the powerful warrior was not interested in such an arrangement, your father was willing to give you to him regardless, so that he could garnish favor with him."

The shock of his words had Hannah stumbling.

"I could not have that. It would mean Warrick might someday lay claim to the Clan MacFillan. But I did think it fitting that you should suffer and die at the very place your father had intended to send you."

Nial's deception knew no bounds. He truly was an evil man.

"I never counted on your strength," Nial said with an angry snarl.

Hannah grew fearful that Nial had no intentions of handing her over to her husband. He manipulated and caused suffering in everything that he did and she had no doubt he would do the same in facing defeat. He would make others suffer for his failure.

Nail fastened the rope connected to her shackles to the saddle as he spoke. "Your husband thinks he has won, but I will not suffer defeat or death without seeing my enemy suffer greatly before I die."

Hannah's own anger rose up, sending a shot of heat through her and chasing her chill if only for a moment. She had not survived thus far only to die in the end. She did not know what Nial had planned, but she would do whatever was necessary to stay alive.

"You are quiet. You know your time is near with your husband so close. How bittersweet that must be for you. Not far from you… but too far too save you."

Hannah kept silent. All too aware that her words would do little to improve her situation or save her. Nial was determined to have his way, but so was she.

~~~

Slain watched Nial approach with an apprehensive awareness. Something was not right, he could feel it. Nial was a madman and madmen never surrendered.

He was proven right when Nial stopped well before reaching him.

"If you want your wife, come get her," Nial shouted and raised the end of a rope he had fastened around his waist to make it seem that he held the rope holding Hannah prisoner. Then he gave a kick to the side of his horse. The animal took off, jerking Hannah off her feet to be dragged along the ground.

Slain stared in complete disbelief as he saw his wife being dragged behind Nial's horse. He responded instinctively and with a fierce rage and dreaded fear he had never felt before, spurring his horse after Nial. Slain rode as if the devil was on his trail and suffered every bump he saw his wife suffer. He could not imagine the pain and fear she was going through, though it would be nothing to what he would make Nial suffer.

His horse flew like a mighty wind that swirled down over the land swallowing everything in its sight, though it was not fast enough for Slain. When he finally got close enough, he hurled himself off his horse at Nial, making sure he snatched the rope out of Nial's hand, freeing his wife, before sending them both tumbling to the ground.

Slain's tightly curled fist smashed into Nial's face as the man struggled to get to his feet, again and again his fist pummeled Nial. Hands soon grabbed at Slain and voices screamed at him, but the savage had control of him and all he wanted to do was beat Nial to death.

It took Nial's strange laughter to stop Slain, only then did he hear the voices clearly.

"Hannah is being dragged by the horse," Imus shouted.

Slain hurried to his feet and looked around. His heart nearly stopped when in the distance he saw Hannah being dragged along the ground behind the runaway horse, Roark and some of his warriors rushing after her.

Slain signaled his horse and the animal was at his side in an instant. He was barely mounted when he urged the horse forward. Prayers fell from his lips, begging for his wife's life. He had been a fool, thinking his wife would be safe once he got Nial off the horse. Defeated men could never be trusted. They would do whatever they could to hurt the victor one last time.

The only thing that gave Slain hope was knowing that Roark was one of the finest horsemen that he had ever seen. If anyone could catch the runaway horse and bring him to a stop, he could. That would leave him to see to Hannah and that was what he wanted the most, to hold his wife in his arms and see her safe.

Slain once again flew over the land and he nearly roared with relief when he saw Roark fling himself off his horse, land on Nial's horse, and bring the animal to a stop. By that time Slain was almost upon them, his eyes focused on his wife lying lifeless on the ground.

He jumped off his horse before the animal fully stopped and ran to his wife lying face down. He dropped down beside her, fearful of touching her, fearful of finding her dead. With gentle hands, he eased her onto her back. He cringed when he saw her swollen jaw and blood running from her cut lip, Nial no doubt having hit her, worsening her previous wound.

Mud and grass was smeared everywhere over her, on her face, in her hair, on her garments that he realized were wet. Why were they wet?

He brushed her hair away from her one eye. "Hannah." He let out a relieved breath when she responded with eyes that fluttered open.

"You neglect me, husband, I am cold and need warming," she admonished him with a slight smile that brought a wince with it.

Her teasing reprimand brought a smile to his face. He eased his arms underneath her to move her slowly and gently up into his arms, though stopped when she cried out.

"My arm," she said, a tear hanging from the corner of one eye.

He silently spewed oath after oath as he gathered her as gently as he could against him.

Roark stepped forward silently and held his shroud out to Slain. "To help warm her."

Slain gave him a grateful nod and the two men worked to wrap her in it. Hannah winced and grimaced as they did, Slain suffering every pain along with her.

"Home, Slain. I want to go home," Hannah said, resting her head against her husband's chest, listening to his heart beat madly as his heat seeped into her.

"Aye, wife, whatever you want I will give you," Slain said, standing.

"You already have," Hannah whispered. "You have given me your love."

Chapter Thirty-five

A few weeks later.

Hannah smiled at the work that had been done to the room at the end of the east wing. All the torture devices were gone and heavy tapestries had been removed from the two windows. The stone had been scrubbed and the large fireplace repaired. It was ready to be occupied. "It will make a perfect bedchamber for us."

Slain kissed his wife's rosy lips, his arms circling around her back. "The other two rooms will be finished soon enough, then I will have our things moved into this wing."

"It will be alight with laughter and love, one room awaiting future bairns and a retreat room for me where I will stitch."

"Something I did not know about you. You know how to stitch," Slain said and loved that there were still things he was discovering about his wife.

"Well," Hannah said, "I may need some help since my mum said stitching did not come easy to me."

"Nonsense, I will show you how it is done," Helice said, entering the room. "You should be resting. You are still recovering from that ordeal."

"I feel good," Hannah said with a smile, having come to love Helice more and more since that ordeal. The woman had tended her like only a mum could, refusing to leave her side when Slain had ordered her to, insisting he would tend Hannah himself. Between the two she had been well looked after. Helice had also worked tirelessly applying comfrey poultices to Hannah's bad arm, in hopes that it would help. It had relieved the pain and was doing well.

"And you will continue to feel good if you listen and rest when I tell you," Helice ordered.

"Mum, the women in the kitchen will not give me any food," Conlan said, sticking his head around the open door.

"Did you not just eat supper?" Helice demanded.

Hannah smiled. Conlan had taking to calling Helice mum as he recovered from his wound and Helice had not stopped him. Hannah was happy to see the pair had found what they both had been missing... one a mum and the other a son.

Conlan hurried over to Helice and wrapped his arm around hers. "I cannot help it if your food is so delicious that I cannot stop eating it."

"That tongue of yours charms more by the day, but it will not work on me," Helice warned.

"I love you, Mum, and I am starving," Conlan begged with a mischievous smile.

Hannah was glad to see Helice smile, something she had been doing more and more of as of late.

"I will feed you and then you will return to bed and rest, for you still need to heal," Helice ordered.

"Anything you say, Mum," Conlan said and blew her a kiss.

The two left the room, laughter drifting behind them as they walked down the hall.

"They are good for each other," Slain said, pleased with the many changes taking place to the keep. The Great Hall was filled with talk, laughter, and song once again. Slain had begun hearing disputes and settling them. Women were eager to work at the keep and men as well. And Slain's army of warriors were busy building more cottages and storage sheds for the food that would serve the large clan for the winter.

"All is good now in the keep," Hannah said and gave him a poke in the chest. "You have yet to tell me what you did with all the torture devices."

He had avoided speaking to her about it, not wanting to stir painful memories for her, but since he had sworn to himself there would be no secrets between them, he said, "I destroyed most, though a few Roark took."

"Then your debt with Warrick is settled," Hannah said with relief.

"Aye. Roark received word that my debt to Warrick is no more, though his warriors are always available to me if necessary."

"That is good." Hannah nodded and turned in her husband's arms. "I never told you that Nial informed me that my father offered me to Warrick as a wife or however he wished to use me."

Her words sparked his temper, but the savage was too content to raise his head. "Warrick will never wed."

"Why?"

"I do not know. He would not speak of it and none would ask, though he made it known, in the strongest terms, that he would never take a wife. He couples with willing women, less often than most believe. So your father had no chance of Warrick accepting such a request."

"I am glad all is settled," Hannah said, "and we have each other." She hugged her husband.

He hugged her in return, loving the feel of her in his arms, where to him, she always belonged. He thought about all Nial had told her and he knew there was still more to settle for her.

"You should go talk with Melvin. Neata says he does better and he will do even better if you speak the truth with him," Slain encouraged.

Hannah hesitated. She was not sure if Nial had spoken the truth to her. He was a consummate liar so how did she trust that what he had told her, that Melvin was her da, was the truth?

"It is the only way you will know for sure."

Hannah smiled softly. Her husband often knew her thoughts and she was glad of it, for it solved many a problem without her ever mentioning a word.

"I will walk you there," he said, urging her gently out the door.

"Are you sorry you did not kill, Nial?" Hannah asked.

"That he is dead is all that matters. That it was Imus who drove a sword through him in his last attempt to escape makes it all the better."

Slain stopped in front of the door to Hannah's old bedchamber. "I will wait for you in our bedchamber."

Melvin was recovering though not as fast as Conlan had, but then Neata had explained that Conlan was young and resilient and far too stubborn for his own good. It was different for Melvin. He was older and tired from far too many battles and while he was improving, it was slow, some days proving more challenging than others.

Hannah entered her bedchamber that Melvin had occupied since the night of the incident. His wounds had been too severe to even think of moving him and now that he had settled in, it made no sense to move him.

Melvin was sitting up in bed with his back braced against a couple of pillows, looking much too pale and tired. Though when he saw Hannah, he smiled.

Hannah hesitated at the open door. "I was going to talk with you a while, but you look tired."

He waved her in. "No, please come in. I would enjoy talking with you."

Hannah moved the chair closer to the side of the bed and sat.

"There is something troubling you?" Melvin asked.

"I could never hide anything from you."

"It is your eyes. Your mother had the same look when something bothered her."

"I miss her," Hannah said, the old pain of losing her mum returning to stab at her once more.

"I do as well," Melvin admitted with a sadness in his aging eyes that said more than he realized. "Speak your mind, Hannah, for it is obvious you have something heavy on it."

Hannah sighed. "Nial told me that you were my father. That when my mum learned of my father's—Ross MacFillan's—infidelity she feared his mistress would give him a child so she turned to you for help."

Melvin shook his head.

"He was lying to me?" Hannah asked, having hoped for once Nial had told her the truth. Having found love with Slain, she hoped her mum had at least gotten a chance to find love with Melvin.

"Your mother arrived at the MacFillan keep with such hope and promise for a good union. It did not take her long to realize she would not have it with Ross MacFillan. Our love developed over time and grew deeper through the years."

Joy filled her heart upon hearing that her mum had known a good love. "So you are my father."

"I gave your mum my word…" he shook his head, saying no more, tears collecting in his aging eyes.

Hannah reached out and took his hand. "No more secrets, Da."

The tear slipped down Melvin's cheek. "I am so very proud of you."

They continued to talk and Hannah had the courage to ask, "Did my mum suffer so badly when she delivered me that she no longer could be a wife to Ross."

"Your mum made it seem that way since she no longer wanted to be a wife to Ross. But then he was no husband to her. I wanted your mum to leave with me, have the three of us start a new life together. She insisted Ross would search for us until his dying day to have his revenge and see you dead along with us. As much as I wanted to disagree with her, I knew her words held truth. Ross MacFillan would have been furious at such a betrayal and would have thirsted tirelessly for revenge."

"So you both stayed to protect me."

"We stayed because we loved you and wanted you safe."

"Do you think Ross knew I was not his daughter?" Hannah asked.

"I often wondered if he did, though he never made mention of it and I doubt he would have, since it would have reflected badly on him. At least having one child no one could whisper and gossip that it was his fault no bairn was born to him."

"It must have been difficult for you all those years, having to love my mum from afar."

"It was not the life I would have chosen, but it was the life I was given, and I would not change that for anything, for I got to know love at its unselfish best and I got to be part of my kind, beautiful, and courageous daughter's life."

"We have much time to make up for, Da," Hannah said, having much to tell him about what Nial had said and what he had done to her mum, but that would wait until he was stronger.

Melvin squeezed her hand. "That we do, daughter."

Hannah stood and leaned down to kiss his brow. "Sleep good, Da, and grow strong. I do not want to lose you."

"I am not going anywhere, daughter."

Hannah smiled, pleased to see determination had replaced the sadness in his eyes. She left the room, promising they would talk more tomorrow.

Slain looked up from where he waited in bed for her when she entered. Her head hung low as she turned and closed the door. She raised it when she turned and he saw her eyes bright with tears ready to spill.

Hannah watched her husband rise naked out of bed, his muscles firm and his movements precise, and she stood where she was, waiting for his strong arms to wrap around her, and they did. She let him smother her in his warmth and love. Let it soak deep inside her and feel it stir her heart and meld with her soul.

"Happy tears?" he asked after a few moments.

She nodded against his chest.

Slain lifted her in his arms and went to the chair near the fire and sat, settling her in his lap. He wanted to make love to her and fall asleep wrapped around her, but that would wait. Now, she needed him to hold her, listen if she wished to talk, or remain silent along with her. Whatever she wanted, needed, he would give her.

"I am glad Melvin is my father," she said.

"He is a good man," Slain said, having grown to know the man well.

"So many secrets," she sighed and lifted her head off his shoulder.

"There will be no more secrets between us," he said and sealed his word with a kiss.

"None?"

"Aye, not one," he said

Hannah tool advantage of the moment. "Then, please, tell me of your first wife."

Slain stood and carried her to the bed, sitting her down upon it, then turned away from her a moment before turning to face her once again. "It is truly Helice's story to tell."

"She told me it was for you to tell me." Hannah reached out and took his hand. "I am sorry for the painful memories, but I would like to know about your wife that came before me."

He slipped his hand out of hers and cupped her chin. "What I tell you is for us alone. No one is to know of it."

She nodded, wondering why did he not want anyone to know of his first wife. Was the memory so painful that he wished to bury it? Bury everything about her?

"I was on a mission for Warrick to a Viking village on a small isle just off Scotland when I met Helice and her daughter Astrid. They were slaves of the Vikings. Astrid was a beautiful, shy, fragile young woman… and extremely ill. My first meeting with Astrid was when she collapsed in my arms during a trade meeting. The Viking chief grew angry and told Helice he had had enough and that he intended to sell Astrid since she was worthless to him.

"His actions did not surprise me since he was a hateful chief, laughing when Helice begged him not to do so. She came to me that night and begged for my help. She told me that her daughter was dying. The village had been hit with a bad fever a few years ago and Helice had lost her son and the man who had fathered both children, and who had protected them, to it. Her daughter survived the fever, but it left her weak and she had grown weaker through the years. Helice believed she did not have much time left and she wanted nothing more than for her daughter to die a free woman, but she knew that was impossible. She asked if I would purchase Astrid and take her away so that she could at least die in peace."

Hannah remained quiet when Slain stopped and looked off as if he was back there at that moment in time, reliving it all over again.

"I agreed without hesitation. Astrid's eyes had haunted me since catching her in my arms. They were the most peaceful blue color I had ever seen, but it was the helplessness that I saw there that made my decision easy.

What I did not count on was the Viking chief laughing at me when I asked to purchase Astrid. And what he did not count on was me agreeing when he told me the only way I could have Astrid was if I wed her.

"Helice was happy that her daughter would die a free woman. Astrid was not happy she would leave her mum behind. So after a quick ceremony, I asked Helice to help settle her daughter on my boat and say her good-byes. I set sail before she could leave, my archers standing ready to unleash on the Vikings if they should object.

"The Viking chief laughed and yelled at our departing boat, shouting that I was welcome to Helice and would be sorry I took her."

He grew quiet, and again Hannah waited silently for him to continue.

"I was never sorry I took Helice with me and I am not sorry I wed Astrid. We were a day away from shore, the night sky was brilliant with stars. Helice and most of the men were asleep. Astrid was awake, shivering beneath the mound of blankets and furs Helice kept piled on her. She had grown weaker each day, but her smile never faltered and either did her words to me of how grateful she was that she would die knowing her mum was free and away from the pain of so much heartache and loss. I joined her beneath the blankets and took her in my arms to warm her. She asked me for one last favor."

Slain looked away again but not before Hannah caught the sadness that filled his dark eyes.

He turned after several silent moments and continued. "She asked for a kiss from her husband."

He grew silent again and Hannah fought to keep tears from falling.

"Her lips were soft and warm and she smiled afterwards and told me I was a good husband. She died that night in my arms. Astrid is buried here on MacKewan land. Helice preferred that no one knew. It was enough for her that her daughter died a free woman. I granted her request and I ask you do the same."

Hannah jumped up and threw herself at her husband, hugging him tight and letting her tears fall. She sniffed them back when she raised her head. "You are no savage, husband, you have the kindest heart of all."

"And it belongs to you now and always," he said and was about to kiss her when she kissed his lips quickly and stepped away from him, shedding her garments as fast as she could. "Eager to have your way with me, wife?" he asked with a soft laugh, that brought a deep joy to his heart that he had not felt in a long time.

"Eager to have you plant our first bairn, one of many to come, in me so that Helice and my da will have grandchildren to fuss over and Conlan will have family to fight with, and we will have a home filled with love, laughter, joy… with family."

Slain scooped her up in his arms. "I do love you, wife."

She nibbled at his ear and whispered, "Show me how much."

And Slain did.

Subscribe to Donna Newsletter so you never miss a new book release! You'll also get to read excerpts of future books and take a chance on special giveaways.
Go to donna@donnafletcher.com
to subscribe.

Titles by Donna Fletcher

Highland Warriors Trilogy
To Love A Highlander
Embraced By A Highlander
Highlander The Demon Lord

The Pict King Series
The King's Executioner
The King's Warrior
The King and His Queen

Macinnes Sisters Trilogy
The Highlander's Stolen Heart
Highlander's Rebellious Love
Highlander: The Dark Dragon

Cree & Dawn Series
Highlander Unchained/Forbidden Highlander
Highlander's Captive
Cree & Dawn Short Stories
Highlander's True Love
Highlander's Promise
Highlander's Winter Tale
Highlander's Rescue

Warrior King Series
Bound To A Warrior
Loved By a Warrior
A Warrior's Promise
Wed To a Highland Warrior

Sinclare Brothers' Series
Return of the Rogue

Embraced By A Highlander

Under the Highlander's Spell
The Angel & The Highlander
Highlander's Forbidden Bride

The Irish Devil
Irish Hope

Isle of Lies
Love Me Forever

For a complete list of Donna's titles, visit her at
donna@donnafletcher.com

About the author

It was her love of reading and daydreaming that started USA Today bestselling author Donna Fletcher's writing career. Besides gobbling up books, her mom generously bought for her, she spent a good portion of her time lost in daydreams that took her on grand adventures. She met heroes, villains, and heroines that, while usually in danger, always found the strength and courage to prevail. She traveled all over the world and through time in her dreams. Some places and times fascinated her more than others and she would rush to the library (no Internet at that time) and read all she could about that particular period and place. After a while, she simply could not ignore all the adventures swirling around in her head. She had no choice but to bring them more vividly to life, and so she started writing.

Donna enjoys living on the beautiful Jersey Shore surrounded by family and friends and a cat who thinks she's a princess, but what cat doesn't, and a dog named after a favorite hero…Cree.

Stop by and visit with Donna at her website www.donnafletcher.com or join her Facebook page where she keeps her readers updated.

Made in the USA
Middletown, DE
17 September 2025